Electric Grace

Still More Fiction by Washington Area Women

Edited by Richard Peabody

Several of these stories and novel excerpts have been previously published: Teresa Bevin's story, "The Sylphs," is reprinted with her permission from her collection *Dreams and Other Ailments* (Gival Press, 2001); "Cherry Bomb" from *Rattlebone* by Maxine Clair copyright © 1994 by Maxine Clair. Reprinted by permission of Farar, Straus & Giroux, LLC.; Brenda W. Clough's story, "Times Fifty," is reprinted with her permission from the October 2001 issue of *Christianity Today*; Merle Collins's story "The Visit," is reprinted with her permission from *Rain Darling*, first published by The Women's Press Ltd. 1990; T. Greenwood's story, "Instruments of Torture," is reprinted with her permission from the fall 2001 issue of the *Western Humanities Review*; Catherine Harnett's story, "Her Gorgeous Grief," is reprinted with her permission from the spring 2005 issue of the *Hudson Review*; Faye Moskowitz's story "Completo" is reprinted with her permission from *Story Quarterly* #37 (2001); Barbara Mujica's story, "Dear Erik Estrada, I Love You," is reprinted with her permission from *Sanchez across the Street and Other Stories* (FLF Press, 1997); Mary L. Tabor's story "Riptide," is reprinted with her permission from *The Woman Who Never Cooked* (Mid-List Press, First Series Award, 2006).

ISBN-10: 0-931181-25-9
ISBN-13: 978-0-931181-25-2
First Edition
Published in the USA

Book design by Nita Congress.
Cover by Jody Mussoff, © 2007, "Electric Grace" (colored pencil 30" x 22").
Printed by Main Street Rag Publishing, Charlotte, NC; www.mainstreetrag.com.

Paycock Press
3819 North 13th Street
Arlington, VA 22201
www.gargoylemagazine.com

For two women who
opened my eyes and mind—
Jo Radner
and
Lenore Horowitz

What you risk reveals what you value.

—Jeanette Winterson

Contents

Acknowledgments

Kudos to Nita Congress and M. Scott Douglass without whom our books wouldn't happen. A big shout-out to Robin Ferrier who knocked herself out setting up gigs and working PR on *Enhanced Gravity*. Politics and Prose provided us with a superb launchpad. Special thanks to Robert Giron, Alma Katsu, and Olga Tsyganova who helped us out at the BEA. Plus thanks to Mary Collins and David Everett for the Johns Hopkins launch. Tons more thanks to: Doreen Baingana, Kate Blackwell, Hildie S. Block, Carol Christiansen, Brenda W. Clough, Cleve Corner, Ann Downer, Martha Tod Dudman, Barbara Esstman, Sunil Freeman, Mike Giarratano, Barbara Grosh, Margaret Grosh, Cara Haycak, Derrick Hsu, M.H. Johnson, Wendi Kaufman, Mary Ann Larkin, Wendy Lesser, C. M. Mayo, Terri Mertz, Faye Moskowitz, Steve Moyer, Marianne Nora, Jiwon Park, Joel Pollack, Kevin Sampsell, Lane Stiles, Julie Wakeman-Linn, and Mary-Sherman Willis.

Introduction

Okay, here we go again with a third volume of strong passionate fiction by Washington area women. For those who're counting, this makes a grand total of 1,206 pages of writing by 117 different women scattered throughout three thick volumes. And some folks laughed after I assembled book one—*Grace and Gravity*—saying "you mean there are more than a dozen women writing fiction in DC?" Indeed, there are. And in my literary hunting and gathering, I've already assembled enough additional names for a fourth volume.

For the record, I never planned on publishing this series. I simply saw a need and stepped in to provide something I felt was missing from my own bookshelf. And then I attended the Southeastern Independent Literary Magazine and Small Press Fair at Agnes Scott College in Atlanta, and had the good fortune to attend a panel discussion moderated by Joyelle McSweeney of Action Books on "Women's Role in the Publishing Industry." The panelists—Shannon Ravenel (Shannon Ravenel Books), Helene Atwan (Beacon Press), Nicole Mitchell (University of Georgia Press), Brigid Hughes (A Public Space)—were young and old, feisty and dedicated, energetic and droll. It was absolutely the best panel I have ever seen or heard. (I wish somebody had audio- or videotaped it.) These women were on fire, and they had a lot to say about how things have changed and yet stayed the same in the lit world. Hughes, after all, had just been unceremoniously dumped by the *Paris Review* despite being George Plimpton's hand-picked choice to helm his legacy at the magazine after his death. She got a raw deal, and her new venture—A Public Space—is an impressive addition to the lit world. The first four issues are solid and memorable—and she's still in her early thirties.

Ravenel, who founded Algonquin Books in Chapel Hill with Louis Rubin, said that if she knew then what she knows now about the state of the biz, she never would have done it. That speaks volumes. Ravenel has a professional eye and ear and is quick with an anecdote, but she's also a realist. You had to be there. It was a revolutionary moment and those in attendance were set aflame with purpose and a desire to proselytize about what could be achieved in the grim commercial world of publishing.

So that's it. The goal here is to spread the word—DC is a vibrant and creative place to write and publish. It's not New York, not by a long shot. And yet what we have here in this anthology is another combination of big names and newcomers, established literary magazine denizens and genre writers. This is a diverse group of women whose fiction covers the literary waterfront. It gives me great pleasure to present relative newcomers like Corrine Zappia Gormont, Susan Kellam, Victoria Popdan, Joy Reges, Jessie Seigel, Debra Sequeira, Sheryl Stein, Sheila Walsh, Robyn Kirby Wright, Hananah Zaheer, Anna Ziegler, and Christy J. Zink, alongside literary nomads Teresa Bevin, Merle Collins, T. Greenwood, and Sarah Grace McCandless, plus established names like Maxine Clair, Brenda W. Clough, Joanne Leedom-Ackerman, Faye Moskowitz, and Barbara Mujica.

The result is a literary call to arms if you will. Huzzah.

—Richard Peabody
Summer/Fall 2006

Teresa Bevin

The Sylphs

TERESA BEVIN was born in Camagüey, Cuba. At the age of eighteen, she was sent to Spain to wait out her visa approval into the United States. After three years of working and growing up quickly and independent of family, she came to the States, joining her younger brother—a minor who had emigrated through Mexico and was living with relatives. Her books include *Havana Split* and *Dreams and Other Ailments/Sueños y otros achaques*, a bilingual collection of short stories. Bevin is currently putting finishing touches on the first of a series of bilingual children's books and is contributing to a collective study of women and immigration. She is a professor of Spanish and an instructor in psychology, group dynamics, counseling techniques, and activity therapies at Montgomery College in Takoma Park, Maryland.

"And now girls…Suck in those stomachs!"

Miss Adelfa poked with her cue stick, creating ripples on the soft abdomens of little girls raised on whole milk and tender beef.

"Watch me!" She demonstrated. "Your right hand should be on the bar, like so! And the left on your waist, like so!"

For the few girls who actually had a waistline, that was simple enough, but for girls like Goyita, the waistline was an indefinite place between the armpits and the navel.

"Straighten up!"

When the postures appeared sufficiently forced and uncomfortable, Miss Adelfa indicated her satisfaction with a sharp, nasal "Eeeee!" and began banging with her stick on the wooden floor, keeping the rhythm.

The gaunt pianist beat the piano with exaggerated gestures that she seemed to equate with the true mark of a virtuoso. In the meantime, Miss Adelfo, attentive to the girls' postures and painful moves, stretched her neck several inches above her shoulders, like a turtle peeking out of her shell.

With each count, she hit the floor with her stick.

"One! (Bang!) Two! (Bang!) Three! (Bang!). No! That's not the way! Wait! Stop! No, no, no! (Bang! bang! bang!)"

The piano fell silent and the bile inside each girl turned solid. Awaiting sentence, they all shut their eyes tight, and held their breath.

"Carmencita! I told you not to do it that way, child! You have to do it without bending your knee! Do you understand, child? With-out-bend-ing-your-knee!"

Roughly, Miss Adelfa grabbed the girls by the arms and pulled them away from the bar.

"Move away, everyone! Carmencita is going to do it all by herself if it takes her all afternoon! C'mon, child! Let's see you do it!"

Carmencita puckered her lip and held back tears. Standing in the first position, with her back very straight, she held firmly onto the bar. When she closed her eyes, two tears rolled down her cheeks. The other girls cringed in sympathy.

"Eeeee!"

The pianist's shoulders threatened to pop out of their sockets with the first strident chords.

"One! Two! Two, I said! Two-two-two! Not like that, child! Not like that!"

Carmencita, before her classmates' compassionate gaze, fell to the floor in panic. Her mouth opened squarely, and she sobbed with all her heart, slobbering like a baby.

"Ababah! My bab-bah!" It was impossible for her to form any clear words with her lips so stretched out by anguish.

Miss Adelfa too was beside herself. Her hands met above her head and she looked up at the ceiling, as if expecting divine assistance from there. Still, she seemed the only one who understood the basic language of Carmencita's hysteria. With her hands made into tight fists, she suddenly turned to face the source of her upset.

"Go ahead! Call your mamá! And while you're at it please tell her not to send you here anymore! You are a disaster! You will never be a ballerina! It's a blessed miracle that you can actually walk, you clumsy thing!"

In all this commotion, Goyita felt relieved, because this time it wasn't she who had to pay for the teacher's outbursts of artistic zeal. But she could not help feeling very sorry for the new victim.

Hiccupping and shaking, the distraught Carmencita moved away from the bar to take refuge within the group's anonymity.

Miss Adelfa paced the mirrored room from one end to the other like a caged animal, her worn slippers pointing outward. Her hair escaped its ties, and in a matter of seconds, she had transformed herself into a much older version of the demented Giselle.

Terrified girls in black leotards and pink tights huddled together in a corner, embracing their little bundles of clothes.

"None of you spoiled brats know discipline or dedication!" She shook her fist. "Why would you know anything about it? Why? And why should I waste my time on you?" Her tone became suddenly solemn, and she turned her back to the girls. "When I studied under the direction of the great Alicia Alonso, everyone knew the value of her instruction. That was discipline! We did what we were told, and we practiced every day, religiously. And why?" The teacher suddenly turned around to face her terror-stricken students once more. "We had what it takes for ballet! We had love for it, and we had talent! TA-LENT! Do you know what talent is? Is there anyone with talent around here? Is there any talent in this country anymore?"

Miss Adelfa started to walk out of the studio with her indexes on her temples and her pinkies pointing to the heavens. "The lesson is finished for today," she spat the words as she climbed upstairs to her quarters. "You may call your mothers to come and pick you up, but I'll talk to no one. I'm indisposed and retiring for the day."

The pianist stood up and stuffed the music sheets in her briefcase. She turned to look at the girls with disdain, and she too walked out, slamming the front door behind her.

By this time, Gabriela, the youngest of the group, had let her bladder loose for fear of asking for permission to go to the bathroom. She quietly shuffled away from the small puddle and dashed for the phone to call her mother.

When the girls were done with the phone calls, Miss Adelfa's housekeeper pushed them out into the garden, closing the door behind them unceremoniously.

Goyita never phoned her mother when the class was dismissed before the regular time. And on this day Carmencita didn't do it either. Both girls quietly sat at the edge of the porch to wait for their mothers. Goyita, ashamed of her previous relief when Carmencita was at the mercy of Miss Adelfa's rage, smiled in solidarity.

"You hate ballet too, right?" Carmencita asked in a weak voice.

"Yes. My mother makes me..."

"Mine too," she lowered her head.

Both remained silent for few minutes. But soon Carmencita seemed to perk up. "Look," she showed Goyita a pack of gum. "My sister sent this from Miami. Want some?"

"When we chew them up a bit, let's put the wads in Miss Adelfa's door lock!"

"Yeah!" Carmencita gazed at the front door and for the first time that afternoon, she smiled.

Eventually their mothers arrived at the same time, though coming from opposite directions. Recognizing that something was wrong upon seeing their daughters still in leotards and tights, sitting quietly on the front steps, the mothers did not react. They greeted each other politely, saving their feelings of annoyance for when they got home.

Several shamefaced mothers had already attempted to telephone Miss Adelfa, each hoping to be the one to calm her down. When they found the line busy, their frustration grew.

"Miss Adelfa is so distraught that she has left her phone off the hook!"

Goyita's mother was mortified. After all, Miss Adelfa had been a pupil of the great Alicia Alonso, which amply justified the steep price of her lessons.

"A well-educated girl must take ballet lessons," Goyita's mother started. "I know you don't want to be a ballerina. You don't have to say it again. The fact is that as a girl, you must learn to adopt feminine postures and graceful movements, and ballet is the best thing. When you make your debut in society, you must look the part." She paused for a few moments, biting her lip. "I hope this debut of yours will happen in Miami because here we have no fit society in which to introduce a young girl anymore." She sighed, looking at her daughter. "Don't put that martyr's face on. Everything we do is for your own good. One day you will remember my words and be grateful. One day you will ask me why I didn't force you to try harder when you had the chance. But then it would already be too late. All refined girls should take ballet lessons, that's all there is to it. I would have given anything to have that opportunity. But my parents couldn't afford those luxuries, like we can."

She paused again and bit her lip. "Maybe it won't be the same way in Miami. Who knows when we'll be able to afford ballet lessons again," she paced, wringing her hands dramatically. "You are being ungrateful. Yes, I know, I know that what you really want to do is play basketball, which is such a violent game. Tomboys and girl athletes don't get married because men don't like girls like that. Girls playing tough sports look like sweaty male goats jumping around. Girls must cultivate their beauty and femininity for when the time comes for them to get married and make their husbands proud. The least you can do is take advantage of how fortunate you are. Girls…"

While her mother continued delivering her customary speech, Goyita sank in her father's favorite chair, breathing a sigh of relief. At least there she didn't have to fear the poking of the cue stick in her lower back. It was comforting to know that at least for the rest of that day she would be surrounded by the familiar, what she saw and heard every day, and every night. She knew her mother's speeches very well, and she had learned to let her thoughts wander while she still appeared to listen in contrition, her head low.

Her fingers played distractedly with the buttons of the leather char. She always found tobacco from her father's pipe trapped within the folds and corners of the seat. She carefully extracted the particles and slipped them into her mouth. It filled her with wonder to think of how such a diminutive speck could have such a strong, spicy flavor that remained on the tongue for a long time. Her imagination took flight, while keeping her mouth busy playing with tobacco clippings.

She saw herself as a world-famous comedienne, poking fun at the ballet *Swan Lake*, which she had renamed "Ugly Duckling Puddle." She would adorn her head with duck feathers, and have not simply a tutu made with them, but a complete duck suit, with a tutu.

She could talk some of her classmates into joining an absurd *corps de ballet.* They would all enjoy dancing to a choreography especially created to make fun of ballet.

Her mind entered a new dimension, far away from her mother's sermon with all of its drama. It was a dimension of greatness, of glory, of fun and entertainment for all audiences of the world. Deafening applause and laughter echoed all around her, completely drowning her mother's distant litany.

Her mother could dedicate her spare time to the creation of costumes for "Ugly Duckling Puddle." Didn't she love sewing and everything related to traditional women's work? Didn't she admire tiny, undetectable stitches and finely cut dresses, blouses, and skirts? Well, she should be happy to be given the chance to see her name in the program, even if it appeared in very small characters on the back of it.

Goyita held no grudges.

Jody Lannen Brady

Babies Don't Bowl

Jody Lannen Brady is a freelance writer and editor living in Arlington, Virginia. Past winner of the F. Scott Fitzgerald Short Story Contest, her fiction has been published in journals and anthologies including *At Our Core* (Papier-Mache), *The Adoption Reader* (Seal Press), and *A More Perfect Union* (St. Martins).

I've just spent ten minutes checking the weight of every ball on this rack. I'm looking for a ball that my children and my nieces can pick up. The ball selection here would be great for a league of body-builders, but I can't see my ten-year-old daughter flitting down the lane with one of these boulders. She insisted on coming here after seeing a commercial on TV. I am on record as voting against this particular outing, but as a mother I have apparently been officially designated a "good sport" whose vote does not count except when it comes to matters of safety, schoolwork, and bedtime. I walk to the cashier stand to inquire about balls lighter than sixteen pounds, and a fat man with a pencil behind his ear ignores me until I ask him a second time.

"What you want is a six-pounder."

"Okay," I say.

He rings someone up for shoes. I wait while he finds women's size six and men's size eleven. I wonder if they're made ugly on purpose—who would steal a pair of blue and red and puke tie-shoes?

"We don't have any," he finally says to me. "We used to have a few of 'em, but—"

"We have 'em," a woman interrupts.

I turn to look at her. She's a big-haired woman leaning on the counter and sucking on a cigarette. Her bouffant looks more helmet than hair—perhaps a wig? As she puffs out a stream of smoke, I realize that I've forgotten what we were talking about.

"Check each lane for orange-colored balls," she tells me. "The orange are the lightest. We usually save 'em for the children, but if you want to use one, there's nothin' stopping you," she says.

I start to explain that the balls *are* for children, but she moves on to interrupting the next customer attempting to talk to the fat man with the pencil. I begin to wonder if I look like someone who needs the lightest ball. Or do I just look like someone who would deny small children their fun? You have to understand that I've been on the edge of losing it long before I got to the bowling alley. After a rainy weekend, stuck in my sister's house with both our families, I'm not sure I like *anyone* anymore.

I walk and look, walk and look. Finally, I find two of the orange kiddy balls at the other end of the alley. They're on the rack that belongs to a lane where two hard-looking women are bulleting balls at their pins. These are big women.

"That's our rack," one of them says when I reach for the balls. She looks at me, with one hand on her hip and one hand swinging a towel; she is daring me, I think, to reach for one of the balls.

"Oh," is all I can think to say.

The other woman turns around. They're wearing matching T-shirts that say "BALL BREAKERS" on the front. Two bowling balls are under the words, stretched over D-cup-size breasts. These are not the kind of women I am used to. My kind of woman is not defiant; I don't like to admit it, but "apologetic" would be a better description of women like my sister and me. These women scare me. I look down.

"For your kids?"

I'm not certain which one has spoken because of my feigned interest in my ugly bowling shoes. So I nod at the space between them.

The closer one leans over the rack. I have to will myself not to back away. She scoops up an orange ball and holds it out to me.

"How many kids?" she asks.

"Four," I say.

She whistles and shakes her head. It's a response that registers both sympathy and amazement; I realize that she thinks I meant all four children were my own but before I can think of a way to explain, she leans over again and lifts up the other orange ball. She half hands, half tosses me the ball, but I cradle it easily with my free arm.

"Have a good one," the other Ball Breaker says. They turn back to their lane. Without another word, the one on the left picks up a ball, steps up onto the lane, and, in a clean sweep of grace, sends the ball racing down the lane. It crashes loudly into the neat set of pins and sends them flying everywhere.

I want to do that.

I'm walking back down the lane, each arm cradling a ball. I'm replaying the woman's strike in my mind. Seamless, that's what it was. No hesitation—just one flowing rush of power. A kid is racing down the alley; I step towards the concession stand to clear a path for him. But he clips me anyway, banging my arm, and the ball pops out and lands on my foot in an explosion of pain. My toes must be broken. I drop the other ball to the ground.

"PUL-LEASE." It's the concession lady—she's shaking her hair at me and giving me her best expression of disapproval. "No dropping balls," she says.

"Good move," I hear. A snorting laugh. This is my brother-in-law, the smart-ass from hell. He's a research engineer, and in his scheme of the world that puts him somewhere just below God. Once, he offered to set me up for a date with one of his fellow deities from work; when I refused, telling him that I didn't feel ready to go out, he assumed the real reason was that I was too intellectually intimated to go out with his kind. He actually told my sister that.

But I don't buy into his hierarchy—so I'm wondering why it's always me that goes after things like these balls. And I'm wondering why it's always my brother-in-law who gets to snort at my efforts. I want to sit down and hold my toes and cry. I want to tell him where he can go, but I'm not allowed to do that. I am a peacemaker. So I shake my head, shrug my shoulders, and let out a little laugh. It's meant as an apology to the concession lady and a joke at my expense for my brother-in-law.

I pick up one ball and wait for my brother-in-law to grab the other one. But he doesn't; he turns back to a rack of balls, inspecting a blue marble number as though his ball selection is going to make a big difference. I have a flash of bad sportsmanship and use my good foot to give the ball a push towards my brother-in-law's exposed ankles. The concession lady with the hair is saying something to me, but I don't care. Maybe she'll do me a favor and get me thrown out of the alley for kicking a bowling ball. Instead, my brother-in-law recoils when the ball smacks the back of his leg, gives it a blank stare, and then walks back to our lane. I bend and awkwardly retrieve the second ball.

My toe is still killing me, but I plant a fake smile on my face and present my kiddy balls to the children: my twelve-year-old son Mike; the ten-year-olds, my niece Pam and my daughter Sam; and my six-year-old niece Jen.

"I don't want an orange ball," the six-year-old niece whines.

"I don't need that, Mom," my son says. "I'm using this one." He is staggering under the weight of what is no doubt the heaviest ball he could find.

My daughter puts on her fake smile and puts her hands out. I'll take one for you, her expression says. It's her martyr face and I don't need it.

I turn away and walk to a ball stand by the concessions. I put the balls on the rack. Another mother on the prowl snatches one of the balls the second I put it down and then—and only then—my gang suddenly finds orange balls desirable. My son and the girls race past me. Mike grabs the lone orange ball. But then the other mother, rebuffed by her children, returns the second ball to the rack. The ten-year-olds grab it. Sam stands up, triumphantly holding the ball over her head.

"We'll share," she says to Pam.

"And it's not for you," my niece leans down to direct the words into her sister's face.

And so my little niece begins to pout and sniffle. I have a sudden wish to be the kind of person who could just slap them all and be done with the anger that is gnawing inside me. But, in a second, I'm back to myself again and I know that I don't want to slap anyone. All I want to do is leave. Or have a drink. Or both.

My little niece makes a bigger pout. When no one responds, she turns on the tear faucet. By the time my sister hustles over, Jen has two streams rippling down her cheeks. I stand staring stupidly at the scene, while my sister gives me her best pursed-lip, you-caused-this look. It's hard to believe at times like this that my sister and I, when we're alone, can be reasonably intelligent and humorous. We can even be friends.

"*I'll* get a ball for you," my sister says.

"But I want *that* ball," my niece manages to say in between sobs. She points at the ball held triumphantly by the smug ten-year-olds.

"Mike will share his ball with you," my sister says. She doesn't see the face my son shoots at her. It's his "fat chance" look.

"I want *that* ball."

"The girls have it."

"I saw it first."

"Well...," my sister says, and the girls go flying away with the ball.

Jen pushes her unhappiness up a notch and begins a high-pitched howl. But she has miscalculated, and her howl sends my sister over the edge.

"Babies don't bowl," my sister says in her tight-lipped voice.

Jen knows that voice means business. She opts to turn off her howl.

Mike steps up to the lane. His bowling form gives away his preference for baseball—ten feet down the lane the ball he has pitched thuds down on the wood. I cringe. The ball heads straight for the gutter.

"Nice start, champ," my brother-in-law pipes in. He laughs and gleefully switches on the overhead projector so that everyone in the ally can watch the auto-score machine record a zero in Mike's frame.

Mike hangs his head.

"I can't bowl," he says.

"Just use a heavier ball," comes a voice from the next lane.

Mike looks up. I look too. A skinny man is leaning on the bench that separates our lanes. He smiles at Mike. He's young. He has a T-shirt on that says something, but I don't want to stare at him long enough to read it.

"You're too strong for that ball. Try a ten-pounder," he says and turns away, moving back to his lane. I watch him bend over the ring of balls and study them. He stands up suddenly and swings back around towards us.

"Here," he says, holding the ball out to Mike. "Give yourself a couple frames to get used to it. You'll do fine."

Mike grins sheepishly, and he shyly moves over to take the ball from the man. I watch him walk back on the lane and I concentrate; I will the ball to behave this time. Mike holds the ball like a shot put.

"Keep it low," the man coaches.

And then it hits me. If Mike had a father, it would be his father saying these words. Suddenly my chest hurts, and I put a hand over my heart. It's as though I need to hold it in place. Heartache is supposed to be a cliché. This has happened, now and then, for three years now—but it still takes me by surprise every time I find myself missing my dead husband in a literal rush of pain.

Mike awkwardly flings the ball down the lane. It bangs down but not as hard as the first time and it makes a long, wobbly path to the gutter. I think: his father never got to bowl with him. And then I have to laugh at myself for my ridiculous, sentimental thought. Michael wouldn't have gone bowling. He would have sent us off, and he would have stayed at home to watch a baseball game. Baseball is America's sport, he liked to say. Bowling, for Michael, fell under the same category as mud-wrestling and monster trucks—unredeemably redneck.

"That was close," the man says to Mike. "Next frame."

"Nosey SOB," my brother-in-law mutters once the man has turned away. "Who's up? Let's go."

"I'll go," Pam says.

But before she can stand, Jen has leaped up with a screech. "Me," she says. "Meeeee, me."

Pam and Sam give one another a look; their look says that they know that Jen will get her way and they are above arguing. I like that look.

⁂

It's Jen's turn to bowl yet again, but she won't go. She has cried her way through two frames of gutter balls. My sister has alternated chastising Jen's crying and encouraging her to try. "Hey, Jen, did you turn two or three this year?" my brother-in-law calls out. "Maybe Mommy can share some of her style points with you," he adds with a snort. He has kept up his sarcastic commentary, and, despite myself, I am amazed at his capacity for uninterrupted put-downs—maybe he and the other engineers spend their lunch hours swapping insults for all occasions.

"Why don't I help you this time?" my sister asks.

Jen sniffles and nods.

My sister takes hold of Jen's hand and pulls her up to the red line of the lane.

"I thought babies didn't bowl," Mike whispers loudly to the big girls. They laugh until I shoot them a scowl. I hear something and look over to see the man in the next lane muffling a laugh. So he's been watching us, I think. Suddenly I feel self-conscious. My face feels hot and I wonder what he's seen me do.

"Does my butt look big?"

My sister leans over Jen, asking us this question between her legs.

"Naw," my brother-in-law howls. "Just blocks out the sun."

What wit, I think. And my sister is convinced this guy is some kind of brilliant. She says she has to humor him because the rest of us don't understand how frustrating daily life is for a genius like her husband.

"Does it look *really* big?" she asks.

I want to scream. I often want to scream when I'm around these two. I want to ask her: Have you no dignity? Why do you set him up? Why is it okay for them, our men, to laugh at us? And, come to think of it, why was it that when I laughed at something Michael did or said unintentionally, it was suddenly *not* funny? Laugh at his jokes, laugh at his wit—but whatever you do, don't laugh when a man says "rod iron" instead of "wrought." Years later, I can still feel his ire over that one.

My sister counts to three as she and Jen swing the ball back and forth between their legs. Then they shove the ball, and it slowly, slowly makes its way down the lane. When it reaches the end of the lane, it has just enough force left to push over a pin. Jen is squealing with delight and my sister jumps up and down like an idiot, smiling dumbly at her genius husband. She is performing for his benefit, as though she owes him something for putting up with all of us. I know, because I have felt myself do that—and that, I realize, is exactly what I don't miss about Michael.

I miss the smell of him—still, after three and a half years. I miss the way his hair looked when he woke up in the morning. I miss his frantic energy when he got ready to head out to watch a baseball game. Sometimes I go through this list just to make certain that I still remember him. It keeps me grateful for what he gave us. It keeps me single. But, as I stand here and watch my sister clown my brother-in-law into good humor, I start a new list. And it begins with this: I don't miss feeling that the children and I were something Michael had to put up with, and I don't miss feeling that I owed him gratitude and obedience for putting up with us.

⁓

My sister jumps out of her seat to applaud her husband's spare. She offers up a squeal of approval; he rewards this with a sneer and an eye roll. Then he looks over at me. He's trying to bait me. When it's my turn to bowl, I chant under my breath: ignore him, ignore him. I pick up Mike's ball this time. This is supposed to be fun. I swing my arm back, take a couple steps, and let the ball loose. It makes a beeline for the gutter. Some fun.

"Sign her up," comes my brother-in-law's jeer from behind the scoring screen. "Bowling for dollars."

"It's your thumb."

I know that voice now. In the next lane, the skinny man is looking seriously at me. He has his own thumbs tucked in the pockets of his jeans.

"My thumb?" It makes me smile.

"Can I show you?"

I nod, and the man puts a hand on the top of the bench and then hops it. It's like he's on the moon, the way he defies gravity. The children look up at him; I can see that they're impressed. My brother-in-law leans around the screen to stare at me. Certainly he thinks that I have lost my mind. Now I'm having fun.

"I'm Toby."

He doesn't say anything else. I don't know what to do. I look at him long enough to notice his long sideburns. He's older than I first thought. That's not good. Finally I realize what he's waiting for—my name.

"Beth."

"Well, Beth," he says, and I get the feeling he likes knowing my name. It makes me uncomfortable—like he has a claim on me now. "You just have to think about your thumb."

"Uh-huh," I mutter. I want him to hop back over where he belongs.

"Point your thumb up," he instructs.

I point my thumb up obediently, hoping it will make him leave.

"That's it," he says and grins.

Instinctively, I look to my brother-in-law for a reaction. He rolls his eyes.

"Let's see you try it now. You just swing, keeping that thumb on top and keep it up there as you release."

I grab my ball and stick my fingers in. He's watching me, but I focus on my thumb. Thumb up. I hold the ball in both hands in front of me. Thumb up. I swing the ball back. Thumb up. I step and swing the ball towards the pins. Thumb up. I release it. The ball cuts a clean path to the pins and smashes eight of them out of the way.

"Wow," is all I say to Toby when I turn around.

It is enough. He smiles back, then hops back over the bench to his own lane. We all watch him. He gives me a double thumbs-up and grins. Then he picks up a ball and sends the ball down the lane. A strike.

If I had started bowling this way, I'd be ahead of our entire group now. As it is, I've beaten everyone, including my brother-in-law, for the last four frames. Though clearly it's working for me, it seems that the rest of them either aren't trying or can't master the thumb advice.

When my sister gets up to bowl with Jen, I jump up. I've had it with the butt comments from my brother-in-law. What I need is a beer.

And who do I find at the stand? Toby's here, smiling away at me. He looks at me with his unblinking blue eyes as though we know one another. I get uneasy.

"Buy you a drink?" he asks.

This is awkward. If I let him buy me a drink, then I owe him something: talk, time, possibly something more. Taking something from a man is a promise. I have studiously avoided this situation since Michael died. It's easy to use the grieving widow face as a shield when a man knows your back story. But if I say no to this man, then I'll have ungratefully rebuffed a kind stranger who just revolutionized my bowling. I look back to our alley. I can feel my face flushed with embarrassment. I have to answer him.

Just then my brother-in-law looks up. His jaw drops at the sight of me and Toby standing together at the concession stand.

"Sure," I say to Toby. "I'd love a beer."

"All right," Toby says to me. To the concession lady he says: "A pitcher, please. And two mugs."

I am in for trouble now.

⌘

The beer is cold and Toby is funny and my brother-in-law is in shock. Sitting here chugging down my second mug, I just can't bother feeling neurotic. It's as though I've turned off a switch.

Pam and Sam are sitting on either side of Toby. I don't like that his T-shirt says "Eat My Shorts," but the girls don't seem to have noticed it. They are mesmerized by Toby's tattoo. They have never talked to anyone who had a tattoo before. They tell Toby this. So he rolls up his sleeve so that they can get a good look at the Chinese dragon that covers his upper arm. He has a lot of muscle for such a skinny man. My sister calls Pam to bowl. She has to call a second time before Pam can tear herself away from Toby. Now Sam scoots closer to Toby.

"Did it hurt?" she asks Toby in a low voice.

"It nearly killed me," he says to Sam in a whisper.

Her eyes open wide. Pam calls her to bowl.

"Do I have to?" Sam asks, pointing down at the lane.

I nod yes, and Sam takes one more look at the dragon as she walks away.

"I don't like to lie," Toby says, watching Sam line up to bowl. "Just didn't think you'd appreciate me encouraging your daughter to get one."

Toby fills up my mug. I don't say anything to him because I can't tell him what I'm thinking: that it wouldn't matter what he said, that we aren't the kind of people who get tattoos. That despite my aberrant behavior in agreeing to drink with him, we have nothing in common. That despite his being a man and my being a woman, there could never be anything between us. I don't say these things but they embarrass me as if I had. I take a big chug of beer and then I use a napkin to dab at the foam on my upper lip. I am a snob getting drunk with a redneck who is quite possibly trying to pick me up.

Mike comes to the table after his frame. We haven't finished our first game but he wants to quit.

"It takes them," he points to the rest of our gang, "*all* day. And I can't get any pins down. Can't I go to the game room?"

"You can't quit," I say.

"You like candy?" Toby asks Mike.

Mike perks up. He nods.

"How 'bout a candy bar if you get five pins down on your next frame?"

"All right," Mike shouts, and he's raced back to the lane to tell everyone before I can protest.

Now the girls have flocked around Toby.

"Us, too?" Sam asks.

"Yep," Toby says and grins at them. "A candy bar for each five pins."

"For the rest of the game?" Pam asks.

"Now, wait a minute," I say when Toby nods to Pam.

"Me, too. Me, too." Jen is looking both happy and angry at the same time. She is ready for either way Toby's response might go.

"You, too," he tells her.

⸙

The children work hard at their bowling. Mike gets six pins down, and Toby saunters over to the concession stand with him. Mike comes back with a big chocolate bar.

"That's too much," I say.

The girls pull Toby down to the bench to watch them. Sam gets her five pins but Pam doesn't; Sam says she'll share and they run off with one of Toby's dollars to pick out their candy.

It's Jen's turn. My sister walks up to help, but Jen insists on bowling by herself. She kneels by the foul line and pushes the ball. The ball heads slowly for the gutter and Jen whips around, ready to cry.

"How 'bout I bowl your next ball?" Toby asks her, and he stands up.

Jen nods at him and hands him her orange ball.

"You stand with me," he says.

He scoots her ball down the lane and knocks over most of the pins. She takes his hand. And this is, finally, too much for my brother-in-law.

"Jen," he calls her and pats his side as though calling a dog, but Jen doesn't let go of Toby's hand.

"Jennifer," he says, his face turning red. "I'll buy your candy."

Jen flings Toby's hand out of hers and runs over to her father. He looks over at me with what looks like a sneer, as though he's showing me that he's won some kind of battle here and he's daring me to confront him. But I don't play his game; I won't be baited into saying something stupid when none of this means anything.

I smile at him. "I got my five pins down. Get me one, too; something chocolate."

⸙

It's my turn now to bowl my last frame. As I'm swinging into my release, I think of the Ball Breaker and the way she shot her ball down the lane, and I feel a surge of power. My ball speeds down the lane and crashes the pins—only one left standing. If I can get the last pin, I'll have a spare, and by now even I know that a spare on the last frame means I'll get an extra ball to bowl. I want the spare.

"Slide to your left," Toby instructs me. It startles me because he's come up close behind me. "Just pretend you're in the middle of the lane. No hooking that way." He gives me a pat on the shoulder.

I panic. Strangers don't touch. That was not the touch of a stranger, I think. This man thinks we have something going on. I look around. Jen sits on her father's lap, happily stuffing M&Ms into her mouth. My sister has an arm around Pam and an arm around Sam, who are both chewing the last of their second candy bars, their third ones clutched in their hands. He has bought us candy, shared his beer with me, given us bowling lessons—and now he has touched me. This man isn't going to go away, I think.

"So bowl," my brother-in-law calls to me. "The suspense is killing us."

"Get a spare, Mom," Mike calls out. He's just returned from the snack bar, and he flashes me a thumbs up with the hand that isn't holding his candy bar.

I get up to the lane. But the air feels hot and heavy suddenly and it looks to me like the pin is swaying. I want to know: what have I gotten myself into?

I swing and the motion feels jerky; the ball awkwardly spins off my fingers and I know my thumb isn't remotely pointing up, as Toby has taught me. I turn away from the lane.

"What is that?" My brother-in-law looks dumbfounded.

"It's spinning back, Mom," Mike says. "Look, I think it's going to make it."

I turn around and see that the ball is somehow, miraculously, aiming down the lane in the direction of the pin. It moves closer and closer but, finally, it passes by the last pin and drops out of sight. A miracle ball, nonetheless, because I'd challenge anyone to explain how a ball launched totally out of control with no chance of connection ever made it that far.

Toby flashes a smile at me. He shrugs.

"If they all went the way we planned," he says, "it wouldn't be a game, now would it?"

I get the feeling he is talking about more than bowling and I feel I owe him an apology, that somehow he knew all along what I was thinking about him. I don't know how to answer him. But he doesn't seem to be waiting for an answer. He walks over to me, his hand out.

"It was nice meeting you all," he says and takes my hand. He pumps my hand up and down and then lets go. "Bye now, everyone."

Toby flips his baseball cap onto his head, and the children are all calling "bye" and "thanks" to him.

"Bye, Toby," my sister says.

Only my brother-in-law and I say nothing. Toby gives us a wave and then he's gone. I watch him as he passes the big-haired concession stand lady and gives her a nod. I watch him as he pats a man on the shoulder and I watch him as he walks out the door of the alley. Only then do I believe that he could really leave without asking for my phone number.

"Your boyfriend's dumped you," my brother-in-law says as he walks past me.

"That's what you think," I say for no particular reason, but I am rewarded anyway by a genuinely puzzled look from my brother-in-law. The thought that he just might not know everything must be troubling for a genius like him. It is for me, and I'm no genius.

Michelle Brafman

Her Antonia

MICHELLE BRAFMAN's fiction has appeared in various literary journals and was nominated for Best New American Voices 2009 and an AWP award. In 2006, she won the F. Scott Fitzgerald Short Story Contest and the *Lilith* Fiction Contest. A graduate of the Johns Hopkins University MA in writing program, she lives in Glen Echo, Maryland, with her husband and two children.

Phil shells pink pistachios at breakneck speed, leaving the detritus for Georgia to vacuum up later. The Redskins are winning 13–10, and the sportscaster's baritone blends with the hum of the dryer tumbling a load of Phil's whites. This afternoon the sound annoys Georgia. Without glancing up from her book—she's reading *My Antonia* for the fourth time—she knows it's halftime by the feel of Phil's stained fingers rubbing the inside of her arm.

She puts down her book and leads him upstairs to her bedroom, where she made up the bed with a fresh pair of sheets—one thousand thread count—moments before his arrival. Six minutes later, she rests her head against Phil's chest, a faded gold from his summer tan. Spermicide trickles down her thighs.

"Did you go?" This is Phil's language for inquiring about her orgasm.

"Hmmm." *In six minutes?* At least he asks. Her sister is right; ugly men are better in bed because they have to try harder. Phil is better-looking and younger than Georgia, and the fact that he calls on schedule, wipes down the toilet basin after he pees, and blogs about the conflict in Darfur compensates for his deficits as a lover. Plus, she likes the way his ropey arms feel wrapped around her torso—her trimmest body part—and for the past seven months, this weekly arrangement has been enough for her. She turns her head into his sparse chest hair and breathes in his scent: Dial soap and cat. Her nose starts to tingle as if she's going to cry.

God, she's been so needy since her cat died. It's been almost six months already. Pathetic.

Start to finish, they spend about seventeen minutes—roughly the length of a halftime show—in bed; Georgia times it. Phil sneaks downstairs to catch the second half of the game, while she sprays Shout on the pink thumbprint stains he left on her new sheets.

"Georgia?" he calls up to her in a kind voice. "Mind taking my clothes out of the dryer?"

Georgia does not yell. Ever. She walks down the two stairs of her split-level condo in her terry-cloth robe. "Done." She turns around on her heel, climbs back up the stairs to her bathroom, washes herself, and puts on a fresh pair of panties and the jeans and blouse she had been wearing earlier.

She pads over to the fridge, sliding her feet into her slippers. "Hungry?" She also never uses more words than she needs to, which makes people talk too much and subsequently become uncomfortable around her.

"Always, after some good loving." Without looking away from the game, he grins at her and reclines on the couch.

Georgia loves to cook. *Next week, I'll pick up a hearty bread and some butternut squash from the farmer's market. I'll make a nice soup. And I'll buy fresh ginger root and Asian pears from the vendor with the Coke-bottle glasses,* she muses while retrieving two television trays from her front hall closet. Shopping and preparing a meal for Phil give her Sundays structure, and the leftovers carry her through the week.

"You spoil me." He finishes his last bite of poached salmon and then pats his stomach as lean people sometimes do to draw attention to, and consequently generate compliments on, their waistlines.

"You're right." The edge in her voice surprises her. Maybe she's going through the change; her sister began menopause in her mid-forties.

"You okay?"

For the first Sunday in seven months, she doesn't feel okay about their routine: cable television, bad sex, laundry, and a home-cooked meal, followed by the cell phone call on Wednesday afternoons. "I miss Willa." This is true, but it also lets Phil off the hook.

He pulls her toward him and strokes her hair. "How long were you two together?"

She likes the way he phrases this question and the look of concern in his pale blue eyes. "Eleven years." Georgia and Phil had initially bonded over the similarity in their cats' names—Hobie Cat, to remind him of the free ocean winds, and Willa Cat-Her, after her favorite author—while she edited a pitch tape for him last year. Funny how such a simple exchange of information could incite their absurd coupling.

"Whoa. It's just going to take time." He kisses the top of her head. "It took about a year after my first kitty died before I was ready for another one. Now it feels like Hobie's been with me forever."

He wraps one of her curls around his pointer finger, and his tenderness embarrasses her. "I've got an early morning tomorrow." She extricates herself from him. Extra touching and soft words are not part of the deal.

After he leaves, she closes up the downstairs and runs a hot bubble bath for herself. The water burns her skin, but she doesn't care. She welcomes the little bit of warmth.

The next morning, Georgia awakens at five o'clock, unsettled from Phil's visit. She makes herself a cup of green tea, and even though it's Columbus Day—a company holiday—she heads to the office to work in peace. She edits a scene for "The Mettle of a Marriage," a reality television show that tests the strength of a seemingly happy marriage—an institution she rebuffed back in her thirties—by sending the husband or wife on a date with his or her first love.

Working on reality shows makes her feel greasy, but six months ago, the day after she put Willa to sleep, she split a tooth and needed money to foot the hefty dentist bill. Soon thereafter, she began to suffer panic attacks over her meager savings and the fear that she would grow old alone. She swapped her earnest broke public television colleagues like Phil for hungry young producers sporting hip eyewear.

She stuffs her exchange with Phil in the back of her mind and parachutes into a stack of field tapes. Her brain is well suited for video editing; she has a knack for mining key images and moments from yards of footage. She then registers, sorts, and spits them out in perfectly rendered scenes.

Today, she zeroes in on wife Sheila hunting down a pair of "miracle jeans" that will hide what gravity has inflicted upon her rear end. Bingo. Georgia ignores her producer Heidi's script and begins cutting a sequence of Sheila's shopping trip.

Heidi breezes into the edit suite at nine thirty with two skim lattes. Even though she's young, she has the look of a woman who has dated too many married men.

"What are you doing here?" Georgia calls over her shoulder, knowing the answer. Heidi is a bit of a control freak, even though she relies on Georgia to make her look good.

"Stupid-ass holiday." She hands Georgia a tall cup and removes her cell phone earpiece. "So what have you got?"

Georgia dims the lights and presses the play button on her computer.

When the sequence is over, Heidi whistles in genuine awe. "Fucking wizard, Georgia." Heidi puts down her latte. "That shot of Sheila struggling with her waistband is killer."

Georgia is disturbingly good at her job, which makes her feel a little proud, but also ashamed. Her editing prowess enables her to exploit this poor middle-aged woman, whose thighs look like her own—like someone stuffed a vat of cottage cheese into an old pair of pantyhose.

Heidi pulls up a chair and sits too close to Georgia. "I totally nailed that interview. What a boo-hooer! She was so into that high school flame. They like played in a band together or something. And her husband Joe is a marathon runner, he's probably Viagra-dependent from all that exercise. She weighs more than he does for sure, bet she could take him in a fight. Don't you think?" Heidi prattles, and Georgia knows this is her cue to tell her how brilliant she is for digging up this story. But she continues to shuttle through footage in silence, willing Heidi to just stop talking. "Major flippage in store for this one," Heidi snorts.

"Flippage" is the network term for the moment when the spouse moves from mild interest to obsession over his or her first love. Flippage makes a fool out of perfectly normal people, makes them do crazy things. *Good job, Heidi. Congratulations on ruining another marriage.* "You sure know how to pick 'em," Georgia mutters.

"Hey, that's why they pay me the big bucks." She simultaneously laughs and hacks—in the way that smokers do—wheeling her chair toward Georgia.

Georgia catches a whiff of Heidi's scent: spearmint Altoids and Camel Lights and Clinique Elixir. "Heidi. Space." She points to the desk behind the edit carrel.

Because Heidi respects bitchiness, she returns to the producer's chair without argument, and then her cell phone and Georgia's line ring simultaneously. Georgia does not own a cell phone. What would be the point? She's only received a dozen phone calls since she began working here, mostly short ones from Phil, on Wednesdays, during the early evening, while he walks to the Y for his weekly racquetball game with his college roommate Neil.

"Hey there," he croons in his playful baritone.

"Hi." Georgia puts her finger over her free ear to drown out Heidi's raspy laugh.

"Would anyone object to us having dinner tonight?" He shifts to his fake debonair persona.

Dinner? "What's up?" She shuttles through footage of Sheila enduring a bikini wax.

"Can't a guy take his girl for a meal?"

His girl? His use of this simple pronoun gives her a start; she's not so sure she wants to alter her status with Phil. Feels dangerous. It's the dead-endedness of her relationship with Phil—not his dimpled smile or compassion—that appeals to Georgia.

"Okay. I'm taking off early," Georgia announces to Heidi, who raises one eyebrow.

Heidi removes her glasses and folds her hands on her lap.

"Dinner plans."

"But there's more, chérie. Do tell." She gives her best deadpan.

Georgia considers telling Heidi about Phil; she doesn't have many close girlfriends, particularly for a woman who has chosen the single life. Her married friends eat their dinners without chewing and try too hard to pretend that they have room in their lives for more than their kids and husbands, and her single friends seem too desperate sometimes. Heidi is actually an articulate listener, which is why she's such a good interviewer. But she knows that confiding in Heidi will make her feel good while she's talking but soiled afterwards.

"It's a holiday, Heidi," she mutters while she shuts down her computer.

Georgia waits for Phil to arrive at the Basil Café. She follows a perky hostess to an empty table and downs two glasses of merlot. Fifteen minutes later, she plays a game she invented to help her survive social situations. She scans the room for images and sounds, imagining that she is editing this real-life scene: *Establishing shot of restaurant, six p.m., gorgeous light; medium shot of older couple laughing; tight shot of man's face, cut to wedding ring encasing a plump, freckled finger. Natural sound has potential: glasses clinking, grinding of the espresso machine, laughter, water pouring from a pitcher, pianist tinkling. Gershwin? Nice. Very nice. Lots to work with here.* A man in an ill-fitted mohair coat and a strong jawline glides past the hostess with a wink; he looks like a Kennedy. Phil.

"So sorry I'm late." He extends his hand, and when Georgia tries to shake it, he scratches his head. "Gotcha." And then he points his finger at her as if he's shooting her and gives her arm a good squeeze.

Why would anyone think it feels good to have the flesh of one's tricep pulled from the bone?

"Whatcha drinkin?" He points to the wineglasses.

"I don't drink." She glances to the end of the bar, at a handsome young man wearing a carefully coiffed ponytail and clogs.

"He sent you these?" He looks toward the man with interest.

"Gotcha." She fake-shoots him back, exhibiting her sassy side for the first time. This exchange incites a flirtatious charge between them.

"That's good. Good." His eyes twinkle, as he motions to the waitress and orders a glass of port for himself. They eat penne out of bowls the size of Frisbees, while Phil describes a grant proposal he is writing for some documentary series about the rise of hate crimes in Ontario. His passion charms Georgia, making her ache to ditch Heidi for the chance to work on a real film again, something that might matter. She wants to ask why they are drinking too much wine in this Italian bistro on a Monday night, just one day after their routine date, but she doesn't. Georgia is good at waiting.

The air is balmy for a Washington October night. Phil grabs Georgia's hand as they walk from the restaurant to his Georgetown apartment; she can't remember the last time a man grabbed her hand. It feels good. His English basement apartment smells less like cat pee than she had anticipated it might. She shrugs her sweater off, aware that he is watching her.

"They're nice." He points at her breasts.

Her cheeks are warm from the bottle of wine they split at dinner, and she can't wipe the goofy smile off her face. "Where's Hobie?"

"She's shy." He disappears into his bedroom and returns with a ginger tabby under his arm.

"Hewwo kitty cat. This is Georgia." Beneath his baby talk, his voice reveals gentleness. That uncomfortable feeling from the day before returns but softer around the edges, porous enough for her to welcome another kind of sensation. She wants to stay more than she wants to flee, so she intuitively reaches for the silky fur beneath Hobie's chin and rubs the sweet spot until she purrs.

"She only likes special people." He nods.

Special people? How many women have met this cat? A pang of something like ownership surprises Georgia.

"Can I get you something to drink? A glass of vino maybe?"

"Sure." She doesn't know what to do with herself while he fusses with the corkscrew, so she paces around his small apartment. She spots a photo of a younger, goateed Phil slinging his arm around the shoulders of a handsome gray-haired woman wearing a lavender sun dress. Same dimple, same jaw. *Must be his mother.* "You two look alike," Georgia comments.

"She passed away five years ago." Phil's tone is matter-of-fact.

Before Georgia can respond, he comes up behind her and kisses her neck, leaving just the slightest bit of moisture on her skin. He kneads her shoulders, and she feels tension dissolve into her body. And a full hour later, when he asks her if she has "gone," she answers him truthfully with a yes. Sleep finds her with Phil's arm slung over her belly and Hobie's heat curling around her toes.

Georgia wakes up the next morning with a pounding headache and a mouth that feels like she's been chewing on old gym socks. Phil is shaving in his bathroom, wearing a pair of Redskins boxers that Georgia recognizes from doing his laundry. "How'd you sleep, Georgia girl?" His voice is full of mischief. "You were something last night."

She buries her head under the covers, embarrassed by all her thrashing and thrusting.

He laughs. "Hey, listen, remember that conference in Toronto I told you about last night?" He washes thin lines of shaving cream from his cheeks. "Do you think you could take care of Hobie while I'm gone?"

"Yes." She strokes Hobie's stomach; she feels like she's thawing. She imagines herself with Phil in his apartment reading the paper on Sunday mornings, like normal couples do. Sipping hot vanilla-flavored coffee, petting Hobie, licking butter and jam from the sides of each other's mouths. Or maybe they'd be like one of those freshly showered couples she endures while she breakfasts at Café Luna with her Sunday *New York Times.* The ones who laugh too hard at each other's jokes and gorge themselves on pancakes and eggs, ravenous and hung over from their rigorous lovemaking. *What are you doing? Think, Georgia, think. Remember the stale jokes and the Metallica CD you spotted on his bookshelf. And don't forget last night—that caper shrapnel dangling from his chin and how it made the leggy waitress he'd been flirting with look away.*

He finishes dressing and then sits down next to her on her bed. "Okay then, we'll talk details later. Sleep as long as you like, tiger." He cups her chin. "Roar."

She smiles. "Bye."

"You should do that more." He runs his finger over her lips. "Pretty."

She couldn't stop if she wanted to.

Is this happening? A vague sense of recognition orbits around her head as she tries to name the feeling that is taking hold of her. Holy shit. Flippage. She doesn't flip. She won't flip, not like her mother and her sister, always waiting for some husband (seldom their own) to phone to tell them that they will be ten minutes, twenty minutes, two hours late. Don't wait up for me babe, the sure warning sign that they have had their fill. Georgia has done an excellent job of insulating herself from this by dating men she doesn't really like, and she certainly isn't going to let anyone, even someone with a cat as fine as Hobie, come along and turn her into a heap of goo. No thanks.

She dials Heidi's cell phone to tell her that she will be late.

"Phil Wagner?" Heidi teases. "The PBS hottie?"

She hates caller ID. "Just feeding a friend's cat, Heidi."

"You know that cute promotion producer, the Sheryl Crow with baby-fat. She had a huge, and I mean like, rabbit-in-the-bathtub, stalker-huge thing for that guy."

Georgia is glad that Heidi can't see her ears redden with pride.

"Nice work. Hope you got some."

"Get over yourself. We used to work together," she snaps. This morning Heidi's crudeness makes Georgia cringe, particularly after last night, after she had made herself so vulnerable.

Phil extends his trip to eight days; he tells Georgia that he's following up on some hot funding leads from the conference. While he is away, Georgia thinks about him on days other than Wednesday and Sunday, perhaps because she stops by his house every day to play with Hobie. She visits her favorite pet store and buys organic catnip and a furry toy possum attached to a fishing pole. She runs around the living room dangling the possum, with Hobie in hot pursuit. She brushes Hobie's fur and strokes her while she reads and drinks Phil's coffee. She smiles for no reason and edits meandering scenes of special moments between

Sheila and her husband. Heidi complains that she has lost her edge, that her sequences have become maudlin. She covers her gray with an auburn rinse and picks up a brochure for Lasik eye surgery as she leaves her ophthalmologist's on her way out of her optometrist's appointment. She buys a pair of pointy black shoes, the kind Heidi wears. She returns a pale pink cashmere sweater to Saks and then drops the $173.32 into her old lover's mail slot, hoping that he will spend it on a woman who can reciprocate his feelings, one who might look better in pastels. She calls her sister and listens with interest while she describes her new boyfriend, Hank, who is nothing like her last husband, Steve. She buys her niece an iPod for Christmas.

Phil is scheduled to return home on a Monday night. On Sunday afternoon, clad in her hip new shoes, Georgia visits her vendor with the glasses. She buys eight juicy Stayman apples. She'll bake Phil a pie. A mélange of yellow, red, and gold leaves blankets the streets. It's a crisp fall day, one of the last of the season, she figures. The cool air cuts through her sweatshirt, hardening her nipples. *Nice.* She blushes remembering Phil's comment about her breasts. During the entire cab ride to Phil's, she replays that night over in her head a million times. It just came out of nowhere.

She lets herself inside Phil's apartment and stands still in the entryway ready for Hobie to greet her. This ritual has become the best part of her day, waiting for Hobie. She listens for Hobie's meow, kneeling down, fingers poised for the touch of her smooth fur.

Today the phone rings and she watches the little red light on the answering machine flicker. The caller is one of those rambling types, "...not sure if you're back from the great white north. Let me know if you want to play on Wednesday." *At least it isn't a woman.* "Sorry again I couldn't help out with your cat. Hope that chick who does your laundry came through for you. Okay then. Call me. Later."

Blood rushes through Georgia's body, and paisley-shaped blotches multiply on her face and chest. She sits down on Phil's couch dumbly. Hobie climbs up on her lap, and looks up at her with her steely gray eyes; as if she knows what an asshole her owner is; as if to say thanks for the gourmet grub, but didn't I try to warn you? Her cheeks feel hot. How could she have been so stupid? Flippage, schlippage. What a dunce. This is her punishment for ridiculing poor Sheila and everyone else who has ever been naïve enough to participate in her slimy television show. Why did she have to tinker with her arrangement with Phil? Think that it could ever be more than it was? That someone who could date some Sheryl Crow look-alike would really be interested in a middle-aged woman like her? That she could ever be more than the "chick who does his laundry"?

God she is tired. Tired of doing this whole living thing solo. She closes her eyes for a second and forty-five minutes later, Hobie is licking her cheek. A fresh wave of anger takes hold of her, as she reaches to stroke Hobie's arched back. What a fucking cliché, a forty-something spinster with a fierce attachment to her cat, who is whoring out her one real talent so that she can store a few more pennies for her twilight years, when her contemporaries will retire and travel cross country in Winnebagos, or live off of their spouses' life insurance policies or 401ks. There will be no children to visit her in a nursing home when she has lost her teeth and hair and the wits to pee in a toilet. And as reckless as her mother and her sister are about love, at least they aren't going to rot alone, like her.

It's dusk when she ventures outside for some air. The temperature has dropped and her shirt—dampened from sleep—sticks to her body. Gooseflesh breaks out on her arms and legs like a bad case of poison oak. She walks until the back of her heel grows hot with the promise of a blister. Scenes from the last month bombard her in rapid fire, as if she can't operate the controls on her video deck. The machine jams on the same damned images of the night Phil made love to her in his bed; his delicate kisses on her forehead and belly and wrist. And for the first time since that night, she allows herself to think about those seven months of Sundays when she forgave him his selfishness. Had she known that he had some skill as a lover, she would have made him work harder for the meal and laundry service. Or worse, maybe poaching salmon and sorting his fucking underwear—not to mention the road-kill sex—was a fair price to pay for a reason to hunt down fresh ginger on a Saturday afternoon and a measly postcoital hug. Her eyes burn, but she doesn't cry. Her limbs feel like rubber, but she doesn't slow down. She enters a gourmet deli and notices her crazed look reflected in the storekeeper's eyes; he quickly rings up a pound of hot-pink pistachio nuts.

She walks back to Phil's apartment and opens a bottle of his wine—hoping he was saving it for a special occasion—and pours herself a full glass of red. Then she sits on the couch and cracks the nuts in half. She stuffs the meat into a Baggie—she hates the taste of pistachios—leaving a mound of splintered shells on Phil's carpet. She gathers up his polyester white sheets with her stained fingers, which creates a pink tie-dyed pattern of sorts.

"Come here Hobie cat." She picks her up to say goodbye; truly this is her intention. But just as she leaves, just as she should release Hobie back into the empty apartment, she bows her head and whispers, "Let's just call you Antonia. *My* Antonia." Her muscles loosen, and her mouth forms that goofy flippage smile as she shuts Phil's door behind her. She walks past the Basil Café and her vendor's empty apple stand and the darkened gourmet deli. The hard leather of her shoe zests a layer of skin from her heel, but she ignores the warm blood trickling toward the arch of her foot. She just keeps moving. Her arms cradle her new cat to her breasts, shielding her against the first cold breath of winter.

Laura Brylawski-Miller

from "The Shadow of the Evening"

LAURA BRYLAWSKI-MILLER was born and raised in Milan, Italy, and is now a resident of Arlington, Virginia. She has a BS in allied health from George Washington University and an MFA in creative writing from American University. Her publications include two books of poetry—*Luna Parks* (1985) and *The Snow on Lake Como* (1991, winner of the Washington Writers' Publishing House poetry competition)—and two novels—*The Square at Vigevano* (2001) and *The Medusa's Smile* (2006), both winners of the Washington Writers' Publishing House fiction competition. Her creative work has appeared in numerous literary magazines; she has also published surgical articles in medical journals. She is at work on her fourth novel.

I was fate's instrument. The chosen agent. This is why I had to come to this place, I know it now. I didn't want to believe that fate controls us, yet I have to accept it. Predestination has robbed me of free will—and of absolution. I didn't know this—not that a choice was ever involved—so how could I have changed what happened? Yes, there were signs. And I refused to heed them.

So I'm guilty. My guilt is the guilt of the storm that drowns the sailors, of the avalanche that buries the village. Death went through me. I'm not death, I'm only a tool, but I brought death with me. Instruments of evil should perish, and yet I wasn't destroyed. I was spared. I'm a spare part.

The catalyst was the air. Oxygen holds a dangerous, delicate balance. It supports life, but it can combust inside you till you explode, turn to ashes. I needed air. I had to come out and go sit under the pines, away from the tomb, breathe the sea air into the my lungs. I heard the sea calling, my lungs recognized the sea in the air. Our lungs were sponges when we were part of the sea. We came from the sea, but now the sea can drown us. We can't use the oxygen in water. H_20. I had to get out and sit under the pines. The lack of oxygen destroyed me, but the oxygen destroyed him. I saw him vanish in front of my eyes, and Vanth saw me. She stood up behind him, the great wings spread out to comfort him. Her torch illuminated the tomb, the shadows came forward, the long dark shadows of the sunless world. I should have known we wouldn't return unscathed.

They're guilty too, but they deny it. To deny is to pretend. They are pretenders, because they're not what they seem. Like *Phersu*, they wear masks. Agamemnon wore a mask of gold in his tomb and when the mask was lifted his face turned to dust. Life only gives you dusty answers. I'm life, therefore I'm dust.

I have been imprisoned in my room for two days in order to avoid them. I know they're asking for me because the man downstairs told me, when I went out tonight. His name is Benvenuto, the same as Cellini. He's a good man, so he should be welcome. I'm a prisoner, but my room is not a jail, nor a hospital. It has a lock with a key in it and Benvenuto wears a uniform, not like a real concierge, but similar. He looks like a guard, but he's not a guard. He didn't stop me when I went downstairs, only asked how I was, and I could tell he meant his words. I talked to him because I could trust him with my words. He's not a pretender—there is goodness in his face.

When I finally went out, it was dark and the sky was full of stars. Some twinkled, but others had become fixed and opaque, dead masses reflecting borrowed light, like planets. I tried to recognize these new planets, give them the reality of a name, but they were moving fast, some streaking through the sky so rapidly I couldn't calculate their orbit. Perhaps they came from another galaxy. planets of portents, scarring the sky with omens. Earth must still be spinning on its axis, perhaps faster than before, and that takes time away. I thought it had only been two days but Benvenuto said tonight was the twentieth of August. I don't know what happened to that lost time. An Italian poet called the earth an opaque atom of evil. In Italian, *male* means both evil and illness. Maybe they're the same thing. I am a male, and I've turned opaque, the fire dead in me. But I'm not evil, because I did not will this. Evil is live turned on itself.

Diana keeps calling.

"Are you all right?" she says. She's worried about me, or maybe about herself. Her voice filters from the phone into my ear, reaches my brain, and I have to decide. Is the voice real? I thought I could find out if I went to see her. I need to know what is happening, no, what has happened. But what is real? Reality has so many facets, like the compound eye of a fly. Thoughts fly through my head, compound my burden. My synapses have been rearranged in a tangled web, the cortex is having trouble keeping the revolution down. I'm leaking acetylcholine, how can I have free will? I love her more than I knew I could love.

I took a long shower and shaved, because I wanted to look good to her. Mina said I was good-looking, but she was just being kind. The kindness of strangers bandages lost souls.

I was surprised at how steady my hands were while I shaved, how solid and wise in their stereognosis, recognizing their position in space even with my eyes closed. As agile as acrobats, the fingers sure and alive, with little pale moons at the base of the nails. Lunulae. The moons on my fingers. Lovers have stars in their eyes, a song says, and that makes them blind. I'm blinded by stars. Women have been heavenly bodies for my hands to hold. I love the body of a woman, the sensuous comfort of a woman's skin under my hands. My wise, strong hands. I thought I saw my hands fall apart this morning when I tried to lift my coffee cup. The fingers were disintegrating, first the nails with their waning moons and then the tips. They'd lost all feeling, the innervation gone dead as in Hansen's disease. Leprosy. The mute skin, someone called leprosy, because there is no feeling left. I have no feeling left. I am a leper but my hands are again strong and solid.

I went out today and the sun was too strong, a sun to destroy the living dead I am becoming, but I wanted to see Diana. Has she changed as I have? We must all be wearing the mark of what has happened. I saw people staring at me in the street, but I knew they couldn't see the mark, because the mark is invisible. Still they kept looking, and I could feel their eyes trespassing behind the sunglasses.

"You had us all worried," Diana said. "Why didn't you answer our calls? Where were you?"

"Nowhere. In a place I can't remember," I told her, and I saw the glance between her and Roberto. I was upset to see him there, because I'd hoped to be alone with her.

"You should be in Florence," I said to him. He pretended not to understand but he did. "You should go underground. We all should. That's where we belong."

"Alexander, please. Don't do this," Diana said. "You look exhausted. Talk to us, don't pull away now. We're doing everything that can be done. Trust Roberto."

"Can he reverse time?" I said.

"You know there is no answer to that," Roberto said. "It's devastating. And so unfair."

"Oh, what good does it do to torment ourselves..." Diana said. She looked right through my brain. "Alexander, don't go and do anything rash. This isn't the moment."

Her hand was on my arm, like a caress, a fierce caress, the fingernails digging in. I love her. I am a leper, but my skin is not mute under her hand. Her touch shoots through me like a current. They no longer do electroshock, there are drugs now. Even executions are by lethal injection.

"Who executes the executioners? I asked them.

And I saw the fear in her eyes. She has eyes like stars. But they were fearful stars.

"Alexander, come to Florence with me for a few days," Roberto said. "I think you need to get away from here. Perhaps see somebody."

He means a doctor. They always mean a doctor, though they never say the word. But then words are for hiding thoughts, are they not? I think Talleyrand said that. Except I see through such words.

"We're worried about you," Diana again, repeating the same lie.

Why? Nothing happened to me. "Nothing happened to me," I told them. They're worried about themselves.

"Nothing happened because Claudio dragged you away. You didn't know what you were doing. We were afraid you would get hurt."

Claudio, the hotel owner. Then I remembered. My hands remembered digging. There were no shovels, so I used my hands. But hands are useless against the gods.

"We all had to get out of there," she went on. "There was nothing else we could do."

"We should not have been there," I said.

"What good—" She started to talk, but Roberto was looking at her. I saw the signal in his eyes. They don't realize how well I can see their thoughts.

"We're all too shaken to make any decision," he said. "What we need is time. We'll talk again in a few days."

"I don't want to stay here," Diana objected. "I'm coming to Florence with you.

Roberto was looking at me. "Will you come to Florence too, Alexander?"

"What good would that do? Orestes couldn't escape the Furies," I told him. "I must stay here."

"Then stay with him, Diana."

Again there was fear in her eyes. "I don't think it's wise," she said.

She's afraid for me. Of me. I am in her hands and she's afraid of me.

The voices have come back, relentless. They fill the room with fragmented phrases I can't quite understand, enigmatic answers to questions I haven't asked, coming at me from every corner, till I find the strength to go out and escape them. It is better outside. Other noises seem to mute them, though the assault doesn't quite cease. I long for silence, the long, white silence of a deserted, snowy landscape.

One of the voices is Etruscan—the young man in the tomb. He speaks though he has no mouth, no larynx. Is this why he hid his face in the Guarnacci? Did he know I would come to destroy him?

Diana keeps asking about the photographs.

"I lost the camera at the site," I told her. But she doesn't believe me.

"When did you last remember having it?"

"I don't remember anything."

Last night I went down to the Balze and threw the camera over the cliff. That was an Etruscan site. So the lie is no longer a lie.

I should go to the police, give them the photographs. But it would be a useless betrayal. I betrayed myself long ago. And there must be a reason why the photos were spared. They're mute witnesses. Maybe they're tarot cards. They hold the future in them. But the future is slipping away, and I cannot read it.

I know what to do. I will send the photos to David—I can trust him. They'll be safe across the ocean. A message in a bottle, for fate to do what it wants with it.

I drove to Pisa to mail the photos this morning, slipping out early so no one would see me. But a few miles out I noticed a black Mercedes following me. It wasn't trying to pass me, even when the road gave the opportunity, which was suspicious. Italians don't drive that way. Roberto has a black Mercedes. Mercedes means mercy. I am at the mercy of a Mercedes. I pulled into a gas station and pretended to ask the attendant directions for Tirrenia, in case anybody asked. The Mercedes went by. It was driven by a bearded man. Beards are for disguise. Then I felt ashamed. Roberto is in Florence, trying to get things "right," Diana says. Not that she believes it. Not that things can ever be right again.

The sun filled the sky with lies as I drove on to Pisa.

After I mailed the photos I stopped on one of the bridges and watched the Arno flow away toward the sea. Words were written on the water, the water was like a screen on which words were written. A message I couldn't read. The voices were silent, perhaps they were writing the words instead of speaking them. There was noise around me but I only heard the silence. D'Annunzio called Pisa one of the "Cities of Silence." I watched that message flow toward the sea and wondered what the sea does with words written on the water.

The earth is crushing me.

Dr. Azzini came to see me this morning. All dressed up in his three-piece suit, in spite of the blazing heat. Perhaps his suit is his armor. A suit of armor. But his pale face is unprotected, soft as bread dough.

"We're concerned about you," he told me. "You look tired. Are you sleeping well?

"Are you?" I said, and he gave me a lost look.

He's a stupid man, a stuffed shirt stuffed in his suit, but his is a sincere stupidity. The others are clever. Too clever. "Sleep?" his eyes behind the gold-rimmed lenses looked as forlorn as goldfish in a bowl. "No. I'm not sleeping too well. How could anybody? But it's you I'm concerned about." He sounded as if he really meant it. "Please trust me. I think you need help."

He needs help too. "I think we're beyond help," I said, "you and I."

"Don't say that." The dough face deflated. "But it's you I'm worried about," he repeated. "And please trust me—as a physician."

The voices started to laugh. Yeah, trust a doctor.

"Stop," I told them. The room filled with silence.

"Dr. Woodford," Azzini said.

I had forgotten he was there. "What?"

"Forgive me." He was staring at me. "But...are you perhaps hearing..."

A stupid man, but a good doctor.

"I hear the daisies growing over me," I told him. He stiffened, and I took pity. "I'm only quoting Keats," I said. "It's not about us, Doctor. Only the good die young."

"Dr. Woodford. Alexander. Please let me help you. You need some rest. If you don't have anything, I can write you a prescription," he said. "A mild sedative. What do you take usually? Just so you can relax. Later...Later we can discuss things. All right?" I'm back into my prison. So I just nodded.

I haven't filled the prescription. The voices are getting clear. They are the voices of demons. We let them loose when we opened the tomb. I should have known you don't return unscathed from the underworld—the gods won't allow it. I hear Luigi's voice, and then I feel the wind through the pines, salty and bitter. The wind is not wind. It's Vanth, her great wings beating in the still air, waiting...

It's night. The wind now comes from Balze, where the earth swallowed the old Etruscan city. The voices are in the wind. They're calling...

Maxine Clair

Cherry Bomb

MAXINE CLAIR is the author of *Rattlebone*, a collection of short stories, which won the *Chicago Tribune*'s Heartland Prize for fiction; the novel *October Suite*; a collection of poems, *Coping With Gravity*; and a fiction chapbook, *October Brown*, which won Baltimore's Artscape Prize. Born and raised in Kansas City, Kansas, she worked for many years as chief medical technologist at the Children's Medical Center in Washington, D.C. She is now an associate professor of English at George Washington University and lives in Maryland.

It was two summers before I would put my thin-penny bus token in the slot and ride the Fifth Street trolley all the way to the end of the line to junior high. Life was measured in summers then, and the expression "I am in this world, but not of it" appealed to me. I wasn't sure what it meant, but It had just the right ring for a lofty statement I should adopt. That Midwest summer broke records for straight over-one-hundred-degree days in July, and Mr. Calhoun still came around with that-old-thing of an ice truck. Our mother still bought a help-him-out block of ice to leave in the backyard for us to lick or sit on. It was the summer that the Bible's plague of locusts came. Evening sighed its own relief in a locust hum that swelled from the cattails next to the cemetery, from the bridal wreath shrubs and the pickle grass that my younger cousin, Bea, combed and braided on our side of the alley.

I kept a cherry bomb and a locked diary in the closet under the back steps where Bea, restrained by my suggestions that the Hairy Man hid there, wouldn't try to find them. It was an established, Daddy-said-so fact that at night the Hairy Man went anywhere he wanted to go but in the daytime he stayed inside the yellow house on Sherman Avenue near our school. During the school year if we were so late that the patrol boys had gone inside, we would see him in his fenced-in yard, woolly-headed and bearded, hollering things we dared not repeat until a nurse kind of woman in a bandanna came out and took him back inside the house with the windows painted light blue, which my mother said was a peaceful color for somebody shell-shocked.

If you parted the heavy coats between the raggedy mouton that once belonged to my father's mother, who, my father said, was his Heart when she died, and the putrid-colored jacket my father wore when he got shipped out to the dot in the Pacific Ocean where, he said, the women wore one piece of cloth and looked as fine as wine in the summertime, you would find yourself right in the middle of our cave-dark closet. Then, if you closed your eyes, held your hands up over your head, placed one foot in front of the other, walked until the tips of your fingers touched the smooth cool of slanted plaster all the way down to where you had to slue your feet and walk squat-legged, fell to your knees and felt around on the floor—then you would hit the strong-smelling cigar box. My box of private things.

From time to time my cousins Bea and Eddy stayed with us, and on the Fourth of July the year before, Eddy had lit a cherry bomb in a Libby's corn can and tried to lob it over the house into the alley. Before it reached the top of the porch it went off, and piece of tin shot God-is-whipping-you straight for Eddy's eye. By the time school started that year, Eddy had a keloid like a piece of twine down the side of his face and a black patch he had to wear until he got his glass eye that stared in a fixed angle at the sky. Nick, Eddy's friend, began calling Eddy "Black-Eyed Pea."

After Eddy's accident, he gave me a cherry bomb. His last, I kept it in my cigar box as a sort of memento of good times. Even if I had wanted to explode it, my mother had threatened to do worse to us if we so much as looked at fireworks again. Except for Christmas presents, it was the first thing anybody ever gave me.

But my diary was my most private thing, except for the other kind of private thing, which Eddy's friend Nick was always telling me he was going to put his hand up my dress and feel someday when I stopped being babyish about it. I told that to my diary right along with telling the other Nick-smells-like-Dixie-Peach things I wrote every afternoon, sitting in my room with the bed that Bea and I shared pulled up against the door. I always wrote until it was time for my father to come home and take off his crusty brogans that sent little rocks of dried cement flying.

One evening after supper, I sat on the curb with Bea and Wanda calling out cars the way my father sometimes did with us from the glider on our front porch. The engine sounds, the sleekness of shapes, the intricacies of chrome in the grillwork were on his list of what he would get when his ship came in. Buick Dynaflow! Fifty-three Ford! Bea kept rock-chalk score on the curb until Nick rode up on his dump-parts bike. Situated precariously on the handlebars, he pedaled backwards, one of his easy postures. He rode his bike in every possible pose, including his favorite invention, the J.C., which had him sailing along, standing upright on the seat with his arms out in mock crucifixion.

"You wanna ride?"

Of course I wanted to, but Nick was stingy when it came to his bike, and I knew he was teasing.

"It's gettin dark, but I'll ride you up to the highway and back if you want to," he said. He sounded like he meant it.

"Okay, but no fooling around," I said, and at once I was on the seat behind him, close up to his Dixie Peach hair. Pumping up and over two long hills, we rode a mile in the twilight. Later with our knees drawn up, we sat to rest on the soft bluff overlooking the yellow-stippled asphalt road, calling out cars. Beyond the highway toward the river, I could see the horizon's last flames. The faint smell of bacon rode sweetly on the breeze from the packing house upshore.

"Star light, star bright, the first star I see tonight, I wish I may, I wish I might…"

At first Nick wouldn't look up. "I don't see no star," he said.

I pointed. "See right up there, it's the North Star."

"How you know?"

"My mother showed it to me."

Then he looked. "Bet that ain't."

"Bet it is. When it gets all the way dark, it'll be on the handle of the Little Dipper."

"If it's on the handle by the time the nine o'clock whistle blows, you get to ride my bike tomorrow all day. If it ain't, I get a kiss."

"Uh-uh, Nick," I said. "Let's just bet a hot pickle."

"Okay, Mama's-Baby, okay, Miss Can't-Get-No-Brassiere, Miss Bow-Legs," and he rubbed my leg.

"Quit!" I said, and brushed his hand away. He did it again and I knocked his hand away again.

"Bet nobody ever touched your pussy."

"Ain't nobody ever going to, either."

"See if I don't," and he pushed me backwards, stuck his salty tongue in my mouth. His groping fingers up the leg of my shorts scratched when he pulled at my underpants. Then, like an arrow, fast and straight, his finger shot pain inside me. I punched him hard and he—"Ow, girl!"—stopped. I jumped up—"I'm telling"—and ran. He grabbed my ankle. His "Don't tell," then his "You better not" filled the air around me. But my own steely "I ain't scared" walked me all the way home. Halfway there I heard the pad of bike tires behind me on the brick street, and Nick sailed by, standing on the seat, his arms out in a J.C.

"Girl, I send Eddy out looking for you, where you been?" my mother asked.

"I was up by Janice's house," I told her.

That night the tinge of pink in my underpants said that I should put epsom salts in the bathtub and hope that nothing bad had happened down there. When my mother asked me what I was doing with epsom salts, I told her, "Chiggers."

But I spelled it all out to my diary in I-am-in-this-world language. Nick: his shiny black-walnut skin, the soft fragrance of Dixie Peach in his hair, the cutoff overalls he wore with only one shoulder strap fastened so that I had to hold on to his bare shoulders even though they were sweaty. And in but-not-of-this-world language I told my diary the wish I had for him to get some kind of home training, go to church, act right, and not want to feel in my panties, and the soft kiss I wanted him to learn. I also told my diary how Eddy was pretending to be able to see with his glass eye, but how I heard him crying at night because he wanted to go with

Wanda Coles and she made a fool out of him by having him watch her hand move back and forth in front of his face.

The next morning, when I gave my father his lunch box and his ice-water thermos and held the screen door for him, I saw Nick leaning and looking to be noticed in the Y of his apricot tree across the alley that was the boundary between our backyards. It was washday, a good opportunity for me to ignore him.

"Four loads before the sun gets hot," my mother said, and we rolled the washer off the back porch and into the middle of the kitchen, with two rinse tubs set side by side on my father's workbench. I stripped the beds still full of Bea and Eddy and the tobacco smell of my father and soft scent of my mother's Pond's cream. Underneath the mattress in their bedroom I always saw the same envelope of old war bonds, the small book of old ration stamps. And this time I found a magazine, *True Romance*, and inside it a card with roses on the front and a my-love-grows message, unsigned. At first I thought it must be from my father to my mother or vice versa. But as I ran to the kitchen with my discovery, I suddenly thought of my *private* cigar box, and slowly I went back up the stairs to sort out the knot of bedclothes on the floor.

Nick waited until the last sheet was stretched and pinned and the long pole was jacked up to raise the clothesline higher before he said a word.

"Found a new pedal for my bike," he yelled. I went inside the screen door but turned to see him sliding down from his perch.

"You can ride all day," he said through the screen. "Aw, hi, Miss Wilson."

"What you doing running around this early?" my mother asked him. "I know your mamma left something for you to get done 'fore she gets home," she said. "I bet you haven't even washed your face yet."

"I already did everything," Nick lied. The naps on his head were still separate.

"Then you can get your friend Eddy out the bed, and y'all can go to the store for me. We need some more starch."

It tickled Nick that he had gained entrance to the goings-on of our house, and he raced up the back stairs calling out, "Hey, Eddy, let's go!"

I was hanging up line number two when they jostled down the unpaved alleyway, picking up rocks and throwing them at birds. "Come on, girl," my mother called. "We got a mess of overalls in here."

On washdays, when my mother said "Catch as catch can," we reveled in the break of routine, eating whatever we could find raw in a bowl for breakfast—and whatever we could get between two slices of bread for lunch. That noon, in my mother's got-to-get-this-done expression, I tried to find the secret that must have brought her the card of roses. Suppose Nick gave me such a card. But I could not picture my mother looking at the man holding the woman on the front of *True Romance.* I made mustard-and-onion sandwiches for me and Bea and wandered among the clotheslines, waiting for Nick to ride by so I could ignore him some more.

When the sun was at its highest point, Eddy and Nick came into the kitchen for a cool drink of water. Nick grinned at me through Eddy's entire speech to my mother about how hot it was, how the Missouri River had backed up enough from recent rains to fill the hole that wasn't even stagnant this summer, how the still water was so clear you could see the tadpoles, and how my father had said even *he* used to swim over there.

As Eddy went on, Nick said I could go swimming with them if I wanted to. I couldn't swim, and I knew that he knew it, which made his asking sweet.

"I saw the Dipper last night," he said. "You can ride my bike tomorrow since y'all have to wash today."

"I don't want to ride your bike," I said. "You don't know how to act. Besides, my father is building me one for myself, and it's going to be a girl's bike."

"You can't *make* a girl's bike," Nick said. "They don't throw away those kinds of frames at the dump."

"Okay," my mother said to them. "Y'all can go. But Nick, you watch out for Eddy. He can't see as good as you can, so don't be cuttin the fool in the water. Y'all be back here 'fore supper, you hear?"

Nick winked at me. Rolling my eyes had become my best response. Undaunted, he pushed Eddy toward the screen door, and by the time it slammed, they were on Nick's bike, headed for the Missouri River hole.

My best friend, Cece, lived with her grandmother over the summer, too far away from our house. And so I hung around with Wanda most of the time, though I usually told her none of my secrets. Really, the only thing I had against Wanda was her long, straight hair in bangs and two braids that she made even longer with colored plastic clothespins clamped onto the ends.

"Can you come out?" she asked through the screen.

"Sprinkle the shirts and ball them up, and you can go," my mother said. I filled the ironing basket with sprinkled clothes and left with Wanda. Out under our crabapple tree we sat rubbing chunks of ice over our legs and arms in the still afternoon.

"I came to tell you something," Wanda said.

"What?"

"Guess," she said.

"I don't know."

"It has something to do with this," she said, and reached into the elastic band of her shorts. She struggled with the size of the thing until it cleared her pocket and she held it up. "See."

It was a small, thick diary, a tan color, with letters that read FIVE YEAR DIARY in gold on the cover, and when she felt around in her pocket, a small key—all just like mine. Then deftly she unlocked the lock.

"Read this," she said. I took the book from her and confirmed that each page held a lined section for each day of five years. It was enough to see that Wanda, who wasn't even my friend, had managed to secure for herself the same precious thing I had done Miss Gray's chores for. Because Miss Gray next door was grossly overweight and couldn't get her arms up, I had oiled and braided her thick, sticky hair. I had swept her house, rugs and all. Since she couldn't get around very well, I had run to the store to get her messy tobacco, and got the boneless ham too that she said she ought to cut back on—all in order to collect two dollars' worth of dimes in a sock for the journal that would record the most vital facts about five years of my life.

That was enough without Wanda insisting that I read it.

"I can't read your writing," I said.

She took the book from my hands. "It says, 'Today I became a woman. I didn't get the cramps live everyone said I would. Now I can wear heels and red-fox stockings, and know that I have put away all the childish things I used to do. I am truly happy.' You know what that means?" she asked me.

"Yeah, that's nice," was all I could muster.

"I think every girl should have a diary, because it happens to every girl and it's a day you should always remember. You ought to get one."

"Yeah," I said.

By the time my father got home, I had done my two-faced best to convince Wanda that she would look like Lena Horne if she just wore kit curlers to bed. All the while I delighted in the way her bangs fell like a stringy rag mop in her eyes that day.

By suppertime I was sick of Wanda and happy to go looking for Eddy and Nick at the river. My mother insisted Wanda should keep me company, and so off we went, hopscotching our way on the bricks until we came to the new concrete sidewalk with cracks to avoid in the name of good luck. Down the soft slope above the highway we scooted, and when the whiz of cars broke, we flew across the highway and ran down the muddy hollow to the plain of wild onion, garlic, asparagus, and no telling what kinds of snakes to the place where the stand of short trees leaned, and the noisy rush of cars gave way to the noisy rush of river to come.

There on the ground just through the trees, Eddy lay on his back with his arms careless at this sides. Something wavelike through me made the hairs stand up on my arms, and I took off running to him just long enough to see his blind eye staring before he jumped awake, opening his other eye. In that instant I realized that not since the cherry-bomb accident had I seen Eddy asleep, and therefore did not know that he slept with the eye open.

"What are you doing laying here like this? Where's Nick?"

"I got too tired and Nick didn't want to come out yet," Eddy said, and he got up, pulled on his undershirt, and picked up Nick's bike at his side.

Wanda and I went to the bank of the cloudy green pool and called for Nick to come out. We called again and again. "Nick! Nick! We're going to leave you here and take your bike!"

"Nick!" Eddy called from across the water. "Nick!" Eddy called again and it went through the hairs on my arms. Wanda and I couldn't hold back our "Nick! Come on!" We looked in to the pool but saw nothing through the muddy green.

We ran around the pool to Eddy's side.

"You don't think he went on over to the river, do you?"

"Not without telling me," Eddy said.

"Then were is he? Where was he when you came out?"

"He was right there." Eddy pointed. "Right out here in the middle. He can swim better than anybody. Let's just wait, hear?"

"Uh-uh," Wanda said. "We ought to get somebody. Suppose something happened to him."

I hated Wanda more than anybody and anything. "Let's just wait," I echoed Eddy.

"I'm going," Wanda said. As she ran, she yelled, "I'm going to get y'all's daddy. My mamma's going to be mad. I ain't got no business by the river."

"Nick's gonna get it. Nick's gonna get it," Eddy kept repeating as we stood looking toward the river, hoping to see Nick's white-toothed, nappy-headed self come bopping through the short trees, looking for his bike to go off on while we walked home, probably meeting my father on the way, probably telling him never mind, and most likely rolling our eyes at Wanda, who always acts like she knows so much.

Nick's gonna get it. When I get my girl's bike I'm not letting him touch it unless he swears he will not show off like it's some piece of junk he doesn't have to treat right. Unless he says we can ride together up to the highway and he says he's sorry for not acting right. I am in this world, but not of it. I am in this world.

Eddy and I waited, watched the pool turn deeper green, and the sun slant light like fire through the trees.

First came my father, the sweat on his face and head shining, his arms wagging out at his sides as he sloshed through the tall grass toward us. Then mamma behind him in her flower-print wash dress, calling us like she couldn't see we were standing right there. Then, really bad, Nick's mother with her gray and crimson elevator operator's uniform still on from work, running in high-heel shoes, calling Nick. Then Bea with Wanda and Mrs. Coles holding Puddin's hand, walking fast, then standing still outside the realm of confusion. Then the questions and Nick's mother shaking Eddy and my mother snatching her away from us and my father jumping in with his overalls on and Nick's mother crying and my mother saying, "Hush, now, it's gonna be all right," and Eddy closing his good eye tight and me saying the Lord's Prayer for us all. Then my father spitting out water and hollering and going down again and up again and hollering. "Get them kids away from here, get 'em away!" and Wanda and her mother running toward the highway, and my mother making us go stand over by the trees and Nick's mother pulling away from Mamma like she was going to jump into the water herself.

When my father laid Nick's body on the grass, I could see that Nick's hands were curled like they could never be straightened. Mamma walked his mother over to him and they held those curled-up hands until the ambulance people came and covered up his face. Nick's mother and Mamma went with them. Wanda's mother took me and Eddy and my father and Bea home in their Dynaflow.

That night Mamma held her waist and cried a lot. Eddy put his bed up to his door so that nobody could go in. My father said that I could stay up as long as I wanted and he sat out on the porch with his cigarettes. I could hear the glider creak every now and then, and I knew he was dozing and waking in the dark. Bea was so quiet in our room, she was almost not there. I sat awake in our bed for what seemed like the longest time, as if I had been sentenced to wait for something that could never come. I didn't feel at all like I would cry. Blank was what I felt, blank and swollen tight.

Groping my way, I parted the coats between the mouton and my father's rough wool, stretched my arms, and walked my hands down the ceiling to the box. Although I could not yet bring myself to throw away a month of my recorded life, my diary would not be useful, I had nothing to write. I found the cherry bomb. In the kitchen, I took the box of matches from the shelf over the stove and crept out the screen door. The glider creaked, but I stole out of the yard across the alley, through Nick's yard, out to the sidewalk and on.

From the soft bluff, I could hear the rush of the river above the hum of locusts. A fingernail sliver of moon laid out the highway gray and bent. The Little Dipper tilted. I struck a match and lit the green stem. When it sizzled, I threw it high and far, exploding the whole summer.

Brenda W. Clough

Times Fifty

BRENDA W. CLOUGH has written eight novels, including her most recent, *Doors of Death and Life*. Her short stories have been published in numerous magazines, including *Analog SF Magazine* and the anthology *Starlight 3*. Other work has appeared in *SF Age*, *Aboriginal*, *Marion Zimmer Bradley Magazine*, and many anthologies. She was a finalist for both the Hugo Award and Nebula Award in 2002. She teaches at the Writer's Center in Bethesda, Maryland.

Danielle is fifteen and a half, and her sweet tooth is still untamed. When she heaps three spoonfuls of sugar into her peppermint tea, Wendy rolls her eyes: "That's her, you know."

Danielle drops the teaspoon clattering to the buffet. "Aah! Don't say that! I'm switching to honey, as of right now."

Another girl with "Amanda" on her name tag says darkly, "You must have found out by now that we're allergic to honey. And cilantro tastes soapy. They're both genetically linked traits."

Danielle quickly sets her mug down. She surveys the drinks table, where cans of soda are nestled in a plastic tub of ice. The crowd of girls has cut into the supply of orange sodas and colas, but a dozen cans of lemon-lime are untouched. Danielle snatches up a lemon-lime. She takes too big a gulp and almost chokes. It tastes dreadful. She glowers at the forty-nine girls milling sullenly around the hall. Every one of them is also fifteen and half years old, brown-eyed and lean and well-muscled, five-foot-five or -six, brimming with good health, and sporting a stick-on name tag. But at least none of them is drinking a lemon-lime. Danielle takes another defiant swig.

And at least none of them has her hair. All of them are dark and curly, but their hairstyles are in the best teenage spirit of continual experimentation. Danielle can pretend she is looking at a hairstyling webzine, or one of those customized beauty programs at the mall. She sees her own hair short and velvety, or in a huge cloud of ringlets, or tied back in a sheaf of sleek braids. The neat topknot over there on Lora looks the best—she'll have to try that when she gets home. But every nose around her is narrow and aquiline. Every mouth under the different lip glosses or glazes is firm and dimpled. Mortification creeps down her spine.

"I hate you all," she announces.

Nods of agreement. "You'd feel better if you drank cola instead of that disgusting lemon-lime.," Olga remarks. This girl looks around, nerving herself to mention the taboo subject. "Do any of you do—sports?"

"Soccer."

"Soccer."

"Soccer."

"Softball!" Danielle announces. The other girls glare at her with undisguised envy, each scowl an exact replica of the other.

"But you're good," Tia predicts in flat tones.

Danielle's well-toned shoulders slump. "I'm a sophomore, and I'm already on the varsity team. It wasn't like Mom and Dad pushed me into it or anything. It just happened."

"Does any one of us do anything of our own?" Bev almost wails. "Drama, or cooking, or building miniature railroads?"

Danielle can't bear to drink any more lemon-lime. Meeting for the first time like this sickens her stomach, the eerie revulsion in the unnatural act of meeting yourself forty-nine times over. Mom has tried to help, talking about Sleeping Beauty. Danielle is Princess Aurora in the movie, the beloved daughter, treasured for her natural gifts, farmed out to nice folks who would raise her as their own until she was old enough to meet her destiny. Until, Danielle says to herself, the wicked witch comes knocking at her door. That day is here—times fifty.

No one replies to Bev's question because the hall's double oak doors swing open. One man holds the door while another pushes the woman in the wheelchair through, and a third man—tall and wide in his brown suit—follows behind. They push her up the ramp leading to a little stage so everyone can see.

Danielle has been told that Tanya Haynes is only forty-five. How many other girls get to see what they'll look like in thirty years? A frizz of gray on the temples, those deep curving lines around the mouth—the wicked witch, Danielle thinks. She studies the wrinkles around the older woman's eyes and resolves to start moisturizing and using sunblock.

The tall, wide man must be Earl. Daniele has heard about him. He beams down at the assembly, his hands clasped behind his back. "Now don't they look great, Tan? We got here the makings of three or four of the most dynamite soccer teams in history. You ever see such a beautiful crop of girlhood in your entire life? Girls, you are bee-you-tee-ful."

A hostile silence, broken by Tanya saying, "I've been trying to think what to call you, dears. You're not my daughters—you have parents, all of your wonderful adoptive parents around the country. Not my sisters. My twins?"

Earl grins. "They're your clones, hon."

"I won't call you that," she says to the girls. "Let's just say I'm your aunt, your Aunt Tanya. And when a niece comes to visit, Auntie has a present for you. Earl, take your boys and go up to my room. Get those big bags down."

"Bill and Ricky can handle it," he says, dismissing the flunkies with a wave.

"No, you go too, Earl. There are three bags, heavy ones. I'll be fine right here."

Muttering under his breath, Earl takes his boys and goes. Tanya waits until the door shuts behind them and then rolls her wheelchair to the edge of the little stage. "You, dear," she says, pointing at Danielle, who is nearest. "Come a little closer, would you please? My eyes aren't good enough to read name tags anymore."

Back in South Carolina, Danielle's parents raised her to be polite to elders. She hops up onto the stage and sees the metal braces on the older woman's knees. A car crash when Tanya Haynes was twenty-nine—Danielle's parents showed her all the newspaper files and sports videos last month, when they broke the news to her about the cloning. The great athlete, the most stupendous female soccer star ever, has never walked again.

"Danielle," Tanya says, reading the name tag. "I can't hold fifty hands, so I'm going to hold yours, all right? As a representative. The rest of you, listen to me, please."

The hands clutching Danielle's are lighter than hers, and the skin is looser and rough. But the fingernails are exactly the same, the distance between the joints, even the little bump on the outside of the wrist bone. She has no words for how strange it is, looking down at two pairs of identical hands of different ages. Silently Danielle measures her palm and fingers against them. Exactly the same length.

Tanya's voice is harsh. "My dears, this wasn't my idea. I would never have consented, if I had known what it meant. Earl thought that—he just couldn't stand the idea of the U.S. women's soccer team without me. And the soccer federation had its heart set on another Olympic gold. They filled up my head with all this stuff about the legacy of the sport and the future generations of soccer players, and then when Earl offered to pay all the medical bills if I'd contribute the tissue cultures..." For a moment she falters. Then she says, simply, "I'm sorry, girls."

We're slaves, Danielle thinks—not even that, we're photocopies of an original. Danielle's entire future has been laid out for her in sports, and there is nothing she can do about it, in this chain gang with her forty-nine sister-selves. She wants to cry. Instead she says, "Do we apologize for being alive, then?" Then she wants to stuff the angry words back into her mouth. But several of her—sisters? twins?—nod their approval. Their sullen, hurt faces show her what she must look like.

"Don't you ever do that." Tanya's older mouth purses instead of dimpling when she sets her teeth, but otherwise the expression is one that Danielle has seen in her own mirror. "They cloned me to make all fifty of you. The plan is for you to dominate sports for the rest of the century. But you are your own women, do you hear? They wanted to give you my legs, my lungs, my muscles. But I'm giving you my heart. Don't you let these sports moguls run you. They made you in petri dishes and paid for your births, but they don't own you. Seize your lives, and make them yours. You can do it, because you are champions, girls. It takes one to know one."

The strength that won Tanya Hayes the gold medal in 2008 radiates out of her as she leans forward in her wheelchair, not the long-gone strength of the broken body, but deeper, hotter—the strength of her spirit. Danielle can feel the heat of it in the bony hand clasping her own, and it is like a burning match touching an unlit new one. Tanya—Aunt Tanya—isn't the wicked witch. She's the Sleeping Beauty, trapped in a tower shaped like a wheelchair and guarded by creepy fat cats, and she will never escape now. But she has given them—her twinned progeny—the key.

The will and power flare up in Danielle's middle. She is a champion too—of her life. She can be whatever she wants to be. They could make her, but they cannot mold her. "And don't forget," she says, "we're teens—rebellious by nature."

Tanya grins at her, at them all. "You go right ahead and rebel, dears. Explore the world. Find your place."

Then the door opens again and it is as if a curtain falls over Tanya's countenance. Earl staggers in hauling a large canvas duffel bag, the other two following behind with more. Tanya smiles at him as he drags the bag up the ramp. "Now aren't you sweet. You know I can't do very much these days, girls, but I've taken up lace knitting. And luckily I didn't have to worry about the colors that would suit you! Danielle, dear, try this one."

She takes a vivid blue scarf from the bag, neatly folded and tied with a ribbon. Danielle carefully slips off the ribbon and shakes the scarf out. "Oh, it's beautiful!" the glorious blue color and the pattern of interlocked triangles seem perfect for her alone. Danielle wraps the scarf around her neck. It is light and warm as a hug. She looks up and meets Tanya's eyes, exactly the brown of her own. The older woman smiles and gives her a wink.

Beside her Amanda unfolds her green scarf, awed. "And look at that," she says. "Mine has hearts!"

"They're different—every one is different." Danielle grins back at Tanya. And all fifty of them look just as dangerous and beautiful.

Merle Collins

The Visit

MERLE COLLINS was born on September 29, 1950, on the tiny island of Grenada in the Caribbean. She holds BA degrees from the University of the West Indies in Mona, Jamaica, in English and Spanish. Her books include the poetry collections *Because the Dawn Breaks* (1985) and *Rotten Pomerack* (1992), the novels *Angel* (1987) and *The Colour of Forgetting* (1995), and the short story collection *Rain Darling* (1990). She has appeared in numerous publications, including *Penguin Modern Poets Volume 8* (1996) and *The Oxford Book of Caribbean Short Stories* (1999). She is a professor at the University of Maryland, focusing on literature and Caribbean studies, as well as on creative writing.

The woman sat leaning slightly forward. Left elbow on leg, left hand holding up her chin, clamping shut her lips. Not hiding their look of sullen disinterest. From the doorway, her daughter watched her. Took in the droop of the shoulders, the emptiness in the heavy-lidded black eyes.

"You watching that program?"

Miriam shrugged, not moving her hand, not moving her eyes from the television. Catherine sighed, leaned in the doorway, and turned her eyes towards the television. "Jensen's Dream!" The woman was trying to prevent Jensen from getting the deal on the plantation. Catherine hoped that he would find out in time to stop her. She glanced over at her mother. Lord! Look at her! Just look at her! She had to choose the most uncomfortable chair in the room, quite in the corner over there! and look at her face! Anybody come in here and see her looking like that must think I making her see trouble! Just look at her! Catherine sucked her teeth and turned away from the doorway, moving back to the kitchen.

Martin looked up from his job of washing dishes at the kitchen sink. He chuckled. Stepped back and blocked his sister's path with his elbow. "Behave yourself, non!" he said in a low voice. "Leave the lady alone!"

Catherine matched his tone. "Go and watch her! Go and see how she sit down poor-me-one as if somebody thief she best clean-neck fowl!"

Martin laughed quietly, the sound staying down in his throat. He picked up a glass and placed his hands back in the water. "Behave yourself," he repeated, "leave her alone!"

His answer was a prolonged sucking of the teeth as his sister moved towards the refrigerator.

Jensen was confronting his secret adversary. He was beginning to suspect that something not quite right was going on.

Miriam had heard the whispering. Guessed that it had something to do with her. She removed her hand from under her chin, frowned, looked cross-eyed at the door, shifted herself sideways in the chair, crossed her legs, and leaned her head cautiously back. Her right ear just touched the cushion.

An advertisement. Some kind of sauce. Miriam didn't hear what sauce it was. A far-off memory came back to her. An advertisement on radio years ago. "Don't just say Worcester! Say Bee and Digby's!"

Miriam cleared her throat and hunched her shoulders. Couldn't they do something to make it a little warmer? Put on the fire or something? Miriam yawned. She would have liked to go and lie down. Cover up. She smiled. *Kooblay* up! But for sure Catherine would want to know if she was ill or something. Quietly, so as not to be heard, Miriam sucked her teeth and turned in the chair. Her body was curved, head down, her back turned now towards the television.

April in England. Catherine and Martin had said when they wrote that it was a good time to come. Not very hot, but good weather. Springtime! Good weather! Well I wouldn't like to see bad one! Last week, when they had gone to visit Cousin Bertrand in Huddersfield, it had snowed! Miriam shivered. Martin who wasn't a bad child, really...Not like his sister. Is as if she think England is hers and she doing me a favor to have me here! Favor? I want to go home, yes! I want to go home where me is woman in me own house!

Martin said that Huddersfield and that whole area around there was like that. Always cold. Always cold. When there was snow in Huddersfield, he said, it didn't mean that there was snow in London, too. In fact afterwards they knew that it hadn't snowed in London that day. But snow or no snow, it well cold! It well, well cold!

I tell you, eh, it hurting me heart. Catherine! Look at Catherine, non! I remember how I nurse that child! Puny, puny, she did nearly dead, yes! They didn't even think she would survive! And now acting with me like if she think she is queen!

When she had sat there in Peggy's Whim, high up on the hill above Hermitage, writing Martin and Catherine here in England, she never would have thought that England was like this. No. 30 Rose Mansions, Bedford Street, London NW…NW…either 3 or 5, she could never remember. Those England addresses were so long! Rose Mansions! Rose Mansions! She had expected…she had expected…well not a *mansion*, but something different to this. This high, high building, all the markings on the wall downstairs, and you had to travel up in a dark, dark elevator! Like a hole! And even those steps! Miriam lifted her head, turned, looked around her. I mean, when you reach inside here, it not bad. It nice, she conceded. They have the place well put away! Well put away!

Furtively, she looked around the room. The little carpet well nice, the bookcase in the corner well neat, the pictures on the wall, well…not my choice, these kind of mix-up colors that you don't even know what you looking at, but is all right. Miriam's eyes moved to the records stacked in the corner, the music set on the side by the television. Everything well put away! Is to be expected. Both of them know from time how to take care of a place. They didn't grow up anyhow, if even self we was poor. Her eyes traveled around the room. She looked down at the corners. The place clean. The place well clean. Catherine could work. I know that. And Martin never had nobody servanting for him. He accustom cooking and looking after himself. He spend enough time looking after the house and seeing after Catherine while I go to work! So they all right. They could see after theyself from time!

But...Miriam looked around the room again, sucked her teeth softly, leaned her head back against the cushion. So this England is place to live too, then? Only coop up, coop up inside a house all the time? Miriam sucked her teeth again, too loudly this time.

"You all right, Mammie?" Catherine asked from the doorway, unbuttoning her jeans at the waist to ease the pressure.

"Yes," Miriam answered in an almost questioning tone, a resigned sort of tone that infuriated Catherine. "Yes, I all right, yes."

"Well Mammie, how you doing *kabusé, kabusé* so? As if you seeing trouble?" Miriam sniffed, held onto the arms of the chair and drew herself to a more upright position. "Why you sit down there in the chair looking poor-me-one, poor-me-one so? Lively up yourself, non!"

"Madame Catherine, if you don't want me to sit down in you chair, just tell me, yes. I not beggin nobody for a cup of water, non! I have me house, yes. I didn't ask allyou to come up here. So I could pack me things and go whenever allyou ready! All I will ask you is to drop me on the airport please. And even self you don't want to do that, I sure I could find me way. I not beggin nobody for a drop of water, non! I could go back home in me house this evening self, self!"

Martin pushed past his sister, walked towards his mother, laughing. "So who is allyou now?" he asked. "Who you cursing in smart there?" He sat on the arm of the chair, hugged her, leaned his head against hers.

"You smell of onion, boy! Don't try to mamaguy me at all! Move away from me!"

"Come on, Mums. Don't take things so hard." He put his other arm around her. Catherine grumbled something and moved back into the kitchen.

"I want to go home, yes," said Miriam. "Youall just drop me on the airport let me find me way, please. I don't want to come in people place come and give them trouble!"

"Mum, why you acting as if you with strangers? How you mean in *people* place come and give them trouble? Who is this *people*?"

"I don't have time bandy words with you and you sister, non! I..."

"My sister? You daughter, yes! Come on, Mums!"

He shook her gently. “Is just a short holiday. Relax and enjoy yourself. You’re so tense up! Is only because Catherine wants to see you happy. You just sit there looking so sad, hardly eating…How you think we feel?”

“I not trying to make youall unhappy, so let me go where I happy. I don’t like this place. It cold, cold; you can’t move; if it little bit bright, which is hardly, and I want to take a walk outside, I have to say where I going, as if me is some little child; I have to ring doorbell to annoy people for them to let me in again…How people could live like that? In a house, in a house all day long?”

“Mums, that’s the way it is here. And it’s more difficult because we have to be running around, getting Carl to school and to the baby-sitter; we couldn’t take our holidays same time, so I have to be rushing off to work sometimes; it’s different! But it’s just a short holiday! Enjoy yourself! We want to see you feeling happy! And look, you even have a chance to meet your grandson for the first time!”

“That self is another thing. Perhaps you should have send that child home for me since after the mother dead. The two of you letting him do exactly what he want. The child talking to you just as he want, saying what he feel? No. Is not so. Is so England children is, then? No wonder it have so much bad thing happening all over the place!”

Martin removed his arms. Linked his fingers, unlinked them, and leaned towards the small table to pick up the remote control for the television.

“You not watching that, non?”

“What?” His mother’s eyes followed the direction of his glance. “No. No. I not watching no television!”

Martin pressed a button on the control. The image faded. “Carl’s all right, Mum. He’s doing pretty well at school and…I encourage him to express his ideas.” He leaned forward again, put down the control, sat looking at the photograph of his son on the side table. Carl was holding a ball, looking straight into the camera, his tongue out. That had been taken last summer, up on Hampstead Heath. Carl was wearing a T-shirt and shorts. Martin’s long face was serious, thoughtful, as he watched his son’s laughing face. He turned his eyes towards his mother’s face. “Carl’s a fine child, Mums.”

"Papa, take care of allyou children as allyou want, you hear. Is your responsibility. I just want to go where I living!"

"You only have two more weeks, Mum."

"If you could organize it for me to leave before, I will be very grateful."

Martin hunched his shoulders. Cracked his fingers. "Okay," he said. "Okay, Mum. Whatever you want." He sat there a while longer, then stood up and moved back towards the kitchen.

I know he feeling bad, but I just don't like this place! Not me and England at all! After a while, Miriam pushed herself up from the chair and walked slowly out to the kitchen.

"We're almost finished," Martin said.

"Nothing I could do?" Miriam asked.

Catherine turned from taking something off a shelf. Picked up the jug of juice. "Just put this juice on the table for me, Mammie. And if you want, while I setting the table, you could take out those clothes in the washing machine and hang them up in the bathroom."

"All right."

It had started from the time she reached the airport here, really. Before that, Miriam had been excited about the visit. It was only when she reached Heathrow that she started feeling perhaps she should have stayed at home.

Walking up in that line and waiting to go to one of those customs officers. Was customs, non? Customs, or immigration, or something. One of them. Just standing in that line she had remembered school, all those donkey years ago. Standing in line for the ruler from Teacher Alfred. And that man was a beater! She remembered a day when she didn't know all of her poem. She could even remember the book! Royal Readers, Book...book...She couldn't remember which number Royal Readers, but it was Royal Readers, anyway. And the lesson was

Lives of great men
All remind us
We can make our lives sublime
And departing leave behind us
Footprints on the sands of time

Footprints that...

And that's the part that she had forgotten. Standing in line at Heathrow Airport, Miriam realized that she *still* couldn't remember it.

Standing taking clothes out of the washing machine, she didn't remember it still. Miriam laughed at herself, out loud. Said, "Well yes, wi!" Catherine and Martin exchanged glances.

The man at the airport desk had asked a lot of questions. And Miriam had started to feel guilty. She didn't know why, because she didn't have anything to hide. But she had felt really guilty. It was as if he thought she was lying about something.

"You say your daughter and son invited you here on this holiday?"

Miriam had cleared her throat, put her hand to her mouth, said, "Sorry!" Inclined her head slightly. "Yes, sir."

"And this here; this is the address you're going to?"

"Yes, sir!"

"What does your daughter do?"

"She's a teacher, sir."

"Your daughter is a teacher in this country?"

He had looked up at her then, lifting his eyebrows questioningly.

So what the hell? You think I can't have a teacher daughter her? "Yes, sir."

He kept her waiting while he looked through her passport again. There was nothing to see. She had only traveled to Trinidad on it before. Many times. To sell things in the market there. And to Barbados once. He seemed to examine each stamp. Then he picked up her ticket. Examined that, too.

"Will your daughter be here at the airport to meet you?"

"Yes, sir."

"You'll be here for three weeks?"

Well look at the flicking ticket, non! "Yes, sir."

Finally, he had looked up at her and his eyes seemed to say, "Well, I guess I'll let you go through, even though I'm sure you're lying." His lips didn't say anything more. He stamped her passport.

By the time Miriam had got through customs and walked out to find Catherine, Martin, and Carl, Martin's six-year-old son, waiting for her, she was near to tears. Something that hadn't happened for a long time. Her shoulders were hunched and she was feeling as small as Cousin Milton's little Maria back home, Maria who usually stayed with her in Peggy's Whim.

She had felt strange with her children and grandson from the beginning. She found that she just couldn't laugh and talk with them as usual. Especially when Carl said, "*You're* my nan?" And she started off wondering why he had said it like that.

And then she found that Carl wasn't like a child at all. He asked big people questions, talked all the time, and Catherine and Martin just wouldn't shut him up. That must be England style. They didn't grow like that at all.

And Miriam's voice began to sound strange in her own ears, especially when Carl talked to her in that funny accent of his. It made him sound even more like big people.

Two more weeks away! The second of May. Miriam wondered if Martin would try to get the date changed. She wouldn't say it again, but she hoped that he would remember.

It rained on April the twenty-seventh. They traveled by the underground train. Took a taxi to the station, hurried out in the rain, and went with the two suitcases down the escalator to take the Northern line to King's Cross. Then they changed to the Piccadilly line, which went all the way out to Heathrow Airport.

At the BWIA airline counter, Miriam began to brighten up. She smiled often. Even seemed to be holding herself back from exploding with laughter. She touched Carl on the head and said "Young Mister Carl, eh!"

"You must come again, Nan," Carl said.

"All right, son." Miriam laughed, glanced at Catherine.

"You know you're only saying that," said Catherine, leaning across and straightening her mother's collar. "You didn't like it at all."

"Well, Miriam shrugged, still smiling, "all place have their people."

"Yes, Madam Diplomat," said Martin.

Miriam laughed again, leaning back in the way that they remembered. Martin and Catherine looked at each other and shook their heads. Catherine's smile was disbelieving. "So Mammie you just start to enjoy yourself, then?" she marveled.

"Child, leave me alone, non. Is home I going, yes." Miriam touched her daughter's face. "Don't mind. Don't mind that!"

"Well I never!" said Catherine.

They sat in the airport cafeteria and drank orange juice. "This orange juice could have do with a little touch of something stronger in it!" laughed Miriam. "But," she added with a laugh as they both looked up at her, "is all right; is all right; I will make do."

Catherine folded her lips and said nothing. Martin laughed. "The lady start to enjoy sheself when she going, yes! Yes. Mammie! Ye-e-s! You not joking!"

Miriam leaned back and smiled at her grandson.

"You're nice, Nan," said Carl, looking at her critically. "When will you be back?"

"Son, I don't know, non. Is you to come to visit me now!"

"Yes!" said Carl enthusiastically. "Yes, Nan." Carl looked from his father to his aunt.

"Don't look at me," said Catherine. "That is you and your father's business."

"Dad?"

"Yes. We'll have to plan it. We're overdue for a visit."

"Well that is all you'll hear now until the date is set." Catherine drained her orange juice, leaned across, and handed a tissue to Carl. "Wipe your mouth, Carl."

The three were quiet as they watched Miriam walk through to emigration. She turned and waved, her round face smiling broadly, the light brown hat that she liked to wear perched almost jauntily on her head, her body looking smaller than when she had first arrived, but her face shining with health and happiness. Martin looked down at his sister. Back at his mother. "Is now I could see how much you two look alike," he said. "Short same way. Same round face. And then both of you stubborn same way."

Catherine chuckled. "She not joking in truth, you know."

"Your mother looking well young, you know, girl."

They waved again. Miriam disappeared around the corner. Carl shouted, "See you in Grenada, Nan!"

They stood for a while looking at the wall around which Miriam had disappeared. "Never me again," said Catherine, as they turned away. "Never me again."

"Never me again," said Miriam to Cousin Milton the next morning. They were sitting under the tamarind tree on the hill just near to her house. "You see that little devil?" she asked in a lower voice, looking down the hill towards a boy of about six who was moving backwards, staring at them, finger in his mouth. "Is me tambran he coming after, you know. See he see us here, he backing back now. But is me tambran he was coming after."

Cousin Milton glanced at the retreating youngster, turned his attention back to Miriam. "But girl, how you mean you don't like England, dey? So England is place not to like, then?"

"I don't care what you say!"

"All round you, you seeing England pounds putting up house; all who stay in England for thirty years and more coming back put up house to dead in luxury, you self saying you don't like England? How you mean? Girl, don't talk this thing hard make people laugh at you at all! Keep that to yourself!"

Miriam laughed. "You all right yes, Cousin Milton. Anyway, that is one episode that over! Dead and bury. Not me and England, non. Never me again! Give me me place where I could sit down outside and see people, do what I want. Not me at all. All place have their people! Never me again!"

Milton sighed. Opened his mouth and seemed about to say something. Lapsed into thoughtful silence.

"Never!" pronounced Miriam.

Julie Corwin

The Lesson

Julie Corwin is a writer living in Bethesda, Maryland. She graduated from the Writing Seminars program at Johns Hopkins University in Baltimore. She has published nonfiction in the *Wall Street Journal Europe*, *U.S. News & World Report*, and the *International Economy*, among other places.

Claire hated cars and anything to do with driving. She took the bus to work and walked whenever possible. Driving was one of the few things that her husband Frank was actually good at. But Claire had finally grown so irritated by Laura's constant efforts to get her father to take her out for driving lessons that she offered.

Laura would ask him as soon as he got home. Did he feel like taking her out for a drive? Wouldn't it be fun to show her how to drive? After getting a quick no, a soft shake of the head, or a mumbled nonresponse, Laura would wait, biding her time until there was some slight sign of a better mood moving in.

Perhaps Frank would laugh at something on TV. Then Laura would laugh, too, a little too loudly, a little too late—not that he would notice how or whether she found the show as funny as he did. He didn't notice anything outside of that narrow column of air between his yellow corduroy chair and the television. As the closing credits rolled, she would ask him again. He would say no, grimacing slightly, pick up the newspaper, or go into the kitchen to pour out some more peanut M&Ms into his bowl. This went on for at least two weeks, until Claire could stand it no longer and volunteered.

Claire always felt something go a little rigid inside herself when her friends at work would express sympathy for Yolanda or Becky, who were raising their children alone—without a husband. "She's not married," they would say, shaking their heads with pity. "Lucky her," Claire would say occasionally. They would laugh, assuming she was kidding.

Claire had a husband, but she still raised her children all by herself. If it hadn't been for his paycheck, she would have gotten rid of him long ago. All he did was take up space, eat M&Ms, laugh too loudly at inane sitcoms, and occasionally pay attention to the children so that they cherished absurd hopes he might do so again. She knew better.

There was nothing Laura could do or not do that would grab his attention, short of setting his chair on fire. Claire had considered that once.

It was Christmas time. One of the bayberry candles on the end table near his chair could so easily get knocked over. She pictured the flames lapping up around him. She could smell the burnt corduroy, but she still couldn't imagine him actually getting up. She would have to yell to budge him. She would end up having to save his life, and the chair would be ruined.

But how could she tell Laura he was hopeless? Laura would have to figure that out herself. Someday she would have to wake up and give up. What caused his few brief bursts of enthusiasm—those rare moments when he not only seemed to have more than just a pulse but actual energy—was a mystery—sort of like the weather but completely impervious to any kind of scientific analysis. It was better not to wait around for him to liven up.

"I'll take you out on Sunday," Claire finally said one evening, looking up from a new mystery.

"Okay." Laura looked surprised and not entirely as pleased as she should have been.

"You'll have to get out of bed early. I don't want to do it when there's a lot of traffic."

Frank, meanwhile, showed no sign of having heard a word.

True to habit, Laura did not get out of bed early. She could not possibly have been asleep. Claire had been running the vacuum since eight o'clock. It was pure stubbornness. Around nine o'clock, she stood in the doorway of Laura's bedroom. "If you're not downstairs and ready to go in a half hour, then you can forget about the driving lesson. There are plenty of other things I can do."

Laura pretended to continue sleeping, but she was downstairs, standing in the doorway by 9:35. Her brown hair was uncombed and unwashed as usual, and she was wearing the same khaki pants she had worn for the last three days. She could be a pretty girl with the slightest effort, but Claire had decided not to waste her energy by commenting. She assumed she would need all of her strength.

Claire started the car herself, before she realized she should let Laura drive to the parking lot where they would practice parallel parking.

"You ought to drive. That is the point, isn't it?"

Claire got out of the car and walked around to Laura's door. Laura, looking a little frightened, slid over slowly, her thighs clenched together tightly. She realized Laura would not have been so scared if her father had been with her. Say what you will about Frank, but he was always pretty damn calm.

Laura shifted the car from park to drive, and the car lurched about a half a foot forward down the black gravel driveway.

"Reverse. You want to be in reverse."

"Right, right. I forgot."

As Laura shifted again, she looked in the rearview mirror. The car very slowly inched backwards.

"You want to actually look backwards and not just rely on your mirror."

Laura quickly looked backwards over her shoulder and accelerated. Claire noticed that she was pressing her own right foot against the floor mat—on the brake that wasn't there.

"Slow down. You want to make sure no traffic is coming before you pull out. Remember this is where that idiot hit me driving too fast through the alley."

A teenager in a beat-up maroon Camaro had slammed into the side of her car, and when he got out, he had had the temerity to start yelling at her. Later, he begged her not to report the accident. He said his father would pay for the damage, that both of their rates would go up, but she didn't believe him. She also wanted to punish him.

"Right, right." Laura looked up and down the alley three times and up and down the street before she pulled into the street so slowly that another car could have emerged from any direction and rammed right into her. Fortunately, there was very little traffic on Sunday mornings.

"Let's drive over to the liquor store parking lot. Go up Fairview Avenue and make a right," she said and then added, "Stop at the stop sign first." Laura rolled her eyes.

Laura was driving too slowly—about fifteen miles per hour—but better too slow than too fast. She might get rear-ended a lot that way, but then it's the other driver's insurance that has to pay. Laura was staring intently ahead. She had that kind of unfocused, catatonic expression that her father assumed most of his waking day.

"Are you paying attention to the road?"

"Yes." Laura blinked and sighed heavily.

"You really have to pay attention when you're driving."

She pulled up to a stop sign and in an exaggerated way snapped her head to the left and to the right.

"Signal."

Laura flipped on her right-turn signal and turned. There were other cars on the road so she started driving faster. She seemed nervous and kept checking her mirror constantly, as if she were being tailed. After her speedometer inched up to thirty-five miles per hour, Claire said, "Do you know how fast you're driving?"

"No, but you're looking at the speedometer, aren't you?"

"Listen, Miss Smart-ass, you can get out of the car right now and walk home. I have better things to do."

She braked slightly and looked at the indicator panel. "Thirty."

"The speed limit is twenty-five. Turn left up there. On Catalpa."

Catalpa was a longer route to the liquor store, but it was a quieter street and had fewer cars. Claire remembered when she learned how to drive. It wasn't so much the driving that bothered her as the other cars. You never knew what they might do. They might turn on their signal, and then never turn. She would have loved driving if she were the only person allowed on the road.

Lined with catalpa trees, the street was thickly shady and felt about ten degrees cooler in the summer than anywhere else in the city. She had always wanted a house there, but it had become clear to her long ago that they were never going to make enough money to afford one. The O'Haras' collie was standing on the sidewalk in front of their faux English Tudor, barking insistently at their car as they approached.

"You better honk so it doesn't jump in front of the car."

"No, we might scare it."

"Honk. Dogs are stupid," she said and reached over to the steering wheel to push the horn. Laura put up her right arm to block her hand, inadvertently turning the steering wheel left. They could hear the metal trim on their car skim the side of a parked station wagon.

"You hit the car," Claire said, grabbing the steering wheel and jerking it to the right. The car sped forward.

"Slow down!" Claire screamed. Laura braked firmly but it was too late. They felt a thump and heard a loud sharp whine.

"I hit the gas pedal instead of the brake," Laura said. Her voice was shaking. Claire looked over to see if she was all right. Her face looked contorted, as if she was going to start sobbing, but she wasn't bruised or bleeding. Her seat belt was fastened.

"Stay in the car," Claire said and got out. She walked toward the rear of the car to avoid seeing the dog. The station wagon had a long scrape along its side, but it was nothing that a touch of paint couldn't fix. She forced herself to look at the dog. What if he was still alive? He might bite her. As she approached the hood of the car, she saw a large pool of blood fanning outward. The dog's eyes and mouth were still open. It had to be dead. It had a large gash on top of its head from which the blood was flowing. One of its legs looked smashed, its bones and flesh pulverized. The smell was awful like blood and urine mixed together.

She glanced quickly at Laura, who looked like she was still in shock, but fortunately had not started crying. Then she examined the O'Haras' house. The curtains on a large picture window on the first floor were open. She could see the outline of the chandelier in their dining room. The house looked empty. There were no cars in the driveway. Ten o'clock on a Sunday, they must be at mass like everyone else on the street. The accident had not created a lot of noise. No honking. No squealing of brakes. Just a dog barking, and it stopped. The thing to do was to just leave. The dog was dead. Nothing could be done. The car just needed a paint touch-up, and she certainly didn't need another accident or the insurance would go up for sure. They couldn't afford it. And Laura didn't need a reputation as a dog killer.

She opened the driver's side car door. "Scoot over," she said.

As Laura slowly slid over, she asked in a quiet voice, "What are we going to do?"

"We're going home," she said and backed the car up into the O'Hara driveway and headed back down Catalpa the way they came. She was careful not to drive too quickly—that might attract attention.

"We can't leave the dog there," Laura whispered intently.

"It's dead. Quite dead. There's nothing we can do for it. The last thing we need to be known for in this neighborhood is the killers of the O'Haras' dog. Trust me." Of course, it wasn't really a "we"—it was Laura, after all, who had hit the dog. But she wanted her to know that she was going to support her. She wouldn't stand by like Frank would have done, as all of the dog's blood slowly drained away and the police arrived.

"But we have to tell someone. We have to call the hospital or something."

"Leave that to me," she said, raising her voice. "I'll handle it."

Laura didn't say anything more. She just sat, pressed against her door, biting her lower lip until she started chewing on the ends of her hair. When they pulled into the driveway at home, Laura made no effort to get out of the car.

"Why don't you go upstairs and read in your room. I'll handle everything."

When Laura didn't move, Claire spoke to her again more loudly and with greater impatience, "Did you hear me?"

Laura got out of the car and ran in the side door.

Claire could hear her footsteps on the front stairs from the open hall window. She walked around to the front of the car to see if it had sustained any damage. The metal trim on the left side of the car looked a little loose but that was all. There was some blood on the grill and a little smeared on the right headlight. She pulled out the long green hose and turned on the water. It took only a few seconds to clean off any traces. As she held the nozzle of the hose down to the driveway's surface, she thought she saw a few tufts of white fur, but the force of the water rinsed them away into the grass. She hosed off the entire car, so it would not look like she had wanted to clean a particular spot.

If she had learned anything from P.D. James and Ruth Rendell, it was important to act as normally as possible. The less one deviated from one's usual routine, the less one drew suspicion.

It occurred to her that someone might have seen them, but she had already decided what to say if confronted. She would say that she was worried about Laura. "She looked like she might snap. She's such a sensitive girl. The dog was already dead. I feel bad for the O'Haras, of course. I love dogs myself, but I'm a mother first and foremost. I had to think about my daughter's welfare. We were definitely going to come forward. I just wanted to give her more time to process." Surely, if no one called or came by in the next couple of days, then they were in the clear. She was surprised that she felt mildly exhilarated. After wrapping up the hose in a neat coil, she went inside to make herself a cup of tea.

Laura remained in her room until supper time. Claire set the plates out in front of the small television set in the breakfast nook. *60 Minutes* was coming on, one of Frank's favorite shows, so she allowed them to eat dinner while watching it. Laura came to the table with her eyes red and puffy. When she plopped in her chair, Frank glanced briefly at her but quickly returned his gaze to the television, looking away occasionally to spear his carrots and his roast beef on his fork. Claire worried briefly that he might ask Laura what was wrong. She should have known better.

At the second commercial break, Laura cleared her throat.

"We went driving today," she said. Claire shot her a warning glance, but she was looking only at her father.

"Oh?" he said, diverting his eyes ever so briefly away from the television.

"We drove down Fairview and Catalpa towards Schneider's liquor store. I didn't—"

Claire interrupted her by turning the volume on the TV set louder. "Look, the show's back on," she said. It wasn't. It was just a preview for a one-hour CBS news special, but Frank found that absorbing enough to resume ignoring Laura completely.

Laura continued staring at him for a full minute, but he showed no sign of asking her to continue her story. She looked so sad, so bitterly disappointed, that Claire decided to forgive the fact that she was trying to betray their secret. Maybe Laura was finally starting to wise up about her father.

Janet Crossen

Desire for Good

Janet Crossen lives in Bethesda, Maryland. When she's not writing, she practices international banking law and performs chamber music. She has degrees in piano performance and law and expects to receive an MFA in creative writing from Warren Wilson College in July 2008. She recently returned from a year in Switzerland where she worked for an international organization and taught a writing workshop at Centrepoint in Basel.

Sondra is not afraid of snow. Or ice. Or the slush that tires sculpt into ruts and knolls. But people trouble her, and especially drivers who don't know how to drive on snow.

Like the man in the next lane. He is one of the gray men. She's been using that term lately, though she's not sure why. It was in some children's book; the gray men were rock creatures or time thieves or devotees of the Dark. She can't recall and it doesn't matter, because she doesn't mean it that way now.

Her bosses at Farringdon, Black are gray men, but she would never say so to their faces, because she needs the job. And the man in the car to her left, though a stranger, is one too. He wears gray, drives gray, blends with the pressing clouds and iced pavement.

There are bright beach towels and plastic tumblers in the windows of the big Crate & Barrel. Patio umbrellas too. Ridiculous on this bleak March morning.

They are stopped at a light and he leans toward his steering wheel, as if by doing so he can cause it to turn to green.

Thomas is a gray man. Marjory too. All of them. They're gray because they think they are significant, and they aren't.

It's not a big snow—there are only inches on Massachusetts Avenue—but it coats the cars, all of them the same. The garaged Porsche and Sondra's battered Dodge that spent the night on the street are equals in the automotive glacier flowing inexorably from the Maryland border to the temples of government, the downtown law firms, the trade associations—the offices with their desks and computers and bustle and receptionists who say, Good morning, Briley, Brig & Golliwog, or Good morning, Frozen Foods of America, and on and on.

The man in the next car is contemptuous of the weather. He wears no coat over his suit jacket.

The light changes to green. He slides, recovers, accelerates. He treats the pavement as if it were one of his staff. To be used, but not noticed for its particular qualities. It's there to do the job he wants done.

Slide into someone else, Gray Man, Sondra says under her breath. She imagines the sound of crushed metal and feels a twinge. Is it the pleasure or agony of destruction?

She opens her ears to the world. The snow crunches under tires. In the distance, a siren whines. Her windshield wipers thump, squeal, moan.

In Manaus, the summer before sixth grade, she was the only child in the party and she slept on a mattress on the floor in the hot room while Gran Alice and Roger shared the small bed. It had been Gran's idea, to take Sondra away so she wouldn't be there when her parents finally separated.

The earnest grown-ups from Roger's church said, you're a lucky child. You're seeing the rainforest, and in twenty years it won't be here, unless we save it.

On most days the group of ten piled into two small boats, and their leathery guides with powerful arms took them into the forests. The adults extolled the brown river and abundant grasses and trees. Sondra waved to the almost-naked children sitting on listing wooden walkways between shacks with oversized TV antennas.

Why would you watch television if you lived in such a remarkable environment? one of the ladies in the boat asked. She wore a violet sun hat and bought herbal teas to take back to Kalamazoo. When they stopped at a little hut for soft drinks, she had Guaraná, because it was a local drink.

The guides turned the boats into creeks and steered between submerged trees and roots. A guide pointed to shiny round mats of green floating on the surface. Giant lily pads, the Guaraná-lady exclaimed. Plant hold child, the guide said in thickly accented English, and seemed ready to put Sondra out of the boat.

One day, she and Gran wandered into a neighborhood of flaking concrete houses where weeds grew from every crack. A woman in an apron ran out of a house and spoke frantically. When they didn't understand, she screamed and waved and they could still hear her when they got to the top of the hill and to the street that led back to their hotel. Was she warning us or scolding us? Sondra asked her Gran, and her Gran said she didn't know.

Sondra is not afraid of snow and ice. She is from the north; knows that snow requires a special etiquette. Slow movements, but natural. The way one might deal with a wild animal in the woods. Don't notice me, one must say to the animal, to the ice. Southerners don't realize how the dance is done. And northerners who move south can forget.

When she approaches American University, she sees that the gray man is still with her, a little ahead in the next lane. They creep around the traffic circle while big, bronze Mr. Ward, in a patchy snow mantel, gazes from his podium. University students in puffy jackets and shaggy boots step into the crosswalk without looking. They assume everything will stop for them.

Gray, gray, gray.

One hour ago, she watched the snow fall in Thomas's backyard while he slept upstairs. The snow mounded on the patio table, the one he should have put in the garage at the end of the summer, but he didn't because his wife wasn't there to remind him.

The day Sondra met Thomas, there'd been open bottles of wine on that patio table. She'd drunk chardonnay in a plastic glass with a detachable stem that fell off if she didn't hold it with just the right amount of pressure.

An office party. The sun was bright. Their lovely Spring Valley home. The grass was green. Chemically enhanced, but could that be? A nice part of town.

Thomas's wife was her boss then. Her boss at the Conservation Institute. A dream boss at a dream job.

Sondra, this is my husband Thomas, Marjory said that summer day as she opened the lid of the massive gas grill and poked an oversized fork at the swordfish steaks. Marjory was tanned and muscled, and wore a tangerine linen sundress and flat, gold sandals. She was nine years older than Thomas. She had wrinkles at the corners of her eyes. She'd been a field biologist before she got her MBA. At the office, the staff joked in private about their boss's young husband. The men still in their twenties asked, why would a young guy want a forty-five-year-old woman?

Sondra drank her third glass of wine and felt Thomas's eyes trace the zipper up the front of her tight denim skirt. Sondra had a good figure and long brown hair. She was twenty-eight. He must be drunk. Did Marjory care that he looked at women this way?

"Are you going to Nu'utele too?" she asked him. Marjory was leaving for Samoa in a week.

"Not my thing."

She must have tightened her mouth. He put up both hands—mocking, as if fending off an attack.

"You're going to lecture me because I don't care about the *Didunculus strigirostris,*" he said, then repeated the words with unnatural emphasis as if they were ancient wisdom and not the Latin name of the endangered Samoan pigeon.

He was a law professor, writing a book on the law of eminent domain. "Takings." He said the word with a lift of his eyebrow. "My work is to change the world with words."

He wore a tan blazer over his jeans. The cut and fabric looked expensive. Someone at the office said he had family money. A strand of dark hair fell in his eye. He wore shiny loafers and no socks. Sondra remembered thinking how she usually hated the look of slip-ons without socks. His slim ankles were as tanned as Marjory's arms.

"It takes more than words," she said. She felt the pleasure of her zeal.

"You're all so fervent," he said.

She turned away.

"Except Marjory. She's got it just about right."

Sondra didn't respond.

"I admire good," he said softly to her back, and she sensed he was not referring only to the appeal of a worthy cause.

She joined two of her colleagues under a white rose trellis; they were discussing biodiversity in Africa. Thomas lounged on the chaise and held his wineglass aloft as if toasting everyone on the patio.

When only a few guests remained, he helped her carry dishes into the kitchen and his hand brushed against her breast. It was barely a touch, but it was as if all her nerves gathered to that place, and she felt a body's worth of touch.

Good is when you change the world. When you've rescued a slope of cloud forest and preserved the bromeliads that press their roots in the damp bark.

In high school, her AP biology class went to a lecture in East Lansing on clean water. In one slide, a gaunt woman dipped a wooden scoop in a brown puddle.

Sondra was always good in science.

You do good by learning the names of five thousand plants and animals and the titles and section numbers of a dozen environmental bills. You do it by going to graduate school in Ann Arbor and doing nothing but work.

Her friends couldn't believe she'd landed the job with the Institute right out of grad school. Who'd you sleep with? Ricky said. He asked questions like that. She had sex with him once because he pestered her. It was the only reason. He was hurt. I liked you, he said. She didn't believe in relationships, she told him. Passion was for work.

Sondra met Marjory at a B-school conference on industry and the environment. Marjory wore a gold bracelet of thick chain links. When she gestured to the graphs and diagrams on the screen behind her, the bracelet slid but slightly. High quality. A perfect fit.

Her presentation was direct and to the point. She was the kind of woman who had no doubts, who would never apologize for anything she did. After the lecture, Sondra waited to speak to Marjory and said, I want to be you when I grow up, and the older woman laughed and took a copy of her resume back to Washington, and that was how Sondra got the job.

Sondra's car is old and battered, but it is blue, the color of a pale winter sky. She can be calm as a pale winter sky. She must respect the ice and snow, must get to the law firm and sit at the receptionist's desk and say, Good morning, Farringdon, Black, How may I direct your call? It was the only job she could get. Thomas said he'd help her get a better job, but he didn't. The nonprofit world is small. Everyone knows everyone. Affair with boss's husband? Even her friends, who wanted to help, couldn't. Maybe she should go to law school, he said. Be like him.

Where is that gray man in his gray car? She wants to keep track of him, to stay clear of him. The other motorists clench their steering wheels and crane their necks. Some try to go faster, but give up when they start to slide.

The apartment building at the corner of Mass Ave and Wisconsin is old, refurbished to grandeur. The townhouses are new, made to look old. What is old, what new? A sign offers luxurious properties for sale in the "high brackets."

People stand in the bus shelter wearing heavy coats with hoods. Their faces say that nothing changes.

After they'd been lovers for four months, Sondra tried to understand how it started. She never told anyone else the story and she thought that must be why she couldn't explain it to herself.

He started it. She had no experience with seduction. And why would she do that? A couple weeks after the party, they ran into each other on the sidewalk in Georgetown. Sandy? he'd said as they passed on the street. You work with my wife, right? And she corrected him, that her name was Sondra, but yes, she worked for Marjory.

Sondra didn't have her car. It was raining. He would drop her at Farragut North to get the Metro home. But then he decided to drive her home. I want to see where a young environmentalist lives—field research, he said—and when they walked into her small living room, he put his hand on her shoulder and squeezed it slightly. Only the first time did they make love at her place. Afterwards, she went to the house in Spring Valley when Marjory was out of town or late at meetings.

What will your wife say? Sondra asked after he kissed her. Let me worry about that, he said, and she knew she wasn't the first. But she stopped thinking, because the longing was so great, and it seemed familiar, and therefore right.

Last week, if someone had asked Sondra, are there many churches on Mass Ave? she would have said, some, a few, I don't know. This morning she notices all the holy places. Church, church, seminary, church, synagogue, church, church, cathedral, church, all snowed on from Above. Soon she will reach the mosque. They are square, brick, stone, grand, modest, with pillars, with signs that advertise their particular brand of righteousness. They claim connection with a high good. Sondra does not understand this kind of holiness.

The cars move on, slowly and more carefully now. Pedestrians shuffle and slide on the icy sidewalks. She looks for the black-haired woman whose three-legged cocker spaniel usually hobbles happily by her side, but she's not there; it must be difficult to walk with only three legs, but the dog doesn't know that, does it? And what about the other woman she nearly always sees on her morning-after drives, the anorexic who runs on stick legs in bright Lycra tights? Perhaps it is too cold for a woman who is only bones.

Her windshield wipers strain against slush. The heater, on high, pumps out baked air and fumes.

Why does she miss the woman who prances because she's made her body as light as air?

When she came into the Institute that last morning, Marjory's door was closed. She wants to see you *as soon as you come in*, the project leader told Sondra. She's in a terrible mood. What in god's name did you do?

"Do you remember what you said to me that first time we met?" Marjory asked, her voice breaking, and Sondra closed the office door behind her. "Does what we do here mean nothing to you?" Marjory, standing behind her desk, pressed against it and fingered the gold bracelet that she was never without. "Do you care nothing about your job?"

"No, this is everything..." How could she explain the need for that little bit more? And it was little, nothing really.

"Wanted to be like me. And you think that means screwing my husband?"

"I didn't, I mean, there must have been, what did he?"

"Get out," Marjory screamed. "Out of my office, out of this building, and never come back. Never." Marjory tugged hard at her bracelet and it fell to the floor at Sondra's feet. When Sondra leaned over to pick it up, Marjory shoved her away and retrieved it herself. She clenched the bracelet in both hands.

The other commuters don't notice what they pass, but Sondra sees everything, because nothing will bring her to this part of town again. She notices the tree branches, thickened with the wet snow, bending toward the pavement. She says out loud the names of countries whose embassies line this bend in the road. Finland's glass box with vines. South Africa. The British embassy with its new flower box fortification. In their midst, the Vice President's gun-guarded acres. Bolivia. Brazil. They coexist in an eccentric geography. The wind blows snow from Bolivia to Finland to South Africa. In a matter of minutes.

When Sondra pulls into the right lane of Mass Ave to get onto Rock Creek Parkway, the snow is so thick that the minaret of the mosque is hidden. With her imagination, she puts it where it belongs while she waits for the light to change to green.

Seven hours before, she'd been at Caddie's in Bethesda with two Michigan classmates and a couple of their friends. They all worked on the Hill. She had a story ready why she wasn't at the Institute anymore; she'd tell it quickly—boss a bitch, political infighting, glorified-file-clerk work, not what you think—discourage questions and ask if they knew about any interesting jobs. But somehow she couldn't do it. The others complained about their hours, their jobs, their bosses, their incomes. They ordered more beer. They cheered the game on the televisions above the bar. Sondra was the first to leave, and she walked to the garage alone.

She headed toward the District instead of east to her apartment. The snow was coming down hard, and the county trucks with their flashing yellow lights spread salt and sand on Wisconsin Ave.

It had been four weeks since Thomas had walked her to Farringdon, Black and introduced her to one of the partners. Since then they'd had one phone conversation. One email. Lay low, he said.

The windows were dark when she pulled in front of his house. Marjory's car was in the driveway, snow covered. Why here? Sondra knew that Marjory was in Madagascar because she'd produced the original outline for the trip briefing book a week before she was fired.

It took a long time for the porch light to come on after she rang the bell. He stood elevated on the step behind the glass storm door, dressed in jeans and a white undershirt. There was no smile, no welcome.

She turned the handle, but it was locked. "Aren't you going to let me in?"

His arms remained at his sides.

"It's snowing," she said.

He unlatched the door and gave it a nudge but let go as soon as she took the handle.

"I can see that it's snowing."

"I want to talk." She tried to sound dignified.

The corners of his mouth were pinched. "I thought we said we were taking a break."

"I can't," she said.

She rushed toward him, expecting him to take her in his arms, but instead they stumbled together against the wall and she wedged her hands behind him and cried against his chest. After a while he held her. She waited for the warmth and yearning to take hold, but they didn't. In his bed, they went through the motions, roughly, and her wish to feel something, anything, faded until nothing of that hope was left.

Sondra should have gotten in her car then and driven east, across Military Road, east and north, to her part of town. She shouldn't have stayed until morning in the extra room with its low bed and brushed steel night stand. But she imagined the drive home as an endless journey, and Thomas was asleep, and what did it matter where she stayed?

Morning came at last, and she put her clothes on. Black pants and sweater; no one at the law firm would notice they were the same as yesterday; they never looked at her. She found some juice in the refrigerator and took a half of an English muffin from a package on the counter. When she sat at the table by the back window, she saw Marjory's big document bag next to the counter. Sondra was staring at it when he came in. He was in jeans and a T-shirt, same as the night before.

"I didn't mean for it to happen like this," he said.

"You mean you told Marjory you wouldn't screw me anymore?" She kept her eyes on the document bag. "Are you going to tell her about this?"

"You're so young," he said, as if that explained everything.

"You never cared; god, you never cared," she said, and cringed when the words rang out like an afternoon soap opera, and she knew they meant absolutely nothing.

She swerves on a patch of ice as she turns onto Waterside Drive, and when she pumps her brakes to regain control, the car behind her honks. Bastard, she says. The single line of cars waiting to get on Rock Creek Parkway is backed up to the alley entrance, and she stops behind a large white van with diplomatic plates. Minutes pass. They move about the length of one car. The snow is turning to sleet. She looks over the edge of the ramp onto the parkway, and sees that traffic is moving, so it doesn't make sense they're stopped. They move another ten feet, around the bend, and she sees the car crossways on the road, aimed into the hedge by the small row of townhouses. At first she doesn't recognize the car, but then she sees that it's the gray man. She'd forgotten him, but here he is making trouble, making an ass of himself. An SUV bounces over the curb and into the wooded area to the right of the road in order to pass the stopped car. A sedan starts to follow, and stops.

She could help. She knows how to do it. She has a shovel in her trunk, wire grids to get him off ice. She could even push his car. She's done it dozens of times. But she turns on the radio and the announcer says there's a snow storm.

The random congregation of drivers is strangely docile while they wait for something to happen. What do they expect? Her windshield wipers thump offbeats to a jingle for a carpet cleaning company.

The sliding door of the white van in front of her opens. The man who exits is huge and bronze; he wears a Kente cloth robe of gold, yellow, and brown, his legs swathed in the same patterned fabric, a small matching cap on his head. He seems a creature of sun and wild landscapes, unexpected in this cold, gray place.

The traffic reporter warns of hazardous conditions.

He strides to the gray car, leans and says something to the driver, then moves behind. His goal is simple. To remove the barrier to their journeys. He embraces the car and leans against the wetness, calling out something while the man gives the car gas and turns the wheels until he once again is on the ramp headed toward the parkway. The gray man drives cautiously, as do the drivers who follow.

Sondra regards the road, now open in front of her, the narrow passage through the arch of snow-coated branches and brush. She imagines stopping there forever and letting the snow and ice bury her car. But the car horns behind her are loud and angry.

She is certain there is something she is destined to save, if only she could figure out what.

Rosie Dempsey

Walking the Grounds

Rosie Dempsey writes fiction and essays for the *Gettysburg Review*, the *Washington Post*, the *Cleveland Plain Journal*, the *LA Times*, and the *Las Vegas Review Journal*; KNPR and NPR radio networks; and *Desert Companion* and *The Sun Runner* magazines.

"When we pull into a gas station," Cathy said, "Ian has to drive a circle around the pump before getting the car into position. He reminds me of a goddamn cat."

"Dominic's the same way. Every time we pull in he has to ask me which side the gas tank's on," Susan said.

They walked past a tour bus in the driveway of the Hillwood Museum and Gardens, the former home of Mrs. Post. Cathy ran her hands through her hair to fluff it up in the oppressive heat. "What's he going to be like in another ten years?" she said.

Cathy let Susan pick the table in the small house that had been converted into a café. They were seated in a far corner where no one could easily overhear them. Cathy quickly decided on the goose liver pâté with pickled slaw and closed her menu. She looked past Susan to the old people outside who were stepping off the tour bus. The café was a brick and gable miniature of the main house. It reminded her of her childhood doll house that was big enough for her to sit in as a child. Many times, the big bad wolf had tried to blow it down, but she had thrown stones until it ran away.

Sipping her water, Cathy recalled how Susan had called and invited her to lunch at a fancy restaurant five years ago. They knew each other only from a local women's shelter where both had briefly served on the board. Cathy went to the lunch out of curiosity, presuming that Susan was trying to jump-start her career. She kept meeting Susan because she enjoyed going to museum shows and then on to restaurants where dinner for her and her husband would be too expensive, but a Dutch treat lunch wasn't. Yet, back then, Cathy had felt there was a trace of charity about the time she spent with Susan.

Susan had exuded an unspoken desperation in those early years. But all they discussed was the art they'd seen and stories from the newspaper. The recent feats of their children were usually dispensed with in the first few minutes. Over time their conversations expanded into more intimate realms.

"I'm ready, are you?" Susan said, finally putting down her menu.

She did not order her usual glass of wine, and Cathy wondered if she had given up drinking. Had it become too much of a habit? Their friendship was composed of spontaneous confessions, and now Cathy found herself anticipating another. Two months ago, they had eaten at the Smithsonian's Old Castle on the Mall, after hitting a *trompe l'oeil* show at the East Wing. Ever since Susan's husband had lost his job, they had stopped lunching at expensive restaurants.

"I feel like I'm withholding myself from him," said Susan. Hesitancy edged her voice. Cathy remembered how she used to envy her friend's sex life—Susan implied an almost nightly act that seemed to supplant any time spent relaxing in front of a TV—though Cathy couldn't imagine giving up her cozy evenings in bed with her husband, Ian, watching old black-and-white movies while their girls slept.

"I understand. I use my time out of the house, my job, to soothe myself. I know you hate the idea...but if you went back to work, you'd find—"

"No," Susan interrupted. "I couldn't do that. Things are bound to get better...right?"

Susan was fragile-looking and strikingly thin despite the elaborate family dinners she cooked nightly. Her ginger hair and a freckled face matched fair skin that never required makeup the way Cathy's did.

"Sure they will," Cathy said. It was a comfort to see other people's blind spots. She dug her fork into the purple cabbage. If only she could have both Susan's miniature appetite and her desire to spend hours cooking.

"When you say 'for better or for worse,'" Susan said, "you can't imagine what the worse is. What if he was in a car accident and paralyzed from the waist down? Why not sexual frailty as a disability?" Cathy noticed that Susan had yet to touch her food.

"So things still aren't working in the bedroom?" In Susan's presence, Cathy found herself believing that her own marriage was more likely to improve.

"No..." Susan said, methodically cutting her curried chicken breast to pieces.

"Men hit middle age and it's a big shock to them," Cathy said. "Sex gets complicated. The prostate exam comes along. They feel violated. They worry about cancer. We've been going to gynecologists all along who say things like, *you're just going to feel a little pinch.* Then it hurts like hell." She wondered when, exactly, Dominic's golden parachute would hit the ground.

"True, true," Susan said in a faraway voice. "Isn't the orchid lovely?"

A small vase on their table held the arching purple plume.

"Dominic's depressed," Susan continued, her eyes tearing. "Not that he'd admit it. But I'm not in denial. I can't pretend..."

"When he finds a job everything will go back to normal," Cathy said. She had resisted doing a web search to find business articles detailing Dominic's professional demise. If Susan didn't want her to know how he had lost his mid-six-figure job, she felt honor bound not to seek out the reasons. "A CPA can always find a job. Don't worry, Susan."

"Dominic says he's not interested in taking the little blue pill or any of them. I can't even say the V-word in his presence. He's competitive with me. I told him, 'You're not letting me proof your letters.' He tells me he spell-checks them. I saw a typo in the first sentence. He'd written 'posses' for 'possess.'" They laughed.

"Ian leaves so much of the practical management of our lives to me," Cathy said to balance the score. "I hate my own competency. I used to want to be in charge. Not anymore. Marriage has its phases, but this one's lasting too long."

"I have half a mind to grind up Viagra or that new one into his food," Susan said and downed her double espresso. She had already ordered a second one.

Cathy smiled with her mouth shut to conceal her stained teeth. Tetracycline had ruined them when she was a teenager. She twirled a soft strand of her dark hair for comfort, another old habit. Revealing marital secrets was hard for her. She liked being alone with her thoughts in Susan's presence where she could grapple with her despair without feeling lonely. She could take aspects of her marriage and realign them as if making moves on a chessboard, plotting a strategem for a more harmonious future. Cathy admired her friend for revealing details that seemed to beg to be kept hidden.

"Dominic can't talk honestly about it. Neither can I because he can't handle it," Susan said.

"You'd be grateful if your husband was more accessible, and I'd be grateful if mine was more stoic." Cathy considered ordering the lemon tart. America was going fat. She didn't want to go with them. What was she forgetting to ask or tell Susan? That was it…a poem. Susan often brought a copy of a favorite poem to share.

Cathy would take the poem home and tape it to the inside of her closet door where most of the others were. While dressing, she often read a stanza. A line might come back to her later in the day, like a keyhole into another life. It could make her forget that for too long she had been running blood drives for the Red Cross. "I really could use a poem today," she said. She licked the last of the pâté off the fork.

"Oh, I almost forgot," Susan said and looked up from the bill. She fished in her purse and handed over a sheet.

Cathy unfolded it and scanned to the middle:

Green crops sheared the train of her vantage
Plains flooded and grew boats before her
Chaos coursed round goosenecks of land
And swept them over the fall of time.

Yes, that was right. Middle age was like going over Niagara Falls in a barrel. The poet was unknown to her. Cathy stuffed the poem in her purse and pulled out money. When had she last put a dollar in the wide-mouth wine jug in the corner of her bedroom? Ten days ago. The habit had begun when they lived in a group house, sharing a room flanked with windows. It had been Ian's suggestion. Every time they had sex, they dropped a dollar in the green jug. Its base was woven and hooked up to the throat of the bottle, which offered a grip when plucking the bills out with chopsticks. Often, back then they'd used the booty when they were broke to go to their favorite Mexican restaurant. That was before the twins, the little girls they had wanted for so long. Now, the cask filled much more slowly, but they still pulled bills from it. Today even, she had maneuvered ten ones out and fattened her wallet with them. They were all that she had left after pulling out fifteen dollars for lunch. She was amazed that the cask had never broken.

"Ready?" Susan said, plucking the bills from Cathy's hand and adding her own for exact change, tip included.

Cathy stood, and heard a glass crash. She saw water pooling on a nearby table and then an elderly lady leapt out of her chair, ice cubes falling from her wet lap. For a second, Cathy thought she had caused the accident. She followed Susan out and past two men, one clad in a loud Madras plaid jacket with matches in his hand, the other with his pants cinched by a white belt. She heard him say, *Why'd I agreed to go on this trip? She's really getting on my nerves.* The first man nodded and bit into a cigar and looked away.

They walked along a bank of cutting flowers grown for indoor display. Cathy thought of the phlox moss flowers of early spring that grew over her front stone wall. Nothing could trick the phlox moss to bloom longer or later in the season. Susan led them to the greenhouse where they found thousands of orchids shielded from the sun by whitewashed panes. They bent over to sniff the rich scents. "This is aromatherapy," said Cathy. She thought of pre–air conditioning days when some women stored their underwear in the refrigerator. What other old tricks were forgotten? "It's too hot in here," she said.

Their footsteps crunched against the pebble drive. The immense brick colonial towered ahead. Inside, cool air flowed among columns of veined marble, a grand urn of flowers, and busts that filled the grand foyer. They wandered into the long pantry and each chose a favorite from the demitasse sets displayed in high glass cabinets. Cathy pictured the chaos in the pantry on the evening of a large dinner party, the huge silver trays pulled from slots and polished in preparation. She had worked in catering during college but hated the effort required for hosting dinner parties herself. Susan entertained, but without ever speaking of it Cathy knew she and Ian would never be invited to such a gathering. Sharing secrets precluded them from sitting around a dinner table as couples.

Off the hugest kitchen Cathy had ever seen was a dimly lit antechamber that held Russian religious artifacts: a miter, robes, and icons behind glass. "Fancy spending your nights drinking wine out of that," Cathy said of a chalice completely encrusted with large jewels. She found it hard to believe the colored stones were real.

"I can," Susan said, her fingers reaching towards the stem. Susan often picked out objects and art at the exhibits they went to and commented on where they would *look good in my house*. She always seemed happy in those moments of make-believe. She had dined many times at chef's tables right inside the kitchen, where reservations had to be made a year in advance, and the chef personally doled out samples. Before Susan, Cathy had never even heard of such things.

They walked through more rooms cluttered with *objets d'arts*. "A world built on frozen peas and breakfast cereal," Cathy said. They paused over the photos of Mrs. Post all done up in her eighties. "What's the latest on your mother-in-law?"

"She doesn't recognize anyone anymore," Susan said, "and Dominic still doesn't visit her. A few weeks ago the nursing home called. 'When we went in to give her her afternoon pills, your mother was in a state of undress and consensual congress with a male resident. We like to keep the family informed,' they said. Apparently, completely losing your inhibitions is the silver lining of dementia."

They both laughed as they lingered in the boudoir.

"She won't live forever," Cathy said. "You'll inherit and that will ease your finances." In a drawing room, she imagined sweeping her hand and clearing the tabletops of expensive junk. Once, she had thrown a paperweight at her husband and missed. Cathy would never reveal that. She was grateful that Ian kept track of her menstrual cycle on his computer. Her emotions went haywire just before her period. She wished there was a way to sidestep her meltdowns, let alone Ian's, which were less predictable and more frequent than her PMS.

"Dominic says I'm faithless," Susan said as they walked on. She stopped and gestured around the enormous room. "There's no art here I'd want on my walls."

"You're right, Fabergé eggs and vanity portraits mostly," Cathy said, wondering what kind of *faithless* Susan meant?

"I wouldn't want to be this rich," Susan said with earnestness.

"Oh, you could just give me what you didn't want," Cathy said, and laughed. They walked out to a slate veranda and sat side by side in wrought-iron chairs set before a drop-off in the land.

"The outside of the house is really rather ungainly," Susan said.

Cathy nodded from her vantage over the sloping hillside of mowed grass that ended in a horseshoe of dense forest. The tip of the Washington Monument could be seen because the tops of the trees had been badly hacked in the middle distance. There was a further horizon of trees, and these, she guessed, were on the other side of Rock Creek Park near the zoo. When she and Ian lived in a group house over there, they had woken to the animals' roars and screeches on the wind, and found it inspired morning sex.

"Cool drinks are being brought on a tray," Susan said playfully.

"By the naked pool boy."

"Oh, my…Yes, the naked pool boy."

"We're getting the hang of it," Cathy said. "That's what Mrs. Post must have done in her dotage. There were always young men on the social scene that wanted to benefit from association with a wealthy matron. There still are. Can you imagine?" Cathy thought of herself and Susan as widows, riding the carousel astride wooden horses, their relationship having lasted decades and geographic distances that had intervened, their laughter drifting across the green corridor of the Mall, the Capitol like an oversized doll house at one end.

"How about working your way through four husbands?" Susan said.

"It does make them seem rather disposable." Cathy's eyes turned from the view and acknowledged Susan's glance. They both faced the distance. "I didn't get any sense of those husbands, even the last one."

"There's no imprint of them in the house," Susan said.

"Yes...She was a woman who simply bought too much."

"Remember the gleam in her eye in that photo in the boudoir," Susan said. "Where did that look go?"

"I'm moving to Europe when I turn fifty. They still make sex goddesses out of women our age. Here, we're nonentities. When's the last time someone seriously flirted with you?" When Susan didn't answer, Cathy said, "Shall we?"

In the Japanese garden, cool air misted off the man-made waterfall and cut into the dense humidity. Cathy thought of the zoo animals pacing off their cages. The women walked the circular croquet lawn, a thick carpet of manicured grass. Between the knotted patterns of sheared hedges, Cathy moved against the invisible resistance of heavy air. In spite of the bird songs drifting in from the forest beyond, the grounds were unimpressive. Some imbalance marred the effect—a threadbare quality to some of the beds, deadwood left to rot, the plain house as backdrop. "Our houses are going to look smaller when we get home."

"Mine's going to look good," Susan said.

Cathy heard the effect of the espressos in Susan's giddy voice. Her friend's big Victorian did suit her, thought Cathy, and perhaps her own little bungalow did, too. She and Ian had never wanted a big mortgage, and loved their yard, argued over its care just last weekend. "These gardens aren't as nice as the grounds at Dumbarton Oaks," Cathy said. "Did I ever tell you that when I was sixteen my best friend and I sneaked in there after hours and went swimming?"

"Yes," Susan said, her tone heightened. "You know I once went bareback riding...naked. I was staying with a girlfriend who was house-sitting at a farm way out Route 29. The horses jumped into the water."

"A pool?" Cathy said, startled.

"No. A pond. We left our clothes behind at the stables."

"Why not be outrageous like we were back then?

"You mean like vacuum the house naked?" Susan said.

"Oh, I don't know. Something," Cathy said. "I'm saving adultery for when I'm sixty-four. You know the Beatles's tune." She laughed and began to make a mental list of all the unusual places she'd done it with Ian: up a tree, on a train, in bathrooms at parties. Now, they preferred their own bed. But once in a while she wanted something else—the backyard, the dining room table. Ian rarely agreed.

"Aren't we lucky that the rain held off," Susan said. "You can almost slice the air." They crossed the pebble drive to the visitors' center. It had been converted from the head gardener's office and its elegant symmetry belittled the big house. They sat indoors for a minute.

"Next time, how about the de Kooning show at the Hirshhorn?" Susan said, her datebook open. "The *Washington Post* says he's a misogynist. I think it runs through August." She pulled out the article from her purse, and they looked at the canvases featured in the photos that were described as *Dominated by women's bodies bisected by pink and black slashes.* They walked towards the cars.

"Poor Elaine de Kooning. Artistic geniuses make terrible husbands," Cathy said, and turned her ignition. Where had she read that boredom was the one emotion no marriage could survive? Sometimes, it seemed that children were the only reason to marry for life. One day her beautiful girls would go off. She collapsed their futures into milestones: graduation, degrees, careers, marriages, and children of their own. And then, when you became a grandparent, people said your long, enduring path suddenly made sense. But she wanted her life to make sense now. For a moment, she felt she might cry. What was that line from today's poem...*over the fall of time.* She adjusted her sunglasses, glad to find them on her nose as she steered down the curving drive.

"I've wanted to come to Hillwood for years," Susan said.

Cathy cocked her head to the right. "Want to see what's down that street?"

"Sure," said Susan. "When will I ever be back here?"

"It really is an in-the-know destination." They passed houses marked by the overbearing imprint of an architect's hand. Some were downright ugly: bunkers, industrial. One, painted muddy orange, was right out of the 1970s. A for-sale sign stood in the front yard.

"That house must be going at a discount," Cathy said. They rounded the dead-end circle and headed back out.

"I'd never buy that clunker," Susan said.

Such an inheritance was within Susan's reach, but Cathy knew it would never be in her own future. She drove past the zoo and into the Mount Pleasant neighborhood, hardly paying attention to Susan's comments about her younger son's latest soccer feats. Cathy noticed that the business strip seemed livelier than ever, and more than recovered from the riots when Latino immigrants had protested police mistreatment. A window of the barrio restaurant was filled with a large gangly plant. The hand-painted sign over the storefront was unchanged. Cathy knew Susan wouldn't go to such a place, its food too basic, and its décor too low brow.

But she and Ian had often eaten there when they lived nearby twenty years ago in that group house. Somehow the Rio Bravo Restaurant had stayed the same while other businesses were transformed. The bakery had added outdoor seating. The shop where she used to have her Raleigh bicycle repaired was gone. It startled her to remember she had ridden a bicycle everywhere in those days.

On these sidewalks, they had once strolled arm in arm. She wanted to go back with Ian and order the enchilada special with the green tomatillo salsa. She wanted him to tell the old stories again—like the one about how he had bought a second-hand stove from a man who later became the governor of Maryland or the time he had drunk homemade corn liquor and dandelion wine in a garage with elderly black men still proud of their country ways, honored by their invitation. Back at the Rio Bravo, she and Ian could order another bottle of wine, perhaps one shaped like a fish. She would bring it home and put it on her vanity, and let the girls fill it with coins.

She gave a peck to Susan's cheek at the Metro. As usual, Susan did not offer a peck back. Cathy drove on and was a few blocks from home when she decided what to do with the rest of the day. Her bedroom needed a thorough vacuuming. It would be easy to accomplish with Ian out with the girls for the afternoon.

The old tubular Hoover was kept in the upstairs closet to use on the wall-to-wall carpet in the bedrooms. It felt like holy work, this long overdue cleaning. When she finished the corner by her bureau, she turned and yanked the Hoover along. It hit the jug which cleanly shattered into its own basket. She stood there in amazement. After bagging the shards, she wiped the dollars one by one, and hid them in her underwear drawer in an envelope. She vacuumed the corner several times, carefully, before putting the vacuum away.

That night, the girls in bed, she and Ian settled in for their Saturday night video. It was a Hungarian film, *Time Stands Still*, an old favorite they had first seen in the nearly empty five-hundred-seat Circle Theatre on Pennsylvania Avenue.

"Hey, what happened," he said. The FBI warning played on the screen as he pointed to where the wine cask had sat for a dozen years. She walked to the bare corner and dropped her kimono. "It was an accident," she said, posing. "Come here and I might tell you where I put the dollar bills." She stood there naked until he turned the movie off. As he walked towards her, it occurred to her that they had never done it in the corner before.

Mary Katya Doroshenk

Real Last Names

MARY KATYA DOROSHENK is a short story writer who's been published in the *Washington Post* and *Not What I Expected: The Unpredictable Road from Womanhood to Motherhood*. She lives in Arlington, Virginia, with her husband, Chris, and her muse, daughter Madeline True.

I don't know what's the matter with me, but ever since Cole was born, I cry at everything. I used to think I was a tough guy, a guy's guy. I like beer and lawn mowers and raw bloody steaks. In college, I lived off a Kegerator and a Fry Daddy for a good seven months. If someone merges too slowly or cuts me off, I give 'em the finger whether they're truckers or minivans or little old women. I can put my entire fist in my mouth, seal my lips around my wrist, and hang out like that for hours. I defend the Philadelphia Eagles, even though they're a bunch of worthless shits and they piss me off. I'm just kind of like every other man I know—except sometimes I hold little Cole and cry.

For instance, I've spent all afternoon waiting for my wife, Claire, to come home, so I could go see my brother Edgar. I need to talk to Edgar about Dad. An hour ago, Cole was wailing, driving me absolutely bat shit. I had planned on using the afternoon to take down the brown paneling in the back room that I always hated. Instead, I couldn't get Cole to stop crying. I changed his diaper, fed him, gave him a bottle, rocked him. Nothing. He was shrieking away.

But then the dog jumped on the sofa and licked Cole right on the face, and Cole stopped crying. He opened his eyes, formed a little smile, and made this content little sound—all while Toby slobbered all over him. I swear to god it took my breath away. We just sat like that for a while—Cole, Toby, and me. And the next thing you know, I felt pressure behind my eyes, and I was about to cry.

Same thing happened a couple of weeks ago, right after Dad got sick. My wife Claire and I were going back to the hospital, and it had already been just a hell of a day. We found out the ceiling was dripping in the back room, Cole had been crabby, and Toby knocked over the garbage and tracked spaghetti sauce all through the house. We don't have the money to replace the roof, and neither of us has the time to scrub up the tomato sauce that was all over the carpet. It wouldn't have taken much more than a broken shoelace, and I would have thrown my Bob Vila home repair book right out the window.

But as we were leaving, I placed little Cole in his car seat, and he was gazing up. He was mesmerized by the dome light and wouldn't stop staring at it, but then it shut off. It lit back on, and he looked at me, dumbfounded. He reached up his little baby arm and pointed his slobbery pint-size fingers to the light. He wanted to make sure I saw it. I started tearing up all over again.

Claire and I got into the car, and I leaned my head back into the driver's seat, bit my lip and held it in. I thought I did an okay job of holding it back, until Claire fished through her purse for a travel pack of Kleenex, dabbed her nose, and, in a not-so-discreet way, left the pack on the dashboard.

I look out the window to see if Claire's home yet and wonder what the hell's with me. Last time I cried I was eight years old, and my brother Edgar had slammed my fingers in the car door. My dad never cried that I can remember. My dad was a Navy sea captain. We called him "Captain The Ted." Plenty of times I'd seen him frustrated, annoyed, and definitely pissed. But never crying. He's kind of big—tall and muscular in a compact sort of way. When he got mad, his arms would lengthen, and his shoulders would freeze up. He'd bite down on his upper lip, which was already kind of thin. His whole upper lip would disappear, so you could only see his teeth. If that lip disappeared, my dad was going to explode, and Edgar and I would scram. Oddly enough, I really would love to see my dad all pissed off again. Or even better, delivering the punch line to one of his stories. When I think of him in his hospital bed, I feel sick to my stomach.

His first night in the hospital, they made Claire and me sit forever in the waiting room. I hate those places. Nothing but old copies of *Prevention* magazine and *Modern Maturity*. It was too cold, so I kept switching chairs, trying to avoid the air vent. When we finally did get in, Dad was propped up in the hospital bed. His skin was gray, and tubes were coming out of his arm. They had him in a white gown with blue flowers. I sat in the guest seat. He didn't look at me. I wanted to say something, but the room was depressing, and nothing came.

Claire sat on the edge of the bed and rubbed Dad's shoulder, almost like when she puts Cole to bed. I thought of her resting Cole in his crib, smoothing his hair, and whispering to him. A calmness that I couldn't manage surrounded Claire while she sat by my dad. Sure enough, Dad relaxed at Claire's touch. The whole time I sat there with nothing to say.

Claire finally gets home, and I get in the car to leave. I get to the on-ramp and roll down the window. The scent of the hospital room seems to be stuck in the car. It's a sterile smell that mixes with the faint scent of body odor. The sick feeling in my stomach returns. I turn on talk radio.

With Cole being born, I thought I was getting immune to gross smells. My buddy Sammy once said to me, "You can be in the middle of lunch, have to stop to change your kid's diaper, and go right back to eating your sandwich...no problem."

One time Cole was real sick, projectile vomiting. I was holding him, trying to comfort him, had no shirt on, and he began to vomit. I looked around trying to figure out where I should point his mouth. It was either the carpeting or the front of my chest. I didn't want to have to clean the carpet, so I held his mouth near me, trapping the vomit between the two of us. You don't do that for anyone but your kid.

I wonder if my dad did that for me. He's been great with Cole. In fact the night we first realized Dad was sick, he had Cole laughing just by saying *Cole* in a deep foghorn voice. That night was my birthday. Number thirty-two. Edgar and his wife, Cecilia, had us all over for dinner.

"Hey! It's my long-lost brother, Mackie!" Edgar announced as we walked in.

Dad gave me a firm handshake and slapped me on the back. "Happy birthday, Mackie! Enjoy it—because this is it until next year!"

We weren't there ten minutes when my dad started telling one of his favorite stories about the Navy. His face lit up, and his hands were going. He's got a slight receding hairline, so when he gets wound up, you can really see his forehead wrinkle and loosen. The gist of the story was that he was inspecting some shipyard in New Orleans where the contractor was way behind. These guys were telling the Navy it would take three million dollars to get the project back on track.

"So the contractors are giving me this big sob story, telling me they have three hundred men working twenty-four hours a day, but it's not enough to get the job done. So I pull one of my petty officers aside and tell him to go count how many men are on the job. We go on with the tour, and the contractors keep giving me this big song and dance about three hundred men. Meantime, the petty officer comes back and tells me he only counted seventy-four. So I slap my wad of travel money on the conference table. *Here's two hundred bucks. What do you say we pull the fire alarm, everybody empties out, and we count how many men show up. If it's three hundred men, you guys get to keep the cash.* Well, these guys get all flustered and whiny. *I don't know, Captain, that wouldn't be ethical.* So I shout back. *Yeah? That's because you guys are bullshitting me!*"

Everyone laughed. I started to relax and loosen up as the conversation flowed. Claire had her brown hair pulled back in a ponytail, and her face looked really soft. We hadn't been able to sit with other adults and talk for ages.

We were all huddled around the dining room table, candles lit, with the stories rolling. We went back to when Edgar and I were kids, and when my dad was a kid. Stories about when you got into a scrape and weren't quite sure if you would make it out, or when you outsmarted the other guy—or he outsmarted you. Everybody swapped tales, but my dad's drew everyone in. Sure there'd be some he'd tell that we could finish for him, but as always, he came up with some new ones that made me bust a gut laughing.

After dinner, I finished telling a story about my friend, the diving welder, who used to raid the lobster traps and leave lobster in the trunk of my car. My dad picked up little Cole and began another one. Edgar's son Ryan, who had been sliding in his socks across the wood floor, skidded into a jackknife under the table. I stuck my head under the table to tell him to settle down when I noticed my dad's leg shaking.

"You know, when Mackie was about eleven, I used to take him to the Eagles games at the Vet," my dad began. "Well, every week we sat by the same guys who'd get high and fall asleep by half-time. Remember I took Aunt Gloria that one time, and she kept saying, *What's that funny smell?* And I said, *Glor—that's pot.*" My dad shifted Cole to his other leg, and Cole wrapped his little fist around my dad's finger.

"Anyway, each game I'd go out to get a beer at half-time. I'd shake those guys and yell, *Wake up! The Eagles are losing. You guys should be cheering.* So those guys would flop around a little, yell *Go Eagles!* and go back to sleep. Well, after we moved from Philly, I'd swear it had to be a year before we got to go to another game. No lie—we're back a year later and one of those potheads gives me a nod with his eyes half shut and says, *Hey man—missed you last week.*"

We all laughed, but my dad wiped his forehead with his hanky. He motioned to pass Cole to Claire but then seemed reluctant to pry loose Cole's clutching fingers.

"Dad? Are you feeling all right?"

"Huh? Oh yeah. I just need some water."

My dad got up and gripped the back of the chair.

"I'll get it, Dad. You sit down. We need to get Mackie's cake anyway." My sister-in-law Cecilia brought out the cake with a big Three-Two on top. It was my favorite. German's sweet chocolate. Everyone started to sing.

Happy birthday to you! My dad's voice usually booms, but that night he didn't sing. He had an odd expression on his face, and his cheek was twitching.

Happy birthday to you! Half my dad's thin lip went up, and the other half tugged down in a grim semi-smile. The skin under his eye crumpled.

Happy birthday dear Mackie! My dad's cheek was pulling back and down away from his mouth, almost rippling in a grotesque sort of way.

Happy birthday to you!

There was silence at the table.

"Happy birthday, Mackie!" my dad said. Only he slurred his words.

Edgar got up. "Dad, are you feeling okay?"

The number-two candle on the cake had collapsed. My dad tried to pick up his fork but dropped it, despite going after the fork with an overwrought grip. His free hand slipped, hitting a saucer, which shattered on the floor. I called an ambulance.

I pull into Edgar's driveway and bang on the door, while letting myself in.

"Is that you bro?" I hear him yell. "You're missing the game." I go in their TV room to find Edgar leaning back with his gut sticking out and his two-year-old baby girl sitting on top. He looks exhausted. Ryan is on a rampage. Edgar tells me that lately Ryan's been obsessed with climbing on top of their round glass coffee table. They got the glass table because the wooden one they really liked had square corners, and they didn't want to see one of the kids crack their head open on an edge. Now they're much more worried that Ryan is going to crash through the glass center.

Edgar yells at Ryan to settle down and turns back to the Eagles game. "See, me and the baby got it all figured out," Edgar says. "I eat potato chips, she eats animal crackers." The Eagles fumble the ball. Interception.

"Eagles losing?"

"Yeah."

I grab some of Edgar's potato chips. "Remember the story about Dad in college, when they lived off potato chips for a whole month?"

"No shit," Edgar says. "I don't remember that one."

"Yeah. They lived right behind these train tracks, and one day, a potato chip truck got stuck on the tracks. A locomotive smacked right into the truck, cracked the thing right in half, and blew bags of chips everywhere. So Dad and his buddies run out there and grab armfuls of bags of potato chips. Dad says they lived off them for a month."

"Sounds like Dad," Edgar said. The Eagles shank a field goal wide right, and Edgar and I both groan.

"You know, Claire and I went over to see Dad last night."

"Good. I think we're going again tonight. How's he seem?"

"Well, Dad got a story wrong."

Edgar looks at me. His forehead wrinkles, just like Dad's.

"He messed up a punch line," I said. "He started telling the one about the old neighborhood. The one where all the Russian, Italian, and Slovak kids were playing together. And some lady from the good side of the street with a name like *Mrs. Daniel* called Tony Masciangelo a *Dago*."

"I know the one, Mackie."

"The punch line is, *Yeah? At least we got real names, lady—all you got is two first names.*"

"Mackie—I know the story."

"Well, Dad confused it with the story about his Aunt Jules making him exchange his coat when the salesman ripped him off."

Edgar doesn't say anything. He doesn't look at me, but he puts Morgan down.

"Anyway, Claire and I told the doctor about it. I just thought you should know." The whole point of me coming over was to bring up bigger issues of Dad's health and long-term care. We need to talk about Dad living alone, driving, hell, even cooking. What if he leaves a burner on? What if he has another stroke, and no one is around? What if it gets to the point where he can't eat, or bathe, or crap?

Edgar and I watch Dallas run the clock down. Kneel down. Kneel down. The game is over.

That night, Claire's parents have Cole because we are supposed to go visit my dad and then go out to dinner with Bill and Suzy. Suzy's my wife's best friend, but I don't care for her husband Bill. Actually, I can't stand him. Bill wears too much Aqua Velva and talks with an English accent even though he only lived in England for two years. He tells stories that go nowhere and always asks me what I do even though I've told him about seventeen different times.

We're getting ready to go, and Claire has the stereo on. She's singing along to Carole King. Claire keeps singing the same lines over and over again even though the CD had gone to a different song. Toby starts barking at the kids screaming across the street. The way they screech, who knows if they're truly beating the hell out of each other or if they're just playing freeze tag. I yell at Toby to shut up, and for the eighth time that night, I hear Claire sing, "Holding you again would only do me good. How I wish I could, but you're so far away," while Carole King sings a different song entirely. My jaw tightens, and it's not going to release until Claire can at least get to the next line. But here it comes again, "Holding you again would only do me good. How I wish I could, but you're so far away."

"Goddamnit Claire. Would you either stop singing or turn off the stereo?"

"Excuse me?" Claire looks at me like ice. It's a warning, but a warning I ignore.

"I'm sorry. All I'm asking is for you to turn off the stereo. Jesus, between the dog barking and the neighborhood kids, it's giving me a friggin' headache. I feel like I'm stuck in one of Bill's stories." I imitate Bill in his fake English accent, thinking I'm being really hilarious. But Claire is tired too and not about to put up with my shit.

"Mackie. I haven't seen Sue in a while, and I'm not asking for much here, so if I were you, I would stop."

"Actually, Claire. You are asking for a lot," I begin to raise my voice. Or maybe I'd been raising it for a while. "All I want is to see Dad and spend my weekend with my wife and baby…" Claire tries to cut me off, but I talk louder, "With my wife and baby and not waste three hours listening to that fathead. But since that won't happen …" Claire tries to cut me off again, but I talk louder still, "Since that won't happen, maybe you could at least turn down the stereo. Or maybe I'll just turn the goddamn stereo down myself." I grab the remote, cut off Carole King, and pound the sliding glass door. The pane cracks, occupying the air with accusation. The glass fractures stare at me with unmistakable violence. I didn't mean to hit it that hard. But it's too late. Claire has left.

Claire is gone for what seems like a really long time. The house smells dank. I can hear the drip in the back room, and I wonder if there is permanent water damage. I climb up to the top of the roof and jury-rig a tarp, so it won't leak the next time it rains. I fight with the damn thing for an hour before it finally seems secure. Then I go to the back room and start ripping up the brown paneling I've always hated.

I think of my dad in the hospital bed. He was sweaty and tired. It's like his six-foot frame had shrunk, and his muscles had begun to age from spending hours upon hours in bed. But that wasn't the worst thing.

The worst thing was that he knew he was getting the story wrong. *All you got is two first names.* I wanted to say the punch line for him. I wanted to say it so badly. My dad was pulling and pulling, pausing and searching, but he couldn't get the line. He kept stammering, telling some tangled and twisted repetitive version of the story, looking at me to help, looking at me to sit on the bed, rub his shoulder, and untangle it for him piece by piece like old fishing wire until he got it right. *All you got is two first names.* But I didn't do that. Instead I turned away.

Around ten, I go over to Claire's parents to get Cole, telling them our night ended early. When I get home, I bathe Cole and put him in his yellow terry-cloth pajamas. I walk him around the house, look at the fractured windowpane, bury my face in his little body, and wonder if I'm going to start friggin' crying again. Instead, the stomach sickness returns. *At least we got real names, lady. All you got is two first names.*

I think of the last time we were all together before my birthday. Edgar, Cecilia, Ryan, and their baby girl; Claire, me, and little Cole; and of course my dad.

We went out for a walk, and Ryan ran ahead with his arms tucked inside his jacket and his sleeves flapping empty at his side. My dad carried Cole, who started to fuss. My dad cuddled and kissed him and then held him to his chest in a way that let Cole look out over his shoulder. He held him with a steady ease that calmed Cole and calmed me. Dad was a natural. It was a small and quiet moment, but as I think of it, a roar starts in my chest and takes over every part of my skin.

Claire finally comes home near midnight and finds me in the basement working on the paneling. She's brought me cold KFC. In between prying off the paneling with a crowbar, I tell her about the time my dad ate all of Jerry Frola's chicken. He had been home from college and was taking the bus back to school with my mother. His roommate, Jerry Frola, was from the same hometown, and Jerry's mom made the most amazing fried chicken. She gave my dad a whole batch to take to Jerry. Only he and Mom started eating it and couldn't stop. They ate every last piece of chicken. Jerry greeted them at the bus stop, all excited because he heard his mom sent food. My mom and dad looked at Jerry, looked at each other, and smacked their heads. *Oh no! We left it on the bus! We forgot the chicken!*

The story seems empty when I tell it, and Claire barely smiles. I jimmy off another strip of paneling. I wedge the crowbar in between a seam and throw my weight against it. The paneling cracks off, but half is still stuck on the wall. I look at Claire and sink down against the boards and tell her I'm sorry. She holds me in her arms and brushes my forehead with warm kisses.

The next day, I go to the hospital by myself. I stand in my dad's doorway, looking at his nameplate before pushing the door open. He is in bed, as he was the last time I saw him and the time before that. His face looks heavy. His hair is greasy, and he smells of sickness. I don't like the color of his skin. He looks like he hasn't slept well for days and needs his rest. He doesn't look at me.

"I just had a physical six months ago. The doctor wrote on my report that I was in much better health than most men my age. He said I didn't look like I was sixty-five."

"I know," I say, grateful that it's him sitting here with me.

"I just can't believe it. I eat right. I take an aspirin every day. I go to the gym a few times a week."

"I know."

"I really have no idea when they'll finally let me out of here."

I look at my dad. His face looks like Cole's, whose face looks like mine. But there is something more. His lips are tight, resembling Cole's when he is distraught. His breathing is uneven like Cole's when he is troubled, and his forehead wrinkles like Cole's when he is afraid.

I move to the edge of the bed, ease the bed down, and scoot closer to my dad. I want to hold him and tell him it will be okay. Tell him not to be afraid because I will take him home. That if it ever comes to it, I will be the one to care for him. That I will be the one to feed him and bathe him and rock him in my arms. That I will care for him like a father or a mother. That I will care for him like he cared for me.

But I don't say that. Instead, I take his hand. The tight expression on his mouth relaxes. His fingers are heavy and cold, but it's okay. I hold his hand, and his breathing steadies. I watch the late afternoon sun fall and cast some light on the plastic gray hospital chair. The creases on his forehead loosen. We are reluctant to release each other's grip. His fingers warm in my hand, and we sit like that for hours.

Cynthia Folcarelli

Kitchen Talking

CYNTHIA FOLCARELLI lives in Washington, D.C., with her husband, writer Len Kruger, and their dog, Toby. A longtime health, mental health, and disability rights advocate, she currently directs the Vanner Street Group (www.vannerstreet.com).

My father had a job then, a job he didn't like. He would come home at the end of each day, jacket slung over one arm, eyes meeting no one's as he disappeared into my parents' bedroom. Minutes later, standing in the kitchen in his casual clothes, he would fix his first drink of the evening, and talk.

Talk—but not to my mother, even when she was in the kitchen with him, making our dinner. He wasn't talking to me, even though I spent my days in Mrs. Hunter's first-grade class and that, I felt, qualified me as a legitimate news source. He didn't address my brother, Danny, who spent his days with our mother. He was only four then, and I pitied him for being too young to go to school.

My father did not speak to any of us. Stirring his drink with a butter knife, his kitchen talks consisted of low and growling chains of words that circled around to come back to him, disinterested in anyone else in the room. Though his words ran together in a barely audible stream of muttering, sometimes I would hear the name of the Company, or his boss, leap out of the monologue. The word was like a candle in a dark basement, giving just enough light so that you know where you are, but not enough to find anything.

During dinner, my parents sometimes talked to each other, though my mother usually started the conversation. Always the last to sit down, she would push her hair away from her face, then reach for the food to serve Danny and me. Like my father, she would look down at her plate while she ate, but unlike my father she would soon put down her fork and look up at the three of us. Her eyes quickly settling on my father, she would watch him silently, intently, like a museum-goer searching for something in an abstract painting.

And she usually found it.

"Your tie," she announced one night, "has a stain on it."

"Hmmm?" my father looked down at his tie-less shirt.

"When you came in," she explained. "I saw a stain on your tie."

"I got my adding test back," I said. I waved my fork in the air a bit, to attract attention. "I got a gold star. Mrs. Hunter says I can do minus signs pretty soon."

"When did you spill on it?" she asked. "I mean, how long did you go around the office today with a stained tie?" She stabbed her fork into a cooked carrot.

"Do you do games at school?" Danny asked. He was staring across the dinner table at me, fascinated by my comment about the math test. Now that he didn't use a baby chair anymore, his face barely came above the table's edge. "Games like, ah, duck duck goose?"

My mother leaned over the table, scooping carrots onto Danny's plate. "Of all the days for your clothes to be dirty, this had to be the worst." She sat down and smoothed her napkin in her lap, shaking her head.

My father's face moved downward. From where I sat, it looked as if it was almost touching his food. Huge forkfuls of shepherd's pie moved into his mouth, so fast that there were no breaths between some of them.

Watching my father, my mother's eyes grew wide, as if startled by something. She leaned forward again, her look intent.

"Did you ask?" She spoke slowly, an emphasis on each word.

My stomach started to hurt then. "We play duck duck goose, yeah, sometimes," I said quickly, a little louder than usual.

"For the raise?" Still leaned forward, her hands were pressed tense and flat against the table.

My father looked up. I put my fork down. I could feel my lips pressed together, hard, like they were trying to keep something out.

"No," he answered. His voice was quiet, but when he reached for his drink, his hand shook a tiny bit.

"No," he said again, a little louder this time. "I did not." Danny was sucking on his spoon now. I knew it had no food on it because I saw it go in.

My mother sat still, and we were still. We were all inside of her stillness, waiting.

And then she reared back.

Her hands flew into the air.

"*Jesus*, why *not*?" she cried. "You know we need it!"

Her voice was high, loud now. I wished she would stop.

"What is it, Tom? What are you not telling me?" Her eyes grew narrow, the way they did when Danny wet his pants, then told her he didn't.

"You're not going to lose this job too, are you?" she asked.

My father's chair fell backward as he stood up. His face was red.

"That's IT!" he shouted. "That's *enough*!"

He pointed at her, his hand shaking. "I don't need this from you right now. Keep it up, and see what happens!"

He left the table and disappeared into the hallway. We could hear him slam their bedroom door behind him.

There was a moment of silence before my mother looked at me and Danny.

"Finish your dinner," she said. I picked up my fork, but it didn't go into my food.

"Go ahead," she said, "Eat." She was wiping at her eyes.

"But Mommy," Danny protested, "I have a headache. In my stomach."

She looked up at the ceiling, and sighed. Her arms were folded across her chest.

"Go to bed, then," she told the ceiling. "Just go to bed."

My father played baseball in high school. He wanted to go to a camp and, as his father told me, be a famous player. But my father wasn't good enough to be famous, Grandpa said. He wasn't good at a lot of things, Grandpa said.

My mother knew him in his baseball days. There was a picture in our living room of them then, my mother smiling broadly, her dark hair tumbling over the shoulders of a flaring polka-dot dress. My father was standing next to her in his gray high school uniform. His arms behind his back, he stared straight into the camera from beneath his baseball cap, smiling only a little but enough so that you knew he was happy.

I liked that picture. Sometimes I sat on our living room couch and held it in my lap, staring at it. They looked perfect, like the parents on TV. I wondered why my grandfather didn't think he was any good.

Sometimes, my father would play baseball with Danny and me, teaching us how to bat, showing us how to throw and catch. Standing in the street in front of our house, I would hold the bat tight in my hands as my father gently lobbed the ball toward me.

"It's Lucy Stanton at bat!" he said in his TV-announcer voice. Danny laughed. "And just look at that batting stance. Here comes the pitch—" I swung and heard the ball thud against the wooden stick.

"Look at it go!" he cried as the ball rolled down the street. "It's a home run for sure! Nice job there, Lucy!" He clapped while Danny jumped up and down.

"Okay now, Lucy," my father said, gesturing toward the rolling ball. "Go get it, and then we'll have a conference on the mound."

The three of us pressed together. My father brought his face down to ours, his arms around us, whispering conspiratorially. I could feel his breath in my hair.

"Okay now, we're at the bottom of the ninth." He looked at each of us and smiled. I thought for a moment he might kiss us.

"Lucy's looking good, Danny's looking good," he went on. "But can we do it? Can we pull it out here, can we win? What do y'think?"

Danny balled his fists together in concentration and excitement.

"Yes yes!" he cried, standing on tiptoe.

"Me too!" I yelled. I wasn't sure what we were winning or who we were winning against, but I wanted to win just the same.

"Danny," he whispered, "It's your turn at bat. Are you ready?"

Danny nodded vigorously. My father stood up and clapped his hands.

"All right then, let's go!" he cried.

In the distance, I could hear our front door squeaking open. "It's time for dinner!" my mother yelled.

My father waved a hand in her direction, as if shooing something away. "In a minute!" he yelled back.

"It will get *cold*," she shouted. But there was no movement in her direction. "Well fine, then!" She slammed the door.

"Okay, Danny," he finally said. His voice had changed. "Here's the pitch."

The ball arced forward, and Danny swung wildly at the air. The ball flew past him and fell to the ground. I ran to retrieve it.

"For Christ's sake, Danny, you've got to concentrate!" my father yelled. He rubbed his forehead with his hand, then used it to catch the ball I tossed back to him. "Okay, now, try it again."

The ball flew forward, and this time the bat caught it, whacking it against the ground with enough force that it rolled quickly to the side of the street and into the gutter, where it kept rolling.

"Go get it!" my father cried in alarm. "Danny, get that ball!"

Danny and I leapt toward the gutter, running for the ball as it rolled toward the hole in the curb where the drainage went.

"*When* are you coming in for dinner?" I heard my mother yell.

I could feel the breath in my chest, my arms reaching blindly forward at the ball that was now less than a yard away. The gutter drain loomed, a black rectangular hole, and in the next moment the ball disappeared into it.

I stopped, panting, feeling the tears spring to my eyes. I could hear Danny skid to a halt behind me.

I stared into that dark hole, afraid to turn around and face my father.

"God*damn* it!" he cried. "Did you *lose* the goddamn ball? For Christ's sakes, you kids. What's wrong with you?"

His footsteps pounded toward me.

"Answer me!" he roared. I felt his hand on my shoulder as he swung me around. "You think the ball is free? You think we can just go and get another ball, just like that?"

"No, sir—" I stammered.

"Don't 'no, sir' me! I saw you stand there, I saw you stand there and watch it go down that drainpipe!" His red face was an inch from mine. "You think that's funny? You probably think that's funny that the ball went down there. Do you?"

"No, I—"

"I should make you go down there and get that ball. I should make you go down, in the gutter, and get the fucking ball. Ah," he stood up, disgusted. "Get the hell in the house."

I was shaking as I ran to the door, where my mother had been standing for several minutes. I looked up at her, but her face was closed.

"Well," she said, turning away from me. "I hope your supper's not cold now."

The first time it happened, I can remember that my mother was behind, behind in getting dinner ready. Traffic was slow to the drugstore, traffic was slow from the grocery store, traffic was slow everywhere that day. Now it was six o'clock, and dinner was barely started.

I knew all this because I heard her say so while she was chopping vegetables for salad. She had taken to kitchen talking herself lately. Danny and I would sit at the kitchen table, drinking milk and sort of listening to her.

She stopped talking for a moment and looked up from her pile of cucumber slices.

"Lucy," she said. "Go into the garage, and get us some soda."

I slid off my chair and took the short walk to the door that connected the dining area of our kitchen to the garage. Next to the door was a cupboard, and I wished that we would put the soda in there instead of just plates and cups, so that I wouldn't have to go into the garage so often.

Visiting the garage was not my favorite thing to do. Once the door shut behind me, it was a race against time to do whatever had to be done so I could be back in the house again. It was a scary place, gray and damp and usually cold. It had no windows and only one light bulb overhead. To me, it was a cement box full of strange items that I couldn't identify, and wasn't supposed to touch. Any grotesque thing, I decided, could hide in there if it wanted to.

I found the case of soda beneath my father's workbench, and grabbed a bottle. Cradling it in both arms, I hurried back into the house.

"In the fridge," she gestured. "Put it in the fridge for now." She wiped the back of her sleeve against her forehead.

"He'd better not complain," she pronounced to the cutting board. "We're having what we're having, and that's it."

The front door slammed. My mother jumped and the knife jumped with it; I saw it sink a little into the edge of her finger.

"Dammit!" she muttered, and dumped all of the choppings into the salad bowl. She threw the knife into the sink. She was sucking on her finger when my father came into the kitchen.

Still in his suit, he didn't even bother to change clothes before mixing his drink that night. He poured the two bottles into a glass while my mother started making the sandwiches. She opened the refrigerator door, and frowned.

"Not enough," she said. "Not enough soda. Danny, go into the garage and get us another bottle of soda."

Danny let out a small wail.

"I don't want to go to the garage, Mommy," he said. "It's ugly in there."

"Awww, come on, big baby," I said.

"Danny," she snapped. "I don't have time to fool around. Go get that soda."

"No," he said, turning toward my father. "*You* get it, Daddy."

They stopped.

My father looked up from his drink, my mother from her sandwiches. Both looked at Danny before briefly glancing at each other.

My father turned to Danny.

"What did you say?" he asked in an almost-steady voice.

Danny stood still, mouth half open.

My father stepped forward, moving his hands toward his waist.

"I asked you," he was much louder now, "what did you *say*?"

He began undoing the buckle on his belt.

Danny began to cry.

"I don'—I don'—" he was flailing for words, afraid to say something and afraid not to.

Within seconds, the belt was off my father's waist and in his right hand, folded in half to create a loop of leather. His left hand clamped down on my brother's upper arm, whom he half-dragged, half-lifted to the garage door. When the door shut behind them, the first thing I heard was my father's voice echoing from the garage.

"Is that the way you talk to me?" he yelled.

"No!" Danny cried. And then I heard it—that snapping sound—and a scream.

"Who is the boss!" my father bellowed. "Who is it? Huh? Do you think it's you? Huh? Do you? *Who*," he roared, "is the *boss* in this *family*?"

But there was no time for Danny to answer before the next snap, and the next, and the next. I looked at my mother, who was listening too.

She would stop it.

My mother walked toward the garage door with purpose. Her hand reached forward.

She unlatched and opened the cupboard door. She pulled out a stack of plates, then closed the cupboard again.

"Lucy," she said. "Help me set the table."

Have you ever heard a child cry? I don't mean the grocery store cry, the cranky cry, the cry while he wrestles his hand out of an adult's, pulling away, wanting to be somewhere else.

I mean *cry*. A cry laced with the screams of a small throat. A cry of *stop* when it is not in him to stop. A cry of response to large hands and hard objects, biting straps, collisions of flesh.

And you cannot escape that cry. It comes back to you through stairwells in elevators sometimes at your desk as you stare at an empty monitor, your hands shaking a little on the keyboard. In the night when you wake and the wall looms against you, your face wet with tears and sweat, the terrible emptiness the terrible sadness the screaming and somehow in the middle of the screams the most terrible thing is the other voice, the calm voice, the voice that puts its hand on your shoulder and then it says: *forks on the left, spoons on the right.*

When my father was finished, he came back into the kitchen. Danny darted in behind him, his face red and wet, and disappeared down the hallway to his room.

My father remained standing. His skin was glowing with a fine mist of perspiration, his hands pink but relaxed at his sides.

As my father sat down on the table, I gripped the seat of my chair so hard that my fingernails hurt. There was silence for a moment. Then my mother spoke.

"How was your day today?" she asked.

He shrugged and put his napkin on his lap. "Not too bad. About usual, I guess. I'm pretty hungry," he said politely. "Are those sandwiches ready yet?"

"Yes—yes of course," she answered. She put the plate of sandwiches on the table, and then the bowl of salad.

Eyeing both of them, I held fast to my chair like a tiny boat in a strangely calm sea. For at that moment, all of the kitchen talking had been sucked out of them. It had moved through our kitchen like a lost and desperate animal, its head sick with bumping into walls and darting from corner to corner, until it finally found its place in the vault of our garage.

My mother stood beside my father, serving him. He watched her as she dipped the spoon in the salad bowl, gently ladling the greens onto his plate. His mouth grew soft, almost like a smile.

Barbara Goldberg

Writings from the Quattrocento

BARBARA GOLDBERG, senior speechwriter at AARP, is the author of six books of poetry. She received the Felix Pollak Poetry Prize for *The Royal Baker's Daughter*, forthcoming from University of Wisconsin Press in 2008. She is the translator, along with Israeli poet Moshe Dor, of *The Fire Stays in Red: Poems by Ronny Someck* (University of Wisconsin/ Dryad Press) and *After the First Rain: Israeli Poems on War and Peace* (University of Syracuse Press). The recipient of many grants and awards, including two fellowships from the National Endowment for the Arts, her work appears in such magazines as the *Gettysburg Review*, the *Paris Review*, and *Poetry*. She lives in Chevy Chase, Maryland.

From letters and journal entries of Tommasa di Benedetto Malefici, wife of Paolo Uccelo (1397–1475), Renaissance painter and sculptor best known for his perspective theory.

The Birth Day of Our Lord, 1425.
My Lord, you have gone far. I see it by your letter from San Romano. I am pleased the hunt goes well. Here in my chambers, I dip the needle through the green silk of your robe.

Feast of the Epiphany, 1425.
My dear, it rains. Days are like thick gloves covering my fingers. I have not the heart to sew. And yet, there is much to do. Adalfa has taken to stealing eggs from the guinea hen. Lorenzo lacks your skill with the horses. They balk and grow fretful. I am not with child, as we had hoped. I beg you to be patient. I am still young and in good health. Your brother tries to taunt you about your manhood. He has always been jealous of

you, the firstborn. His Marta is like a sow, dropping piglets as though they were eggs.

Candlemas, 1425.
Paolo. The nights are hard. I cannot sleep for longing. And yet, if I lie perfectly still, I sometimes hear the tunes you used to play within my font.

Shrove Tuesday, 1426.
Just yesterday Ghiberti sent word that your services are required. Yet another set of gates, this time of Paradise. Do you suppose that these will also take twenty-five years like the North Baptistry Doors? I once asked him if he had not grown bored with his doors, with quatrefoils to last a lifetime. Do you know what he said? "My doors are entry ways to the spirit." "But Signor," I replied. "Your doors are so magnificent one never wishes to open them. Those doors keep people out." I was feeling gay that day. This was before little Paolo's fever.

Whitsunday, 1426.
My husband. I know you still grieve. I know the sight of me is loathsome to you. You see in me his eyes, his chin. He was dear to me too. Especially today. One year ago he was baptized in white robes. What is it you need to hunt for in that thicket? Surely not the Holy Ghost in the lost limb of a tree.

Journal Entry, All Saint's Day, 1427.
To him it is a game. I could crack an egg, or pull my hair, it's all the same. He looks up with a baffled mien before returning with ardent concentration to his compass and protractor. He maps out a multitude of intersecting lines, and shifts an angle here, an angle there, in the wild hope that all lines will meet in the infinite distance. I know he wracks his brain—how can the appearance of near and far be rendered on a flat plane? This intricate quest absorbs him, keeps him young and buoyant. When we dine I feel his years fall upon me in the candlelight. After soup and fish and flan the lines around my eyes and mouth define themselves more deeply. If he raised his glance to really look at me he'd see how near and

far are merely metaphor of present, past, and future. Ah, but his realm is space and all its variations, while mine is time. The two realms intersect, of course: for instance, when he went far, I ached for his return. Now that he's here I feel a greater distance. And when he strokes my breast I know he thinks of orthogons and where to plot the vanishing point. My Paolo truly serves a higher Master. But I am young to renounce the pleasures of the flesh, once having known its mad trembling. I should be grateful for his fidelity. He does not cast an eye at other comely women. If only I were an ordinary chalice to be analyzed! He would view me with greater fascination and I would be held in dearer regard.

Journal Entry, Childermas, 1428.

I hear the hoofbeats so I know he's gone. My faith, I'm red all over. He caused my blood to rise by his knowing look, his insolent smile. And thus he struts before my husband, his older brother, with such an air of cheerful malice. It's as though he lifts my skirts and slips inside, at home in the darkness of my inner soul. But no, I cannot even think that way. Soul I said, but I believe the soul to be pure spirit, not cognizant of heartbeats or that slow spreading warmth between my thighs and yes, I feel his touch, his knowing root inside me, rocking to our own sweet music. And nights I've lain awake and felt his lips, his cock just so, just so, dear Lord, I've always been a gentle woman but this is new, new and strange. I must be confused, to have such shameful thoughts with no sense of shame. I must find useful work to do. Alas, there are no children and I've been warned against another misadventure. After little Paolo's burial I did not wish to live—another sin, and so I fortified myself but truly against my will. It is written, *This too shall pass.* Shall this pass? For the everlasting fate of my soul I pray it does. But if it should be that after death there is only darkness, then I will swallow with bitter rue, bitter rue, all that I could have done but did not do.

Journal Entry, Saint John's Eve, 1429.

Praise God, the heat has passed. I see him for the coxcomb that he is, vain and spiteful, not without a certain charm but lacking depth like a shallow pond. I even feel some pity for that cocksure man, his Marta like a leaden bell around his neck. He's the one who bears the weight of inattention. I feel a stranger to that fool who wrote at such a fever pitch. What I seek now is harmony. Fra Benveniste has been my learned guide on the tortur-ous path to righteousness. His serenity inspires me. A humble man, he does not judge but waits in faith that I shall come to see the error of my ways. Thus I am free, free and light as steam rising. The yoke of longing has been broken. My soul is even as a weaned child.

Michaelmas, 1455.
Francesca. I am glad our Mother counts the coins again. It means her strength is back. Enjoy your feast of plump roast goose, and may your year be profitable! Adalfa says I mustn't brood, it turns my skin to paste. I do not know why I listen to her tedious chatter. Yet I seem to crave the kitchen warmth, the flutter of floury hands, the fragrant dough rising. Nothing rises in me. Always a bitter flavor in my mouth, no, a taste of pepper. No matter what is placed before me, it might as well be pepper. Adalfa says I must let go of Lucrezia's soul.

Martinmas, 1455.
My sister. Please come. We are less than two day's journey from Siena. Surely Giorgio could accompany you and vouchsafe your arrival. I miss your sweet presence. Remember that day winding seed pearls through your hair? I beg you to reconsider. The house is so empty, and how true, how true. I cannot let Lucrezia go. Strange, I barely think of Paolo now, though he lived to clutch my skirts.

Feast of Fools, 1455.
Cara Franca. Have you heard the scandal concerning Fra Filippo Lippi? I have no quarrel with his painting. He was appointed chaplain of the convent in Prato. It is said he shares himself with the nun Lucrezia (how that name still causes my heart to ache!), her sister Spinetta, and five other nuns! And more, Lucrezia has already presented him with a son. Why God should favor such a heinous coupling remains to me a mystery.

How my heart swells at your wondrous news! Of course, travel is out of the question now. You must be sure to only listen to harmonious music and to avoid garlic and rapscallions! The joy that awaits you!

Maundy Thursday, 1456.
Little Franca, poor Franca, I weep with you at your loss. I know the way you feel like the inside of my mouth. I'm glad you find solace in the garden. Paolo has found his solace in perspective and endless diagrams of distance. He jokes of his obsession, calls it "my sweet mistress." Often he forgets to enter my bedchambers. He makes light of it, but you must know how it pains me. The peppery taste still lingers. I find some measure of peace in our chapel. Franca, it seems mere days ago that we sat at Mama's rosewood desk and built that soaring house of cards.

Corrine Zappia Gormont

Unya's Vacation

CORRINE ZAPPIA GORMONT holds an MFA in creative writing, won a Mary Roberts Reinhart award for short fiction, and was a finalist in Scribner's Best of the Fiction Workshops. Her fiction has appeared in *Five Points.* As a self-employed professional writer, her work has appeared in numerous trade publications.

Unya hadn't done anything to prepare herself for her mother's ankles. Her sudden ownership of the same slightly bluish set, flattened and thick across the back as if hammered and fired, came with a number of symptoms, jittery and undependable, like the possible onset of flu. It was a rainy August that year. Sinus weather, her mother said, and so now Unya said it too, suddenly incapable of suppressing.

She was obsessed with sex. No, love. No, sex. Loneliness. Crusty and curled around the edges. It was pointless trying to discern. Whatever it was, she was obsessed and had to hold herself back from rubbing against people, a cat silently winding through a room full of legs in search of a hand, low and open with blunt fingernails. She woke in the middle of the night, her insides like oil on fire: greasy and hot, capable of smoking for days. Don't encourage yourself, she thought, surfing through channels catching glimpses of pinched flesh, inflamed, briefly visible between the colored lines of scrambled stations. Her husband Mark's beautiful smooth bones, drained of purpose, silly as a Halloween puzzle, were three years in the grave. Her daughter Helen was obsessed with butterflies "which mean love," and walking into walls and crashing her bike into bridges, chasing tiny thumping wings too small to be seen.

Whatever it was, she should get laid, she reasoned.

Could it be that every office has one?

Like searching for a drug dealer, you follow rumors down dark alleys. You put your money on gossip and hope for the best.

Unya stalked Gail in the cafeteria, ordered the same cup of chicken broth, two Saltines, and black coffee and then asked to join her as her body uncontrollably erupted into a shameless girly perkiness: all goofy smile and hair tossing, only moments away from a bouncy hello cheer.

According to rumor, Gail and her husband had a marriage so open, they chose sexual partners for each other. They held parties where people didn't need to get too drunk or too high to take their clothes off. A suspension of good judgment every single Friday night.

Gail was pale and remote. A hologram of a woman, comfortably wavering between two worlds. She suffered from the unstoppable confidence of someone under the constant spell of seduction. Unya could have fallen into the blank slate of her.

"My God, the weather," Unya said. "If it doesn't stop soon, we'll all be swinging in the rain.

"Did you hear that Melanie is pregnant again? Rumor is, the baby could be anyone's. *Anybody's*...except her ex-husband's. Well, good for her, I say. I wish it were me. Well, not the baby, though, childbirth is such a mess, but the getting there, I mean if it's true, about all the possible men and women, well not the pregnant part, that'd be hard to pull off with the women..."

It went on for quite some time.

"...I mean it's liberating, really. What is sex after all, if not just an expression, a..."

It was unbearable.

"We don't call ourselves swingers," Gail finally said. She had a way of sitting remarkably still while appearing to pull herself up to her full height.

Unya quickly leaned in, elbows pressed into the Formica tabletop, shoulders braced to snatch the words before they could carry across the communal surfaces of the agency's cafeteria. Her cough had moved from her chest into her throat, and she reflexively traced its path with her fingers, caressing her neck. A Victorian pose, she thought, suddenly embarrassed by herself.

"Sinus infection," Unya said pointing to her nose. "I wouldn't wish this on anybody."

"You can't come with a cold," Gail said. "And you have to bring someone." It was as if she knew the impossibility of people's lives. Unya felt the familiar collision of hopefulness with desperate last acts.

"Bring someone? You mean like a gift exchange?"

She laughed a little too hard at her own joke. Gail stared. Her eyes were brilliant green with large flecks of brown, like extra pupils. They had a dizzying effect on Unya, who suspected she kept them open when screwing.

Unya took every possible combination of decongestant, pain reliever, fever reducer, and antihistamine on a strict four-hour schedule, regardless of the package instructions. Her head bobbled when she moved quickly. It floated in a jar; her nose tapped against the glass. Can someone let me out of here?

She was losing her passion for the real estate business, for houses themselves. All those properties lovingly disinfected and left for the right price. Her own had become inconsolable without Mark. The pantry door refused to swell and stick and smack its lips open in the summer. The dishwasher stopped chewing glass. The third shelf of Helen's closet no longer crashed to the floor in the middle of the night. It was as if all of the house's inconveniences packed up, leaving not a house, but a resemblance of a house. There's no one here to fix us anyway, they said over their shoulders, never quite as attached to Unya as to Mark. They laughed at her floundering career.

And yet she was obsessed with the tragic stories of houses: the daughter abducted by the estranged father; the haunting after Mrs. Henderson's suicide; the mold behind the walls that made the woman-of-the-house go insane. She collected them from work. She just heard one about a woman whose wedding ring was stolen from the trunk of her car at her gym.

Early one morning, Mrs. Martinelli parked next to the only car in the lot, retrieved her bag from the trunk, replaced it with her ring, went inside, worked out, returned to the car, opened the trunk to swap her gym bag full of sweaty clothes with her ring, and found it gone. The passenger's window was smashed with a rock that was left in the driver's seat.

Her husband left her a month later.

Why do horrible things keep happening to wives, Unya wondered. The ring was said to be priceless. The house, however, priced for quick sale, went in less than four hours for $679,000.

Helen was the kind of six-year-old you worry about seeing on the front pages one day. She refused to talk about her heartbreaks and disappointments. She collected everything butterfly and tracked her brief friendships on a chart she taped to the refrigerator. Hannah, Lindsey, Caroline, Brittany—small pink and purple lines that lasted as long as three days and as short as a phone conversation. Where did all the Elizabeths and Marys go, Unya wondered? Helen had played the baby Jesus when she was three months old in a neighborhood Christmas pageant. She lay quietly in a manger for forty-five minutes. Didn't that count for something?

Six years later she stayed silent but took it out on Butter the cat. She chewed the inside of her lips until they bled and then blamed him. She had pizzas delivered to the neighbors in the middle of the night and blamed him. She whacked him on the nose twenty times a day as he tried to get to his food bowl.

"Honey, we don't treat animals that way," Unya said. "They're helpless and count on us to take care of them."

"Oh, she doesn't mean anything by it," Unya's mother Bea said.

Helen hid under her grandmother's skirt. Literally. She pulled it over her head and stood, hands on hips, elbows creating a Marie Antoinette silhouette.

Since Mark's death, Bea and Helen became inseparable. Their mourning took the form of a fifties musical. Late night, giggly sleepovers followed by all-day pajama and hair-curling parties. Unya recognized her own secret wish that her mother, a competent widow herself for many years, would become the de facto man of the house, and she resented the budding sorority. Unya, the housemother, the cleanup crew.

Now the girls were busy with a project. They carried paintbrushes and sloshing cans of paint into Helen's room, locking the door behind them. Giggle, giggle, giggle. Not until the transformation is complete, they said. My God, not another mirage, Unya thought. Bea was a muralist and well known for the trompe l'oeil in the coffee shop on 17th. The one with the tricky corner that caused customers to bruise their elbows and hips while trying to negotiate the illusion of a corner painted to look like a corner in a mirror somewhere remote and tropical. How many butterflies does it take to fill a ten-by-nine room with love?

Unya's own room was the color of a yellowing sickness, the temperature of a fever. She slept in the sweatpants and T-shirt Mark wore before his last trip to the hospital. The smell of him long replaced by her own scent, dry and itchy as a sunburn.

She lay on his papers. The typed notes listing warranties; insurance agents; who to call to trim the trees, clean the ducts, remove a wasps' nest. The occasional script in blue pen, bubbly little encouragements designed to increase her and Helen's chances of survival. *Oh ya! try to remember to change the furnace filter every couple of months. It'll help to keep Helen's asthma in check. You won't forget, will you?* As if either of them ever changed the filter more than once every two years. Nothing made Unya miss Mark more than his obsession with how life should look without him: a remarkably improved version.

Despite the heat and humidity, Unya chose to wear a silk blouse, the old holiday standby with a shock of red across the middle. She had hoped to convey a sense of adventure, but when she left the house for the office on Friday morning with more than her usual light dusting of powder and lipstick, she could almost hear Mark saying from above, if there was an above, "Time for the company Christmas party already?"

She had difficulty making pupil contact with Gail, who was photocopying the new listing on Starlight Lane. A remodeled Greek revival with

Corian counter tops, cherry floors throughout, and "a hot tub warming as we speak," said Gail.

"You actually do this in our properties?" Unya tried to sound more impressed than accusatory.

"If you're over that cold, you can come," Gail said.

"I'm feeling much better," Unya said. Her voice shook and wheezed like an old boiler, and her nose dripped uncontrollably.

Gail just looked at her. If you could call it that.

Advice from coworkers: It's time to take your ring off. Wear flared pants to cover your ankles and give the illusion of height. Put a little lipstick on. Go on a date.

"A date? Rhymes with mate, wait, too late? There isn't anyone interested in me, and there's no one I'm interested in. The world and I have found ourselves locked in a STALEMATE, a checkmate. Why do I find the word mate wherever I turn?"

"My ex-husband is *very* interested in you," Melanie told Unya. "No one expects you to fall in love, just have some fun, wear a little lipstick, go on a date."

"Will there be alcohol?" Unya asked. "There must be alcohol."

"It's settled," Melanie said. "Come to the party early. Bob will be there eating all the steamed shrimp before the others arrive."

Starlight Lane was a desirable old neighborhood, each house designed and built to the owner's taste: Tudors, Colonials, Victorians. Unya had been cautioned about parking too close to the house, drawing unwanted attention to the property. The sidewalks were slick from the rain that had only stopped an hour before, and the streetlights were fashionably dim and sparse, making the two-block walk in spikes treacherous, ridiculous.

Inside, the house was lit only by candles. The large urn in the vestibule and the few pieces of beautiful reproductions were rentals that had been chosen by the agency to convey a promise of status to potential buyers.

Melanie and Bob were in the kitchen sharing a glass of wine over a large plate of shrimp, peeled and pink and unnaturally posed.

"The secret lives of prawn," Bob said to Unya as she approached. He held two up in a sixty-nine position before biting into them.

Unya had always found Bob unsettling. He was just beyond quirky, shifting between charming and weird and vacant so suddenly that she ended up questioning her own social skills. Melanie swore by his brilliance, his knowledge of all things science, but in the end, she just couldn't live with a man who saw the world from the inside out. "He's an awfully nice guy," Melanie said after the divorce. "It's just I don't give a shit about how many germs can fit on the head of a needle. I mean his big bang theory is miles from my own."

People silently entered the party as if the house concealed extra doors and tunnels. By ten thirty, at least thirty people were there. A nice round number, Unya thought, a dirty number, now drunk and used to strangers' nakedness, as if her eyes finally adjusted to a darkness. Gail was the grande dame, dry palms and lips lingering on cheeks, bare shoulders, backs, private jokes whispered into hairlines. Her husband moved like an eel, sliding around and between people, feeling with his entire body. Unya sat on a kitchen stool, dressed and clutching, her feet wrapped firmly around its legs. Just one more drink, she thought.

Bob's invitation was a tongue in her ear, or maybe a shrimp. He had been talking about the newest HIV/AIDS strain that can develop into full-blown AIDS within four months, assured her of the strength of condoms, and then stuck something wet in her ear. The act somehow seemed appropriate, and if she could squint her imagination long enough, it was mildly seductive. He ushered her out of the kitchen, his hand placed lightly against the small of her back, led her to the dark staircase where they stepped over an entangled threesome flopping and groaning as if in the throes of suffocation.

"I had hoped for more beauty," Unya said.

"I had hoped for a Fulbright," Bob said.

Unya had been developing a theory over the years. A person's body is a lot like a house. In the empty bedroom, Bob lit a candle, folded his sport coat inside out and laid it on the floor as a cushion, rolled his socks together and placed them across the toes of his loafers. He was a Foursquare, Unya thought. Simple, Midwestern, unadorned, drafty. He was neither heavy nor thin and offered no excess of light or surprising details. He was average. He was also predictable. You could do worse than a Foursquare, Unya thought. And he treated her as if she were a Foursquare, although she thought of herself as a Stick, a decorative, lighthearted resort home, without the ankles. Bob the Foursquare toured her body evenly from left to right. Ear nibble symmetry, shoulders, breasts, hipbones, thighs. Who am I to complain, Unya thought, relieved to feel nothing but the warmth of her own body.

Mark had been a Queen Anne, with wide eyes and slightly protruding brow. His arms were a large, welcoming verandah. He would coax her to speak softly in his ear. His large hands held her head firmly against his own, held her until she matched his verbal and doubtless love. Surrender, she thought, only love would make an act against oneself seem reasonable.

Bob made things easy. He required nothing much of Unya, so she could open her eyes and close them, caress him briefly or leave her hands by her sides. She felt confident that a minimum of germs were being shared.

Afterwards, and it seemed to take much longer than Unya had expected, Bob stared out the window as he quickly dressed. It occurred to her that he was considering the distance of the drop.

"Well, that was kind of silly, wasn't it?" Unya said. She had never been good at wrapping things up. Her goodbyes were painful and uneven, hiccups really. In the end, Mark held a thin finger against her lips. His veins could be seen withering just beneath the surface of his skin.

"Not to be repeated," Bob said. He pulled a tissue from his pocket and dabbed at something on the side of Unya's mouth. She suddenly hated this Bob the Foursquare.

"I think we should try to escape through the window," he said. "The police are here."

It took two paddy wagons to move the party to the jailhouse. Despite the impending embarrassment and sure loss of careers and reputations, the atmosphere was strikingly jovial—an overwhelming sense of righteousness and accomplishment, as if the occupants were dragged in for standing against a great injustice. An older man with hands and fingers as large and delicate as a pianist's led a chorus in "We Shall Overcome," with an emphasis on the last syllable to the great pleasure of the others. Unya was surprised to find herself smiling too. She even played with the idea of saying something like, "Well now, this is certainly anticlimactic, isn't it," but she wasn't quite sure that it was as clear a crowd pleaser, so she kept it to herself. Bob sat across from her and smiled. She didn't hate him enough to not smile back.

It was one thirty a.m., and Bea had to disturb a neighbor so that she could leave Helen to retrieve Unya. The car was on its last legs; shorts and mechanical problems moved through it like a slow shutdown of a power grid. There was no interior light left, which made it hard to find the ignition. The AC coughed.

"Spare me the details," Bea said. "I hope this is only grief."

Butter met Unya at the door whining and clawing for attention. Unya picked her up and carried her up the stairs and down the hall towards the smell of paint.

Helen's room had been transformed into another world. Images from floor to ceiling. Tricks of light and perception. Secret hollows and sudden openings. The butterflies, as Unya expected, were overwhelming. They swooped and floated and fluttered all in one direction, as if caught in a river of air. They held and swooned over the image of Mark, a remarkable likeness from Unya's favorite photograph of the three of them, a year before they knew of the cancer, a regular Saturday with a new camera. He was holding his body at a peculiar angle, and Unya used to joke that it was hard to tell if he was coming or going.

Mark's image broke Unya's heart. He looked more at home hovering and suspended in an illusion than he did the whole last year of his life when he was turning to dust before her eyes. This new Mark had a smile that conveyed the most amazing sense of purpose. A wave goodbye, a kiss blown from a car pulling away. I'm leaving…leaving…gone, he smiled.

Unya pressed her body against the wall, suspended herself, briefly, between denial and acceptance. He's dead.

"It's beautiful, isn't it?" Bea said. She was standing in the doorway beaming at her work. "We weren't sure what we were headed towards, Helen and I, but it just kind of painted itself."

The next morning, Unya didn't feel guilty about Bob. She didn't feel sorry about being fired, which she surely would be, or even worried about what would come next. She could easily picture Helen's room painted over in a nice warm white, bright and appealing to prospective buyers who are always more interested in the bones of a house, its future rather than its past.

T. Greenwood

Instruments of Torture

T. Greenwood, MA, MFA, is the author of three novels: *Breathing Water*, *Nearer Than the Sky*, and *Undressing the Moon*. She has received grants from the Sherwood Anderson Foundation, the Christopher Isherwood Foundation, and, most recently, the National Endowment for the Arts. Two of her novels have been BookSense76 picks, and her short stories have been published in *Quarterly West* and *Western Humanities Review*. Her fourth novel, *Two Rivers*, will be published in 2009.

The Iron Maiden

The Iron Maiden was used primarily in Germany, the most famous version being the Iron Maiden of Nuremberg. This apparatus was essentially a large container, shaped like a woman, equipped with two doors with adjustable iron spikes. Legend has it that a German who had forged coins was shut inside the Iron Maiden on August 14, 1515. His arms, legs, belly, chest, bladder, genitals, eyes, shoulders, and buttocks were slowly pierced by the spikes causing excruciating pain but not death. The Iron Maiden's embrace, much like many other investigative methods, was designed not to execute but to torture.

It was inside the Instruments of Torture exhibit at The Museum of Man that I figured out why I hate Francesca. Somewhere between the head crusher and the impaling rod it dawned on me. She was Jack's *what-if* girl, the one he would have (perhaps should have) slept with before I came along, but for some reason never did.

Testing the sharpness of an iron spike, she could have been the same girl in faded Levi's and sandals we knew at school ten years ago. I'd been looking for some evidence of change in her face since she arrived the night before, but the only thing I found was a new dark freckle on her bottom lip. And Jack, I was beginning to realize, hadn't changed much either. So, as she and Jack leaned into the various displays of chastity belts and stockades while I waddled behind them, eight months pregnant with hemorrhoids and sciatica, Francesca came to represent everything Jack's life would have (perhaps should have) been had I not come along.

When Francesca called and said she was going to be in town for the weekend, Jack waited almost three days to tell me. I know this, because I heard him talking to her in the baby's room that used to be the office. I didn't need to hear him say her name. I just recognized that *tone.* When we were all friends and all lived in the same city I used to *hate* that tone. I remember once lying in his bed while he talked to her in the bathroom, wanting to gag at the way he picked up her accent, that soft Brooklynese that was about as far from his native Wisconsin tongue as Chinese or Swahili. It was that weird adopted New York accent I heard coming out of the office turned nursery-in-waiting, but rather than acknowledge that I'd been eavesdropping, I merely waited for the bomb to drop. And *he* waited until I was at my now weekly OB/GYN appointment before he dropped it.

"Frannie's going to be in town this weekend," he said, casually flipping through a weekly pregnancy guide.

"Hmph," I said. I couldn't help it.

My doctor was up to the elbows, so to speak, but looked at me when I grunted.

"Sorry."

"It's not *you*," I said.

Jack looked at me over the top of an illustrated uterus, scowling.

"When does she get here?" I asked.

"She's actually here already, in San Diego, I mean, at a conference, but she'd like to stay with us for the weekend."

"Hmph."

"Everything looks great, Elaine," my kindly and almost-handsome doctor smiled. "See you next week?"

"You bet," I said, flirting a little, ignoring Jack's hand as it reached out to help me off the slippery table.

By the time we got home I'd figured out a zillion reasons why she shouldn't stay with us.

"Where will she sleep?" I asked.

"In the office," Jack said.

"In the crib?"

"On the air mattress."

"Isn't she allergic to cats?"

"Pollen and strawberries. Jesus, Laney."

By the time Friday arrived, I'd given up.

Branks or Scold's Bridles

These devices, often elaborately designed, were employed to punish those who challenged prevailing conventions in general and male authority in particular. These victims were predominantly women, and the primary ruling was against women who spoke out either in church or in the presence of a man. Consequently, many branks were placed in the victim's mouth, ultimately mutilating the tongue with its inner spikes and blades. The victims were often forced to endure this method of torture in the public square, vulnerable to the whims of the crowd who subjected them to a variety of beatings and humiliations. They were frequently defecated upon and even fatally wounded in their genitals or breasts.

She has this knock. I've never remembered anyone's knock before, but after I heard her suitcase rolling up our sidewalk and then the sound of our screen door creaking open, I knew exactly what to expect. *Knock, pause, knock-knock-knock.* A little tap dance of knuckles on wood that recalled a whole other era of my life. With that single rhythmic gesture, I was in Jack's studio apartment in Seattle again, tangled up in the sheets and Jack's legs. There was probably a thick dripping candle on the windowsill. Everything smelled like candle wax those days. Even sex. *Knock, pause, knock-knock-knock.* She was always interrupting things. I'd never seen Jack get out of bed so quickly, his hands flying to the top of his head to pat down the mess we'd made. And I remembered not bothering with real clothes, just pulling on Jack's flannel shirt and my panties, hoping that my attire would indicate that she'd chosen a bad time.

But now when I opened the door, she wasn't standing there rain-soaked with a soggy backpack and a half-eaten gyro in waxed paper, but rather tan and smiling, holding out a bunch of irises.

"I picked these up at the Farmer's Market up the street. What a great neighborhood this is! Doesn't feel like southern California at all. And the ocean smells so good. I can practically taste the salt. The closest I get to this in New York is the smell of the pretzel guy down my street. I don't mean the guy, but the pretzels."

"*Hi*," I said in a way that an old friend should, taking the irises and hugging her. I held on an extra few seconds, pressing my big belly into her as hard as I could without seeming weird. When we stepped back, she touched my shoulders and examined me like a dress.

"Look at you! You're just beautiful," she said, motioning to my stomach. "Does everybody want to touch it?"

"The pizza guy asked last night," I nodded.

"I'd love to take some pictures," she said. "Could we do that? Maybe on Sunday?"

Francesca is a fashion photographer. She works freelance for a number of different high-end magazines, the kind that you can't buy at the drugstore, and that if you do find them cost $12.95 and feature snapshots of socialites and debutantes. At UW she was a double major in Fine Arts and History. That's how she met Jack. Medieval History.

"Oh, I don't know," I said.

"Please?" she said, giving the dress a little squeeze. "It'll be fun. And it's not like it's some studio photographer, it's just *me*."

"We'll see," I said. "Maybe Sunday."

"Where's Jack?" she asked, letting go of me.

"He's at school. He's got office hours until three o'clock, and then he's coming home. We've got reservations at this Italian place for six o'clock. I figured Italian was okay. I can never remember whether it's Italian or Mexican you don't like."

"Sweet Jesus, don't let my Italian grandmother hear you. God bless her soul. Actually it's Thai. And Indian. I'm not such a huge fan of Indian."

"Good," I said. "Italian is good then."

"Oh, I almost forgot. I have something for you," she said, bending over to unzip her suitcase. Her waist-length black hair swept the floor. She pulled out a wrapped package, brown paper tied with a rustic bow of raffia.

"You didn't have to…" I was starting to feel guilty.

"Oh, it's nothing. It's just something I did last fall. It made me think of you guys."

I carefully untied the raffia and unwrapped the package without tearing the paper, pretending I was saving it I guess, and held up the framed print.

The photo was of a teenaged girl and boy, both of them gaunt, their bare arms bearing black and white track marks. They were standing on a stoop missing the second step, holding hands. The boy looked defiant, his other hand stuffed into his tight jeans. The girl looked enamored, gazing at him, her eyes wide and scared, like a child afraid of letting go of her mother's hand.

"They reminded you of me and Jack?"

"I mean, they're junkies and all, but look how happy they are. Holding hands. They held hands the whole time I was with them. Like they couldn't let go or else one of them would disappear."

"It's great," I said. "It's perfect. Thank you."

That night at my favorite Italian restaurant downtown, the one in the Gaslamp District that has all this Italian kitsch (velvet paintings of the Pope, autographed photos of Frank Sinatra, even a ceramic Venus de Milo in the center of our table), Jack and Francesca got drunk on the house chianti, and I drank so much Sprite I thought I'd either explode or go into a sugar coma. Over the bruschetta we shared, I silently vowed I would never let this child forget what I'd sacrificed during my pregnancy. I even thought about stealing a few sips from Jack's wineglass while they were exploring the Sistine Chapel Room, but knew that gray teeth and stained lips would give me away. I ordered the veal parmigiana, fully aware of the ironies. I also ordered a salad and more bruschetta. Francesca, who didn't need a pregnancy to alleviate her food guilt, ordered the spaghetti with meatballs with extra meatballs and Jack got what he always gets, lasagna. And while Dean Martin crooned and everybody but me got drunk, I watched them.

Jack is one of those men who is better looking when he's telling a story. His face when it's in a state of rest is highly uninteresting: brown hair that falls into his average eyes, smallish mouth, and nondescript nose (not too big, not too small). But when he speaks, when his face comes alive, and he is relaying anything from the weather forecast to his feelings about something important, that's when I remember the flutters I used to get in my gut whenever he was close.

At the Italian restaurant he was talking about the Spanish Inquisition exhibit, about the largest collection of authentic torture devices assembled in the United States. Francesca was positively rapt, and I could tell that she noticed his transformation too. His skin was illuminated by the red glow of the mesh-covered glass candle holder. He was resting his elbows on either side of the plate, his hands fluttering like birds as he described the various instruments of torture.

Francesca had on a simple black linen dress, sleeveless, revealing arms that looked manufactured by a gym, but I knew were just the accidental byproduct of lugging camera equipment around. Francesca was not the gym type. Her hair was up off her neck, but it was hot, and she had to keep pushing stray pieces away from her face. We were all sweating. Being pregnant through the entire summer, I had become accustomed to the misery of being too hot for my skin. But inside that restaurant there was something more than late summer making me uncomfortable. There it was again. Brooklyn coming out of Jack's thin lips.

"They've got an executiona's axe, thumbscrews, spiked collas."

"Collars," I said. "Spiked collars."

"That's what I said," Jack said, looking at me as I sucked more Sprite through my straw. I stared into the red plastic tumbler.

"We could go, tomorra, if you want?" he said.

"Fantastic. Do they allow cameras inside?"

I drove us home, taking the long way around the harbor to avoid the inevitable return to our interrupted home.

When a stranger comes to your house, suddenly you start to see your things in a whole new way. When Jack finally managed to get the key in the door, and I turned on the lights, I tried to see our things the way Francesca might.

We still didn't have a real couch. It was the one expense neither one of us was quite ready to accept. Since college we'd been sitting on Goodwill couches of various plaids and burlap, fantasizing about the day we'd be able to buy one of those couches they always advertise in the Sunday paper's supplements. I favored the velvety type, filled with down. Jack preferred the wooden framed sort, sensible and versatile. And so what we had was a faux patchwork love seat, cushions flipped to strategically hide the tears.

Jack went to the bathroom. Francesca tossed her purse onto the floor and sat down on the couch. I cringed.

"Come here," she said to me, motioning for me to come sit next to her. I set down the Styrofoam container with Jack's leftover lasagna inside and reluctantly went to her. She reached her hand up and grabbed mine.

"Sit," she said.

I obeyed.

"You seem so happy," she said.

I didn't know what she was talking about. I'd been quiet and pissed off the whole night. Maybe my Cheshire cat smile had worked.

"I'm glad everything's come together for you." I wouldn't even know she was drunk if I hadn't watched her down two bottles of chianti with my husband. And go figure, her teeth weren't stained.

"You have everything you wanted," she said.

"What do you mean?" I asked.

She turned to me and looked at me hard. I stared at her eyebrows, their perfect black arches, one raised slightly more than the other, but still somehow perfectly symmetrical.

"I *mean*...the house. The baby." She reached for my belly, smiling, and I had to resist the distinct urge to recoil from her long pretty fingers.

Her expression turned serious.

"Don't you have everything you wanted too?" I asked. "Your job? The travel?"

"I *mean...*" she whispered, leaning into me. Then I smelled the wine on her breath. "Jack."

The bathroom door opened, the sound of the toilet bowl filling with water punctuating the silence.

"Anybody want to play cards?" Jack asked, grinning foolishly, and I wanted to run to him and wrap myself around him, to say, *He's mine. Now go home.* Instead, I said, "Let's play Hearts."

The Saw

This particular large-toothed, four-handed woodsman's saw dates back only two centuries, though historical accounts of its victims abound. The unfortunate subject was suspended upside-down, and the saw was used to split the body in two, beginning at the crotch. Because the victim was inverted, the brain remained adequately oxygenated and little blood was lost, ensuring that consciousness was maintained until the saw reached the navel and even possibly the breast. The saw was frequently assigned as a method of torture and execution to homosexuals of both sexes. In Spain, the saw was rumored to have been used in the armed forces until the end of the eighteenth century. The saw was the chosen method of execution for leaders of disobedient peasants in Lutheran Germany, and in France it provided punishment for witches who became pregnant by Satan.

I found out I was pregnant the same day I got laid off from my third job this year. In the morning, while Jack was sleeping, I peed on the fourth pregnancy stick in as many days, setting it on the edge of the counter while I flossed my teeth. I already knew what the Magic 8-Ball would say (it had been saying the same thing for four days), so I took extra time, flossing and rinsing, flossing and rinsing.

Jack's first class wasn't until noon, so I left the stick on the counter and a note in the leftover steam on the mirror. *Hi, Daddy.*

Then I went to work.

But what I imagined, the phone call saying, *Come home. Tell them you're sick. I'll be there in ten minutes, oh my God I am so happy*...didn't have time to happen.

I had already lived this scene. The first time it had surprised me: the inevitable crying secretary standing at the boss's door clutching a box of tissues and a framed photo of her three children (or cats, or boyfriend), the computer equipment stripped from the desks, the chaos of workers breaking down cubicle dividers, walls falling around people struggling to get their personal emails off the hard drive. And so I emptied my drawer filled with Tootsie Rolls and did what my friend Zelda calls the dot-*bomb* dance (which typically entails lots of profanity and gesturing toward the boss and workers and crying secretary) all the way out the door.

When I got home, Jack was reading the paper, eating a bowl of Bran Flakes.

"Hi," I said.

"Oh shit," he said, like a question. To be polite.

I nodded. "My cubicle was missing. They left my desk, but they took my walls before I even got there."

Jack nodded and folded the newspaper.

"Did you get my message?" I asked.

"What message?"

"In the bathroom?"

"You left me a message in the bathroom? Why didn't you put it on the dry erase board on the refrigerator?"

I sat down at the table and covered my face with my hands.

"Well are you going to tell me?" he asked.

"I'm pregnant," I said, staring at his cereal bowl, at the sensible bran, at the brown milk.

"Oh shit," he said. And this time it wasn't like a question at all.

Over time, of course, we both warmed up to the idea. Jack even transformed into a new but familiar kind of Jack, the kind of Jack concerned with the safety of high chairs and cribs. I was more fascinated with names and how very small the socks and T-shirts were. By the time Francesca arrived, we'd settled into the pregnancy like a secondhand couch.

In the morning, while Jack was still sleeping and the door to the baby's room remained closed, I stared at my naked body in the mirror and thought, *This is it. You will never see your ribs again.* I rubbed a futile handful of cocoa butter lotion across the great mountain of my stomach. I did it in the beginning to ward off stretch marks that defiantly appeared anyway. Now I just did it because my skin was stretched beyond recognition and itched beyond belief.

I pulled the prettiest dress I had over my head, yanking it down over my round middle, and thought about squeezing my swollen feet into a cute pair of strappy sandals. I opted for flip-flops (and a modicum of comfort) instead and went to the living room to wait for them to wake up.

Francesca came out first. She was wearing an oversized T-shirt that just reached the middle of her thighs. Her hair was tangled and she rubbed her eyes like a child. "Morning," she said and disappeared into the bathroom.

Coffee. The other forbidden beverage. I made a pot of coffee out of habit for Jack, holding my nose against the temptation of it all. Jack emerged from the bedroom and, seeing the bathroom door closed, came to me in the kitchen. He wrapped his arms around me and my big stomach, nuzzling his head into my neck. "Thank you," he said and I almost forgave him for letting Francesca win at Hearts.

The Judas Cradle

This method of torture was perhaps one of the most vicious and painful exercised in the Middle Ages. The victim was first stripped and then suspended over a jagged or pointed pyramid. The torturer, using ropes and pulleys, was able to raise and lower the victim so that the point would penetrate either the anus, the vagina, or the scrotum. Using these ropes and pulleys, the pressure ranged from none to the total weight of the victim's body. The victim was frequently made to fall repeatedly onto the point.

Who am I kidding? I guess I've always known that Francesca is Jack's *what-if* girl. She has been his imagined future since Jack and I first met, since the possibility of Francesca became something unknowable to Jack. Something out of reach. But it really hits me at the torture exhibit. Like a chain flail across my back.

Jack met Francesca in the Medieval History seminar at UW. They were friends for an entire year before he met me (at the coffee shop where I worked for one semester before the Starbucks across the street put it out of business and me out of a part-time job). That year of friendship between them was something I could never catch up on. No matter how long Jack and I were together, Francesca will have always known him *longer*.

The first few times we went out, Francesca came along. I was surprised the first time when he arrived to pick me up with Francesca following close behind, snapping photos and cracking jokes. At first I thought she was his sister. They had the same accent.

I never got used to it. Not when she came with us to the French film festival at the Varsity (Jack sandwiched between us, staring helplessly at Emmanuelle Béart, totally nude for four hours in *La Belle Noiseuse*). Not when she knocked on the door in the middle of our first night together with news of her grandmother's death (Jack sandwiched between us on the first Goodwill couch, staring helplessly at the pot of tea on the coffee table in front of us as Francesca cried about her Nonna).It wasn't until we graduated and she moved to New York that I finally felt free. When Jack started applying to graduate schools, I sabotaged the NYU and Columbia brochures that arrived in his post box like small slaps in the face. When he got accepted into UCSD, I packed his clothes (tossing the faded UW T-shirt she'd forgotten once that wound up unwashed, pristine, in his drawer).

And for a while, the amputation of Francesca seemed clean. Jack started and finished graduate school. I got my first job with an Internet startup. And Francesca was nothing more than a phantom limb, making her presence known only in postcards and the occasional message on the machine.

But now, inside the dark recesses of The Museum of Man, there was that year all over again. I might have been having his child, but she had that year. That year that they met before I came along, when everything was possible. That year when they spent their afternoons in the coffee shop where I eventually was hired and fired. When they took the bus to the Pike Place Market and wound up at the sex toy shop giggling over dildos and vibrators and edible panties. That year that they studied Medieval History late into the night, not-kissing.

My back was aching and my skin was itching and my hemorrhoids were burning as we perused the instruments of torture. I wandered away from the Iron Maiden and sat down on a bench near the exit and put my head between my knees.

"Nauseating, isn't it?"

The security guard offered me a cone-shaped cup of water.

Confused, I looked at Jack and Francesca pointing in mutual horror at an iron mask.

"Sickening," I agreed.

"In your condition, you'd think you wouldn't want to be around this kind of thing," he said.

I nodded and accepted the water.

The Chastity Belt

The myth of the medieval chastity belt was that it was used to ensure fidelity. However, wearing one of these devices for any significant amount of time would inevitably lead to lacerations, abrasions, and even sepsis. More likely, a woman would use the chastity belt as a protective device against rape which was an ever-present threat. So, though not a traditional device associated with torture, the chastity belt still represents the barbarism of the medieval male.

Jack and I have not had sex for over a month. In the beginning, it was easy to pretend that nothing had changed, that my body wasn't metamorphosing into something neither of us recognized. But after about five months, I no longer remembered what my old butt looked like, and lying on my back didn't make my stomach appear to be flat anymore. Jack's been a good sport about the abstinence, he gave up trying almost three weeks ago, but almost every joke he makes is of the sexual sort lately. He's become the king of dirty jokes, his frustration channeled into one punch line after another.

"So this nurse keeps sneezing, and the second nurse says, 'Geez, are you all right?' And the first nurse says, 'Yeah, I'm fine, but I can't stop sneezing.' The second nurse says, "That's terrible.' The first nurse says, 'It's okay, because every time I sneeze I have an orgasm.' The second nurse says, 'Wow! Are you taking anything for it?' The first nurse says, 'Yeah. Pepper.'

Jack slapped the table at the Mexican restaurant, and my rolled taco rolled off my plate.

Francesca sipped on her margarita and I sucked on my Sprite. Jack was contemplating another dirty joke, probably trying to formulate it in his mind.

"What would you like to do tonight?" I asked. "It's your last night here."

Francesca licked a bit of salt from her lip and said, "I don't know. Maybe go take a walk on the beach?"

"What about a movie?" I asked.

"Sure," she said.

"Let's get a paper and see what's playing." The idea of killing a couple of the remaining excruciating hours of Francesca's visit by sitting in a dark theater, not talking, seemed like the best idea I'd had in a while.

Then Francesca sneezed. And then she sneezed again. And again. And again.

Jack's hand shot out for the pepper shaker in the center of the table. He handed it to her, grinning with pride.

"Geez, I must be allergic to something around here."

"Hmph," I said. I couldn't help it.

Sitting in the movie theater was its own kind of torture. Not only did Jack find his usual place sandwiched between us, the mismatched bookends, holding the giant bucket of popcorn we were all supposed to share, but it wasn't one of those new plush theaters with the comfortable seats and my sciatica was almost unbearable. By the time we got back to the house I felt like electric shocks were traveling from my hip all the way down my leg.

"Let's go walk on the beach!" Francesca said. "It's a full moon. It'll be beautiful."

"Go ahead," I said, waving them away. Giving up. If they said they were running away together, I probably would have bid the same fond adieu. I lowered myself onto the ugly couch and clicked on the TV.

Francesca borrowed one of Jack's sweaters to wear to the beach. When she pulled it over her head, her hair was trapped inside, and she didn't bother to pull it out. She looped her arm through Jack's and waved. "We'll be back in a little bit."

After they closed the door, I heard Jack saying, "Oh, oh, you've got to hear this one…so anyway, this priest and this prostitute meet at a bar…"

I'd had to do this before—let them go. To a Prince concert one night when I had to study for an exam. To the mountains one weekend when I got the flu. To the grocery store, apple picking, and fishing. Antiquing, bike riding, to when Jack had his wisdom teeth removed. I couldn't be there all the time. I couldn't watch over them in the hopes that nothing would happen. I just had to trust. And so far, nothing had. As far as I knew.

All of a sudden the baby kicked and my stomach dropped.

As far as I knew. I didn't know anything. I hadn't been with them in the mountains. I hadn't been in the canoe with them on Lake Washington, or inside the dusty antique store in Fremont. Was I crazy? The only thing I *knew* was what Jack didn't say. And Jack didn't say much.

My heart beating, my hands sweating, and the electric current in my butt buzzing, I limped into the baby's room and closed the door behind me. Francesca's bags were placed carefully in the corner, the makeshift bed made. The moon shone through the window and through the bars of the crib making a cage on the floor. I sat down on the carpet and opened her suitcase first.

Inside it smelled like her detergent. Jeans, soft T-shirts, a flowery sun dress. The linen dress she wore to dinner and two pairs of stockings. A worn paperback missing the cover and a jewelry bag full of dangly earrings. I carefully reached into the pocket of her jeans and felt the rough edge of a piece of paper. I pulled it gently out and peered at the handwriting. It had been through the wash. *Toilet paper. Film. Benadryl.* My hands were shaking. I shoved it back into the pocket and zipped the suitcase up quickly.

I reached for the black leather book bag next, my leg a live wire, my throat thick.

Inside was her address book, held together with a rubber band. A copy of *Interview* magazine. And a small spiral notebook.

But just as I was about to open it, the air outside exploded. I leapt to my feet, dropping the notebook, almost collapsing. One leg was humming, and the other was asleep. I was completely made of currents. Outside I could see the small explosions of the nightly fireworks display at SeaWorld. This view was one of the reasons why we bought this house rather than the larger one up the hill. A loud crack, and the sky was splintered with red lights. I imagined Jack and Francesca, walking along the deserted beach, noticing the fireworks in the distance. I imagined them holding hands. I imagined everything.

By the time they came back in the door, offering me a warm churro from the all-night taco stand around the corner, I was convinced I'd been wrong all along. Francesca wasn't his *what-if* girl at all. Everything about the way they came in, giggling at Jack's joke about the little boy catching his parents doing it, offering me the long cinnamony stick of dough (a strange compensatory gratuity) said *guilty, guilty.*

The Interrogation Chair

This chair was built of iron and equipped with either wooden or iron spikes (which could be heated up from behind). Also called the "Confession Chair," this chair inflicted unbearable pain to its victim. Still used in some countries to elicit confessions, modern interrogation chairs are sometimes equipped with an electrical current.

In the bedroom I waited for Jack. I turned down my side of the bed, got in, and crossed my arms. I didn't turn out the light. I only waited. I could hear the sound of water running in the bathroom, the shuffle of Jack's feet as he turned out the lights. Francesca's "Night, Jack," and the hesitation before her door closed.

"Why are you still awake?" Jack asked, peeling off his sweater and shirt.

"Don't get sand in the bed," I said.

"You okay?" he asked, crawling in next to me, putting his ear against my stomach the way he did every night. "Good night, baby," he whispered, his lips grazing my belly button.

"I need you to do that thing you do with my back," I said.

"It's bad tonight, isn't it?"

I nodded, feeling like I was going to cry.

I rolled over on my side, and he pressed his bare foot hard against my tail bone. At first it hurt, and I moaned. I thought for a second that Francesca, on the other side of our wall, might mistake my pain for passion, so I moaned again. But then the trick started to work, and for the first time in days the pain was gone. The circuit breaker was shut off, and my leg felt like a leg again.

"Better?" Jack asked.

I nodded and he reached across my giant stomach to turn out the light.

There was sand on my back from where his foot had been, but I just brushed it away and squeezed my eyes shut.

In the morning, Francesca made pancakes in my kitchen and Jack read the Sunday paper. I took a shower, feeling like I'd slept on the beach.

"Let's take pictures today," Francesca said, putting down a plate of steaming pancakes in front of me. "While Jack's at school."

"Why are you going to school today?" I asked.

"I'm meeting one of my students. She's failing, and she couldn't make my office hours Friday. They've got an exam tomorrow."

"Oh," I said.

"It'll be fun," Francesca said. "I promise."

After Jack left, Francesca set up her tripod and umbrella lights that she had in her rental car. She used a large sheet to transform our small living room into a virtual studio. I looked through my closet for something to wear.

"Get something simple. We don't want this to be about your clothes," she said.

I found the one not-so-little black dress that still fit and pulled it on.

"Gorgeous," she said. "Now stand right over there and let me check the lights."

Francesca was actually very good. I forgot for a while that I hated her, and even felt proud of my belly, even when I looked at her bare midriff exposed each time she lifted her arms to raise or lower the lights.

An hour went by before we took a break.

"I'm having such a good time," Francesca said, sitting down on the couch, opening the soda can I brought her. The lights were hot, and we were both thirsty.

"Well, I know it means a lot to Jack to stay in touch."

"I mean with *you*," she said. Then she gestured to my stomach. "And the baby."

I sipped on my lemonade.

"I know you don't like me," she said.

The baby kicked me in the ribs, and I winced.

"I mean, I wouldn't like me either, I suppose."

I didn't know what to say. My face was sweating. I shook my head weakly in protest.

But instead of further explanation, she offered me nothing. Why shouldn't I like her? She was Jack's old best friend. She and Jack weren't exes. They weren't lovers. What was she talking about?

"I want some nude photos," I blurted out. "For Jack's birthday."

"Perfect," she said, and I took off my clothes.

Maybe I just wanted to show her the reality of what Jack and I had. Maybe I thought that my naked stomach and swollen breasts (and ankles) might clarify for her that she might have that extra year, but I had his offspring. His progeny. She couldn't match that. She just couldn't. And so I lay on my back and closed my eyes, while she fanned my hair out like some strange mermaid and took an aerial photo of my very pregnant body. After another hour, I didn't feel shy or strange anymore and I thought that I could live like this. Naked. Wild. Beautiful. Maybe I just wanted to prove that I was every bit as exciting as she was.

I don't hate you, Francesca. I feel sorry for you. That's what I should have said.

What I did say was, "My back is killing me and this baby wants food. Let's call it a day."

When Jack came home, Francesca took a shower.

I sat at the kitchen table and stared at the side of the refrigerator. "I need to know something," I said.

"What's that?" Jack asked, peering into the cupboard for something to eat.

There was a long drip mark running down the side of the fridge. A misplaced magnet. An old lasagna noodle peeking out from under the fridge. I could hear Francesca turning the hot water on, the sound of her clothes coming off.

"I was just wondering if you ever think about what would have happened if I hadn't been working that day. At the coffee shop."

"You mean Latté for Work?"

"No, the *first* coffee shop. In Seattle."

"You mean if we'd never met?" he said, closing the cupboard door and sitting down next to me at the table.

"Yeh. If we'd never met."

He reached out and touched my stomach, absently, in the way both of us had become prone to doing.

"Let me think," he said.

Good idea, I thought.

"Well, I certainly wouldn't have finished school. I probably wouldn't have moved to California. I probably wouldn't have even moved out of that studio apartment."

I covered his hand with my own as the baby wriggled under our fingers.

"I wouldn't have gotten married," he said seriously.

My heart beat in my throat, and I looked at his face. His honest face.

"And I certainly wouldn't have been anybody's daddy."

The baby gave a kick that nearly knocked the wind out of me, and I squeezed his hand.

The Guillotine

The purpose of this device was not torture but execution. The apparatus, comprised of a blade which falls between two vertical columns equipped with grooves, was designed to behead and was used as early as the fourteenth century. It is named after Joseph-Ignace Guillotin, a French physician elected to the National Assembly in 1789 who mandated that all executions be performed by this painless method. Painless perhaps, but scientists soon discovered (and this has been confirmed by modern neuroscience) that a head that is cut off in this swift manner is well aware that it has been beheaded, maintaining consciousness just long enough to perceive this.

Jack helped Francesca load up the rental car and scribbled directions to the airport in her spiral notebook, which I realized (by looking over his shoulder as he wrote) was merely a book of grocery lists and other meaningless notes. I hugged her, and stood in the door touching my belly as she and Jack walked down the street to her car. I went back inside and closed the door. I did not look out the window. Didn't even peek.

When Jack came back I was in the baby's room deflating the air mattress. I unplugged the valve and put all of my 174 pounds down square in the center and listened to the whistle of the air escaping.

"Well that was a nice visit," he said and sat down next to me.

Together we waited for the air to escape, Jack pushing the places I couldn't reach, until we were both touching the ground and the air mattress was completely empty.

Catherine Harnett

Her Gorgeous Grief

Catherine Harnett is the author of two books of poetry, *Still Life* and *Evidence*, both published by Washington Writers Publishing House. Harnett, a native New Yorker, has lived in the D.C. area for over thirty years, and she began a relationship with *Gargoyle* magazine in the mid-seventies. Over the years, her poetry has been published in the *American Literary Review*, *Yankee*, *Fine Madness*, the *Chatahoochee Review*, *Poet Lore*, and *Louisiana Literature*; her translations of native Israeli poetry have appeared in numerous publications. She has recently retired from a career with the federal government, and now intends to devote considerably more time to her writing. She lives in Fairfax with her daughter.

Since you asked, I will tell you this: my mother did seek out calamities, listening for the tragic noise that led her there, to those gatherings of grief I came to know when I was young.

The days would start with her waking me from my deepest part of sleep, telling me in her urgent way that we needed to go, emphatically, now. I would dress quickly in the dark, not in the school uniform I'd laid out the night before, but in whatever I could gather from my drawers that seemed to match: jeans, the pullover, my zippered jacket for the long, cold trip to where this time? I had learned the set routine: ask nothing, crumple my still warm pajamas into the shopping bag kept under my bed, three pair of underwear, another top, one more pair of pants and go, quietly into the cold starred night where my mother warmed the car, its headlights off, till we were long gone down the block.

When I'd return to school in a few days, I'd bring a note which claimed strep throat, or colds, or a sudden family death. Exhausted, I would try to find my place again in mathematics, having missed the crucial steps that day we traveled hundreds of miles to the place that girl had disappeared, or the executed man shivered one last time.

I would sleep in the back seat until the morning light shone in as my mother smoked her cigarettes and listened to the news. Years later I would recall this repeated scene as I rode in the back of a taxicab while the driver sought news of traffic jams, bringing it all back, the certain sound of AM radio.

We would stop for breakfast in a diner or a pancake house, lingering for only a short time because of the urgency, she said, of getting there as soon as possible. Her vocabulary, full of words like *arraigned*, *adjudicate*, *abduct* amazed me, how my mother rattled off these terms like other mothers could recite ingredients for cakes. She navigated highways and strange rural roads while other mothers drove to baseball games and home.

My mother was always put together well on these occasions, her Coty lipstick neat and pink, her ample dress coat and kerchief. On our outings, she would wear high heels and hose, despite the long drives we took, as if we were headed to a sorority reunion, or a dinner date.

There were so many trips, it is hard to remember them all, their particulars. When I look back I count perhaps eighteen or so, but they are jumbled and some indistinct from one another. All of our ventures ended in towns or cities across New York or Jersey and each involved some kind of tragedy: a missing wife, a kidnapped child, house fires, homicides, a hanged college kid. Each trip was a pilgrimage, of sorts, a haj to the scene of the crime, or the home of the disappeared.

She would learn of misfortune by thoroughly combing newspapers she read at the town library each day while I was in school. For several hours my mother would read the *Post*, the *Record*, the *Sun*, the *News*, the *Journal* and every local weekly she could find in the periodical section. What the regular librarians thought of her I do not know; if they found her conscientious or eccentric, their opinions never made it back to me. All I know is that she copied down the names at the center of these tragedies, the addresses of the funeral homes, the makeshift rescue centers, churches where vigils were being held, courtrooms where the victim's case was heard.

With characteristic precision, my mother would gaze at maps and plot our routes, though I only saw evidence of this after the fact, during our journeys when I would sit up front with her as she drove. Each time she created a file with a label she bought at the stationer's across the street from St. Genevieve's. The file would be marked with the name of the deceased, the missing, the accused. She would have Xeroxed articles and photographs, marking particular paragraphs and details. Once I read while she drove, drawn to the highlighted yellow lines written about the young scout who disappeared while delivering papers on his rural route. "At night, Timothy's dog, a black and white spaniel, sits by the front door, waiting. Timothy's aunt, Adrienne, says quietly 'they are the best of friends,' a tear rolling down her tired cheek." In the folder was my mother's to-do list along with the directions to the search headquarters: bring flat walking shoes, flashlight, buy dog bones.

When I asked my mother how long it would take to get to Timothy's she replied "as long as it takes." She reached over and squeezed my knee, and smiled, asking me to quiz her on the contents of the file. "Okay," she said, "ask me how old he was—or is, I should have said. How tall. What he was wearing when he disappeared. His favorite TV show." The list went on and on until she had exhausted every published fact, recited every aspect of his photograph.

Timothy was two years younger than I, his blond crewcut and light eyes staring back at me as I studied his face. This morning we would drive an hour past Albany to the VFW Hall, where volunteers assembled, photocopying flyers, assigning routes for searches through the woods, waiting for leads. When we arrived, hours past my normal lunchtime, my mother parked the car and sighed. "We're here," she'd say, as she did at every destination, and she'd readjust the mirror. "God, I look beat," she'd sigh, applying fresh lipstick and running a brush through her hair. I wondered what the kids at school were doing now, the girl who sat next to me, dangling her skinny legs and writing on her hand with her bright green Flair. They were winding down their day as mine was grinding on, beginning in earnest now.

My mother made me neaten up, made sure my hair was combed and tame, wiped the pancake syrup from my chin. "There," she said, "let's go."

Every time she arrived at the scene, whether a candlelight vigil where posters of the gone would be illuminated in the evening chill, a line of grieving visitors leaving flowers at the blood soaked corner where a struggle had taken place, or now, in this hall; when she arrived she seemed to be familiar with the others who had come, seemed a piece of each community, the victim's intimate. As she arrived at the appointed place, my hand slipped from hers, no longer her accomplice. I sat quietly in the corner of the hall as she consulted with the search leader on the route to take, and with which crew. I had learned from many of these trips to bring homework, books, a deck of cards, to amuse myself, sometimes for three days.

She disappeared into the cold November afternoon, her map in hand. She had never looked so beautiful to me.

On evenings after afternoons like these, after the volunteers were fed, she and I would return to the car. We had the whole parking lot to ourselves; we'd bundle tight our clothes, prepared for the cold night of semi-sleep. Put your head on my lap, sweetie, she would say and stroke my hair until she fell asleep, bone tired from the drive, from hours in the spangled woods.

I was afraid to move, once she slept, and I listened for hours to the sound of cars passing, to the long freight trains that crossed the parallels of night, insistent on their routes, regardless of this town's most recent tragedy.

I never remember good news arriving while we inhabited those strange, tense villages, no relief. The next morning I overheard that hunters came across the small pale boy, his canvas newspaper pouch covering his stunned blond head, tucked among the leaves of oaks and maple trees. "Oh how sad," my mother said, as she sobbed. "That little boy, how lonely his dog will be." A local reporter comforted her as she wept, his photographer capturing her gorgeous grief. Weeks later she would show me the grainy photograph she'd come across as she scoured papers at the long wooden library table, the article describing an unidentified woman's reaction to the grim discovery of Timothy Blake's remains.

There were several incidents which occurred during our many excursions, most of them involving my mother, all requiring that we quickly leave the other searchers and mourners without so much as a goodbye. But I once created an inopportune disturbance in a forgettable Upstate town when I developed a fever of 104 degrees and began vomiting at the scene of Carolee Malone's brutal murder. Her beautician friends created a shrine in front of her duplex, where hundreds of flowers and several handwritten goodbyes diminished in the days of unrelenting rain. My mother expressed her deep chagrin at having to leave before Carolee's aging father arrived to plead with his daughter's killer, most likely that man she had been seeing behind her husband's back. She hurried me into our car, felt my forehead and let out a sound like despair, handed me an empty potato chip bag and told me to try to hold it in as best I could. I don't remember much of the long drive home that night, except for the persistent chills and nausea which have revisited me several times in my life since, always recalling the utter loneliness I experienced in the back seat that night, my mother's cigarette smoke blue and obstinate in the winter air.

On those occasions when we had to leave suddenly or silently on her account, my mother would flush with excitement and speak cryptically to me, her sentences spare and hurried. I rarely knew the particulars but caught fragments as she muttered something about the victim's family demanding to know who she was, or the investigating cop asking her to recall details of the victim's life. People often supposed that she was on intimate terms with the victim, or the executed, or at least with grief, and on that point I believed it too. It was real and palpable, her grief, and she bathed herself in sadness publicly, in its shared, overwhelming waters.

We'd leave quickly, the two of us on the lam, the way I imagined jewel thieves felt after a heist. We sped through towns one by one with their closed factories and signs announcing we entered and then left places where secrets would often lie buried with the gone. We longed for the smell and sheets of our own beds, and as we made our way towards home, I imagined the skeptical look my teacher would give me in the morning when I tendered yet another note. My mother turned the headlights off as she rounded the corner of our street, and crept quietly into the driveway and its protective dark.

But there was nothing like the circumstances surrounding our last trip, the one involving that young mother with the beautiful Italian name.

I did not want to go that morning, early, when my mother woke me before dawn. I had a test that day, one which counted for the biggest portion of my grade that year, and I had studied hard for it. "You can make it up," she said, "Get dressed." While I protested, she pulled me from bed and said again, more firmly now, "get dressed."

She hurriedly grabbed her papers, gloves, keys, tucked a stray hair behind her ear and looked sternly at me. Nothing inside me wanted to make another long drive, to miss school, to sit playing solitaire for hours in the corner of a room I would never see again, in a town I hoped I'd never sleep in one more time.

It seemed my mother smoked more during that drive than she did ordinarily, rapidly switching stations on the radio even before the songs were over, looked impatiently in the rearview and pursed her lips. I watched the empty roads pass quickly by, the farms, the just beginning light. I prayed inside that this time would be quick.

For some reason, perhaps the suddenness of this trip, perhaps my mother's mood, she never asked me to read her articles, or quiz her. Instead, while she hurried into the service station to ask directions after half an hour's aimless drive, I glanced at the front page of yesterday's *Newsday* which arrived each day at four o'clock. There was no map in her file, and all I saw was a photograph of the dark-haired woman, smiling, with three young children on a couch. My mother strode back towards the car, her face expressionless and worn. "Let's go," she said.

During the remainder of the journey, as my mother focused on the exit signs and landmarks the attendant had described, she talked softly to herself, distracted and concerned. "Poor Angela, she said, "didn't anyone see the warning signs? No one gave her help, the poor girl, no one. My God, it could happen to any of us," and her voice trailed off. I didn't dare ask her what she said, since she had forgotten breakfast for me, and it seemed pointless to make myself known to her.

We arrived at the place she was called to, seemingly out of a dark sleep, the place she was meant to be. This small town—its A&P, its pizza parlor, the Catholic church looming on the avenue, the railroad station where fathers left each morning in the dark, returning in the evening dark, bringing back the city's soot and salaries—this small town bred Angela, and all that happened.

"You're on your own," my mother said, "but don't go far." In the parking lot, she smoothed her coat and checked her lipstick one last time before she joined the crowd waiting to enter the church. This time was different in a way; you could tell that something else had happened, something people rarely talked about.

I watched my mother on the steps of St. Rita's, her cheeks flushed with the color that she had in her face when in the fall we walked to school, her blue eyes bright, expectant. Her distraction lifted; she seemed different from the woman in the car, the one who seemed to keep her own secrets, loving each of them as she opened and shut them tight during our long drive that morning.

I am not sure what possessed me this time, after all my obedience, after my practiced invisibility. I waited for the long line of mourners to fill the church and watched from the car for just the right moment. The closed church doors were heavy and I opened one slowly, overwhelmed with the smell of benediction and burning candles, that sweet devout smell that is like no other. The church was quiet except for the mournful organ and the rustling sound adults made at times like this. I watched from the very back of the church, wondering where my mother was sitting, and with whom. From the back, hundreds of women looked like my mother, bent kneeling with bowed heads, kerchiefs or chapel veils covering their heads.

At the front of the church, there were three small white coffins, each strewn with carnations and greens. Each perched on small gurneys, ready to be offered into the earth in just over an hour, the small holes taking them in for their long forever sleep. I was terribly confused: where was Angela, hadn't tragedy befallen her, hadn't someone come up from behind her, sliced her neck or suffocated her as she slept? Who were these small white ghosts contained in boxes, did the same man who harmed Angela take these three too? Perhaps we were at the wrong event, perhaps Angela's would follow.

I am not sure when it all came clear to me; it could have been days later, or two hours, but when I focused on the facts I could not comprehend how or why their mother took their breath away, how she had driven to the river and had locked the doors, had let the car roll down the pier and watched it disappear, the slow maroon of it. Angela who will never see this town again, until she becomes a part of its dirt, who will never be that young mother, hushing three small boys in the pizza parlor on a summer afternoon. Who will never put them to bed again, exhausted from her day, who will never sleep next to the man who gave them over to her keep. And my mother, who understood.

There are nights now when I do not sleep and listen for sounds, for any little thing, for portents. I sit and think, drinking tea and watching the clock. I check on my spouse who takes up half the bed and sometimes more; on my children, the boy and the girl, each in a decorated room, and I remember them all, the ones who are somewhere else now. When I cannot sleep, I watch TV and for hours and hours become steeped in the details of today's missing girls, the accused husband, the young woman who left her apartment and never returned, her bones found a year later, peaceful in the park. See the parents weeping, the best friends, neighbors who saw nothing strange, and we can visit with them at all hours over and again, footage flickering during our long insomniac nights. What my mother did was hard, seeking them out, not waiting for this grief to be delivered, virtual and cold. She traveled far and felt it close and beating, fear, uncertainty and loss, their photographs, their preferences, the pets they left behind; and knew them all. She seems always at my side, especially on these long nights, saying nothing but reminding me of the power of my own hands, the way things turn in an instant, what can be done and what can never be undone.

Jamie Holland

Valentine's Day

JAMIE HOLLAND's stories have appeared in *Gargoyle, Antietam Review, Baltimore Review*, and *Wordwrights*. Her novel, "The Box of Secrets," has been accepted by an agent and is currently under consideration at several publishing houses. She is at work on her second book.

They'd spent four straight nights together at the fancy hotel. The sweet, sensual memory of it had kept Ariel in a trance all week. Now it was Valentine's Day and they had a seven o'clock date at Lutece, a restaurant with a cobblestone patio and small candles at each table. Ariel had passed the place several times in her three months of living in Dallas. It was always packed with couples who looked like they were in that stage between courting and falling deeply in love.

She locked the door to her apartment and went down the steps to the first floor, where the security guard sat in a little adobe hut.

"Bye, Stan."

He nodded. "Hair looks nice."

It was up tonight, pulled away from her face, a suggestion from the saleslady at the empty store where she'd bought the tight pink dress. Ariel let the eager woman fuss with her hair, pulling out tendrils, sticking in barrettes, sliding in bobby pins like a bridesmaid.

"Enjoy the weather!" Stan called. It was unseasonably warm for February.

The restaurant was crowded with couples. Ariel smelled a fusion of perfume, grilled fish, and lit candles. All week she'd imagined sitting across from Jonathan, her bare leg swinging playfully, her tanned shoulders rolling toward him. In the mirror at home, she primped like a schoolgirl, steaming her complexion, applying a new lipstick called "Sparkling Rose." Now she imagined the color coming off on his lips and her wiping it away with a brush of her thumb.

The host smiled as she walked up. "Just one?" He had a closely shaved face but sprouts of hair peeked out from under his bow tie.

"I'm waiting for someone," she said. "Jonathan Mitchell." She imagined saying, *I'm waiting for my husband, Jonathan Mitchell.*

The man looked down at his reservation list, then flipped the page. He set down the clipboard and plucked out two menus. "Follow me." He had an accent but Ariel couldn't place it. Geography had never been her strong suit.

He led her to the famous cobblestone patio. All those evenings of jogging past the restaurant, eyeing the couples, and now she was finally on stage. Opening Night.

The host stopped before a table with a red rose in the middle and gestured dramatically toward it, as if to say, And now your Valentine's Day shall begin.

She sat down, taking in her surroundings. Couple, couple, couple. Next to her a man and woman leaned toward each other, the candlelight dancing on their faces. They were young, probably early twenties. The woman wore a low-cut red dress to match her nails and lips like she'd read an article called "How to Get a Man" and followed all the steps.

Hannah, Ariel's support group leader in Chicago, liked to peer into everyone's face and say, "What life do *you* want?"

After being silent for three months, Ariel finally raised her hand. "I want to be loved."

"Yes," Hannah said. "But first you must—"

"I know."

She was sick of the mantra. Why couldn't someone just love her first and then *later* she'd learn to love herself? Ignoring Hannah, she packed up her bags and left the city that had sent her into a raging depression. As the plane took off, she felt herself changing from a frightened, angry girl to a confident young woman. Part One, Part Two. Before and After.

Now Ariel smiled to herself as she imagined an interviewer thrusting a microphone at her mouth, *And how did you make the difficult shift from spurned fiancée to desirable date?*

"Well, it was hard," she'd say, "but I knew I deserved better." She imagined traveling the country, making speeches to lonely women. "I used to be like you," she'd tell them. And then she'd reveal how she met Jonathan in the local coffee shop—him in a tweed jacket and wingtips, reading the *Wall Street Journal*, and her in black running pants and a sweatshirt, circling ads in the classifieds.

"See, you don't have to be all dressed up to meet your soul mate," she'd say. She wouldn't reveal that he'd taken her that same day to the luxury hotel because some people in the audience might not understand about love at first sight.

A tall man in a black vest towered over her. "Something to drink?"

"White wine, please."

She looked at her watch. Ten minutes late. Maybe he'd stopped to buy a gift. Maybe he'd bought her a bouquet of flowers and while driving in his convertible, they flew out one by one. Maybe he went back to the florist, handpicking each one.

She looked toward the entrance, half-expecting him to appear at that moment. In her mind, Jonathan raced in the door, one hand smoothing back his windswept hair, the host rushing him to the table. She played the scene over in her head, rearranging this, editing that. She dressed him in a light olive suit with a red tie. The suit would match his eyes and complement his skin tone. When he came to kiss her, she'd smell a hint of Bay Rum. Then she jumbled up the images, fast forwarding, rewinding like she did with the creative visualization tapes in her apartment. Then she placed Jonathan in his hotel room, putting on his pressed shirt, sliding a red carnation in the slit of his lapel.

A James Bond type strolled onto the patio and sat near her. Dark hair, tan face. He looked around the restaurant serenely, then took out a book. Some people were content being alone. One glance and it was clear they couldn't care less who was watching them.

At the O'Hare Airport three months ago, Ariel had felt the critical stare of passengers as she lugged her bags through the terminal. Dark, angry eyes, a rubber band full of oily, unbrushed hair—of course they could tell she was a scorned woman—a stupid, stupid woman desperate to throw out her old life and start anew.

She'd never been to Texas; that was part of its appeal. Warm evenings sounded soothing. Weren't the men nice in Dallas? She pictured a big Texan medicating her with rare steaks and margaritas.

The wine arrived. She quickly brought it to her lips, breathing in the alcohol. She thought about Jonathan's mouth close to hers, his tongue lightly tracing her lips. Last week "I love you" was on the tip of her tongue, but she waited. One step at a time, she said to herself. Don't ruin this.

She looked at her watch. Seven thirty. She tapped it with her manicured nail. Some watches ran fast. She played a game with herself. *Let's see how long you can go without looking at your watch.* Then another part of her said, *I'll look toward the entrance one last time, then stop completely.* When she turned, the young couple next to her burst out laughing. Her fingers found the back of her neck. It was moist. Her thumb fiddled with one of the bobby pins, pulled it out and pushed it back in again, until her waiter appeared and said, "Your dinner companion hasn't arrived yet?"

"No," she said, finishing off her wine. "Another chardonnay, please." By the time Jonathan would arrive, she'd be pleasantly buzzed.

All in all, they'd spent four nights together at the hotel. One two three four. Four three two one.

A cell phone rang. The host had a small gray phone pressed to his ear. She thought of her own phone stupidly left on her bureau, pulsing with messages. *Ariel, I'm running late. Ariel, I'm in a stretcher, bleeding to death.*

She looked down at the stomach creases in her dress and saw lines of sweat. She straightened and the material sagged a little. For a flash she imagined herself melting. Jonathan would show up and Ariel, a tiny puddle in the seat, would scream in a small voice, See what happened? See how worried I was about you? He'd say, *Oh Ariel, Ariel, Ariel, What am I going to do with you?* He'd scoop her up until she came back to a normal human shape.

The host walked toward her, glanced at the empty seat, and walked past her. His face was stern. She watched him survey the tables. His lips were moving; she tried to read them. At the entrance, anxious couples waited in droves like teenagers trying to get into a nightclub.

Her wine arrived. She was so eager to pick it up, her hand collided with the waiter's. "I'm so sorry," she said. It felt good to actually speak. If left silent, the words in her head could run rampant.

Right then the host walked over to the waiter and said something under his breath while gesturing toward Ariel's table. Her stomach contracted. Thank God for alcohol, she thought. *I'll finish this glass, then look at my watch.*

The couple next to her ate their dinner. The woman chewed daintily. A bottle of champagne rested in a silver bucket. Ariel watched as the man suddenly reached across the table and, with his hands, cradled his date's cheeks as if she were a gem to behold.

Ariel looked away and her eyes landed on four women in red, clinking glasses, laughing. She longed for them to come sit with her, to cradle her with kind words, and to tell her to stop worrying so much. If only someone could reach into her head and sweep out the mess. Suck it all up with a vacuum.

The James Bond man sat, drinking his dark beer and talking to the host. They laughed like old friends, then the host excused himself and walked across the patio to assist a new couple. The man looked like an ad. Maybe he was a model. Maybe he was famous. Why was he alone? No one went to a restaurant alone on Valentine's Day, unless of course he wanted to meet someone who was also alone.

She was staring at him when suddenly he looked at her. It took a second before he smiled. Ariel smiled back, but it felt forced. *I'm sorry, I'm taken* was how her smile must have looked. It was an awful day to be alone. But then, wasn't it awful to be alone on any day? When Ariel was alone too long, fear took over. Fear of falling, fear of being hit by a car or lightning or a stray bullet, fear of skin cancer and breast cancer and insanity and light and dark and fear of being trapped in an elevator, fear of being found out. Fear froze her heart and her veins and there were times when she could look down at her hands and not know what they were going to do next.

She made herself focus on the place settings at her table: two knives, two forks, two spoons, two napkins. Her wine glass was foggy with fingerprints. One swallow left. As the wine went down, images opened like glossy pictures from a coffee table book: Jonathan's car crushed under a Mack truck. Jonathan sliding the hotel bathrobe on another woman. She willed them to go away, but they stayed in front of her, persistent. She stared at them and they backed off. New ones appeared: Ariel lugging her bags through the airport, Ariel running furiously around the track, running around and around, trying to sweat out the pain. Her head felt light now, dizzy, a rain cloud hovering, about to burst.

She thought, *I'm going to look at my watch now. I'm getting ready to look.* If she said these warnings, maybe Jonathan would appear. *I'm looking right now at what time it is. I'm looking. I'm looking. I'm turning my head about to look. There. I'm looking.* It was eight o'clock.

The nausea vanished, but now she had to deal with her heart banging around in her chest. She spoke to herself the way a mother might speak to a child. *He's just late. It could be a mix-up. Or an accident. This is not about you, all right?*

The thing was, Jonathan had been clear about his wife from the start.

"I love her but I'm no longer *in* love with her." He'd paused then, and shrugged. "Things change." Then he touched her cheek and said, "But *you*. You're a keeper."

And Ariel just about fainted.

"Excuse me, miss?"

It was the host, scowling now. "We're very busy tonight." He flashed an insincere smile. "Do you think your dinner companion has been held up in some way or..."

She brought her hand to her face and, with her thumb and index finger, felt the corners of her mouth. It was a nervous habit, but it also served the purpose of getting rid of any stale lipstick or crumbs that had settled there. Of course there were no crumbs. She hadn't eaten a thing. Why didn't they give her any bread? At the fancy hotel they would've delivered an assortment of warm rolls to the room.

"He should be here," she said. "Let's see, it's—" She looked at her watch. Eight-o-seven.

"We have several parties of two," he said, eying the empty seat.

"I'll call him," she said, standing. The weight of the situation rushed to that space between her eyebrows, where the worry line was deepening.

In the lobby, couples stood expectantly. Was it good? their faces asked her. Was it a good Valentine's dinner? She wanted to pick up someone's champagne bottle and hurl it at the crowd.

At the phone booth she took the coins out of her purse, slipped them into the slot, and dialed the number. Her bare toes were red from being squeezed into too-tight, on-sale sandals. One ring. Ariel swallowed. Two rings. The phone clicked—*he's picking up!*—and finally his voice, "Hello," it said Relief rushed though Ariel's veins. She opened her mouth to speak but his voice kept going: "If you'd like to leave a message, please do so at the tone."

She hung up quickly, not realizing she'd made the movement. Shock had a distinct numbing sensation. If she put her finger against a hot oven it would take a minute to feel the burn.

Halfway back to her table, she was practically assaulted by the host. His brows were raised. "The gentleman is on his way?" He held two menus.

"No," she said. She glanced at the handsome man, now on his second beer. He looked up suddenly and Ariel thought she saw a hint of empathy on his face, somewhere around the mouth.

"Then you'll be leaving?" the host said.

"Yes."

He presented her with the bill and told her to pay inside. Just as quickly, he waved two people over and in an instant the couple were seated. Ariel moved across the cobblestone as if she had some place important to go, as if all along her purpose this evening was to keep the seat warm for someone else.

In the ladies room, she found comfort in the sudden but improbable concern that something really *had* happened to Jonathan. Maybe he had suffered a heart attack while running. Maybe his apartment had caught on fire. Each situation offered relief and then humiliation as she realized how unlikely it was. Relief, humiliation.

She stood in front of the mirror. Her dress was wrinkled at the waist from sitting and sweating. She looked so deeply at her reflection that it was no longer her face she was looking into but something else—a tunnel, maybe. Her heart and soul. There must be some piece of her that she could hold on to, some part of her that would hold all the other parts together. The handsome man could help collect all those shards of her that were breaking off and falling to the floor.

The door swung open and two young women came in, talking.

"And so I'm sitting at work," one girl was saying. "And this flower delivery guy comes and he's like, I have a delivery for Candace Johnson? and I'm like, I'm Candace Johnson? and he's like, Well these are yours?"

"He is *such* a sweetie," the other one said. "You're like *so* lucky."

Ariel focused her anger on their appalling diction. She wanted to tell the girls to speak properly, to stop using the work "like" all the time, and to stop inflecting at the end of each sentence.

She left and stood at the periphery of the restaurant as if she were at an eighth grade dance, waiting to be picked. Relief, humiliation. Relief, humiliation. The new couple at her table sat, moonfaced, sharing a bottle of red wine.

The handsome man was looking at her, as if confused. Then he looked past her, where the entrance was. The water glass across from him was still full, no trace of another person. And he hadn't eaten a thing. She imagined him waving her over, pulling out a chair and saying, "What took you so long?" They could drink champagne together, clink glasses to once being alone and now not being alone. Maybe they'd end up married. Maybe years later they'd look back on the day and laugh about it. "All along I was hoping your date wouldn't show," he'd say. "I thought you looked like James Bond," she'd admit.

Slowly she walked toward him.

She reached his table and said, "Hello," but it sounded hesitant.

"Hello." His face was expectant, his brows an arch of curiosity.

She gestured toward her old table. "I don't know if you saw me or not, but I was sitting there alone and I just—" sweat trickled down the inside or her arm—"I thought it would be nice if we…"

The man was polite, there was not doubt about that. He did not pull out a chair, though, and ask her to take the seat. His face changed to another expression that she couldn't identify—embarrassment? Before she could place it, his face switched once again—this time to joy. In back of her a woman said, "I'm *so* sorry! The plane circled for an hour!"

A small suitcase dropped to the ground and Ariel's first thought was, Jonathan's here! He's whisking me off to the hotel! It wasn't Jonathan. It was a woman with a long neck and perfect cheekbones. The man and woman hugged and kissed, murmuring how good it was to see each other.

Ariel backed away from the love scene. Her body crumbled. Pieces fell to the floor, scattering like broken tiles all over the quaint patio. Hungry customers stepped on them, oblivious. She too trampled over her self, eager to find the door.

On her way out, she thrust a crumpled-up twenty-dollar bill at the host. He took it and said, "Good evening. And enjoy the rest of your Valentine's Day."

She made her way along the sidewalk. Cars passed. The lights blinded her. One beeped quickly and she turned around. It sped off, as if not satisfied. She felt like she was in a bus that stopped and started with quick jerks. It made her dizzy. She was starved and drunk.

Between the blur of headlights, the names of cities flashed through her head—New York, Chicago, Dallas. She thought of the territory people covered running from place to place. A map of her own life would have frantic lines jutting through the states, like the sudden bleeps on a heart monitor screen.

A block away came the desperate cries of fraternity boys barreling down the street. A college town, she thought, hopeful. That was what she needed—cafés and libraries crawling with mature grad students and young, single professors. An ocean nearby. The mountains. *Nature.* That was what was missing. Mother Earth. Rocks. Soil couldn't hurt you, after all. Trees couldn't abandon you in a restaurant. They had roots, a firm grounding. If you needed them, they were there, year after year. Nature wasn't going anywhere.

A clean-cut man in a black car slowed down at the intersection where Ariel stood, waiting for the light.

Her left foot stepped off the curb, but the heel must have caught on something because she lurched forward, falling hard onto the pavement. Her bare knees turned raw and bloody; the soft skin of her hands stung.

The man quickly got out of the car then, and went to her.

"You need help," he said.

Obviously he was a stranger, and she knew all about strangers, but this stranger was right—she did need help. Her wounds needed to be cleaned, bandaged. And she needed a ride home.

She thought, *Don't you dare go with him Don't you dare be an idiot.* Then almost in the same second, she scolded herself for rushing to judgment. *This is different. Someone is trying to help.* Plus, the authoritative way he spoke suggested he knew what to do. A doctor, maybe.

A streetlight shone directly on his face. All she saw was his hand, reaching for her, and she took it. She went with him.

Susan Kellam

For Cynthia and Her Rite of Spring

SUSAN KELLAM has published fiction, memoir, and creative nonfiction in numerous magazines and journals, from the *Baltimore Sun* magazine to *Mass Ave Review*. She was a fiction contributor to Sewanee Writers' Conference (2002) and to Bread Loaf Writers' Conference (2006) and graduated from the Johns Hopkins Writing Program in May 2002. Her day job is senior communications advisor at the Brookings Institution.

March 14: Pushed dried sugar snap peas in soil the consistency of defrosted hamburger. When fledglings shoot from the earth in seven to fourteen days, I'll have forgotten I put them there. Such a burst of life will be a surprise.

Like Cynthia, when she breezed past my desk and said, "Got to talk. It's about Bob." Floral bouquet. A scent she'd never use in the dead of winter.

We're in the same communications shop in a large government agency, one that keeps the pulse of the nation. Because the truth can be unsettling, Cynthia and I are trained in obscurantism.

"What's with Bob?"

"I think I'm going to leave him."

Cynthia separated from Bob? I could hear a saw buzzing between these two perfect growths.

"Why?"

She said one word. Passion. It wasn't there anymore.

Passion is so overrated I tried to tell her. I'd had a history of passion after all, and never one that lasted more than a season. What she had with Bob has weathered into the durable wood of cottage shingles, nearly the same gray-brown as the dirt where I stuck my sugar snaps. She and Bob are organic material.

Clearly Cynthia hungered after the synthetic. Her eyes cast out to the many shapeless forms in the office halls. I noticed a dreamy look on her face I'd never seen before. "Ten years," she said. "I've been married to Bob for an entire decade. A whole generation."

"Look at how much has grown between you."

Cynthia left before she could deny the gentle, mossy field that is their marriage. Perhaps she will reconsider.

March 20: Sorted through lettuce seeds and chose arugula. The loose-leaf varieties flop beyond their allotted portion.

Cynthia is overreaching her boundaries. Everywhere I turn, it seems, are her budding arms.

She toyed with me today as she toys with Bob. I had to sit through a whole speech she wrote for our chief commissioner and tell her when she'd penned a cliché. Usually she is good at putting words in others' mouths. Yet her head doesn't seem into verbiage anymore.

"Not wretched," I said. "Ratchet. We must ratchet up our actions."

"That's what I wrote."

"No, you wrote that our actions are wretched."

Her limbs drooped, and I thought she might cry.

I changed the subject. "Are we on for dinner Sunday night?" Every other weekend we did this. Usually she baked a roast that simmered all afternoon in rosemary and thyme. The three of us sat around and ate it, ourselves lubricated with red wine.

She didn't brighten. "I'm going to tell Bob this Sunday night that it's over between us."

"Why Sunday night?"

"Why ruin the whole weekend?"

"Anyway, it's not wretched."

March 25: Radishes are the worst to plant. Each pebble-like seed rolls into the next. It's nearly impossible not to let them clump. No matter how much care, I'll get radish clusters that taste like ammunition from a spark gun.

Cynthia told me today that she dissed Bob. Her word, dissed. But it's not even a word. You can disseat, or disrupt, or dissect, dissent, or even disturb. But you can't diss.

"All right, then," she said, tossing back her long hair. "I told Bob that I was moving on." She wiggled her ring finger at me. Empty.

I sighed, not happily.

"You've never known anything but his Sunday dinner manners."

I asked about their lovely home, set in five acres of trees, with wood-burning stoves and domed ceilings.

"We've divided the house in half. He gets the bedrooms and the study. I have the living room and guest bedroom. We've established kitchen hours."

"How civil."

She didn't answer me.

With the radishes planted, I had a chance to look over the rest of the garden. There they were: tiny sugar snap shoots. Rows of them as harbingers of the season to come. How lighthearted I felt, for a moment.

Then I thought of Cynthia and Bob's beautiful home divided like a piece of cake. I mentally calculated the number of dinners I'd had there over the past five years. It must have been at least a hundred. There were a few special birthday dinners, too, scattered throughout. Usually it was just the three of us, except on those occasions when I'd dated someone long enough to pass muster. Richard, for instance, with no lion heart. He'd a mane of red hair and funny yellow-blue eyes that narrowed into glowering dynamite sticks when crossed. I'd taken him there for Bob's birthday a year or so ago.

I'd spent the entire afternoon decorating a carrot cake with squiggles from the tubes, a whole rainbow of sugary squiggles. I nearly couldn't keep Richard from running his finger through my hard work, and did catch him at one of the discarded tubes, squeezing until that last squiggle emerged. Blue, like his jeans. Rather than eat it, he let it slither along one of his fingers, which he used to beckon me. How seductively he wiggled that blue line.

I succumbed, eventually, to Richard and his mane of wild hair, streaked with the blue of our passion. Cynthia said nothing when we'd arrived nearly an hour late, except she mentioned that the roast was dried out, and the wine nearly drunk. She and Bob giggled, for emphasis. Bob had that glazed look he got after two glasses.

"No problem," Richard had said. We'd brought two extra bottles with us, along with the squiggly cake. We drank and ate and talked. No one cared that the roast was stringy and the carrots nearly mush. The colors of the cake grew brighter as the night wore on.

I don't recall how many times I saw Richard after that night. Once. Twice. I'd stopped waiting for the low growl of his voice. There had always been dinner on Sunday night with Cynthia and Bob to salve the lonely soul.

April 2: The perennial herbs are springing back to life. The chives are nearly long enough to snip; the parsley is uncurling; the mint, well, the mint is staging its attack. If I don't guard the vegetables from the mint, there'll be fragrant interlopers everywhere. Fragrant and persistent.

Cynthia insisted we have dinner last night, Sunday night, at a restaurant. She chose a dark Moroccan place set on top of another, brighter, cookery. The steps took us past scents of rich tomato sauce, garlic, melting cheese, past folds of woven fabrics that opened to reveal a single room with low tables and cushions. Cumin and cinnamon filled the air, more powerful than the roasted chicken and lamb paraded on platters of rice.

"We eat with our fingers," Cynthia said.

I watched the other diners trying to discover the Arab deep inside their American tailored suits. Too-tight collars held their necks upright even as their legs obediently curled beneath them. White skins glowed in the rosy lights.

But Cynthia had it right. She wore a loose, flowing dress that cascaded around the cushions when she sat. The absence of any jewelry on her arms and hands allowed her to smoothly run pita bread through the chickpea spreads. She chewed thoughtfully; spoke almost nostalgically about Bob.

I had to remind myself that Cynthia had had only Bob for the past ten years. I'd had Richard with the red mane; and the several suitors who came, blossomed, and folded like woodland flowers; Patrick who sliced my heart, and Kevin who lacerated my soul but taught me how to ride out storms.

Could Cynthia grow as a single stalk?

April 15: The cilantro is finally up. Such a wonderful herb, full of sprigs that brighten everything I cook with bold, spicy essence. As seedlings, they emerge from the soil tentatively, like a row of eyeless green worms. They'll leaf out in a day or two, develop those heavy aromatic fronds that capture rainfall and grow ever more broad and scrumptious.

Soon, when I can go out with clippers and harvest a handful of my lovely cilantro, perhaps I'll make Sunday dinner.

I mentioned that to Cynthia today in the office, while we joint-edited a report the intern had drafted with far too many adverbs and adjectives, most of them slashed by myself in red pencil. "Can a downturn ever be anything but quick?" I asked.

"Or painful," Cynthia said, her pencil pointed toward the useless words.

"What about Sunday dinner?"

"This Sunday?" She looked up at me with fresh green eyes.

"Or next Sunday." How tentative we sounded. Only weeks after dinner every other Sunday had been chiseled in our routines.

"At your house?"

At least there was no imaginary line cut down the middle, with poor Bob sequestered to one half. I nodded.

"Only the two of us?"

"Do you have someone else in mind?"

Her hair swayed, and I imagined fresh breezes in our airtight office. For some reason, her eyes lit on our excessive wordsmith of an intern. I would say he was youthful, and leave it at that. But infected by his overblown writing in my hands, I'd have to call him a dewy-eyed graduate with taut muscles and thick brown hair. He has a name of course: Russ.

I asked, "Russ of the lavish vernacular?"

"Russ," she said, her tongue caressing his name.

Moved by the utterances of his one-syllable moniker, our verbose intern strolled toward us, his eyebrows cocked and his high, olive-toned forehead crinkled in question. "Did you call me?"

"It's this memo," I said. "We're going over it now. Just trimming a bit, getting rid of an extraneous word or two. Otherwise," and I smiled, "you've done good."

"Very good," Cynthia echoed. "Turn around."

He obeyed, did a complete turn like a pirouetting dancer.

"Very good," she said again.

A bit of a butterfly, I thought. Too soon out of the cocoon, on a whirl through uncharted territory, or he would be shortly. His brown eyes darted between the two of us, and neither of us said anything. "Can I go?" he finally asked.

By the look on Cynthia's face, I knew she would overreach. She'd ripened into a vibrant display of color right before my eyes. I couldn't stop her from saying to our young friend, "Don't go."

Russ turned again. Preening this time, I thought.

"Forget Sunday dinner," she said before her hands felt for Russ's dusty wings.

April 22: Pollen in the air like a hailstorm. There's nothing to do but sneeze and suffer. I've an entire box of tissues tucked under my arm wherever I go, and a red nose that begs for a cleansing rain that might clear the air, even momentarily. The mint is into the lettuce and I don't have the energy to yank the sweet herb by its fat root.

Cynthia didn't look quite so flush today. In fact, she withered this morning when I reminded her about the monthly report we would have to prepare before May.

"It can't be May yet," she bemoaned.

"By the way," I asked, "What have you done with our intern? He could be doing this work."

She collapsed into the chair by my desk, one thin finger pushed into my arm. "Russ," she whispered, "is a good time."

"How about a few more adjectives. It's only fitting."

Her head hung back over the straight chair, eyes and arms drooped like a water-starved creature. "I'm wrung out. He's a veritable machine. He can go all night."

Poor Bob, I thought. Not a competitor by nature, he'll never measure up again.

"Then where is machine man?"

"Studying for finals. It's that time of the semester."

As I watched, I swore she was going through a growth spurt. The color was fading, but the cells of her essence were furiously multiplying. Her already long legs stretched across the office floor, and I nearly tripped over her when I stood up for a bathroom break.

I was relieved at five o'clock when Cynthia folded back into herself and mumbled, "Time to go home."

May 1: A drenching rain last night sent my sugar snaps running up the ropes I'd hung for just such wanderings. The water smacked my cilantro and all the lettuce into the dirt, but they'll revive with the sun, if it ever returns. Three days of stormy weather, and there's no bright rays on the horizon.

Bob waded through the puddles earlier today to wish me a happy May Day. We both lamented that it was Sunday, but there would be no roast or red wine.

"Do you miss her?" I asked.

He ran his fingers through the wisps of hair that grew in crooked curls above his ears. "We still talk, across our boundaries. I watch her come and go. She's still Cynthia."

"Would you take her back?"

"She hasn't left."

I made Bob tea when I noticed how wet his feet were and detected a slight shiver across his shoulder blades. With such a bumper crop of mint, I'd already picked huge bunches that I kept steeping in a kettle. With honey, it was heavenly.

"Cynthia won't move away," he said, somewhat revived by my potent brew.

"Why are you so sure of that?" Did he know anything about Russ?

He took a bite from one of the fig bars I placed on the table between us. "She's well rooted."

"Would you move out?"

He shook his head.

May 8: The clouds always break on Monday mornings. I'd nearly forgotten what the sun feels like, as I ran from the house to my car and my car to the office. Only briefly did I look over the tall grass at my climbing peas and notice how their tendrils cleverly clung to the ropes, pulling up and up.

A major speech was to be written for our chief commissioner by close of business. Cynthia and Russ the intern took the first crack at a draft that detailed a series of accomplishments, most notably, an effort to reverse our lagging growth. Unfortunately, they detailed every slug in the works.

"How can we improve if we don't admit to our mistakes?"

Both of them looked so naïve. Yes, even the bright Cynthia appeared totally naïve. Yet she knew better. Didn't she?

With the sun so brilliant, what a hard day it was to stay inside and massage those words until they spoke well of us. Every negative, tapped carefully, twirled into a positive spin. Our layoffs began to speak of efficiency; the new ethics bureau highlighted our aggressive fight against misdeeds; the negligent fines we paid were slipped into miscellaneous expenses, and that one pesky newspaper article, the reason we created the ethics bureau, was touted as publicity.

Even young Russ was impressed at what we ultimately produced in that speech. The chief commissioner, a short, balding man, would look amazingly tall on the podium as he delivered our words in his large, husky voice. Kudos to our division, I thought. And to Cynthia, who was really very expert at coaxing sweetness out of the dark. It was her idea to cast the ethics bureau as a preemptive strike against the possible rather than as a way to tidy up after disaster.

In the waning sunlight, the three of us sat at an outdoor café and shared a bottle of very crisp chardonnay. We toasted our ability to tuck and cover the creeping agency blight.

Russ asked, "Is this public service?"

Laughing, Cynthia responded, "People hear what they want, anyway."

"But it's not how I imagined."

"Oh," she said, brushing strands of hair from her sunny face.

"What about the values we heard tell of in the last election? What about full disclosure? What about—"

Cynthia laughed, a sound as clear as the wine, as devilishly potent. The reverberations cut through the early evening, cut through Russ. "Do you really believe the government is all that?"

He nodded, those large brown eyes intoxicatingly fetching.

I said, "Don't pollute him totally."

Maybe it was the withering effect of the long day, or the southern breezes that tickled spring with summer's humidity. Cynthia kept lashing out with her long arms, those wavering fingers, telling Russ how misled he was, how he'd come of age in the wrong season. She kept at him until he upended his chair, and flew away.

May 16: The mosquitoes are out in full force now. But I fought back and staked my tomatoes in valleys between the peas. I slid several cucumber bushes in the sunny corners of my plot, and then found the crevices among the lettuce for the peppers. Only the squash was carefully placed in the open spaces, where they'll spread like a suburban subdivision.

With Russ gone, Cynthia and I have little time for chitchat around the office. We steer clear of the windows for fear the sunshine will draw us outside. Cooped in, work nearly consumes us.

"Do you have something to tell me?" I asked because I know Cynthia so well. Her blossom was gone, that cheery yellow glow that never lasts.

"It's the way that I'm growing. I can't possibly stay within my boundaries at home."

"What's that mean?"

"And to be barred from the kitchen at certain hours is an abomination—"

"So?"

"I'm moving out."

I imagined her in the heat of her new home. I said, "It's nearly summer now."

"Just as it was last year." She smiled that sunny smile, as assured of the seasonal rotations as of herself. No longer bound, she'd assumed more languid curves and a thicker stance.

Just as spring will return next year. So would her blossoms; so would the butterflies.

Eugenia SunHee Kim

Year of the Boar

EUGENIA SUNHEE KIM, MFA, has published stories in *Potomac Review* and other journals; narrative nonfiction work has appeared in anthologies, including *Echoes Upon Echoes: New Korean American Writing*; and a historical novel is forthcoming.

A cold, clotted, December day, with clouds so low they blanketed the neighborhood in damp oppression. As soon as she left the house, icy air misted Esther's hair and cheeks and entered her fragile, arthritic hips, stunning her with a stiffness that almost sent her back inside. She limped to the car, her purse over her head, wishing she'd thought to wear a rain bonnet and a thicker sweater, wishing tomorrow wasn't Sollal, New Year's Day, meaning cleaning, cooking, and waiting for the kids and grandkids who were always late. She struggled into her seat and arranged pillows beneath and behind her, relieved to find her cotton driving gloves on the floor. The Granada backed down the driveway and she pulled out slowly, mindful that she had yet to take the eye exam to renew her expired driver's license. Craning her neck to see over the dashboard, she fed the steering wheel an inch at a time from one hand to the other to turn the corner out of her cul-de-sac. She reviewed her grocery list for the Korean store: rice dumplings, beef bones, green onion, tofu, and one more thing—what was it?

Something thumped. She slammed the brake, the car lurched, and a boy's flailing arm and a bicycle wheel arced over the right fender. "Omana!" she cried, tangled in her seat belt and trying to get out.

A woman in a red sweater ran out of the nearby house. "Oh God! Jason! Jason!"

The boy's blue helmet rose above the left headlight and he waved. Relief flushed through Esther and left her trembling. He was about ten, she guessed, and covered with freckles. She managed to get out of the car and saw him shake out his arms and legs.

In thick, unused English, she said, "You okay? Where come from? You don't see!"

"I'm okay!" Jason said to his mom. He brushed his clothes and reached for his bike.

"Don't move. Jason!" The woman ran to them.

"You okay!" said Esther.

"I'm okay. It's okay, Mom!"

"Oh God! Don't move! You might be hurt. Does it hurt anywhere?" Jason's mother patted him all over with fluttering hands.

He jiggled himself and they hugged. "I'm okay, see? Just dirty. Not even a scratch!" The woman's sweater had Santas and reindeer knitted on alternating green and red panels.

"Dear God!" Esther said.

"You could've killed him," the woman said. "You hit my son!"

"He come from nowhere. How can I see him? He was hit me!"

"The bike's okay," Jason said.

"Are you crazy? You crazy old lady, you hit my son with your car!"

"How can I see him? I drive slow. I stop and turn. He came out nowhere!"

"Mom, I'm okay! The bike's okay. Let's go home." He tugged at her.

"Are you sure you're okay? That's your new bike. It's not broken anywhere?"

"Come on, Mom. I'm fine. The bike's fine. Just mud, see? It was slippery. I didn't see her, either." He seemed embarrassed, maybe ready to cry.

"Thank God you okay!" said Esther, her breath puffs of steam. "See? Not my fault!"

The woman shook her finger in Esther's face. "You are a crazy old lady. You're lucky he isn't hurt. People like you shouldn't be driving!"

The wagging finger made her spit out a mixture of languages. "Wae g'rae-yo! He should look where he's going! You think I have eyes on the side of my head? He comes out of nowhere and not looking, then you say my fault! Jungshin baj'da? You give bike to someone who can't ride. I drive slow and he hit! You praise Jesus he's okay. What kind of mother gives bike to boy who can't ride?"

"You're very lucky, old lady. Stay off the road! You wait so I can write down your license." The woman tucked her son under her arm and turned away. "Can't even speak English. Crazy old Chinese lady."

Esther returned to her car, lips set. "Rude woman. Doesn't know Chinese from Russian! He's not hurt. That boy's okay, just scared, like me. She makes big fuss for nothing."

The woman opened her garage door, and she and the boy went in with the bike.

Esther turned down the street unaware that the woman came outside waving a piece of paper, shouting, "I've got your tag number!"

She drove the remaining distance to Korean Korner, trembling. In the parking lot she composed herself and prayed, "Thank you, Father in heaven, for keeping me safe and for making that boy not hurt. Thank you for watching over that ungrateful family and for keeping me out of trouble." She sighed, "Amen."

In the crowded store, she chose two chickens, beef bones, dense rice dumplings, soup vegetables, and six side dishes. Her two daughters, one married with two children, the other still shamefully single—would pay respect on Sollal by formally bowing to the eldest family member—herself, now that Dad was dead. She wouldn't mention the bicycle to her daughters. She drove home without further incident other than the honks and tailgaters on Viers Mill Road.

The next morning brought drizzling ice and slush. Esther hobbled around the yard gathering newspapers in plastic sleeves scattered beneath bushes and on the lawn. Everything was supposed to be orderly to set the proper tone for entrance into the New Year. The yard looked overgrown but acceptable—the house, she'd given up on long ago. Its pine green exterior paint peeled in sheets due to its northern exposure, further shaded by star maples, mountain pines, and tulip trees her husband had planted decades ago as a reminder of Korea. Sleet swirled. She covered her head with dripping newspaper bags and hurried inside.

Little rumpled Kongju—her main companion since her husband had passed four years ago—skittered her nails on the kitchen linoleum, looking for breakfast. She fed the beige and white toy poodle leftover rice and boiled fish, and listened to the house creak in the winter wind. Some mornings she thought she heard her husband collapsing upstairs in the bedroom, his smooth forehead splitting in a clean gash on the edge of the night stand. When he was laid out for viewing, the cut was hidden beneath a line of flesh-hued putty, an unfortunate permanent ridge. Sometimes she thought about him lying in his casket, dry and safe in an aluminum-lined concrete vault. She visualized him serene—his Haband shoes, black church suit, rectangular fingernails, half-bald, round head ringed with gray, his full lips sealed in a half-smile. But this vision was disturbed by the thin rope of putty on his forehead, and she would leave thinking about him with her brow creased.

At the stove, Esther stirred rice and split peas in water, and turned it low to simmer into mush. On the morning of her husband's third and final heart attack, she'd made this porridge, his favorite breakfast. She remembered how methodically he ate and how noisily he slurped in his unmannerly way, specifically—she was certain—to annoy her.

With a cup of tea, she sat on the living room carpet by a low round table, its mother-of-pearl and lacquer Korean design sealed by an eighth-inch of protective polyurethane. Her arthritis flared and she wished that daughter number one, Stephanie, the professional masseuse—the single one—would visit more often. Although Stephanie was more intelligent than Mina, her brains were hidden in a morose personality. As a masseuse, Stephanie's hands were as firm and skilled as Esther's own mother's. She snorted to erase the surprisingly vivid memory of her mother's fingers pressing warmly into her neck. The house was full of ghosts this morning.

She hadn't seen Stephanie in the months preceding Christmas day, nor, oddly, Mina. However, on this day when Korean children formally honored their parents, she'd see them both.

In the daily *Deongah Sinbun*, she came upon the horoscopes. She knew it was peasant foolishness, but she couldn't resist verifying that this was again the year of the boar—the attribution of her birth year.

> *Boar*—The stubborn boar will find his chivalry tested. Although others may appear disloyal, ignore surface indications. Be patient, innate nobility will overcome strife. What is properly due will be delivered, although it may take time to recognize it as such.

Innate nobility will overcome strife. "Ha, Dad!" she said to the empty house. "Too bad you can't read this." Her husband had said during a rare fight that her pride in her yangban aristocratic bloodline caused only trouble and nothing more. It made her judgmental and argumentative, he'd said. It took her a long time to forgive him. She dropped the grudge when she realized that part of what she thought made him a good Christian was his ability to be humble, to embrace his mediocrity.

The word "disloyal" made her grimace. Where had the girls been lately? And what else could she do but be patient? "You kids with your busy lives never have time," she said to the newspaper. Everybody had jobs, but so did some of the other Korean daughters who drove their mothers to church or the mall.

She crossed her legs beneath the low table and adjusted her hips. After reading the news, Esther found a poem, a rare presentation of literary work in the newspaper. The poet was her longtime friend, a woman in her writing club who had emigrated in the late 1940s, between the Pacific and Korean Wars, as had Esther. Both were widows with the same number and ages of children, except that Mrs. Park had two sons, a fact that Esther thought was made plain too often. Thinking the poem pleasant if not terribly original, Esther decided she'd write Mrs. Park a note to congratulate her on its publication. It was the right thing to do, and besides, Esther had previously presented two poems and an essay in that newspaper and knew it was a notable achievement. Kongju settled next to her on the floor, the dog's breath fishy and its flank like a hot-water bottle against Esther's calcifying hip.

She recalled how the birth of Mina's second baby had inspired the poems she'd published. Unfortunately Mina couldn't read Korean, so couldn't appreciate them fully. Her husband translated for her, but it wasn't the same. The baby was—she'd been corrected more than once on the proper terminology—the boy had pervasive developmental disabilities. Such a mouthful and such a shame—Mina and Timothy's last child. Mina was over forty now, with no indication that another child was planned. Times change, Esther thought. As much as she'd disliked submitting to her wifely duties, she'd tried to have a boy until three miscarriages made her believe the doctor's crude remark that her womb was all used up. After that, she moved into the big bedroom with the girls. She told her husband, "You kick and snore. I can't get any rest." His expression was one she'd never seen before and she was disturbed by the hurt in it, but she never saw that look again and pushed it to the bottom of her mind. The sleeping arrangement joined several other subjects that were never again raised: their former lives in Korea, the humiliating modesty of his government position, her pride and ambition, his lack of pride and ambition, her inability to have borne a son.

Tim had to be unhappy about no more babies, although he acted perfectly content. He cooed and rocked baby Alex like any new father would his first son. When the baby first came home after months in the hospital, he could only be fed with a narrow flexible tube. At the oak table in their shiny tiled kitchen, Tim showed Esther how it was done. With the baby on a cushion in his lap, he threw his tie over his shoulder and inserted the long tube down Alex's throat as casually as if he were threading a needle. Esther had laughed and frowned at the same time to cover her awkwardness at giving compliments. "Yah, junjunee heyo. Go slow. Mina, he makes good father." She couldn't resist saying, "Have another son. Try again soon?"

"Oh Mom." At the stove, Mina sterilized feeding equipment, deftly removing tubes and fat syringes from boiling water with tongs. Their daughter, Becky, who was two at the time, ate Cheerios at the table beside Esther. "Besides," said Mina, "both these children are gifts."

"Alex is perfect. See?" Tim held the baby's face next to his, their eyes identical black lines. The baby was well formed but limp. In Esther's day, there were no such children, at least among her class. They were taken to the monks or abandoned. This had been the subject of her poems. Watching Mina and Tim with this baby had shown her a new family ideal—one she could admire although it remained difficult to accept. She had also written about the glory of daughters, but in reality couldn't quite admit that it made up for the lack of sons.

Esther sealed the note of congratulations to Mrs. Park and decided to use the same stationery for the Sollal envelopes. Earlier that week she'd withdrawn new ten-dollar bills from the bank and now peeled them apart, inserting two each into four envelopes labeled with her progeny's names. She fingered the note cards, edged with gold, and the heavy cream envelopes—a wasteful use of expensive cards, but they were a Christmas present from Tim and she felt compelled to use them in a way he'd notice.

On Christmas the week before, Tim had picked up Esther and Stephanie for their annual holiday dinner. She hoped that time in the car with Stephanie would reveal the cause of her long absence. She twisted from the front seat to regard Stephanie in the back, who looked pale. Her wrinkled skirt barely covered her legs in black tights, and an overwashed black sweatshirt hung like a trash bag on her round body. Her wildly permed hair obstructed Esther's view of her face.

"How are you?" Esther said. Stephanie shrugged. "Did you forget to change out of your pajamas?" She smiled to show she was joking, but Stephanie turned toward the window. Esther talked about people from the Korean community that Stephanie might remember: who died, who married, who had asked about her. She gave up after ten minutes of unacknowledged monologue, and Tim turned the radio on to classical music.

When they arrived she wasn't allowed to help in the kitchen, and Stephanie disappeared upstairs with Mina to see a new computer. She sat on the couch, anxiously idle, while Tim read newspapers across the room. "How's your family? Their farm?" She conversed with him in Korean.

"Good, good. We sent them a big check this Christmas for new fertilizer my brother wants to try." Tim let the newspapers slide to the floor, and she stifled her impulse to pick them up. She stared at Tim's soft pink fingers instead.

"Halmoni, Grandmother, there's something I want to talk to you about."

She shifted uncomfortably on the couch. She hoped he wouldn't embarrass her again by trying to give her a new car. Sure he was the man of the family, but this was America, and Dad's old car was perfectly fine!

His square wire-rimmed glasses exaggerated his narrow eyes. "You know that although I'm the eldest my mother lives with my brother. I'm glad to help them run the farm as I can. It may not be wise—the land isn't always profitable—but it's family legacy, and that's wisdom enough."

"True." What was he talking about? She rummaged in her purse for a toothpick to avoid looking at him. When Mina first brought him home, Stephanie said that he was handsome enough—for a Korean guy—but Esther thought he looked puffy and plain, his eyes like two slits in a block of tofu.

"You see how we live. This house is full of rooms we never use."

Why did he have to rub his feet in front of her? "You do have a large house. Many rooms for Mina to clean."

He cleared his throat and clasped his hands. "Well, since I have less responsibility for my mother, I want you to move in with us when the time comes. Whenever you're ready. You won't have to worry about anything. This is your home, too."

She dug at her gums with the toothpick. She wasn't dead yet! And the idea of being under obligation to Tim made her suck at her teeth. "Mina doesn't need more work, she needs someone, like an American husband, to help her." Esther knew he wouldn't disrespect her by defending himself. She couldn't avoid a kernel of pleasure in being blaming to his face.

"Halmoni, we have a cleaning lady."

"Must be expensive. I'll come and clean. You pay me!" She smiled but her voice was grim.

"Yes. Ha-ha." He retrieved the newspapers and shuffled them in his lap. "Halmoni. Naturally, I'm not talking about tomorrow. You have lots of time to think it over. Years. I don't want you to worry about what will happen later, that's all. We'd love to—we'd be honored to have you. Okay?"

She picked at her teeth, one arm wrapped around her waist. Tim waited a moment, then raised his paper.

For the remainder of the evening, she could only think that Tim was like a spider gloating over a helpless, juicy bug in its web. She ate very little of Mina's elaborate dinner and found the number of gifts under their tree obscene. Every time she opened a present from Mina and Tim—a cashmere cardigan, silk blouse, velvet scarf, La Prairie night cream and the expensive note cards—she felt the web of obligation to him tighten. On the way home she surreptitiously gave Stephanie the shopping bag that held the sweater, face cream, and scarf.

The note cards felt heavy in her hands. She decided to tell Mina when she saw her that she was long from being sick or dead, and Tim's idea was preposterous. She printed in Korean so her girls could read it easily: "A year of good health and prosperity. Grandma." She went back and added "Love," in English. Had it been Stephanie or Mina? She couldn't remember who, but recalled a messy time when one of them had yelled at her, "How come you've never said 'I love you?'"

"I love you! I love you!" Esther had shouted back. "This isn't a soap opera. I'm your mother—that should be enough!"

Afterward, she resolved to try to be more demonstrative, but she forgot. And even now, writing it down felt undignified and common. "Well," she rationalized, "it's their way."

She slid the envelopes under a flat pink pillow that lay in the center of a yellow plastic woven floor mat. It covered most of the green living room carpet like a square island on a stained and faded sea. She would sit on the pillow while her family made deep formal bows. They'd be self-conscious and clumsy and Esther would laugh along, pretending the old ways really didn't matter. She'd give them their money gifts after they bowed.

She put away her writing things, smelled something burning and hurried crookedly to the kitchen. The porridge had boiled over and thick smoke crawled up the walls. She scorched her fingertips pulling the pot off the burner, the black mess inside thick as slag. "Aigoo!" Another saucepan ruined, and now the house stank of burnt peas. She turned on the exhaust fan, sprayed Lysol, and chastised her forgetful mind. She soaked the pot to salvage it and decided to make the soup.

Filtered through high rain clouds, feeble afternoon light eked into the kitchen. The chickens and beef bones were set to boil while Esther chopped onions. The phone rang, and she blew her nose and wiped her eyes on a paper towel. "Hyung-neem," said Mrs. Park fondly. They exchanged New Year's greetings and spoke in the shorthand that comes from speaking at least once a week for decades. "How's your soup?" said Mrs. Park.

"They're not here yet. Yours?" Esther leaned against the counter, picturing Mrs. Park at her old-fashioned telephone table, her thin wrinkled legs curled up on the seat, her gray hair still long and plaited into a tidy bun.

"They came early. How they bowed! Nobody could do it without laughing—all on the floor like tickled dogs. Wonderful! I gave them money and now I'm broke. What time are they coming?"

Her kids *are* like animals, thought Esther. She was surprised to see it was two o'clock. "Soon. How's everybody? Working hard?"

"Same. Howard's practice got bought out by another big company. I don't understand this managed care business, but he says it's busier than ever. His wife wants two more kids, so he better work hard!" Mrs. Park chuckled.

"Tell me everything when I see you at church. I have lots to do before they come..."

"The eldest coming?"

"Any minute. Goodbye..."

"Wait—did you see the *Deongah News*?"

Esther remembered the poem. "Didn't have a chance to really look at it."

"Call me when you've seen it."

"Okay. Happy New Year."

"Happy New Year!"

Esther vacuumed and straightened the living room, thinking that Mrs. Park would get the card before they saw each other on Sunday and that would take care of it.

She bathed and gave Kongju a bath at the same time. Pliant, uncomplaining Kongju shook herself as Esther affectionately toweled the dog's yellow curls dry. The tradition was to dress in all new clothes, but she settled for the silk blouse from Tim and Mina and old gray corduroy trousers. Underneath, she wore one of her husband's undershirts, a habit she had adopted for winter. Except for the bothersome arthritis, she felt good and strong. With sewing scissors, she trimmed the edges of her short hair—almost completely white since she stopped coloring it after her husband died—and tamed it with two black bobby pins on the sides. On this day when everyone traditionally turned a year older, she felt sure she'd fully live another year, her eighty-fourth, and was pleased.

She chopped vegetables into the soup, glad that the girls were late—there was still much to do. Consciously ignoring Tim's idea for her future, she knew she should move to a smaller place but couldn't face going through Dad's papers. No matter how much she cleaned, things still seemed scattered everywhere: sewing or painting projects she was in the middle of, piles of papers she wanted to look through, stacks of dishes and dried foodstuffs she meant to give to her daughters.

Rows of unframed photos of her husband, taped on the shelves next to her little table in the living room, hung curled and lopsided, their tape brittle and yellow. She decided it would be a fitting New Year's tribute to dust and rearrange his photos.

She put Kongju out back for her business, and since it was raining, waited by the sliding glass door with a towel. "You're a lucky dog—no worries about being taken care of in your old age." She dried Kongju's wet paws then checked the soup, warm on the stove with the burner turned off. She'd heat it and add the dense dumplings when the kids came. The rice in its thermal cooker would stay hot and moist all day. With the side dishes from Korean Korner, it was a suitable feast.

She found tape and scissors and sat to straighten the photos. She hadn't really looked at them in years and their images stirred the water of her memory. There was Dad at the beach, at his desk job at the Voice of America, with one or another of the girls through various ages, with Kongju as a tiny puppy, and the retirement party. She dusted and taped the pictures flat. Dad, sallow from heart disease, with Stephanie and Mina on either side, their arms around him. They'd always been affectionate with him, and it gave her guilty relief that they gave him the hugs and kisses she found so awkward. Mina had said something about that once—what was it?

As she reattached the last of the photographs, her finger pressed against the clear tape covering Mina's face, and a cold splash of remembrance washed over her.

Last spring, on baby Alex's first birthday, Mina told her she'd been in therapy for years, ever since Dad died. It was so odd that Mina would take her problems to a stranger—somebody she paid to listen to her!

"A head doctor? Why? You're not crazy." Mina and Esther were picking at watermelon slices in the living room after the birthday lunch, while Tim and Stephanie were in the backyard with Becky, the baby, and Kongju.

"Ma, you don't have to be crazy to be depressed." As usual, Mina spoke English and Esther replied in Korean. She often misunderstood her daughter and wondered if Mina misunderstood her equally. "Stephanie and I are both depressed. I can't say for Steph, but I was having a tough time and couldn't figure it out. It hasn't been easy with Tim."

"What? Your husband? You must be doing something wrong."

"Oh Mom, you don't understand."

That was true. "You miss Daddy, is that it?"

"Yes, but it isn't just sadness. It's more complicated. I mean, look at you. You've been able to go on perfectly fine without Dad."

Esther thought of the many boxes in her walk-in closet, which were filled with audiocassettes of one-sided conversations to her husband after his death. "This is because you girls don't go to church. Where is Jesus in your life? He's the one you should turn to, not some stranger."

"It's not that! God has nothing to do with this!"

"Don't yell. God has everything to do with everything. What's wrong with you girls?"

"There's nothing wrong with us! There's things we have to work out, that's all. It wasn't easy growing up in a Korean house."

"Yah, are you crazy? Korean parents love their children most of all. We did everything for you kids."

"Everything but show us your love! At least Dad could hug us now and then." Mina was crying, big childish sobs. "Things are different here. It was hard for us."

"Why are you crying? Of course I was a Korean mother. The problem is, you girls aren't Korean daughters! Why are you so upset? Stop that before Tim comes back. He'll think we've been fighting."

Mina gave a big fake laugh. She went upstairs. Esther heard her splashing her face in the bathroom and the honk when she blew her nose, the identical sound of Dad blowing his. Mina descended, her delicate bones looking a little sharp at the elbows and knees, her eyes red, but her face otherwise composed.

"You need to eat better. Too skinny." Esther said. "Some vitamins. I have ginseng."

"Tim likes me skinny. See how well I take care of him?"

"There's no need to talk rudely. I'm sure Tim loves you. He's your husband, isn't he?" That was the time when Mina had blurted the question, "How come you've never said 'I love you?'" and Esther had yelled at Mina in return.

After that, they sat in silence, Esther searching her mind for Bible passages that might help her troubled daughter. Mina carried the watermelon dish into the kitchen, and Esther followed her, saying softly, "Mina-yah, parents love their children, and Korean parents are no different. Your parents' first thought was always about you kids. If our approach was different from American parents, that doesn't mean our hearts weren't there."

"I know that, Mom," Mina sighed. "Let's forget about it. It's time for us to go anyway." She left to gather her family. From the kitchen window, Esther watched Mina talking to Stephanie in a corner of the yard and the two of them hugging.

She pressed her thumb over the tape on her daughter's face in the photograph and thought that Mina must be having an identity crisis, like the Korean American teenagers at church. After all these years, there was little Esther could do to help. *What is properly due will be delivered, although it may take time to recognize it as such.* Esther brushed the horoscope prediction from her mind and wondered if she should phone Mina. She began to set the table and thought she heard the doorbell, but a quick look out the window showed an empty curbside and she hurried to answer the phone.

"Happy New Year, Mom," said Mina.

"Hi! Happy New Year!" She tried to sound bright and carefree.

"Mom, I'm sorry, but we're not going to make it. I tried, but I just couldn't get it together today."

This was the vague kind of English that Esther didn't understand. "Come have dinner. I made duk-gook and everything's ready. Your husband will like it and your kids have to learn. Stephanie is coming soon."

"I talked to Steph, Mom. She's not doing too well."

"Is she sick?"

"Sort of. She's really out of it. She barely made it to the phone."

"What's wrong with her?"

"She's depressed."

"You said you were, too, but you sound okay."

"Hers is different. It's chronic and she's debilitated by it. I've explained this to you before. She can't just snap out of it. She's on a new medication now, but it'll be a couple of weeks before she can deal with anything."

"Medicine? Weeks? Is she seeing a doctor? She should go to see Howard Park. I just talked to Mrs. Park, and it seems he's doing great business. He must be a good doctor. I'll call her and give her his number."

"She probably won't answer the phone. Just leave her alone for a while."

"But if she's sick—"

"This isn't that kind of sick. This is depression! Mom!"

"Don't talk back!" Mina was quiet so she continued. "I'm only worried. She should see a Korean doctor, a family friend who would be sympathetic."

"She's under a doctor's care—a psychiatrist, okay? She just needs to be left alone right now."

"So, you know what's best."

Mina sighed. "Do what you want, but I'm just telling you that she's not going anywhere today. I wish we didn't have to talk about her every time we talk."

"Then you come. I cooked and cleaned. Everything is ready. I have money for the babies and all this delicious food from Korean Korner."

"Did you take a cab or did you drive?"

"Hmm."

"Mom."

"Yes, I drove, and I had an accident, too."

"Are you okay? What happened? Why didn't you call?"

"Nobody was hurt."

"What happened? Did you hit something?"

"No! A boy on a bicycle hit me!" She related the story, her anger rising as she talked about the woman in the reindeer sweater.

"Did she get your address? Did she take your license plate down?"

"Nobody was hurt! The car was fine. I didn't bother."

"Are you sure the boy's okay? Are you sure she didn't get your license? You could go to jail! You can't drive, Mom!"

"How can I go to jail? It was his fault! Who's going to drive me? How am I supposed to get anywhere?"

"It's always the driver's fault when someone is hit. I can't believe this! I've told you to call a cab. The number's right there by your phone. I'll send you money, for God's sake!"

"Yah! Don't curse." Esther noisily dropped the soup spoons in the drawer.

Mina quieted. "Please don't drive. Please call a cab next time, will you?"

"Don't worry about me. Come and eat. It's good food."

"I'm sure it's wonderful. I told you not to go to any fuss—that we probably couldn't come. Remember I said that at Christmas? Alex doesn't understand about New Year's anyway."

"Is that sick baby all right? Did you and Tim have a fight?"

"Alex is not sick, Mom, he has disabilities. Tim is fine."

"Are you sure? No fighting?"

"Mom. I'm sorry you worked so hard. At least you got the house cleaned. Put the food in the freezer. You'll have great stuff to eat all week."

"It's too much. Come pick it up. Maybe I can take it over to Stephanie's."

"Don't you dare. You can't drive without a license. Promise me you won't drive."

"Don't treat me like a baby."

"Okay, okay. I've got to go. I'm going now."

"Happy New Year."

"Happy New Year."

Esther cleared the table and turned on the burner beneath the soup, ladling a bowl for Kongju before it got too hot. She served herself in the kitchen and ate four different side dishes out of their refrigerator containers. She called Stephanie and got her answering machine. In careful English, she said, "Yah, I heard you were sick. Maybe you should see Howard Park—you know, Mrs. Park's son, the doctor. I get his number. You call me for his number. You should think about church and read Corinthians in your Bible, okay? I miss you today. I pray for you. Yah, happy New Year. This is your mother."

The cloudy day grew swiftly dark. At her little table she worked on a story she'd begun, written from the point of view of an American poodle adopted by a loving Korean family. She unkinked her legs, turned on the grow lamps over the shelves of houseplants above the photographs, and went to make tea. In the kitchen she saw she'd forgotten to put the dinner things away and do the dishes. No matter. Certainly Kongju wouldn't mind. Esther had named the dog after a folktale princess who had sacrificed everything—including her life—for her parents. Kongju nosed Esther with her moist snout. Old now, but still a good dog. Very smart. Her best daughter.

Randi Gray Kristensen

Look Out

RANDI GRAY KRISTENSEN lives, writes, and teaches in Washington, D.C. Of Jamaican and Danish origin, her publications include creative nonfiction in *Under Her Skin: How Girls Experience Race in America*, poetry in *Caribbean Fire*, and book reviews and articles on African and African diaspora literature. She is writing a novel about female sex tourism in Jamaica.

The summer we sang along with all the "la-la-las" in "Brown-Eyed Girl," I spent the long days with two girls from the French school where my mother sent me. Marie-Ange and Marie-Claire were sisters I called Eight and Nine, their ages, and they called me Seven. They lived next door to Kalorama playground, so I thought we were the luckiest girls in Washington.

One Monday, after the long walk from our apartment through the wet smell of morning, my mother handed me over to Madame, put on her public face, and clicked her heels on the tile to the elevator like a wind-up doll, turning to wave and smile like she was going shopping, not to work. Eight and Nine sat at the breakfast table, eating big slices of buttered bread, and I slid into my chair next to Eight and helped myself to the extra slice they always left for me. Madame trilled about the kitchen, but since school was out I had decided I didn't have to speak French. Madame thought I was slow, because I wouldn't even look at the door to go outside until she changed, "viens, petite, viens" to "come already!"

Her irritation made me feel at home. Every summer before this, as soon as school was out, I took the plane to Grandma's in Jamaica, where summer meant barefoot all day, short showers in cold water, rice and peas every Sunday. Grandma strode around her yard in a floppy straw hat, checking mangoes and bananas and allspice, rarely speaking to me, but just as rarely forbidding me to do anything. This year Grandma was going to come up, so the money for my plane ticket went for hers instead. We didn't know yet when she was coming; we didn't know how we would all fit in our little apartment, but that was why I was here with the Frenchies.

After breakfast, Eight and Nine did their chores. I watched *Let's Make a Deal* and *The Price Is Right*, feeling sorry for the contestants who tried so hard and still didn't get what they wanted. Madame let us go to the playground by ourselves until lunch. Every morning, she opened the living room window and told us to yell if anything was wrong; she would hear. We didn't believe her, but we didn't worry. Now and then I checked the window from the playground. Usually it was empty; once I saw Madame, puffs of smoke coming from her. Startled, I forgot to tell Eight and Nine.

Our orders were to hold hands until we reached the playground. Nine and I put Eight in the middle. I had bullied my way into being the elevator button pusher, so I pressed the down arrow, then pulled the other two in as soon as the door opened. I pushed L, for Leaving, and we let go hands as soon as the door closed. This small rebellion cracked us up, and we collapsed against the walls of the elevator. We had figured out all the elevator's tricks. Push the red button in, the elevator stopped. Pull it out, it started again. Our favorite find was the bell; we took turns reaching up and pushing it just before running into the lobby. Madame told us the bell was a way to call for help if something went wrong. One day we rang it and hid behind one of the couches in the lobby. No one came.

We burst from the building and hooked up hands, in case Madame was watching, and decided to skip to the playground. Their legs were shorter than mine, so to keep us together I tried short skips, or sometimes double skips to their one, but we fell out of time with each other, and Eight was jerked forward and backward between us.

We were first, as usual, to the playground. Eight ran for a swing, planting herself in the center of the rubber strap meant to be a seat. She ran backwards until the metal links squeaked, then stuck her legs out straight into the air and swung forward. She tucked her knees in and pumped herself higher and higher, until at the top of the swing the chains went loose and threatened to tumble her out backwards. She squealed, leaning forward to keep her seat.

Nine stood next to the sandbox for a second, looking around. Most days she took to the slide, while there was no line, no scaredy-cats shivering at the top waiting for a push or, worse, climbing back down and making everyone behind them move to the side or lose their place in line. That day, though, she headed for the roundabout and sat in its center, even though there was no one there to push.

I climbed inside the monkey bars, and rested my arms over a bar, just watching. Eight was still scaring herself on the swing; Nine sat in the center of the roundabout, legs crossed under her in what they told us at school was Indian-style, playing with the hem of her skirt, staring out of the playground gate. She looked the way I felt when I was lonely.

"Hey," I yelled, "what's the matter?"

She looked up in my direction and said, "Nothing. I'm just playing a game."

It didn't look like much of a game to me. "What game?"

"I don't want to yell it," she said. "It doesn't work if everyone knows about it."

I looked around the playground from my perch. "There's no one else here."

"Are you sure?" She smiled like she had a secret. "Can you see inside the bushes, or even the rec room?"

"Well, no, smarty-pants, but no one can fit into the bushes, and the rec room's closed."

"Are you sure?" she asked again.

She had me there. We hadn't checked the rec room when we came in, and I supposed someone could be crouching behind a bush where I couldn't see them, but I couldn't imagine why. "C'mon, there's no one here. Just tell me what the game is."

She thought about it. "I'll tell you if you come down. I don't want to yell it."

I smelled a trick. "Nuh-unh. You just want me to come down so I can give you a push. That's what the game is."

She sighed. "That's fine. You just go ahead and play your game, and I'll play mine."

"There *is* no game!" I shouted.

She just smiled and looked away.

I climbed another rung on the bars. I crawled across flat space until I grabbed the next highest rung and turned around so I could see her again. Eight stopped pumping and was letting the swing slow down. She looked over to her Maman's window. She wanted to jump before the swing stopped, which Maman had strictly forbidden. Nine had untied the bow at the back of her dress, and twirled one of the ends in front of her, like a cowboy with a rope. She did look like she was playing a game.

"Okay," I said, "let's make a deal. I'll climb down and you'll tell me the game, but you won't ask me to give you a push."

She stopped twirling for a moment. "It doesn't matter to me," she said. "I can play this game without telling any of you."

Eight picked this moment to jump. She flew forward into the sand and landed on her hands and knees, the swing going up and down behind her with a little twist in the middle.

"Did you see that?" she yelled. "Did you see it? That was the highest I've ever jumped!" She stood and brushed off her knees, then her hands. I looked at Nine, and Nine looked at nothing we could see. Eight started to put her hands on her waist with her elbows sticking out, like she always did when she wanted our attention, but then she dropped her arms.

"What are you guys doing?" Her voice rose on the "ing," French-style, like a bell.

"She's not do-ing anyth-ing." I imitated Eight's accent. "But she wants us to think she is."

"Suit yourself," Nine replied. "But I'll tell you what it is if you come over here."

"It's a trick," I warned Eight. "She just wants a push."

Eight launched at her sister in rapid-fire French. I knew it was supposed to be a big deal that I went to a French school where everything, even English, was taught in French, and that I was going to be fluent, but I wasn't fluent yet. I had to pay attention. I also knew that I was mostly there because school went almost all day, like a job, so my mother didn't have to worry about me in the afternoons. Plus, it was right across the street from where we lived. They couldn't figure out why I, a neighborhood kid who spoke English and didn't ride in cars with DPL plates, was at the school. I paid them back by coming in first or second in the class every year, but it wore me out. Especially the half year before we figured out I was nearly blind and needed glasses.

Our teacher last year was Madame Parapluie. *Parapluie* means umbrella in French. We called her that because she wore long pleated skirts that fell down around her in a perfect circle like an open umbrella. She hated me. At first, I thought I was doing something wrong, but later I guessed she knew we made fun of her, but she couldn't punish the rich diplomat kids for it. Me, on the other hand, she refused to learn my name. She called me other names, and then punished me when I didn't answer. One afternoon, during nap time, I was wrapped up in my soft brown and green blanket on the mat, telling jokes with my friend Peter. I heard Madame calling some other kid's name. All of a sudden Peter's eyes grew wide, and she grabbed me by the arm and beat me on the behind. I never really relaxed after that. Anytime I heard someone else's name in that tone of warning, I knew it could be meant for me.

But now it was summer, and I didn't want to hear any French. My mother thought it was great for me to be with Eight and Nine because that way I wouldn't forget everything over the summer. But I wanted to forget everything, and start over new next year. When Eight walked over to Nine, still babbling away, I slid down the monkey bars and ran in between them.

"Stop it!" I yelled. "Stop it! If I've told you once, I've told you a hundred times, no French on the playground!" Eight froze. Nine looked back at the opening to the playground.

"Mais pourquoi?" Eight squeaked.

"Because it's summertime, and we're not at school." I said it like a teacher. "No one wants to hear French when we're not at school."

"But there's no one else here," Eight said.

"There are people passing by. We don't want them to know we're different. We want them to think we're regular kids. If they think we're different, they might do things to us."

Eight's eyes widened. "Like what?"

"You know, things. Like the things you're afraid of when you're asleep."

"Why would they do that?" Eight whispered.

"Because people treat you different when they think you're different. So you want them to think you're normal. At school, normal is in French. Here, normal is in English. Be careful." I looked behind me over both shoulders. "Let's hope no one heard you." Eight's bottom lip began to tremble.

Nine glanced at her and said, "Tais-toi, petite, I have the lookout."

We both stared at her. She shrugged. "That's my game."

I climbed on the roundabout with her. Big silvery arms stretched from a pole in the center, bending like an elbow to meet the edge. You held onto the bend and ran around to get it moving, then tried to jump on or just let go until it was your turn to ride. It was painted different colors like slices of pie, skinny in the center and wide at the edge. I thought if you looked at it from the sky when it was spinning, all the colors would blur together like a pinwheel in the wind. I sat on green; Nine sat on blue. Eight held onto the bar at red and bent backwards so the tails of her bow dragged in the dust. I waited for Nine to say more. She just flipped the end of her untied bow in and out of her lap.

I hated when someone knew something I didn't, so I said, "Lookout doesn't look like much."

Nine smiled slightly. "You have to know about meerkats."

"What kind of cats?"

"They're not cats."

I got annoyed. "You just said mere cats."

"I know, that's what they're called, but they're not cats."

"Well, what are they, then?"

"They look like…they look like nothing else. I don't know if I can tell you what they look like if you've never seen one."

"Well, where'd you see one?" I started to get angry.

"Maman let me watch *Wild Kingdom* last night." I felt a pang and wanted to hit her. On Sunday nights, my mother only let me watch *Law-*

rence Welk, which was awful, and *Wonderful World of Disney*, which was okay sometimes. We watched *Julia* on Fridays and the news every night. Otherwise, the TV stayed off. I tried to sneak in a show between when I got home from school and she got home from work, but she always checked the TV to see if it was warm when she came in. Sometimes she was certain I had been watching when I hadn't, and sometimes she was certain I hadn't when I had. Usually I only watched *Speed Racer* and then turned it off, even though *Ultraman* came on right after.

"So, *Wild Kingdom* had mere cats on it?" I didn't tell Nine that *Wild Kingdom* scared me. I loved the animals, but I always got a little sick at the part where one animal chased and caught another, and then ate it while its eyes were still open.

"It's one word, meerkat, not mere cats," Nine said.

"Okay, meerkat. Try to say what it looks like."

She shifted her whole body to face me, although she kept looking out over the playground.

"Okay. You know a cat, right? Make it gray, with white from under its chin all the way down its stomach."

"Okay."

"Now stretch it out. It's like a gray cat with a white belly, but long and skinny."

I closed my eyes again. "Got it."

"Now make its legs short, like, like Mrs. Ellis's dog, and make the tail skinny and long, like a kangaroo's, but much smaller and skinnier…cat-size."

This was getting weird. "Okay."

"Now the head is different. First take off the ears. Then make the eyes big. And…and…"

"What?"

"Shut up! I'm trying to think."

There was a long pause. I tried to make the creature in my head move, but it didn't know where to go without a head of its own.

"Okay," she started again. "You know snakes? You know how their heads are all smooth and run straight into their bodies without, like, a real neck? Well, that's what the head's like, but the eyes are bigger and prettier than a snake's."

"Gross. Is it all shiny like a snake's head?"

"No, dummy. It's furry like the rest, just smooth like that. And they run around on all their legs, or they stand up on the back legs and balance with their tails. They're super-fast."

I liked the sound of that, but I couldn't stand the sight of them, these snake-cats.

I opened my eyes. "Okay, so what's the game?"

"Well," she said, "They're never alone. They stick together, I don't know, lots and lots of them all the time. They live in the desert, and go underground like rabbits, and play tag with each other and stuff. While they play, some of them stay on lookout. They stand up on their back legs, keeping an eye out for trouble. Then the ones who were on lookout play, and someone else watches. They are sooooo cool."

"Lookout sounds boring." I wondered how come Nine hadn't noticed that.

"But that's not all there is to it," she leaned forward, breathless. "When the lookout notices danger, she gives the signal, and they all stop playing and run together and stand up on their back legs, real real close, and the stranger-animal doesn't know what it's looking at, so it goes away. Then they relax and play some more. They're so smart."

Or the stranger-animal's really dumb, I thought. Why wouldn't the stranger-animal just grab one of the little snake-cats, chomp it in half, and scare the rest? Then I remembered how I felt seeing the snake-cat, and thought the stranger-animal wouldn't have to be so dumb.

"Okay," I admitted, "They sound kinda cool. So you're being the lookout snake-cat?"

"Meerkat!" She was through with explaining.

"So if you're the lookout, can me and Eight be the other ones?"

"You already are."

"Well, shouldn't we practice running together if someone comes? You aren't even standing on your back legs."

Nine didn't say anything. Finally, without changing where she was looking, she stood up and leaned against the center pole on the roundabout. "Okay," she said. "You and Eight be the others."

Eight sat in the center of the sandbox, legs apart. She leaned forward to sweep the sand together, looking like she was hugging the ground.

"Hey," I called. "We're going to play a game."

She looked over. Sweat stuck some of her hair to her cheeks. "I'm already playing a game."

"This is important," I said. "It's an in-between game. You can go back to playing your game after we play this one."

"What's in-between?"

"It's…it's…" I remembered the elevator bell. "It's an in case of emergency game. In case of emergency we play this game, in-between your other game."

"I don't want to." She went back to scooping sand.

"Get over here, or I'm going to come over there and pinch you." I wanted to play meerkat.

"Leave me alone," Eight said.

"Okay, you asked for it…" I tried to sound scary like my mother did when she said it. I jumped over the sandbox edge, grabbing the end of her bow just as she stood to get away. Her feet slid in the sand and she was down. I tried to grab a piece of her arm between my thumb and finger, but she was too skinny, so I went for her butt. I held but I didn't squeeze. She squirmed and laughed under me.

"Are you going to come play?"

"Yes, yes," she wheezed, kicking at where her pile of sand had been. "I'll come."

We brushed the sand off where it had stuck in our sweat. She looked like she might run again, so I took her hand and we walked back over to the roundabout.

"Okay," I said to Nine, "let's play."

She had been sorting it out while I collected Eight. "I'll make a noise that tells you what to do. If I do this—yip!—" she made a high sound, from the back of her throat through her nose, "that means pay attention. If I do this—yip-yip!—that means get ready. And if I do this—yip! yip! yip!—that means we all run together."

"Where?" This didn't sound so hot to me.

Nine frowned and looked around the playground. Finally she said, "Just follow me. Wherever I run, you run."

Eight said, "What if you're wrong?"

Nine ignored her. "Move away and act like you're playing."

Eight and I took off in opposite directions. She went over by the swings and started turning the seat around on its chains. When she let go, it spun and swung at the same time. I started digging pebbles out of the dirt with the toe of my shoe. Suddenly, Nine went "yip!" Eight and I turned to look at her. She stared off into the distance. After a couple of seconds, she went "yip! yip!" and I got ready to run, one foot ahead, one behind ready to push off. Finally, she went "yip! yip! yip!" and jumped off the roundabout, headed for the back fence. Eight let go of the swing, and I ran toward them, screaming, until we were all against the fence, facing out, scrunched sweaty arm to sweaty arm. We ran through it a couple more times. Once, Nine went "yip-yup-yap," and Eight and I ran but she didn't. She told us to pay closer attention. Then we went back to our other games.

Every day that summer, I had told myself I was going to get to the top of the monkey bars. But every day I found an excuse. Usually I just waited too late to try and the bars got too hot. They felt more slippery when they were hot, or maybe you just didn't want to hold onto them because they burned. So if I was going to do it, it was going to have to be in the morning, and this was the perfect morning: no one else around, Eight and Nine not bugging me, Madame not watching.

One day, while it rained, Madame took out a big picture book of wonders of the world, and turned the pages for us as we sat on the floor. We couldn't touch the pictures, but she told us the story of each place. My favorite was the Taj Mahal, a big white palace with an onion on top. Madame hadn't been there, but she said it had a sad story. Some king loved a princess, but she died before they could be married, so he built this palace to remember her. Madame said it was a Monument to Love. I didn't know what Monument meant, but it sounded big and important, almost as big and important as the way she said Love, and I knew right then I wanted someone to make a Monument to Love for me. I didn't want to die for it, though. I thought the sad part was that no one lived in the Monument to Love; it was so big and beautiful and empty.

The monkey bars reminded me of the Monument to Love. Once I had seen a house being built next door to Grandma's. First, they dug ditches all around, and then they put metal poles sticking up out of the ditches. I liked it best when it was all ditches and we could run around and jump across them into what would be the rooms of the house. The monkey bars looked like a tiny version of what the metal poles inside the Monument to Love would be like.

I started up. The first level was easy; I had done that a million times. The second was harder; there was no ground to stand on, just squares of air in the flat places. I stood on one bar, like a high-wire walker, and hooked one leg over the next highest bar and pulled myself up. There was always that second when you weren't leaning on the bar you were leaving, and not quite on the one you were going to, when you hung in the air and anything could happen—your sweaty hands could slide and you would go backwards, or a big wind could blow you sideways, or the foot that was still tippy-toe on the bar below could slip, and you would jerk into space, like your foot and the ground wanted to find each other, but couldn't reach. I could almost feel the ground rising up then. I loved it. You could lean on the air. Sometimes it felt like the air was pushing me up, not pulling me down, and I thought that was what flying would feel like.

I went over the bar, and sat on the second level, one hand on a bar that curved up and over to make the dome. Under the dome was a big long empty space, like the place the elevator was in, without the elevator. You could hang from the crossbars and swing your legs until you got tired. I wanted to sit on top of it. I had seen bigger kids stretch out over the top, then give a little hop and turn as they went up, so they landed on their behinds. When they were ready to come down, they just slid down one of the curves until their feet reached the flat bar, and then they could do whatever they wanted. But I was too small for that.

The air tasted different up there, like it was thinner and faster at the same time. I looked over my shoulder, and saw Nine still on the round-about, Eight building a clumsy house in the sandbox. I wiped my hands on my shorts, and grabbed the nearest curved bar. I put my feet under me and pulled up until I stood on the bar where I'd been sitting. I inched my feet along the bar until they were right at the place where the curved bar met the one I stood on.

I stretched my left hand forward, and it stopped, just short of the crossbar. I leaned my whole body on the curve, trying to put it in the center of me, so I wouldn't roll over one way or the other. Then I tried to stretch out my right hand, but it didn't reach as far. I could feel the ground almost begging me to look at it, but I kept my eyes on the crossbar. I needed magic, like Tinkerbell's. My left arm started to stretch and grow tired. I couldn't wait any longer. "Un, deux, trois," I whispered, and pushed off.

I watched my right hand grab the center bar, and pulled. I could feel my body trying to roll over, into the center, into the hole, so I wrapped my knees and ankles around the bar and pulled again. Suddenly I was lying on my chest on the top. I stopped to breathe and figure out my next move. The problem was that now I had to look down, and it looked very, very far away.

I pulled my eyes up to look at the apartment buildings and the trees. I had never been this high before, and everything looked closer. I pulled myself forward until my belly button was dead center on top of the dome, and then I slowly slid my bottom to where my belly button had been. I leaned forward a little bit, and grabbed hold of a bar at each side of me. I had done it! I was at the top! I wanted to yell at Eight and Nine, but for a minute I wanted to feel it all by myself. I was all sweaty and the air felt like river water flowing over the wet places. I could see over the fence and the bushes against the fence, and all the way to the clubhouse and the basketball court beyond that. I looked over at Madame's window. No one was there. She would not have been happy. Although she'd never told me not to do this, I knew.

Once I was breathing all right again, I yelled to Eight and Nine: "Hey, you guys, look at me!"

Eight looked up, and dropped the sand in her hands. "Wow!" she said. "How'd you do that? You better be careful!" I had impressed her again, which wasn't very hard to do.

Nine slowly swiveled her head around. Her mouth fell open, and she, too, glanced at the window. "That's great," she said, and I felt my smile stretch wider. "Just don't let Maman catch you up there."

"I already looked, I didn't see her."

Nine looked back at the entrance to the playground, and then back at me. She seemed to be wanting to do two things at once. Then she said, "How far can you see?"

"I can see everything! The basketball court, the clubhouse, the apartment building, everything except down the hill."

"Okay," she said, "I've been lookout all morning, and now I want to play on the monkey bars. So you be lookout for a while, since you can see everything. It's a very important job, and you're in the best place to do it now."

I never wanted to climb down. I was happy to sit up there all day and look at the world from up high. And now Nine was giving me a reason to do that. "Okay! I'm lookout! Did you hear that, Eight? Now you listen for me to warn you."

"Yes, okay." Eight made circles in the sand.

Nine caught me watching her climb. "Hey, you're supposed to be on lookout!"

"I am, I am," I looked back over the playground, where no one else had shown up.

Nine easily climbed up to the level just below me. She hooked her elbows over one bar, and her knees over the one in front of it, and hung her bottom in the air between. She looked like she was in a metal hammock.

"So," she said, "how'd you do it?"

"If you hadn't been so busy with lookout you would have seen."

"Don't look at me when you're talking to me. You can look out and talk at the same time. So, how'd you do it?"

I quickly explained about shimmying up and turning over. I still didn't want to look down at the ground between my legs, so I was glad to keep playing lookout. I also wasn't sure how I was going to get down.

I heard them before I saw them, laughing and whooping and yessing each other as they came up the steps on the far side of the playground. Nine heard them too.

"Who is it?" she demanded. I could see the first heads popping up from the steps.

"It's Carl and Fernando and three boys." Carl and Fernando were friends of Sara, the preacher's daughter who lived down the hill. I knew them a little bit from playing with her. They were real neighborhood kids, the kind who wouldn't be caught dead in a French school. They went to the public school, and were a little bit older. I liked Carl. His eyes were always laughing at something only he knew, like we were all in some play with lots of jokes. Fernando was his brother, taller and quieter. They looked like my grandma, buttery brown like caramel and toffee. Just seeing them made me happy.

Fernando saw me on top of the monkey bars, nudged Carl and pointed. Carl looked up and I let go with one hand to wave. He didn't wave back. Their friends looked up, too. Then one of them said something I couldn't hear, and the boys started laughing. I wondered what was so funny. One of the boys I didn't know said something else, and the boys looked serious for a minute, then started nodding. They left the sidewalk and started walking, not fast, but serious, across the grass to the entrance to our area. They weren't smiling. I later wondered if it would have been different if I hadn't kept waiting for Carl or Fernando to look at me again, but they didn't. They had their heads facing the opening in the fence. I glanced at Nine, who was still beside me, eyes closed, face up to the sun. "Yip!" I said. Her eyes opened.

"What?"

They were real close to the entrance now.

"Yip! Yip!" Eight looked up. They were at the entrance.

"Yip! Yip! Yip!" I screamed. The boys stopped for a second, looking surprised.

I don't know how I got down off the dome. Slid, grabbed, hung, dropped to my knees, Nine right behind me. Eight leapt out of the sandbox towards us as we came out of the middle of the monkey bars. The boys recovered, and started running at us. We wound up with our backs against the fence, where we had practiced, Nine and Eight on each side of me. The boys were right in front of us, the ones in back pushing the ones in front, and we were all screaming. I felt a hand on my stomach, getting under the elastic of my shorts, and then it touched me, there. I didn't know whose hand, or why, I just wanted it out. I pushed, and pushed, and it pulled back. Suddenly I heard Carl's voice in my ear. "Sorry," he whispered. Eight and Nine were still screaming, and the boys were laughing, and then they were done and running away.

The whole city shut up as I stood, trembling, trying to remember what had just happened. I still felt Carl's hot fingers on my skin, and his breath in my ear. Something inside me squirmed, the way it did when my mother came home angry from work, or Madame Parapluie called out a name, like just my being there meant it was my fault. I wanted to drop to my knees and bawl, but I didn't know why. I pictured the fire hydrants, open on hot days, when I'd tuck my dress into my panties and run through the hard spray to cool off. The feeling was like the hard spray threatening to push me off my feet and roll me around on the concrete ground. In my mind, I screwed a lid on the fire hydrant and stopped the water. The world stopped shimmering, and I could now look at Eight and Nine, who leaned against the fence, as if still trying to push themselves through it to the other side. Eight clutched her tummy, and Nine pulled down on the front hem of her dress. Suddenly they looked at each other across me and I heard sounds again as they started blubbering. Then Nine took off, Eight right behind her, hollering and crying and running. Were we going to hunt down the boys and get them back? But then I heard Eight's "Mamaaaan!" and knew.

"Wait!" I yelled, running after them. "Wait! We can't tell! We can't tell! Don't run, come back!"

But Eight's wail had been taken up by Nine, and now their "Mamaaaans" went back and forth between them like they were singing a round of "Frère Jacques."

I even tried French: "Attendez! Attendez! Ne disez rien!"

But they were too far ahead of me, and I didn't want to be in the playground by myself. I caught up with them in front of the elevator. The lobby felt swimming pool cool after the outside running. I tried one last time.

"You can't tell," I whispered quickly. "If you tell, we'll get in trouble. Nothing will happen to the boys, but we won't be able to go to the playground anymore." As soon as I said "playground," they started screaming again, Eight hiccupping between yelps. I put my hands over my ears in the elevator, and dutifully trooped behind them to their door. Madame had it open before they got there, and scooped her little "bébés" into her arms.

They took turns telling the whole thing in French, while I sulked just inside the door. When they got to the end, they pointed at me and said that I hadn't wanted to tell.

Madame took one look at me. "Ces nègres," she hissed.

I felt myself turning browner in front of her. She thought I didn't want to tell because the boys were black. I didn't want to tell because we were girls. I didn't even try to explain. I heard something about "no more playground" and "change clothes" and "lunch."

We spent the afternoon watching soap operas or napping on the sofa with Madame. I dreamt that the ribbons on Eight and Nine's dresses stretched and stretched until they were tied around the light in the middle of the ceiling, and to the legs of all the chairs at the table, and to the doorknob of the front door, criss-crossing back and forth like a crazy spider web I couldn't get through. I couldn't climb over or under them like the monkey bars because they were cloth and couldn't take my weight. They just stretched and gave and rolled me out onto the floor.

When my mother came to pick me up at the end of the day, Madame gave her an earful of something. I sat in the window and looked down on the monkey bars and tried to remember the feeling of being on top of them, but it was gone, too.

My mother muttered all the way home. I wanted to run into Carl and Fernando and give them each a good kick, with my mother standing there, but they were nowhere in sight. I wound up at home alone with the television set, my mother coming home for lunch, until Grandma could come up and look after me. I never told on Carl and Fernando, and when I saw them again, near the end of that summer, we pretended we didn't know each other.

Joanne Leedom-Ackerman

The Arc of My Mother's Life

JOANNE LEEDOM-ACKERMAN is a novelist, short story writer, and journalist whose works of fiction include *No Marble Angels* and *The Dark Path to the River*. She has published numerous stories, essays, and articles in books, magazines, and newspapers. She is the former international secretary of International PEN and served as chair of International PEN's Writers in Prison Committee and as president of PEN USA. A former reporter for the *Christian Science Monitor*, she has covered national and international issues and won awards for her writing. She has taught writing at New York University, City University of New York, Occidental College, and UCLA Extension.

The arc of my mother's life is reduced to a ninety-degree angle. She sits up in bed, leans back on her pillows, stretches forward, head in her hands. Occasionally she veers to the right, then falls upon her side, a wisp of gray hair and flesh diving into pillows. She has aged quickly these past months. Her skin is loose about her bones, yet taut on her cheeks, her fine jaw still proud; her teeth, large—"all the better to eat you with, my dear." I remember this refrain when I see her, remember her crowding in bed with me as a child, telling me stories under the bed covers. Now I have come to tell her stories.

I arrive from Los Angeles in late afternoon into the blue eggshell room with its partial view of Central Park. She waves her hand to me, beckoning me in. Her long pink fingernails remind me of the woman I know. Clarice is there painting her nails. Once a week Clarice imitates what she has seen manicurists do, dipping my mother's frail hands into a solution of cream and soap, then gently pushing back the cuticles, buffing each nail, lacquering coat after coat of Wellington Rose upon them. When

Clarice finishes, my mother examines her nails and smiles. Here is part of herself she recognizes: the elegant hands that set her apart from the other ranchers' wives. That's what she used to call herself and her friends in Austin, Texas, not that my father was a rancher. My mother wasn't a snob, just a transplant who never took.

There are two kinds of people: Texans and those who wish they were. My father sent her a red, white, and blue T-shirt with that slogan printed on it a few years back. She'd laughed as she unfolded the shirt, not at the slogan, but at my father who never allowed her her own point of view about Texas or him. She gave the T-shirt to Clarice. As far as I see, my mother spent her married life waiting to go home. Then, after twenty years of marriage, she went. Jeffrey, my brother, was starting college, and I was fourteen and still lived at home. We moved the summer after my ninth grade year. My mother packed our bags and took me to New York City, where she bought an apartment with the money she'd saved from her early career as an actress before she'd met my father. The apartment on the Upper West Side had two views of Central Park, one from the living room and this partial view from her bedroom, views that now sustain her as she watches the seasons change outside her window.

It wasn't until years later, when I was marrying Robert, that she tried to explain to me that year and why she'd left and why Daddy had not come with us or after us. My mother and father are still married—neither bothered, or perhaps wanted, to get divorced—but they haven't lived together for thirty years. At the time I saw the move only through my fourteen-year-old eyes, the catastrophe and the glory. I was pulled away from my friends, from secrets and clubs, but I was also endowed with glamour because I was moving to New York City. I aligned myself with the glamour and hid the trauma.

I drop my bag now by my mother's bed and hand her a bunch of lilacs I have searched for in half a dozen florist shops on the way here from the airport. Her eyes light when she sees her favorite flower.

"It must be spring," she says as she sniffs the thick purple blossoms. Their perfume fills the room. She holds the flowers to her face, then finally yields them to Clarice. Clarice is from Portugal and has helped my mother since she moved here. They have become more like sisters than employer and employee.

"Yes, spring," Clarice repeats. "And in the spring everything comes back to life." She sets the creams and polish on the side table, and with lilacs in hand lumbers out of the room. Clarice has added five pounds a year since we first met her so that now she is the size of a refrigerator. My mother, on the other hand, reminds me of a feather duster flung upon the pillows.

"So talk to me," she says in a deep, rasping voice as she gestures to the chair beside her. "Where's Emily?"

"I left her with Marjorie in Houston." Marjorie is my mother-in-law. "Marjorie was driving her up to Daddy's today. He'll keep her over the weekend."

My mother frowns. "By himself?"

"It will be good for both of them."

Mother shakes her head. "You call her every day to make sure."

"She'll be fine," I say, though I have my own anxieties that my father will leave my daughter sitting in the lobby of his office while he works, or will turn her over to his secretary who is a child herself. I worry that my father may fall and hurt himself, and Emily, who is only eight, will have to take care of him. Yet I couldn't bring Emily with me. I needed this time alone with my mother. I need a mother myself right now. And I didn't want Emily to see her favorite person in the world as this gaunt old woman. Too much has turned upside down in our lives these past months. I want her to be safe. One of us must be safe.

"Daddy was going to take her to the armadillo farm today." We both smile; every cousin, friend, and second cousin in the family has made their pilgrimage to the armadillo farm with my father.

"Jeffrey's coming over to see you tonight," Mother says.

"I was hoping he would." I haven't seen my brother in over a year. We've stayed in touch mostly through Mother, who tells us the stories of each other's lives. "How is he?"

She shrugs. "He thinks he invented musical comedy. I'm worried he has too much success." She starts to cough. I offer her water which she waves away. She reaches for a Kleenex and coughs violently into it.

When she looks up, her eyes are watery and defeated. "When I get better," she says, "I'm going to take you and Jeffrey to eat a big steak and lots of scallops and fresh bread and…" she thinks, "and lobster, then we'll come home and eat ham sandwiches and tuna fish sandwiches. You know what I've been doing?" She leans towards me as if telling a secret. "I've been watching cooking shows. I've become a voyeur of food. At five o'clock, we'll watch my favorite: Chef Louis. He's from New Orleans. Today he's making soft-shelled crabs. I love to listen to him talk: "darlin', monsieur, mademoiselle…" She slips into a smooth Cajun drawl, reminding me of her own days on the stage. "I spent my life trying to stay thin, and now all I can think about is the food I wish I had the appetite to eat. I want to grow as fat as Clarice." She sinks back into the pillows. "You know when I lie here, I can be anywhere I want in my mind. Yesterday I was in England with you and Jeffrey."

"What were we doing?"

"Well, you were Ophelia…gloriously mad on the stage of the Old Vic. You got a standing ovation. I was Hamlet's wretched mother."

"Was Jeffrey, Hamlet?"

She laughs. "Heavens no. Jeffrey could never play Hamlet. No, Jeffrey was faithfully in the front row leading the applause. After the performance, he persuaded the Royal Shakespeare Company to do his musical with a jazz ensemble. Then we all went out and ate dinner on the Thames, and Jeffrey called your father and told him he must quit passing legislation and give the citizens of Texas a break. He asked your father to join his summer drama camp for inner-city kids as a counselor in set design, but your father said he'd only come if he could teach directing, and he and Jeffrey started arguing…" Mother's voice rambles on quick and feverish.

"Mother…" I try to slow her down. I place my hand over hers. "You were very busy yesterday."

"No, Jeffrey was. Jeffrey was too busy. He's always too busy. But you…tell me about you. Did you get the part? I'm so glad you're going back to acting. You should never have stopped. I told Robert that time and again."

"Robert didn't stop me from acting. I wanted to be with the children. I couldn't do both well. You know that yourself."

"Well, I certainly couldn't, but I hoped time and life would be different for you. Now that Robert has left, maybe it will be."

She leans forward and suddenly is coughing again. I go around to the other side of the bed and climb up next to her. I wish I could pull the covers over our heads and tell stories. Instead I place my hand on her back and hold it steady...steady...steady. She nods, acknowledging the help. Her hand flashes out, trying to find something on her side table. I reach over her body, feel her thin breasts under her gown and hand her a glass of water. She brings it to her lips and slowly draws water and breath. I wish Robert were here. Whatever my husband's faults, he never flinched in the face of pain. And he loved and cared for my mother. But he has left me. I try not to let him fill my mind, impede my acts, my days, my sense of myself. I am here to get my bearings without him and move on with my life, and, if I can, to help my mother. I don't know where to tell my children their father went; I don't know what to tell strangers or myself. I want to ask my mother how she explained to me the rupture in my own life when she and my father split apart. I struggle to remember what she said. As I sit here cradling her, I realize I never have understood, for my mother could give me only her point of view, which was not the same as my own.

"I miss Robert," my mother says when she recovers. She reaches to the bedside table to refill her glass from a blue and white china pitcher. "He must be lost in his own hell right now."

"That, or he's orchestrated hell and is seeking funds for production."

My mother smiles and nods. We don't talk about her hell; she has never yielded much space to it in her ontology. It is not hell, but the ascent she has insisted upon. I yield her right of way.

"So did you get the part?" she asks again. "I still believe you are a fine actress." I recognize the mothering, recognize what I do for Emily and for Josh. I have come for this.

"I left before the call came. I think I'm afraid to start again and have rehearsals day and night with Emily still at home and disoriented and Josh away at college, and Robert gone."

"Robert has been gone in his way for years," she reminds me. "Josh is fine, and Emily's tough, much tougher than you were."

My mother has never shared my belief in gravity; it is only one of many options. I don't have her wingspan. I've approached cautiously reentering the acting world I left fifteen years ago when I was momentarily popular in a TV series. I've only auditioned for a part at a large community theater. I used my maiden name so no one would recognize me as the wife of Robert Powell. "I left your number as a forwarding number."

"Good. Then we shall expect the call."

With a flourish of dancing girls, tambourines, flags, and confetti, Jeffrey sweeps into our mother's bedroom just as the streetlights are clicking on all over the park. I wonder how he has managed to orchestrate his entrance so well. He doesn't really have an entourage, but that is the impression I always have when my older brother enters a room. Energy flows from him, gathers up the other energy in the room, and returns it all back to him. He flings both arms around me, lifting me from the ground. He is gigantic both in height and girth. He and Clarice could make bookends.

"Sam…Sam, I want you to move to New York. I've already found your apartment. It belonged to Cheryl Rogers. You remember her…played every theater on Broadway? It will inspire you just living there. Morgan will work you back into shape, and I'll save some part for you in "The Organdy Dress." We're opening in November. If Morgan says you're good enough, you can audition for a larger role. Emily can go to school here. I know the headmistresses of two schools. Maybe Josh can transfer to Columbia."

I look over at Mother to see if she knows about this scheme, but her head is back on the pillow, and her eyes are shut. On TV Chef Louis is setting out a platter of prawns. Mother was mistaken; he wasn't cooking soft-shelled crabs today. The crabs don't migrate until fall.

"I have everything here but family," Jeffrey goes on. "There's Mother of course. But you are my family. Mother says you're going back on stage. I could help you."

"Jeffrey, slow down." I remember him suddenly as an oversized boy arranging the neighborhood into clubs and teams and saving a spot for me. "I came to see Mother, not move to New York." I resist the pull into his orbit. If I have learned anything being married to Robert for twenty years, watching his world, trying to hold onto some world of my own, I have learned the price of such security is not cheap.

Jeffrey drags the end of the chaise over to Mother's bedside where I'm sitting. He's wearing khaki slacks, a yellow sweater, a green plaid bow tie. His bow tie is his signature. He peers into Mother's face to see if she's awake, then turns questioning to me. I wonder if she has fallen asleep or merely closed herself down to escape Jeffrey's energy. I motion that we should leave.

In the living room we sit opposite each other in wing chairs by the window, a chess table between us. The living room is large, sparsely decorated in English prints as if Mother meant, but never found the time, to finish decorating the room.

"What about Katherine?" I ask after his ex-wife. "Isn't she still your family?"

"It's not the same. We never had children. We've just known each other longer than anyone else in town and put up with each other."

"That sounds like a definition of family to me."

Jeffrey shakes his head. He begins moving the chess pieces on both sides of the table, playing himself. It is a habit of his I'd forgotten. "Robert and you were smart. You took the time to have children."

"I took the time," I correct him.

Jeffrey looks up. "You still haven't heard from him? Did you know Robert took the movie option on 'Burning Grass,' and now I can't sell it or retrieve it? Do you know anything about that? It's really got me held up."

"Jeffrey…" I protest.

"I'm sorry. I know it's hard. You must be getting this from everyone. But there are a lot of people hurt because of Robert."

"A lot of people have been helped by Robert too." I'm surprised how few people remember that Robert helped them. "Robert put his own money in 'Summer Blues' to get you started," I remind my brother.

"Yes, yes, but I did all the creative work, and he made his money back three times over. I can't owe him for that the rest of my life."

I watch Jeffrey move his black knight to capture his white bishop. I remember him playing chess endlessly at the game table in our living room at home, changing from chair to chair to see the board from the other side. It got to the point that no one in the family would play him. He wore us down; he wore me down first, then Mother, and finally Dad. He wouldn't yield a move and if he lost, he would insist that you play him again. Because of Jeffrey, I have understood Robert better. Because of Robert, I have come to have some sympathy for my brother. I turn and look out the window. "You never change," I say.

He looks up. "Is that a criticism?"

"An observation. Do you remember your twelfth grade science fair?"

He castles with his white king. "Which one was that?"

"The beginning of the end is how I remember." He moves out his black queen, then looks up for my explanation. "You postponed taking that science course until your senior year because you hated science, and you postponed your project until the night before because you didn't want to do it. The way I remember, your science fair disrupted our whole lives. Mother left Dad a few months later."

"Because of my science fair?" Jeffrey laughs. "Did Mother tell you that?"

"No. That's how I remember it. I still remember Mom and Dad arguing on the phone, and Mother coming into your room in her nightgown with wires and batteries, trying to help you connect some sort of generator, and both of you electrocuting yourselves. Dad flew in at midnight and stayed up all night helping you. Then he grounded you for two weeks for procrastinating."

"I remember being grounded. But why was that the beginning of the end? You've never said that before."

"Because everybody except Mother was so selfish. I was pouting because she wouldn't take me somewhere—I don't even remember where—because of your project. Dad was so involved in his work in the legislature, he was never home and got mad at everyone. You didn't want to do the project in the first place so you put it off till the last possible moment. Only Mother tried to help us all. She kept trying to find a way for each of us to get what we wanted. I have no idea what she wanted, except peace."

"She wanted to live in New York and go back on stage. And she went," Jeffrey reminds me.

"Yes. But not until all your science fairs were over, and you were in college. She never made it back on stage really, not in the way she'd left. You realize she'd starred in a major hit on Broadway when she was only twenty and was in six movies by twenty-three. Then she married Dad and moved to Texas."

"She could have kept acting. It was her choice," Jeffrey says.

"How many movie companies were in Texas back then? She did try once. Remember? She took the part because they were shooting outside Fort Worth, and she thought she could commute, only she was away all day and half the evenings. We all complained. Mom and Dad almost got divorced then."

Jeffrey adjusts his tie and shifts in his chair. I'm making him uncomfortable. "So what's your point? That I spoiled Mother's career?"

"I don't know my point. Sometimes I feel I'm living Mother's life, only a B-version of it, without her talent or guts."

"She prevailed in a way," Jeffrey says. "Look at us. We both followed her path, not Dad's. We didn't become lawyers or politicians. I could help you, Sam, if you'll let me."

I look out the window at the haze over the streetlights. The lights look as if they are breathing. Jeffrey's offer to arrange my life is as close to an unselfish act as I can remember from my brother. It's not entirely unselfish because he wants me here for his own reasons. A hole is opening for him with Mother passing, a hole I doubt he even allows himself to see. Instinctively he's stuffing me and my family into it. Yet he is also reaching out. I do the same. I take his white knight with the black bishop before he sees the move.

He looks up and smiles. "You should have told me you wanted to play."

A china bell rings from the other room. Mother is awake. She reaches out her hand to Jeffrey. She has brushed her hair and tied a pink silk ribbon around it like a schoolgirl's, with the bow on top of her head. She has put on lipstick and is smiling. "Sweetheart... Did I fall asleep on you?"

"Hi, beautiful." Jeffrey goes over and kisses her.

"I feel much better after that nap. I'm even hungry. Samantha, did you learn how to make soft-shelled crabs?"

"Chef Louis wasn't making crabs today. They don't migrate until September, I'm afraid."

"September? Oh my." She glances out the window as if searching for some sign of the season. "Well, we'll just have to wait. Perhaps I'll feel like eating them in September. For now, I'll settle for chicken soup and a little Jell-O. I asked Clarice to make you lamb chops and spinach and salad..."

"Shall I go help?" I offer.

"No...no, you just got here. Come, sit." She motions for me to sit in the chair beside her. "Did you get your call while I was asleep?"

"What call?" Jeffrey asks.

"From the theater. Samantha has tried out for *The Sound of Music.*"

"*The Sound of Music*? Who's producing that?" Jeffrey doesn't mean to sound condescending, but he can't imagine producing old plays in community theaters.

"What does it matter? Sam's on her way back. That is the point."

"I don't have a part yet," I say.

"Oh, but you will," Mother says. "You read for the Baroness? Maybe I'll come see you opening night."

"I've been trying to persuade Sam to move back to New York," Jeffrey says. "I found out Cheryl Rogers's apartment is suddenly vacant, and I could use Sam in 'The Organdy Dress.'" Jeffrey offers his plan for my life to Mother as though he's presenting her with a school report on which he expects to get an A, but when he finishes, she says only, "Well, that's interesting." I'm expecting to have to resist Mother as well as Jeffrey, but instead she says, "You should have your own family, Jeffrey. You're good at taking care of people. But Samantha has a rather more complicated situation. She'll have to decide what's best." She looks over at me. Before I can speak to what I think is best for my complicated situation, Mother reaches for the phone and puts it on her lap. "Let's call Emily."

Mother dials my father's number. My mother and father have lived separate lives for the last three decades, but they still talk to each other almost every day. After she says hello, she listens for a full minute while my father speaks. She offers an occasional "Hmm-mm-mm…yes…hmmm…well, I'll try that…" Finally she inserts, "Why don't you let me talk to Emily, then I'll let you talk to Samantha and Jeffrey."

Mother's head is leaning back on the pillows during the conversation, her eyes closed as if it takes all her energy just to listen to my father. She rallies when Emily comes on the phone. "Hello, darling." Her eyes open. "So how were the armadillos?…A baby…I've never seen a baby armadillo…I hope to see you soon. You take good care of your grandfather."

She hands the phone to me and again shuts her eyes. I speak to Emily and then to my father, who instructs me to make sure my mother is drinking lots of bottled water. My father has always ascribed life's maladies and its remedies to water. "I've never been sick a day for twenty years. I drink Spring Valley water and listen to the Lord," he tells me as though for the first time.

When Jeffrey hangs up, he repeats, "I drink Spring Valley water and listen to the Lord." We all laugh, taking comfort in this consistency. My mother also smiles from the pillows, her eyes still shut. I wonder if my father's formula would solve my own complicated situation. I wonder what idiosyncrasies of mine Joshua and Emily will laugh about and be bonded by.

No sooner have we hung up the phone than it rings. When Mother doesn't move to answer, Jeffrey picks up. "May I ask who's calling?" He covers the mouthpiece and mouths, "Santa Monica Theater Company."

He raises his bushy black eyebrows high on his balding head. I feel as if we are children in Mother's room, playing at being grown up, conspirators in the adult world. Perhaps that is why when I answer the phone, I'm not nervous. My plans don't really count; they are improvisation, make believe, and when the day is over, Jeffrey and I will be called in for supper and baths and bed, and our parents will sort out the real world for us and keep us safe.

A question is asked of me; I respond. "Yes. I see. I hadn't considered that, but if you think so. I'll be back on Wednesday. I'll call you then. Thank you."

Mother's eyes are open when I hang up, and she and Jeffrey wait. I can't help but smile. "They say I'm wrong for the Baroness." I pause. "They offered me the lead."

"Maria?" Mother lets out a little gasp and claps her hands.

"But they want me to come in to audition one more time with music and the leading man. I haven't sung on stage in years."

Jeffrey suddenly leaps to his feet. In his alto voice he booms, "Climb every mountain, ford every stream…" He motions for me to join him. I begin tentatively, a thin soprano, but I gain confidence and volume with Jeffrey's accompaniment. We sing a duet for the first time in years.

When I finally look over at Mother, tears are streaming down her face. Her face has turned pale, and she is struggling for breath. Jeffrey and I stop. I hurry to the other side of the bed to hold her steady, my hand firm on the small of her back.

"I…I…" she wheezes. "I was trying to sing with you." She holds my hand, her fingernails digging into my skin.

I talk to her quietly, hold her firmly. I breathe with her. I wish I could breathe for her. Jeffrey paces at the foot of the bed. He can barely look at her. "Why don't you go get Clarice," I suggest. He nods, grateful for the task.

By the time Jeffrey and Clarice return, Mother has regained her breath. I'm sitting up beside her with my arms around her. Her eyes are closed.

"I understand you're hungry," Clarice says.

"I want to have dinner with my children," she answers without opening her eyes. "I want to eat at the dining table. And I want to walk in, Clarice. Leave that wheelchair in the closet. I want to walk in on Jeffrey's arm."

I glance at my brother, who steps over to the bed now. "You can have both my arms," he says.

Clarice pulls out a blue robe from the closet and places it on the bed. "I'll just go warm up the soup. I made you some crème brûlé too," she tells Mother.

Mother waves acknowledgment, then she gestures for me to help her sit up. I fluff the bed covers and the pillows behind her as if I am fluffing and spreading her wings. She leans back.

"Now Samantha and Jeffrey..." Her eyes open. Her voice is quiet but strong. "I will not be morbid, but I may or may not see you together for a while, and I have a few things I want to tell you. Arnold, who's managed my finances for years, has drawn up my will. I have given half of what I have to charity and half divided between you. What you receive will be of no large consequence to either of you. For your parts, you have given me the best gift you could just being here together. I want you to continue to be there for each other. I also want you to watch over your father. My passing will strike him in a place he has long since covered over, but he will feel it. You must watch out for him."

"Mother, please..." Jeffrey protests. "You're not going anywhere but to dinner. I hate it when you talk this way."

She turns to me. "I don't know what will happen for you, Samantha. I assume you will want to stay in Los Angeles, not move to New York. That is where you have built your life. But wherever you are, you must find the man inside yourself and rely on yourself. And Jeffrey..." She extends a delicate, pink-tipped finger towards my brother, who is pacing by the windows. "You must grow comfortable with the woman inside you, listen to her and yield to her. That is what I want to say." She slips her thin legs out from under the covers and sits up uncertainly and then steadily on the edge of the bed. "And now let us all go in to dinner."

Jeffrey and I are silent for a moment. Jeffrey comes over to the bed. Handing Mother her robe, he repeats, "Yes, let us all go in to dinner."

I smile at the words, and Jeffrey smiles at me, for this is our mother's signature line, her ordering of our world. For Jeffrey and me in this moment, her words are a salve, or perhaps the recognition between us is the salve, the bond to the life, the conflict, the peace the two of us have shared, wrapped up in this woman who is our mother and in her words that have meaning to no one else in the same way.

I confirm, "Yes, let us all go in to dinner."

Sarah Grace McCandless

Tricks

When SARAH GRACE MCCANDLESS was four years old, she had very specific aspirations for what she wanted to be when she grew up: a Dallas Cowboy cheerleader or a bus driver. However, neither panned out so she became a writer. A native of the Midwest and graduate of Michigan State University, she spent eight years in Portland, Oregon, before moving to D.C. in 2004. She is the author of two novels—*Grosse Pointe Girl: Tales from a Suburban Adolescence* and *The Girl I Wanted to Be*, both published by Simon & Schuster. She also contributes to a variety of publications including *VENUS* and *Daily Candy*. Currently, she is at work on her third novel as well as a screenplay, while also making sure people know just how much she loves cupcakes and *Law and Order: SVU* via her blog, http://sarahdisgrace.blogspot.com.

I am watching the remains of a fire smoldering in the distance from my fourteenth floor balcony. I have been witnessing this story unfold for what seems like days, though in reality, I think everything was destroyed in a handful of minutes, before the trucks even reached the scene. Their approach from the south was rapid and focused, red and yellow sirens swirling to clear their path, but by the time they reached the location, there wasn't much left to salvage. What was once someone's home was now just plumes of thick smoke the color of coal, circling up like a genie from a bottle towards an otherwise perfectly blue sky. I wonder about the people who'd lived there before, what they would wish for the most now if that genie did appear, and then I realize that they, like the house, might not be left standing.

My roommate Miranda taps on the window that separates us and waves for me to come inside. I am reluctant to leave my post, as though things will change if I just remain vigilant, but the October air is turning frosty and I am not dressed appropriately for the shift in weather in my flip-flops, jeans, and thin cotton T-shirt. I join her in the living room, where she has her freshly polished toes propped up on our coffee table, strands of toilet paper woven across her feet to prevent any smudges.

"What do you think?" she asks, taking a brief pause from the gossip rag she's clutching.

"It looks like most of it is gone."

"No, Laurel, I meant about the color." She holds up one foot for evaluation.

"The color suits you well. And it matches with the merlot sitting next to you."

"Well, you know I do like to coordinate when I accessorize," she says, words not yet slurred. "Have a glass?"

"Too early," I tell her, fighting the urge to look out the window again.

"It's nearly six o'clock," she starts to argue, but then lets it trail off and disappear. Strands of her honey blonde hair escape from her messy ponytail and fall across her eyes as she flips the pages of the magazine again, but too quickly this time, animated and exaggerated like a cartoon.

I turn away from her, fidgeting with the picture frames on our bookshelf and wait for the next question. It comes more simply than I had anticipated.

"Have you heard from him?"

The photo in my hand shows Miranda and her boyfriend Paul in Paris last spring, the Eiffel Tower in the distance behind them like a prop. They're planning a return trip in a few months, and I'm convinced this is when he'll propose though Miranda just rolls her eyes at the suggestion.

"Laurel?"

"No." I set the frame back in its spot, next to an extended arm, self-portrait of me and Miranda on the Metro one day this summer, our hair frizzy from the D.C. humidity, the other commuters behind us blurs of shadows and light. "I hope there wasn't anyone in that house."

"I'm sure they survived."

"But they probably lost everything. It's not easy to start all over again." I meet her eyes for the first time since we started this discussion, and reveal my wishing wells.

"It's after six now," she says, heading toward the kitchen for another glass.

~

Eight days ago, I found the letter stuck between Stone Hot Pizza coupons and the Verizon bill. The familiar handwriting jumped from the envelope, my throat choked by the distinctively small, precise, evenly spaced letters. In the year or so we'd been dating, I had not seen Kevin send an actual letter to anyone—not even once. The only reason I even knew what his handwriting looked like was due to my family birthday cards that I'd forced him to co-sign in the hopes of making a good impression.

We collected our mail from the lobby of our apartment building and I held my breath in the elevator, watching the floors pass below me. I made the mistake of opening the letter just before I reached our doorway, and three hours later, that's exactly where Miranda found me when she returned from her work happy hour, smelling faintly of gin and cigarettes.

"What is it? Are you locked out again?" she had asked, twirling her keys on her left index finger. I reached towards her, offering the note for taking, tossing Kevin's latest pleas for forgiveness around in my mind on a spin cycle that wouldn't stop.

Her eyes scanned the page once, and then again.

"Oh Laurel," she said, sinking down next to me in the hallway. "This wasn't the first time this happened, was it?"

In my hands, I held my head, heavy as a bowling ball, afraid to look up and answer that question.

~

I met Kevin on Halloween at a work party. I was dressed as Britney Spears, pre-Federline days, and he showed up in drag as Britney as well, but really old school—plaid skirt, knee socks, blonde wig fashioned into two braids. He walked in with my cube mate Nick, who, like me, was an account executive for a small graphic design firm that mostly catered to nonprofits. Nick had opted for a Unabomber ensemble, which was remarkably similar to his approach to project management—decidedly simple and lazy.

"Kevin, this is Laurel. We work together." It was all he offered, as though there were no more details of me worthy to be shared. It was what I expected. I shifted my beer to shake Kevin's hand.

"Nice outfit," he said.

"Likewise," I had told him, "though I don't remember Britney having a five o'clock shadow."

"Oh, it was there—the magic of airbrushing, you know."

"Right," I had said. "Well, nice to meet you." I scanned the crowd for Miranda, who had decided to come decked out as part of Charlie's Angels with a few of our other friends.

"Are you on the lam?"

"Pardon me?" I had said, realizing that Nick had long since moved on.

"So quick, so abrupt. This town is so transitional. Everyone always has somewhere else to go." I noticed his eyes then, like two shiny copper pennies, gleaming and sincere.

"Hey, if you've got an inside line to more beer, I've got nothing but time," I had told him, handing over my empty bottle, chalking up my change of plans to a night where we were all told to pretend to be something we were not.

~

Here is what I discovered during the first months of our relationship. Kevin came from a family of professors and therefore, was a man of good intentions. He was raised with an older brother, also a teacher but of sixth grade science, and a sister who made her way selling upscale perfume at Nordstrom, which proved to be more lucrative than one might initially believe. He grew up just outside of Manhattan, close enough to take the train in under an hour to experience all the wealth and opportunity the city pledged, but at the end of day, he really didn't care if it delivered on that promise or not. Our birthdays were only twelve days apart, so I would be turning thirty this year just slightly ahead of him. Kevin was scholarly, literate, a good reader. He was taught manners—insisting ladies order first, holding the door open for them, and of course his pleases and thank yous.

He had his visible ticks—letting his laundry grow into monstrous piles, or his disdain for people who were habitually late. He made his way as a counselor at a private high school in the District, where students were challenged with what comes next in a world that had otherwise been laid out so perfectly before them—privileged D.C. families who were almost worse off than those living from paycheck to paycheck because they were so emotionally bankrupt. Kevin was obsessive about the details—what was it that these people really wanted, and how could he help uncover the means to get where they needed to be.

On paper, Kevin was a good guy, the kind my mother liked to call "marriage material." I tried not to get ahead of myself but secretly I'd started wondering if she was right, and this was exactly what I was thinking about a few months ago when it started.

We were standing in his kitchen after having closed down our local dive bar with a few friends. Now, of course, I remember more details—how Kevin had grown quiet toward the end of the night, how he had seemed bored and distracted as Nick and I got caught up on a tangent about work, how the waitress had begun bringing more rounds without us asking. The July humidity had made the air uncomfortable that night, but we had sat at an outside table, our skin sticky and restless.

By the time we got back to Kevin's place, I was a little drunk, but good drunk, playful drunk, and of course with that, I was also hungry. I rummaged through his cupboards, looking for something easy that would satisfy me for now—cereal, pretzels, or maybe if I was feeling really ambitious, a microwavable Thai noodle cup. But there wasn't much to choose from, and I think I said something along the lines of, "Slim pickings. When's the last time you went grocery shopping?"

When I turned around and felt his hand connect with my face, I thought it was an accident. But there was no denying the glare that followed, his eyes glazed from too many bourbons. My cheek throbbed with a stinging, burning rawness, and I was certain his palm had left an impression. I tried to swallow my shock and find a word, any word, but instead I remained silent. He stumbled to pour himself another drink, and that's when I first realized I'd been sharing my bed for nearly a year with a complete stranger.

⁓

I told no one.

I blamed the mark on my face on furniture, explaining to Miranda and Nick and my boss and the barista at Caribou that I had stood up too quickly and caught the side of a cabinet door. I blended with a sponge to cover the bruising. I listened to the mea culpas Kevin left on my phone, and read his emails full of promises that it would never happen again. I listened as he blamed the alcohol, and then as he recanted and blamed himself. And after a week, I agreed to meet him down by the Georgetown waterfront and sat with him on a bench as he cried. Sailboats and tour cruises drifted by while he insisted he was still the person I'd fallen in love with, the one I'd always known. And finally as the sun began to disappear, I took his hand and told him that I forgave him, because I wanted more than anything to believe that I could—that this was just a freak incident and not a spark from a much larger fire.

⁓

My Metro stop is Dupont Circle, and a few days a week when I emerge from the tunnels below, I see the same young man standing at the entrance. He looks like he's trying to seem more grown-up than he really is, wearing a black blazer over a worn white T-shirt and matching black pants that are in desperate need of a tailor. In his hands, he shuffles a deck of cards, trying to catch the eye of people passing by in the hopes of earning a few bucks by performing a trick or two that will charm and amaze them. Of course, most avoid his gaze—even me. But once I've crossed the street, I turn back and watch from a distance as the cards flutter, waiting for an audience. At a glance his hands seem quick and skilled, but I think if someone would actually take the time to stop and look closely, they would see what I see—that it was all just an illusion.

❧

The second time, we were at his apartment after dinner at our favorite Indian place. He began to insist that I had been flirting with the waiter, and when I told him he was crazy, that I had done no such thing, Kevin grabbed me by the arms, his grip tight, shaking me and then pushing me up against the wall. He demanded to know if I had given out my number, what other signals and flares I sent up to that waiter that night, my head making low staccato thuds with each accusation.

The third time, we were parked in his car on a side street near the Uptown with plans to see a movie and grab a bite after. When I mentioned that I would probably sleep at my own place tonight because I had an early meeting the next day, he wrapped his hands around my throat, searching my eyes for some clue to confirm his misguided suspicions. When he finally let go, I coughed my breath back into place, as the newest round of apologies were already making their way from his lips. Then he flipped again, smashing his fist through the driver's window, shattering something that had been built to sustain even the largest impacts.

After three, I stopped counting.

❧

I am trying to learn how to count in different ways. It was Miranda's idea to keep the calendar on our fridge, marking the days that have passed since my last contact with him.

"Old habits are hard to break," she says, adding another black X through the bunch. "Even the ones you know are really bad for you." The calendar features plants and floral bouquets, and this month's photo is a cluster of red and yellow marigolds.

"If I reach certain milestones, do I get a reward?" I ask, making a small attempt to smile.

"Sure, if you count staying alive a reward." She takes out the ingredients for our Sunday omelets, handing me a red pepper, a block of sharp cheddar cheese, and the carton of eggs. I crack the shells against the bowls, whisking the yolks together until they are smooth while she measures spoons of ground coffee into the filter.

"It wasn't always that way," I tell her once again, though I am not sure if I am trying to convince her or myself. "There was a time when he was a good person to love," but the more I say it, the less I remember when it was true. The coffee begins to brew, the aroma of vanilla nut cream filling up the kitchen I turn on the front burner and place the frying pan over the flame, thinking about when his hands still felt kind on my face. If I close my eyes, I can almost still feel him tracing my features as he would in the morning before we lifted ourselves from bed. His fingers ran a distinctive course—starting at my temple, running around my eyes to my nose, and then along my jawline. And I wonder now if he was just marking his territory.

Faye Moskowitz

Completo: A Triptych

Faye Moskowitz is an English professor at George Washington University and the author of three memoirs and a short story collection, and editor of *Her Face in the Mirror: Jewish Women on Mothers and Daughters.*

Italy, 1990

One

The first-class railroad compartment from Rome to Chiazzo seemed spacious enough when we gratefully stumbled into it, Jack and I, jet lagged, grimly schlepping the far too heavy bags we had bickered about even before we left the States. I suppose nowadays you'd call that disagreement an "issue." No matter how many times Jack offers it, the raincoat-doubling-as-bathrobe packing advice always depresses me, makes me realize that soon I'll be in unfamiliar territory without my "things." "The junk dealer's daughter," he calls me, and I am, collecting the past's cast-offs like a peddler with his burlap pack. Still, spacious or not, the moment the other couple entered our compartment, asking us in Italian if the two empty seats were free, I felt out of breath, felt the air in the room evaporate as if someone had placed a glass dome over us all.

He was a good ten years younger than we were then, fifty or so, grizzled hair edging up his temples, dressed in well-cut tweeds at home on his spare body and fine shoes that shoe like the backs of black beetles; she might still have been in her teens, a tulip of a woman, all creamy surface and beautiful proportion. That her companion delighted in her—I could say worshipped her—was clear even from the way his guiding hand trembled her shoulder, no translation needed. Small wonder I couldn't catch my breath. It seemed to me, a woman three times her age, that she was almost without flaw. Her exotically cut dress, skimming her supple body almost to her fragile ankles, was fashioned of a shimmering cotton sateen in shades of black and gray that dimpled in the sunlight as she arranged herself on the seat opposite him—so he could look at her, he said.

She leaned her head against the seat back and her black hair, barely glancing off her shoulders, swung into place, each filament in harmony with the others. I knew it was rude, but I couldn't help staring; even the cunning brocade box she carried as a handbag, scarcely larger than a pack of cigarettes, fascinated me. Here was a woman who traveled light, and I admit it: I was eaten alive by green-gall jealousy. It seemed to me, then, that in all my life, no man had ever looked at me the way her companion looked at her, not even my husband of forty years who was at that very moment sitting next to her trying to keep his eyes focused on his *Herald Tribune.*

The pair chattered away in Italian during the expectant bustle that accompanies a train's departure. Officious-looking uniformed men carrying clipboards strode up and down the platform, a whistle shrieked, great wheels lurched prematurely a few times, and we were off. For my part, I rummaged in my purse, checking for my passport one more time, feeling the reassuring bulk of my traveler's checks, all the while castigating myself for being so drawn into their drama. I'm always doing things like that, fantasizing about people I sit next to on the bus, constructing a life from the contents of her supermarket shopping cart for the woman checking out in front of me, wondering how others' lives compare to mine.

And then he spotted it: just under the shadow of the woman's seat, what I had noticed shortly before their arrival. So close it almost brushed the hem of her shift, lay a small dead mouse. I had considered warning them about it, but my lack of Italian and the self-sufficiency of their mutual absorption had put me off, tongue-tied me.

"It's impossible," he said in English, not to her but to me. "It's nothing," I said finally, his disappointment was so keen. "Just a little mouse, harmless now." He waved his hand at me impatiently. "That's not the point. They should have cleaned it up." There was no fixing the situation until he could rouse a conductor. If he sat next to her, the mouse would still be under the chair; if he exchanged places with her, she would have to look at it. He told the young woman—and I realized they must have met only recently—"I usually travel second class, but I wanted everything just right, it being a holiday and so many people traveling." As for me, I turned away from them, no longer able to bear his middle-aged anxiety, too empathetic with his irritable unrealistic desire for everything that affected them to be perfect.

Two

By the time we board the night train back to Rome, we have the traveling routine down pat. The train is already in the station when we arrive at ten p.m., and our compartment has been made up for sleeping with two facing seats below and two upper bunks. The conductor hands us pillows and blankets and a plastic bag containing two paper items: a "sheet" and a pillow cover.

At this point, Jack does his usual European train number; he leaves me and goes off to the terminal to forage for an English-language newspaper and bottled water. Once again I tell myself that normal people get to the station early enough to take care of that kind of provisioning before they board, but then what do they do for entertainment once they've been seated? Jack has to prove what an experienced and casual traveler he is, while I, the itinerant basket case, drag along enough old emotional baggage to challenge the very real stuff we're dragging. His anxiety is about locating the proper car and getting me and the bundles settled, while I'm afraid he'll wander off and get back too late, and we won't ever find each other again.

Now I've said I'm not the greatest traveler; as if I don't already have enough troubles away from what's familiar, I honestly believe I'm spatially challenged. In other words, I can't find my way out of the proverbial paper bag. When I finally decided to matriculate after the youngest of my four children entered kindergarten, I had a choice between two universities, each about ten minutes in different directions from my home in D.C. The family joke is that I chose George Washington because I already knew how to get there. Jack says I can only find my way to two places, the Giant Food Store and my school. He underestimates me. I can actually make it out to my daughter's house in the suburbs, too, though no matter how many times I do it, one moment of inattention and I'm hopelessly lost. Obviously, I'm no help as a navigator on motor trips; even if I could unfold a map in less time that it takes to pass the exit we're looking for, the drawings and symbols would make as much sense to me as do the words in the Italian newspaper someone has left behind in our compartment.

Now I curse myself for not having made a contingency plan. It's always possible to get separated in a strange place. I should have memorized the name and address of our next hotel. What sick dependency allowed me to travel without foreign currency? If I was so fearful of getting lost, why didn't I have a copy of our itinerary?

I force myself to stay in my seat; I remind myself this very situation has happened before and Jack always gets back in time. I rehearse fail-safes—American Express, the American Embassy—consider getting off the train so we'll at least be together when it leaves without us. Perhaps I should stay put and wait for Jack who will surely be on the next train to Rome when it arrives in the station at the other end. As well as I think I know him after so many years, I still can't imagine what he would do in my place...probably not panic, for one thing. Though the heat has not yet been turned on in our car, my palms are slick; my thighs grow moist under the fabric of my wash-and-wear slacks.

As if disorientation were not enough, there's my language shortfall to contend with. Jack has no problem with tourist speech in any foreign country. He's already hauled out what he thinks passes for Italian, but I'm too much of a snob to do that. My grad school French and German might allow me to decode a festschrift or two, but once in Europe, my tongue takes on the quality of a football, leathery and inflexible; my brain, in sympathy, turns to cold oatmeal in the brainpan.

I remember us driving through the French countryside one summer when the windshield of our rented car exploded, throwing piles of glass chunks into our laps. Jack pulled over to a narrow shoulder. Shaken, we decided to abandon our now air-conditioned auto, walk into the next town (pop. 510), find the police station, and explain our plight. Explain our plight! My brain started its familiar metamorphosis to mush, the football in my mouth cut off my wind. Jack said, "You will tell them what happened. *You're* the language expert."

So we trudged along the highway while Renaults and Peugeots whizzed by close enough to ruffle our clothes, and I searched the crannies of my memory for the French word for windshield. Sadly, most French critics discussing the Symbolist Movement, say, or the impact of Existentialism on American Literature find little use for auto parts. Finally I decided if I ever did know the word, it was gone now. I prayed for an English-speaking gendarme. Naturally, we were out of luck. The rosy-cheeked policeman in his ridiculous cap knew far less of my language than I knew of his. After a while, he shrugged his shoulders and turned his back on us. If he didn't see us, maybe we would go away.

Jack, by this time, had figured to the penny the cost of the French courses I had taken over the years, and was audibly computing the interest. I vowed to restrict my travel to English-speaking countries in the future, but at Jack's insistence I gave my French one last desperate try. "Monsieur," I said, temples throbbing, "The window of my auto is dead." That did it. In exasperation, the gendarme waved his foot-long ham sandwich at us (we had interrupted his lunch) and blurted out his entire stock of English: "The weather is fine. Where is the dentist?" With that, he took a long draught from his liter of mineral water, resumed munching, and we were dismissed.

If my useful French is barely there, my Italian is nonexistent. The first time I saw *spaghetti al burro* on a menu, I thought it contained donkey meat. I have to admit that even in my present state, the memory makes me smile. I smoke yet another cigarette, realize that getting off the train is not an option because I'd never be able to carry that entire luggage alone. Terrorists have bombed another train station, or so I gather from a photo in the Italian newspaper; that information doesn't help me, nor does the paperback I can't get into. On the platform, a vendor pushing a heavy cart laden with sandwiches and cold drinks raps on my window. The very idea of food turns the contents of my already churning stomach to butter. I sing to myself, an old calming device. I sing "The Raven" to the tune of "Humoresque." "ONCE uPON a MIDnight DREary..." I make it as far as "the dusty bust of Pallas" before I'm out of my seat; I've got to find Jack.

Meanwhile, someone has slid the outer door of our car shut. My heart is doing flip-flops in a chest as taut as a trampoline, and the door won't yield. When I figure out how to open it, I stand between the cars and lean out into the icy air, scouring the now nearly deserted platform for any figure who might be Jack. Suddenly I hear doors clang all through the train. Below me, a fellow in uniform, his authority buoyed by festoons of gold braid, shouts at me in Italian, "Shut the door, Signora." I can't believe this nightmare is finally happening; I keep looking for Jack.

I know all about European trains; you can set your watch by them, even in Italy, and according to the posted schedule we had read earlier, this train is not due to leave for at least seven more minutes. Now my fears are justified. No wonder I've been in such a state: obviously we have boarded the wrong train. Mr. Gold Braid slams the door shut in my face, but I wrestle I open once again. "Is this the train for Rome?" "Si, si." "But you're leaving too early." "Signora..." "Mi esposo!" The dialogue is as witty as an Italian opera. "Signora, shut the DOOR!" and I do and go back to my seat muttering, "If this is all a bad dream, why can't I wake up?" The train begins to rock slowly out of the station.

In a few moments, Jack, who has boarded somewhere down the line, slides open the compartment door. He has confronted the Italian lire, the Italian language, and the Italian rail system and stood them all down. Why shouldn't he be smiling? "I bought us some sandwiches," he says, "in case we get hungry later on." I'm so relieved to see him (and so ashamed of my panic), I don't say, don't ever do that to me again. Instead, I nod toward the bundle he carries and say, "Good idea; what kind did you get?"

Three

Our vacation in Italy is almost over, and we've made it onto the *vaporetto* to Venice, our final destination. A gusty wind, a frigid monotonous downpour, and rush hour combine to create a jam on our boat. Naturally, I am convinced it is overloaded and will sink to the bottom of the polluted Grand Canal, a mini-Titanic begging to happen, and I'm not sure Italians observe the convention of women and children first. Would-be passengers, intent on getting home for New Year's, refuse to heed the conductor's please and insist on wedging themselves into the *vaporetto*.

Meanwhile, still carrying our heavy bags now augmented by an assortment of souvenirs and gifts in plastic sacks, we are a formidable obstruction for anyone near us seeking to get on or off the boar. Not a person stumbles past us without a derogatory comment about the "*bagaglio*." Unaccountably I find myself boiling with rage, and all of my ire is directed against Jack. Forget that most of the luggage is mine. I want him to be as upset and embarrassed about the comments as I am. At this point, the baggage is a given; it is simply there and short of dumping it overboard, which I'm sure Jack would offer to do if I said anything, we're stuck with it. Of course, he has the right attitude; we will never see any of these people again, so what difference does their momentary disapproval make? The difference is it will take me all day to shake it off, while to him the grumbling is as of little consequence as a swarm of midges in summer.

The rain seems to have settled in for the long haul. Venice smells like a damp basement, and I'm so cold that even the concept that somewhere in the world people take central heat for granted is unimaginable to me. By the time we have wandered the streets and neared our pension, I have kissed my toes goodbye. Even Jack has stopped saying the winter equivalent of "It's not the heat; it's the humidity." He buries his head in his shoulders and soldiers on.

We're at the stage we reach in all our trips when we both wonder why we spent so much money to travel so far. Home seems so attractive, everyday life is a comfortable blessing. No decisions about where to eat, no prodding of conscience to leave a comfortable room for the Babel of crowded, cold, rainy streets. We miss the kids, our friends, our language, even the *Eye-Witness News* with its ubiquitous gurneys wheeling out the night's gunshot victims. But then a passageway, narrow as a constricted artery suddenly opens onto San Marco, that perennial wonder. Dazzled, we smile at one another, remembering why we came. We turn, turn in a circle to lights, shops, facades, statues, domes, towers, dissolving like sugar in the mist and the beating wings of a cloud of pigeons, rising, rising.

Now it's New Year's Eve and true to form I've been worrying for days that we will get nothing to eat if we don't make some arrangements in advance. Perhaps it's already too late, the eleventh hour, so to speak, when I'm convinced everything decent will be full anyway. Our reactions represent a perfect picture of our personality differences. The pessimist (me) is certain we are closed out. The optimist (Jack) believes that in all of Venice he will surely find some establishment that is waiting for our business.

So we talk and we talk and I play him like wily fisherman seeking to outsmart the old man of the sea. Don't push him too hard; he will resist out of sheer stubbornness. Don't show him how anxious you are; he will rebel in order to show how very cool in the face of all this *he* can be. Somehow I manage to walk the wire with some degree of balance for a change, because Jack does agree to make a reservation at a little restaurant near the Rialto, or rather, I, for once appreciating his uncertainty in the face of all those language stone walls, tell the lady at the other end of the phone, "*Due* reservations, eight o'clock, *otto*." When she asks our name, I'm simply not up to starting in with "Moskowitz," Discretion is the better part of valor. I give her the name of the hotel instead.

We take a nap then, both of us drowning in deep sleep, barely about to rouse ourselves until after seven o'clock. Then I do begin to nag, just a little, as Jack continues to lie in bed. "I may never get up," he says, burrowing further under the blankets. A surreptitious glance at my watch shows the hands tending none too slowly toward eight. Who knows where the restaurant really is or how long we might wander the labyrinthine streets before we find it?

Finally dressed, we head out of the pension, Jack determined not to be rushed, and I certain the restaurant will give up our places if we don't arrive in time. We loll along, looking in the windows of *trattorias* framed in strings of colored lights, reading San Silvestre menus, but making our way in the direction of the Rialto. Jack indicates that he hasn't reached a final decision and certainly implies that it's a buyer's market, that the choice of a place to eat, even at eight o'clock on New Year's Eve, is still his to make.

Meanwhile the narrow alleys teem with locals buying last-minute food from bins piled high with oranges, pineapples, apples, artichokes, fennel. Some carefully carry white cake boxes tied in gold ribbon, a gift perhaps for the hosts who will feed them dinner. Some amble with no apparent destination in mind in the way of those who have no concern about where their next meal is coming from. Others seem to be striding purposefully, probably to tables at gourmet restaurants they had reserved in July. Jack inquires at some of the more festive-looking spots where black-suited waiters ready themselves for the evening's onslaught of diners. The salutary effect of warm blasts of air, redolent with spices and the charred scent of grilling meats is snuffed out by the apologetic smile, the shoulder shrug, "*Completo, completo.*"

No surprise: by the time we arrive at our destination, the motherly-looking proprietress of the tiny restaurant waves us away with what has by now become a familiar litany. "*Completo*," she says, and seeing that we are Americans, "We are complete." I say patiently, "Reservation. Pensione Academia." "Oh," she replies, pointing to her watch, "*otto, otto.*" "What does she say?" Jack asks. "She's full," I tell him, savoring my bitter victory. For a change, what I've worried about has come true. "We got here too late," and I turn away from him, struggling not to look triumphant.

Then we have it, the blow-up of the trip, in the middle of jostling crowds of people, many of them like us, the hour growing late—without a place to eat on this holiday night. It would have taken a true Christian not to say I told you so, and despite the Annunciations and Assumptions and Ascensions I had assimilated in the days previous, I have not yet been nominated for sainthood. I allow myself a few caustic remarks before we hit the flash point. "Go back to the hotel," Jack says. "If you're going to be that way, take a taxi and go back. I'll find something myself."

And so, I push him, both palms flat against his chest, and I say, "Damn you, I don't want to go back to the hotel. I don't want to ruin the evening, either. I just want you to admit, for once, that maybe, just maybe, I was right and you were wrong." And having said that, I've been married long enough to know this is not the time to press an advantage; it's time for me to chill.

We set out silently in a wretched search for any place that is not *completo.* The hole-in-the-wall that we finally hit on is terribly overpriced, and though we try our best to salvage a bit of the evening, neither the flimsy paper hats nor the packets of tiny Styrofoam confetti balls can lift the cloud from any of us in the room, losers from all over the globe who have landed in a tourist trap because we hadn't the foresight to ensure our presence in a spot of our choice.

At midnight, Jack and I stand for a few moments in San Marco, the walks jammed with onlookers, the Piazza itself open to gangs of young men carrying firecrackers and small displays of fireworks. The explosions and bursts of color coming from unexpected places unnerve us both. We turn into one of the bewildering number of small passageways and head for our hotel. I can't remember a Michigan winter this cold. In a few moments we are hopelessly lost, emerging every now and then onto the Grand Canal, then hitting a dead-end that forces us into yet another spider web of deserted narrow streets. I think of the money we carry, how obvious it is that we are foreigners, how quickly we could be assaulted and pushed into the water that shines oily in the weak lamplight. "Got lost in Venice," the guidebooks urged. "Have an adventure!" Well, we were having an adventure, all right, but one we would just as soon have done without. When at last we see a sign that gives us some bearings, Jack admits that he has been frightened, too, and I find that admission a generous gift.

Back at the hotel, Jack wants to order a split of champagne with which to toast the new year. I thirst so mightily for a Coke with ice I would have traded my passport for it. While Jack negotiates with the front desk, I go to our room and in moments am under the covers, shivering, awaiting the resurrection of my toes.

In a little while Jack comes up with a small tray on which stands a large bottle of mineral water, two inches of honey-colored brandy in a snifter, and, miracle of miracles, my Coke with ice. I see he is as eager as I am to make it up—the blunders of the evening: the second-best dinner for which we paid far too much money, the angry words. In the end, it would be another story to laugh about when we got home. *Completo, completo.* And I think, what's a bad meal in a lifetime of breaking bread at one table?

I reach out my hand as he leans forward proffering the tray—a peace offering—and the heavy bottle of mineral water tips over, upsetting the Coke and brandy all over me, the floor, the blankets. I grab the water bottle and try to right the two glasses, but it's too late. A swallow of Coke remains, a drop of brandy.

Jack sits silently in a little slipper chair while I mop up with a bath towel. "It's not a big deal," I tell him. I'm talking about much more than spilled brandy. His disappointment kills me; I would give my soul to ease it. I love him so much at this moment, I can feel my heart clenching and unclenching like a fist with the weight of it. I think of the man in the railroad car from Rome, how much hope we invest in the small details while the flawed world makes a mockery of the perfection we seek.

Barbara Mujica

Dear Erik Estrada, I Love You

BARBARA MUJICA is an American novelist, short story writer and critic. Her latest novels are *Sister Teresa* (2007), based on the life of Saint Teresa of Avila, and *Frida* (2001) based on the life of Frida Kahlo. The latter was an international bestseller that was translated into seventeen languages. Barbara Mujica's other book-length fiction includes *The Deaths of Don Bernardo* (novel, 1990), *Sanchez across the Street* (stories, 1997), and *Far from My Mother's Home* (stories, 1999). She is a professor of Spanish at Georgetown University.

"Put it away, Toby," I said to my fourteen-year-old.

"Isn't he adorable?" she said, handing me the magazine. "I mean, he really is a hunk."

"Toby!" I said. "Please."

"Yeah, sure, Mom. But you've got to admit that he's, like, really cosmic. I mean like you sure never saw anything like that running around here."

The cover showed a picture of Erik Estrada. His smile was broad and friendly.

"Please, Toby," I said. "Just put it away. Don't leave your things lying around for other people to pick up."

The phone rang. The voice on the other end was medium pitched, not immediately distinguishable as masculine or feminine.

"It's for you, Tobe," I said to my daughter.

"Oh, thanks, Mom. I'll take it to my bedroom, okay?" I put down the receiver and picked up the magazine she had left lying on the sofa beside me. Erik Estrada was wearing blue jeans and a white shirt, open almost to his waist. His chest was massive and brown. A medallion of some sort dangled from a chain around his neck, but I couldn't tell exactly what it was. He was crouching, in a pose clearly designed to show off the curve of his muscular shoulders.

"He is a cute kid," I thought.

"Mom!" yelled Toby from the bedroom. "Jessica wants to know if I can go swimming."

"Fine," I said, putting down the magazine. "Go ahead. Only don't get back too late. You promised to wash the dog."

"Okay."

"And Toby," I said. "Please don't forget to put away this magazine."

I got up and went into the kitchen. The refrigerator needed cleaning and I had promised to bake some brownies for my son's Boy Scout troop meeting. There were some papers left to correct—spelling tests, I think—and they were lying in a neat little pile on my desk across from the sink. "I think I'll dust," I said to myself.

I got out the Lemon Pledge and the rags and went into Toby's room. She had already left for Jessica's. Her jeans were lying on the bed, one of her tennis shoes buried under them. The other shoe was nowhere to be seen. In her haste, she had knocked her teddy bear off the dresser. I stooped to pick it up and wondered why, at fourteen, people were always in such a hurry. On top of the stereo was the magazine. Erik Estrada was smiling at me.

I flipped through the pages until I found the article. It was an interview written by someone named Marisa Walsh. There was a picture of her and her subject sitting on a chaise lounge by the pool in Erik's Los Angeles home. She appeared to be about forty and was wearing a frilly white dress that showed off her California tan. Erik's head was thrown back and he was laughing.

"Imagine," I said to myself. "A woman that age running around interviewing teenybopper heroes!"

Erik at his home in the canyon, the caption read. What canyon? I wondered.

There were four other pictures on the page. One showed Erik in his CHiPs outfit, revving up a motorcycle. One showed him bare-chested, staring into the camera. A third showed him sprawling on the grass, and the last one, in the bottom right-hand corner, showed him dancing with a girl in a blue jumpsuit.

"I don't like her," I said to myself. "Her pants are too tight." It was a stupid thought. I tried to push it out of my mind.

"Mom! Are you reading my magazine?" Toby was standing in the doorway.

"No, of course not!" I snapped, throwing it onto the dresser. "What are you doing here? I thought you went swimming with Jessica."

"I forgot my sunglasses."

"What do you need your sunglasses for, if you're going to be in the water?"

"Oh, c'mon Mom, don't be silly. I need my sunglasses to get over there, and then to get home, and to stand around and fox out the guys. What do you think public pools are for, anyway?"

"Toby!"

"Okay, Mom. Bye, Mom. Enjoy the mag!"

My husband Sheldon got home around seven.

"Whew," he said. "It's hot out there."

"How'd it go at the office?"

"Okay, same as usual. Nothing special. Harrison wants to form a new corporation. Needs for me to do the paperwork. Should be good for a few thousand bucks. I have to go to court on the Bensky thing tomorrow. That woman your Aunt Ethel said she was going to send in, she came today. A little old thing, all shriveled up, but smart as a weasel. She wants me to draw up a will for her. She's got a little bundle. I wouldn't mind handling her estate."

Sheldon went into the bedroom. "Want a cold drink?" I called after him.

"Yeah, a lemonade or a Coke or something."

I heard him click on the television.

"You want to take in a movie?" I asked him after dinner.

"Nah," he said. "I'm too tired."

The next day I left for school early because I wanted to clean the gerbil cages before class. In the warm weather they begin to smell if you don't clean them every other day. By the time I got home the temperature was up to a hundred degrees and all I wanted to do was stretch out and sip a nice icy tea. I went into Toby's room and automatically reached for the magazine. I brought it into the living room and, beverage and magazine in hand, plopped down on the sofa. My kids wouldn't be back for a few hours yet. Toby had gone over to Jessica's to study for a history exam and Tommy had gone to his Scout meeting.

"What if the kids caught me looking at this trash?" I chuckled to myself. "Well, what the heck. I'm exhausted and I need something mindless to look at to help me unwind. After all, thirty-five kids and eight gerbils can do a person in."

There was a story about the increase in teenage pregnancies. I decided not to read it. I had heard enough about that already I turned pages until I found Marisa Walsh's interview with Erik Estrada.

"This is really dumb," I said to myself. "I'm not going to read this."

Actually, the article turned out to be more interesting than you might think. Not that it was brilliant reading or anything. I don't mean that. What I mean is, Erik Estrada didn't come over as bubble-brained as I expected. To tell you the truth, from the interview he seemed like a really nice, compassionate, intelligent young man. Not a genius, of course. Not at all. But there seemed to be a...well, a sweetness about him...Naturally, the whole thing was probably just public relations. Probably his agent was behind the whole thing...trying to build up his image or something like that, but, I have to say, the interview made him out to be a pretty nice guy. He told about how much he cared about the young kids who watch his program, that he thinks that by depicting a policeman in a positive light, he makes kids trust cops more. And he talked about the work he does with crippled children, how he goes to the hospitals and tries to lift their spirits. I mean, it must be a big thrill for those kids that a TV star goes to visit them. And, what else? Well, he talked a little bit about how hard it was for him to get started in acting, being from Spanish Harlem and everything, and that he thought that he was a kind of role model for minority youths because he had made a success of himself through hard work and determination. The interviewer asked him about his Latin background, and he said something about being basically an old-fashioned guy who liked the kind of woman who knew how to take care of her husband, but that at the same time, he had no use for these macho types who want to boss women around. He said he thought that bullies like that were basically weak people who cover up their insecurities with a lot of bravado. He—I mean Erik—is more sensitive and vulnerable, and that's what gives him his appeal.

Well, I mean, all I'm saying is that the guy's not a complete idiot.

The next night was Saturday. "How about a movie?" my husband suggested.

"No," I said. "I'm too tired to go out. How about if we just stay home and watch something dumb on television?"

"Whatever you want."

"Yeah, something really inane. I'm not in the mood to think. I'm not even in the mood to move." I got up and switched on *CHiPs.*

"Boy," said Sheldon. "This is really stupid."

"I know," I said. "It really is."

That night I dreamed I won a prize in some magazine contest: a date with Erik Estrada.

"I'm rather too old to be going out with someone as young as you," I said coyly, as we sipped champagne at the Beverly Hilton Hotel.

"Why," said Erik Estrada (in my dream), "you're not old at all. And besides, you're very pretty. Frankly, I prefer a more mature...how shall I say it?...a more sophisticated type of woman."

"You're very kind," I said, blushing.

"You're very lovely," he said softly.

A few days later, I composed a letter to Erik Estrada in my mind:

May 3, 1981

Dear Erik Estrada:

I am writing you this letter because you have taught me a very important lesson.

I am a fifth-grade teacher at highly progressive elementary school. I have always thought of myself as an intelligent and tolerant person, free of prejudices. Recently, however, I discovered in myself a prejudice that I didn't know I had. My daughter Toby brought home a magazine with your picture on the cover. She asked me to read an article about you, and I refused to do it, because I thought that all Hollywood movie and television people were vacuous and insensitive. I didn't want to waste my time reading about the likes of Erik Estrada. She insisted, however, and I did, finally, read the article.

Mr. Estrada, I feel so humbled. The article—an interview by a certain Marisa Walsh—revealed you to be a highly responsible young man, with a clear consciousness of your duty toward the public. It revealed that you understand that you are in a position to help form the attitudes of America's youth, and that you will try to provide youngsters with positive role models. I was also impressed by the work you do with invalid children.

So, Mr. Estrada, you see, even though I am a teacher, you taught something to me. You taught me that we all have preconceived notions that we have to examine and vanquish.

I am grateful to you, Mr. Estrada, for having taught me this lesson.

Very truly yours,

Mrs. Sheldon Silverstein

"Mom," Toby said to me, "what's the matter with you?"

"What do you mean? Nothing's the matter with me."

"You're standing there with a dishrag in your hand giggling to yourself. You going bananas on us or something, Mom?"

"You never did wash the dog, you know. And another thing. I want you to sit down and write a thank-you note to Aunt Ethel. She took the time to buy you that bathing suit. The least you could do is find the time to sit down and write her a letter."

"That's more like it!"

"Get going."

"By the way, Mom, I can't find my magazine. You know, the one with Erik Estrada's picture on the cover. Have you got it?"

"Of course not. What would I be doing with it?

"Well, I don't know. I thought you might have picked it up or something. I can't find it."

"Go write that letter."

When Toby went out to wash the dog, I pulled the magazine out of my dresser drawer. I must have just put it there by mistake. Anyway, I left it on her bed and went in to start the roast. I decided to make a pilaf to go with it, and got some onions out of the refrigerator and started to dice them. Then I peeled some carrots and chopped them up into little pieces and then, I don't know how—what with all the things I have on my mind—I caught myself thinking about Erik Estrada again.

"This is terrible," I said to myself. "I have to stop it."

But instead, I composed another mental letter to Erik Estrada:

May 3, 1981

Dear Mr. Estrada:

I am not your typical fan. I am not a teenager. In fact, I am quite a bit older than you. I am in my forties and am a schoolteacher with two children of my own.

I recently read in a magazine that you do a great deal of work with handicapped children. I want to express my profound admiration for you. If I can ever be of service to you in your endeavors, please do not hesitate to contact me.

Sincerely,

Clea Silverstein
4329 Hooverton Place
Twin Rivers, New Jersey

Before long, there would be a reply.

May 10, 1981

Dear Clea,

I appreciate your kind letter. It is clear that we share a common dedication to the welfare of children. Perhaps we could help one another. I have a few projects in mind that I would like to discuss with you. Next week I will be in New York. Maybe we could meet.

Best wishes,

Erik

Before you knew it, we would be at the Plaza sipping champagne.

"From your description of yourself," Erik would say, "I expected someone much older."

"I'm forty-two."

"Well, you're certainly a very young forty-two. You're a very lovely lady."

"Oh really, I…"

"I mean it, Clea. You're…you're quite…beautiful. Personally, I prefer a more mature…how shall I say it?…a more sophisticated woman."

"I'm…married. You know that."

"I know, Clea, but…"

"Yes?"

"It's just that you're so beautiful."

"Mom!" Tommy was tugging at my arm. "Hey, Mom. What's the matter with you? How come you're acting so weird lately? Toby says you're going through some change or something. How come you're staring out into space like some kind of a kook?"

"You want some milk?

"No, I don't want some milk. I want you to help me with my composition on prayer in public schools."

"It's a rotten idea."

"What?"

"Prayer in public schools. Although, considering what's going on in public schools, it wouldn't be a bad idea to pray for them."

"C'mon, Mom, don't be a smart aleck. Help me with this thing, would you?"

That night I dreamed about Erik Estrada again. I was attending a teachers' conference in California. Sheldon and the kids weren't with me. One afternoon I decided to ditch the conference and splurge. I would have lunch at the Beverly Hilton Hotel. I put on my best clothes and a fancy, wide-brimmed hat with a lot of white silk flowers on it, and walked into the restaurant. Erik was there with his agent. They couldn't help but notice me. I looked exquisite. I could see Erik lean over and whisper something. I knew he had noticed me. The maitre d' seated me and I ordered a champagne cocktail. Then I began to peruse the menu. After a while Erik stood up and came over to my table. "Do you mind if I join you?" he asked. "You caught my eye…I'm sorry…I don't mean to be too forward."

"Well," I said, "I don't know…"

"I'd be honored…"

"I guess it will be all right. Separate checks, though, okay?"

"I couldn't permit it."

"I'll have to insist."

"Well, if those are your conditions, I'll have to accept," he said, smiling as he sat down. "My name is Erik Estrada."

"My name is Clea Silverstein. I'm a teacher."

"I'm an actor."

"Oh? I rarely watch television."

"Of course. A woman like you…"

"What do you mean?"

"So intelligent…so lovely…"

"Really, Erik. I'm quite a bit older than you are, you know. I'm in my forties."

"You look much younger. You're so beautiful."

"Really, Erik. You can't mean that."

"But I do, Clea, I do. You're the kind of girl I…"

"Yes?"

"I could fall in love with."

"Erik, really!"

"Can you have dinner with me tonight, Clea? At my home..."

"At your home. You mean you want me to go to your house in the canyon?"

"Please, Clea...We're both adults. And I'm so...attracted to you..."

The next day, while I scrambled eggs for Toby and Tommy and Sheldon, I wrote Erik another letter.

May 4, 1981

Dear Erik,

The other day while I was cleaning my teenage daughter's room, I came across a magazine that featured an article about you. I was very impressed by what you said about macho men being shallow and insecure. It is amazing that a young man who is so successful and so attractive, who is himself a kind of symbol of rugged masculinity, should have such insight. I am preparing a study of male attitudes toward machismo, and would love to have the opportunity to interview you. We could meet at my home. It is quiet there during the day, ideal for work, because my children are at school, and my husband is at the office. Please let me know when you are coming so I can arrange for a substitute teacher to take my place at the elementary school where I teach.

I am looking forward to hearing from you.

Sincerely,

Clea Silverstein

Within a week, Erik would be knocking at the door. "I'm here for the interview," he would say. And then, "Oh, I didn't expect such an attractive woman. From your letter you sounded like...a scholar. I expected horned-rimmed glasses."

"I am a scholar. I mean, I'm a teacher."

"I wish I were your pupil!"

"Please come in, Mr. Estrada."

"Call me Erik."

"Call me Clea."

"Clea, you're such a lovely woman…"

"Please, Erik, this is a professional meeting."

"I know, Clea, but you're such a beauty. You're not like those shallow Hollywood blondes that are always pawing me. You're a real treasure. An intelligent, mature, sophisticated woman…the kind of woman I never get to meet. It's such a…a joy to meet a woman like you."

"Erik, I really think you have to understand that I'm not in a position to…"

"Clea, where love is concerned, there's no right or wrong!"

"Erick, please, don't come so close…"

"I can't resist, Clea. I can't…"

"Oh, Erick, please don't. Please…"

"Clea! For God's sake, what's the matter with you! You're burning the eggs!"

"I'm not burning the eggs, Sheldon. They're just a little brown around the edges is all!"

"You losing your marbles or something? Look at the bacon! You trying to burn down the house?"

"I'm sorry, Sheldon. My mind was on other things. I'll make you a new breakfast. Here give this to the dog."

Sheldon just stood there, looking as though he'd seen a flying alligator.

"Hurry up," he finally said. "I've got to be in court in less than an hour."

"If you're in such a rush," I said calmly, "make your own breakfast. I have some rather urgent business to take care of."

I handed him the spatula.

"Listen, Clea," Sheldon said, "I realize this is kind of a hard time for you. You're going through…a change."

"I am not! At forty-two? Are you nuts? I have years left before *that!*"

The kids were standing at the kitchen door.

"Hey, Mom," Toby said. "What gives? Isn't breakfast ready yet? I'm going to be late for school."

"Yeah, me too." Tommy was bouncing a volleyball on the linoleum.

"Listen, Sheldon," I said. "I'm afraid you'll just have to take care of this. I have to do something. There's a letter I have to write."

Sheldon blinked.

"You can handle it, honey," I said. I squeezed his hand. Then I went into the den and locked the door. I got some writing paper out of the drawer of the small utility desk that Sheldon sits at to pay the bills, and then I dug a pen out of the bottom drawer. I didn't have too much time. I had to be at work in another half hour myself. But I felt a great urgency about what I was about to do. I sat down at the desk and took a deep breath. Then I began to write:

Dear Erik Estrada…

Jessica Neely

Annunciation

JESSICA NEELY's stories have appeared in *The Best American Short Stories*, *American Fiction*, the *New England Review*, and other magazines.

It is complicated to teach among the Jesuits. Where else might an instructor, rushing across campus on an ordinary afternoon, be blessed by a colleague? And where else might an annual salary meeting become sidetracked by topics like ritual fasting? But the Jesuits are kind to Julian. They appreciate her teaching. They may well be the last academics who value teaching above publication. They rarely moralize, and when they do, their lectures are so well meaning, so full of fatherly intent, that even a lapsed Catholic like Julian can abide them. Several times in the past months since her separation from Malcolm, Julian has reflected that really, she is lucky to be at St. Loyola College, a school fostering brotherhood and charity. It can stop Julian cold, though, just when she's feeling closest to the priests, to realize the fundamental divide separating herself from them: faith, and not just devout faith, but the absolute, hyper-rational brand of Catholicism that seems nearer to Aristotle than Eckhard or the divine mysteries.

The Jesuits never have to cook. They share a community car. And because they do what they do for the love of God, they can't entirely sympathize with the daily concerns of a woman suddenly on her own: the logistics of her commute from San Francisco, frayed spark plugs, doubled rent payments, or crossing Market Street after dark. Malcolm, Julian's husband, got along brilliantly with the Jesuits, especially in his third year at St. Loyola when he converted to Catholicism. Besides, he published far more than anyone else in the department. It was fairly easy for Malcolm to find a visiting lectureship elsewhere when he and Julian separated. And sadly, this makes her all the more reluctant to mention what a tough time she's having.

It is Wednesday, two days before Christmas break, and the students are frenetic with holiday excitement. Instead of their usual class routine, Julian is taking her modern novel students to see a rerun of John Huston's *The Dead*, playing at the discount movie house in town. She has had them read all of *Dubliners* in preparation, and Friday they will have an essay due comparing the movie to the story. Julian prepares a little speech about this assignment as she makes her way to Father Coughlin's office—he left her a note saying please drop by—not that she needs to explain anything. What she needs is to stop being so defensive.

The door to Father's office is open. He is at his desk, reading some papers beneath a tensor lamp. The last rays of sun rush through the cathedral glass windows behind him, illuminating the wide copper pots on the floor which Maggie, Father's secretary, has filled with African violets. Since September, when Malcolm left the department, Julian's relationship with their chairman has been strained unless Maggie is on hand to mediate with cheerful banter. Julian can barely suppress the urge to remind Father Coughlin that she taught here first. She'd been at St. Loyola for a good two years before Malcolm was hired. *He* came there because of *her*. (And *she* was a Catholic long before *he* was.)

"Julian. How's everything?" Father caps his ballpoint pen and motions for her to sit down in the spindle-backed St. Loyola chair.

"I'm well, thanks. I'm taking my students to the movies. Huston's *The Dead* is playing at the revival house in town."

"What a fine idea." Father's smile is perfunctory. "I haven't seen it yet." He is a handsome, dignified man with precise manners and perfectly white hair which he keeps clipped very short; his heavy black glasses remind Julian of the ones her own father wore in the 1950s, plain and sturdy, but decorated at each hinge with a tiny silver diamond.

"You must be looking forward to the holiday break," Father says. "Going home to visit family?" He asks the question briskly, but Julian can tell from the deepening blue of his eyes that he's suddenly remembering conversations with Malcolm—which must be how he learned the details of her separation—about Julian's lack of a family to go home to. A blush of embarrassment reddens his face.

"I plan to stay here. I've got lots of work to catch up on, articles in various states of brainless catastrophe." Julian's own face is hot, she can feel, with a maddening flush of guilt.

"You know, Julian," he begins, looking at the desk blotter, "it might not be such a good idea to hole up all by yourself this season."

"This season?"

"During the vacation, I mean."

"I really ought to get a paper out one of these years, don't you think?"

"Of course, but there's no pressure on you, not now. Sometimes it's more important to attend to family matters." On the wall behind Father's desk hangs a dark wood crucifix and, to the right, a framed photograph of John F. Kennedy with a small American flag propped behind one corner. "And—Malcolm?" Father glances up. "Does he like Fresno?"

"I suppose," Julian says. "I haven't spoken with him in a couple of weeks."

Father Coughlin meets her eyes now, questioning. "I wish I understood," he says quietly. "Such a fine scholar. And the two of you as a couple. It seemed to us, all of your friends here in the department, that you were truly happy."

"We were mismatched soul mates, I guess." It's glib and handy, a ready-made line. She stands, her chair scraping awkwardly against the floor.

Father stands too. "I've penciled you in for a spring section of 'The International Short Story' if you want it. You're an excellent teacher, Julian. The students are always enthusiastic about you."

With a little wave Julian moves toward the door, but before she can make it out, Father calls, "Don't forget the Christmas party Friday evening."

"I won't."

"Come by around quarter of. You can walk over with Maggie."

Outside it is blowing now, a sharp cold wind that carries the scent of eucalyptus, still surprisingly pungent in December. Julian looks at this campus which has always felt so safe, at the mission cross marking the entrance to the south gate, and all around her the brown-burned pious hills of Santa Rosa. She pulls her coat close and heads for the student center.

Philip Sanderson is at his usual table, hunched over a notebook in the tacky student hangout. Mack's Super Subs is such an incongruous place to find Philip, an elegant man who occasionally wears an ascot.

"Julian, where have you *been* all week?" He gestures to the empty seat across the booth, as though he's been saving it for her. And maybe he has. He calls to the kid behind the counter, asks what Julian's having, and orders her sandwich with a couple of beers.

Philip Sanderson is this year's writer in residence. All the women students are in love with him. Most of the male instructors make jokes behind his back. Julian finds his salacious air both facetious and fascinating, because it is outweighed by his poetry, which is intricate and regularly honored. He is in his early fifties, from Newport, Rhode Island. That's all the data anyone has on him. But the rumor mills churn out various incendiary versions of what might draw a middle-aged man to a one-year post with minimum salary, a monastic dorm room, and the requirement that he be available at any hour to inspire students.

Julian doesn't care to think about Philip Sanderson's reasons. She likes being with him, despite whatever flaws he may have. For one thing he's fun; she's rarely met someone so bitingly cynical yet *so* earnest about everything he does. And no matter what Julian says, Philip listens, leaning across the table in complete absorption.

"I've got to read you something," he says. "How's this for the opening line of an autobiographical essay. Listen: 'I was born during that hell known as the Carter administration.'"

"Geez. Right out of his dad's mouth."

Philip nods rapidly. "Right. That's how he'll vote, too. I don't know what to write about this line. He's funny, but he hasn't the foggiest idea why."

Foggiest idea. Philip uses these old expressions, "the foggiest idea" or "a couple of wet pockets" or "wend my way." Julian glances at the student essay, heavily marked with extravagant notations and loopy red deletions; he's crossed out the whole last paragraph, and written "Drivel" in the margin. At his elbow, the discarded evidence of his supper, a Styrofoam soup bowl, cup, and three empty bottles. Philip lights himself a cigarette. What she's seen makes Julian feel embarrassed.

Her sandwich arrives, along with the cold beers, and Julian looks at her watch. "I shouldn't have ordered. I've got to go in a few minutes."

"Stay a little while."

"I'm taking my students to see *The Dead.*"

"Fabulous," he says, touching his thumb to his lip. "Do you think they'll get it?"

Julian frowns. "They're not that dense, Philip. You just have to cultivate an appreciation for—" She stops, but he's quick.

"The educator as gardener. Let me guess. You're Catholic?" He gives her a little smile, just the corners of his lips.

"Lapsed. Though somehow I'd prefer a different word, like *drifted.* It's less punitive."

"A drifted Catholic. A lovely drifted Catholic."

She can't help smiling back. "Maybe that's why I'm having trouble teaching the concept of epiphany."

"The soul of the thing revealed. Transformation of an everyday object. Put it in religious terms, the manifestation of God. They'll get that."

"But then I'll get a paper next week with something like: 'She felt the presence of God illuminating the soul of the shrimp salad sandwich on her table.'"

Philip laughs, leaning in. "I *like* you, Julian."

She looks away. "I can't believe Father Coughlin. He wants me to go to the Christmas party on Friday with Maggie—you know, his secretary—as my escort. How socially appropriate."

"Why appropriate?"

"Because Maggie's a widow."

"And where's your husband?" Philip pours beer into his Styrofoam cup.

"At the State University in Fresno. He used to teach here. We're separated." Of course, Philip probably knows this anyway. And Julian doesn't like pretending. But he must ask if they are to continue the conversation, and she knew this when she raised the topic. Julian doesn't want to be guilty of withholding anything.

Thankfully, Philip has the grace not to pursue. "Well, I need an escort too. Tell Maggie you promised to go with me."

Julian gathers her coat and bag, pulls out her wallet. She hasn't touched her sandwich or the beer. "Come to the department office at five if you want, and you can take Maggie and me."

The students are restless, bunched together in dark winter coats, smoking, shifting backpacks. When Julian crosses the yard to the department building, several call out greetings. There is a half moon in the sky, hazed by an icy ring; a few threads of cirrus clouds slide past, black against the frosty moonlight. Together Julian and the students make their way into town. It's only a fifteen-minute walk from the college gate to the theater, but it seems to her exceedingly long; she listens absently to bits of their conversation. "She said this was the director's last film?" one student tells another. "I wonder if he knew he was dying when he made it?"

The St. Loyola girls are ultra-feminine. They smell minty, of hair spray and spearmint gum, even the ones who proclaim themselves rebels. They wear black clothes and two-dollar dresses from the Salvation Army, but they also fasten gold chains around their necks from which dangle tiny crosses or mustard seeds encased in bubbles of glass. Many of her female students marry right out of college, settle down, and begin raising children. Julian tries to coax them toward a different vision of their futures, but it's difficult with Catholic girls. And what sort of example is she? She doesn't want to intrude. "Remember: you're molding souls as well as gray matter," Father Coughlin says every autumn at the kickoff faculty meeting. But lately, Julian has grown tired of worrying about the souls. That's not her job.

In the dark theater, she sits in an aisle seat and daydreams through the opening montage, the lace and the clocks and the photographs.

It was around the time Malcolm converted to Catholicism, fueled by his enormous enthusiasm, that he decided he was ready to become a father. He pressured her in a determined, methodical way to which she responded with disinterested curiosity: it felt to her so much like biological imperative, the mating rituals of any mammal. When this failed, he tried to reason with her. He was thirty-six, and Julian was thirty-one. They really shouldn't wait much longer. Julian searched her heart, trying to find the folded-up place where her maternal instinct must be lodged, like a life raft stored for safekeeping. If only she could find the inflation valve. But she could not. Despite all of Malcolm's amorous efforts, and his soulful questions late at night, Julian resolutely did not want to become pregnant. At times she almost wished she *couldn't* have a baby. At least that might take the pressure off.

Perhaps because of this tension—the old lingering belief that all good wives bore their husband's children with gladness and a thankful heart—whenever Julian thought of pregnancy, she pictured a fifteenth century Flemish Annunciation, part of the Merode Altarpiece she had studied years ago in art history. How placidly Mary sits in the painting, surrounded by the furnishings of her husband's home, the settee and table, the fireplace and fine red cloak, the washbasin and white linen towel, all the trappings of middle-class leisure. Mary listens obediently to the angel Gabriel, while the arrowlike body of the Christ child shoots toward her womb, rocketing toward the starburst of white between her legs.

A white dove. A heavenly beam of light. The miraculously formed body of the child. These were just metaphors, she had argued with Malcolm.

"Yes, for the Holy Spirit."

"No, for sex. What they disguise is an enormous disdain for women. Sex was unacceptable. A dove is less vulgar."

"Julian, my love, what are we talking about?" Malcolm had sat up, the sheet falling from his bare chest, and clasped his hands. He was a big man, and this supplicating pose made Julian feel guilty, but it wasn't possible to drop the argument.

"I've never accepted the idea of a virgin birth," she said. "It's pure violence, one step removed from Zeus raping Rhea. Shrouded in a cloudy *mist*? Come on."

"I don't want to argue iconography with you. I want to have sex."

"I'm not arguing iconography either, Malcolm. I'm telling you what I feel. Mary had no choice, did she? The common belief is that she was joyfully compliant *and* grateful. But I can't help thinking she must have felt just a little dazed, or...or terrified. Or how about intruded upon? I mean, what does the annunciation celebrate if not the abrogation of Mary's free will?"

Julian took Malcolm's hand. "You're Catholic now. I'm glad for you—that you feel such clarity. But it's not a church that welcomes me. See, I refuse the logic that because I'm female, my holiest duty is to give birth, or that I should be willing to make love to you without protection. I don't—" she had looked up at him, trying to make the distinction clear and knowing that she would hurt him nonetheless. "It isn't that I don't want your baby. I just don't want to be a mother. Not yet, anyway. Maybe never, Malcolm. I don't know."

Now, watching this movie into which she had planned to immerse herself, absorbing the texture of the images, Julian can't help superimposing on everything she sees Malcolm's broken expression, just as on that day, arguing with him, she could not stop picturing the fifteenth century Madonna, that frightening look of drugged ecstasy. Julian listens to the score, the harp and piano, and the tenor singing a cappella. On Angelica Huston's face, lit from above, the same rapt expression. She is transformed by the music, yes, but something else, something else.

On the evening of the holiday party, Julian brings a poinsettia plant to Maggie. She is a gay-hearted, energetic woman who introduced herself six years ago when they met as "a war bride turned secretary." She's been employed by the university for more than forty years.

"You're red and I'm green." Maggie sets the poinsettia carefully on her desk. In honor of the occasion, she has dressed in spruce-colored crepe, decorated with a battery-operated reindeer pin whose nose lights periodically. All day she's worn a Santa's cap on her head. "And with our haircuts, we're like a couple of Gibson Girls. It's five fifteen, Julian. We ought to go."

They cut through the priests' rose garden, behind the Chemistry building, and past the student commons. Heavy metal and funk blast through open dorm windows, clashing and ricocheting off the sides of the buildings. A cold gust of wind catches the tail of Maggie's cap and lifts it up. "Merry Christmas!" she calls out to a carload of students heading off for holiday break. They toot their horn and speed away. Julian's follow-up class on *The Dead* went extremely well, judging from the stack of essays handed in. She's heartened by their enthusiasm, despite one entitled "The Never-Ending Movie." Suddenly, Maggie slips her arm through Julian's. And the gesture is startling. It's been several months since Julian has touched anyone. Maggie's arm is warm; beneath the wool and the crepe, she gives off a comforting smell of floral cologne. Julian leaves her arm where it is and closes her eyes, feeling the first glimmerings of holiday spirit.

Inside, the mood of the faculty club is sedate. Over the sound system, a choral arrangement of "Caroling Caroling" rings out. Maggie pulls Julian over to the hors d'oeuvres table and begins sampling. Julian, who has never been to these Christmas parties without Malcolm, feels predictably yet palpably shy. The elation of her walk outside is fading, but with a cup or two of punch, perhaps she can revive it. Maggie hands her a cup and a small plate piled with food. "One of each." Then she zips around to visit with the handsome math professor, Bob Mariani, who's brought his adorable wife Diana and their two little girls.

Julian gulps her punch, then ladles a second cup. Sipping, she listens to disjointed bits of the surrounding conversation.

"So I'm taking out some of the seventeenth century lyrics and putting in Aphra Behn."

"... but they're complaining about not having pass-fail."

"You can't cut out Ben Jonson."

"I'm not cutting Jonson, I'm cutting Dryden."

"They're called angels on horseback, I think."

"... that if I divided my salary by the number of hours I spend ..."

Boughs of pine and red ribbons are tied to the exposed wood beams. There's a general peal of laughter as somebody puts on a record of dogs barking out "Jingle Bells." They had a code for moments like these; she would lean into Malcolm, press her cheek against his beard, and murmur, "Steer, please." Then he would do the talking. It felt wonderful with him, the enclosure of his strong arms; she was well loved in those moments, beloved, a priceless and delicate flower and gladly his. Or vice versa, for sometimes it was Malcolm who felt tired or reclusive in a crowd. Julian looks around now for Philip Sanderson, who is standing, she sees after a few nervous seconds, near the fireplace, talking with some people from the languages department.

"Merry Christmas, Julian."

She turns quickly, jostling her punch.

"I'm sorry." Father Coughlin sets his plate on the table. "I just wanted to wish you happy holidays. I hope the break will be restful for you." He is wearing his collar and a half-buttoned cardigan that reminds Julian of the one Mr. Rogers put on during each episode. Haven't they already had this conversation? The second cup of punch has begun to fuzz the deliberateness of the holly and pine boughs; the singing dogs give way to Nat King Cole, and, overhead, the dimmed lamps cast a buttery glow.

"Father," she says, "it isn't rest I'm looking for. I think, in fact, that what I really need is to break loose a little. Do you know, I don't believe I have ever committed a mortal sin."

Father Coughlin stares at her.

"Maybe that's true and maybe not. Maybe I've just lied to a priest and sinned this instant. What does it matter?"

"You've been working very hard."

"Oh, please be honest. You don't believe I work too hard. I know what you think, Father. I know."

"You can pray, Julian. You can take advantage of God's forgiveness."

She stares at him intently, reading his expression. "But why should I? I *don't* believe I've sinned. You never knew Malcolm, Father Coughlin. You admired him, you instructed him. I'm sure that was incredibly intimate, but you didn't—You didn't."

Father looks down; his eyelashes are elongated by the lower lens of his bifocals. Julian thinks of those endless months, the hours Malcolm spent in Father's office, reading, talking, preparing for his confirmation. How betrayed she'd felt by him, in a completely irrational way, like two kids vying for one parent's attention. This was precisely the sort of ritual she'd rejected, after all. Yet she still had her own desires, legitimate spiritual desires; why had she been pressured to accommodate them—to the terms of the high holy church? Or to pretend she had none at all?

"I felt close to Malcolm. It's true." Father meets her eyes now, and she can see that he's being perfectly open and that it's difficult. "He was like a son to me."

"But he was *my* husband. Do you know what sort of food he likes? Or music? He's an old Deadhead. And he smoked pot in college too, imagine that. And his parents kicked him out of the house one summer for sneaking girls into the basement and sleeping with them. His mother found a pair of girl's underwear behind the couch when she was vacuuming. A trivial thing, perhaps, but I'll bet you didn't know it."

Father puts his hand out, eyes closed. She is silent.

In a quiet, measured tone, he says, "You are still in love with your husband, Julian. Call him, talk with him. That's what he wants, he's told me. That's what he's waiting for. You can't escape—"

But she won't listen to this. Despite his intentions, despite the rightness of what he might be telling her. He has *talked* with Malcolm, about her. How dare he. This is a job! she wants to scream at him, not a family! Instead she does something worse. Her stomach gives a tight squeeze, the sour whiskey punch burns the back of her throat. And feeling magnified by the stares of every one of her colleagues, she walks directly to Philip Sanderson, takes his arm, and says, "I need to go. Come with me."

Year round, the Ariba Cantina is decorated with Christmas lights. If she squints hard, Julian can make the tiny colored bulbs explode into fragments. They're drinking stingers, a new drink he's introduced her to, and holding hands. With his thumb Philip massages her knuckles one by one. She hasn't felt so exuberant in months. The mariachi music, garlands of shimmering tinsel, the amber glow of cognac in her glass. Up at the bar two men are shooting liar's dice. Philip asks if she wants to play.

"You would lose," Julian says, "I'm too good."

"I don't believe you." He intertwines his fingers with hers. "Try something."

"Okay. Truth or a lie? I was not disappointed when you stood me up this afternoon."

"Lie. And I'm really sorry about that. I just couldn't. It felt too organized, too much a *spectacle*, if you know what I mean."

"Priests on the front porch with a shotgun? I know exactly what you mean."

He laughs. "But that image makes no sense to me whatsoever."

Julian laughs with him. He's right. It's nonsense.

Philip's arm goes around her shoulders. "Tell me more about yourself. Why did you argue with the reverend father?"

"The irreverent father. There's a line. I'm an unrepentant sinner, and I think I just lost my job by talking ever so slightly off color to a priest. I mentioned...panties."

Philip continues to look directly into her eyes. It's unceasing, this stare of his. She doesn't want to turn away. In the swirl of lights and brandy and crème de menthe, Julian thinks that she's never met anyone whose desire is so intensely focused on her. "Well?" he says. "Why did you mention panties?"

Julian slams back into her chair and sighs. "I had an abortion last summer. My husband left me. He told his priest—his priest who happens to be my boss, our boss, the Reverend Father. I felt betrayed, so I yelled at the priest. The end. Except, I can't break free of the old guilt grip."

"'Trip,' though I like 'grip' better. You had every right."

"Thank you."

"So he left you for that?"

"No." Julian shakes her head, like a child with a temper, she thinks; a little girl saying No I Won't. "Not just that. I wanted him to leave."

"A battle of wills."

Julian stares at the unlit candle on the table. It's an outdoor patio candle, encased in plastic netting. She remembers the overly bright light, like a searchlight, a spotlight positioned between her legs, and Malcom's weeping later, when she told him what she'd decided to do.

"Do you want the candle lit?" Philip leans closer. "Julian?"

"Yes. Whatever you want."

With effort, setting a twisted napkin aflame, Philip lights the candle. "I've a ruined marriage in my past as well," he says. "It's tragic how little we forgive."

"Each other?"

"Or ourselves."

Julian leans forward, but he turns away. "I'm very sorry, Phil. You've never mentioned it."

He shrugs. Then with a practiced gesture, he orders two more stingers from the waiter, "full glasses," and then he puts his palm beneath her chin and presses his mouth onto her mouth and his tongue deep into her mouth, in the kind of kiss that promises an all-encompassing good love, if she wants to have that with him later.

But when the kiss is over, Julian looks at her new drink blankly. Is Philip trying to get her drunker than she is? She steadies her gaze on the sputtering flame, takes a breath, and tries to gauge her sobriety. San Francisco is an hour away; she should have left for home long ago. What she needs is strong coffee—maybe they serve espresso. When she looks up at Philip, his eyes are brown and watery, soft. She can neither trust nor entirely distrust him. He lifts her fingers to his mouth and kisses them, one at a time, touching them gently.

She pulls her hand away. "Philip, I'd better have some coffee. It's late, and I'm really drunk."

"You don't have to go," he says with surprising dispassion.

But she does. And on the way home, driving with the window cracked wide for the bracing cold, she thinks of Malcolm, who would normally be driving, allowing her to doze on the passenger side, and then of the Flemish Virgin again, the dolly-round lilt of her head, the rapt expression. What would happen next, Julian wants to know, after the impregnation? Would she fall back into the soft pillows, or roughly against the stiff-backed settee, bruising her chin, skinning an elbow? Julian can't help but picture Mary falling so, or taste the cigarettes and brandy on Philip's tongue; how dramatically he had kissed her in the parking lot, up against the car, one hand behind her neck, his thigh between her legs, pushing himself against her in a strong but lonely gesture.

On Julian's machine are numerous messages from Malcolm: He's home from Fresno for the holidays, wants to invite her to his sister's house for Christmas Eve; they're going to a candlelight service at eight and then the party, presents. Please come. Another: this time a child's voice; it's his niece Eleanor. "Please come to the party, Aunt Julie." Muffled giggling, then she hangs up. And later, "If you decided to leave town, you could have told me. This is thoughtless."

Shaky, hung over, Julian cries in the shower, then spends the whole of Christmas Eve and Christmas day in bed.

On the twenty-seventh, she's working in the living room when Malcolm's key rattles in the door. There's a brief knock. And before Julian can sort through the concurrent sensations of familiarity, confusion, and alarm, he is standing in the door frame in jeans and a rain parka, removing his shoes. This routine domestic gesture offends her, as does the proprietary manner in which he sets a soggy Macy's bag filled with presents on the table, and announces he's putting on a kettle for tea.

"I need to pick up a bunch of papers and clothes," he calls from the kitchen.

Half of his things are still here. Julian removed most of his clothes from the bedroom closet, but she's been unable to do anything about the study except shut the door. Six months have passed since they lived together, four since Malcolm officially moved out. But during this time she has not taken over the one true study in this apartment. Instead, she has continued to occupy the Formica-topped artist's table in the living room, wedged between two windows filled with hanging plants. This is where Julian is sitting now, in sweatpants and an old lavender sweater, writing. Her hair is down against the back of her neck; she's wearing her favorite wool socks. Earlier she'd started a fire in the fireplace, put on chamber music. And right before Malcolm barged in, Julian had finally rallied the courage to pull out an old article. This is exactly how she's sitting, pen still in hand, when Malcolm brings in the tin breakfast tray with their teapot and two mugs.

He looks directly at her. She gets up and comes to sit opposite the couch. "You haven't taken off your coat," she tells him. He does so, hanging it on the back of the front door. He is wearing a tweed jacket, button-down Oxford shirt, and a knit tie that Julian's never seen. Must be a Christmas present. He sits heavily on the sofa, rests his face between his palms, and stares at her.

"This place is beginning to feel strange to me." He starts to cry, head bowed, hands pressed to his cheeks, covering his eyes.

"Malcolm, let me fix you a drink. Do you really want tea? I can at least put some whiskey in it."

"No." He looks up and scowls, irritated with himself for crying. He's begun letting his beard grow thicker, which makes him look younger and older at the same time, Julian thinks. Wilder, but less concerned with appearances, less precise. It is taxing every layer of her newly toughened soul to keep from moving to his side, putting her arm around his shoulders.

"I miss you," he says, his head still down. "You're my family. I don't want to live by myself."

"I'm not a stoic either." She makes a move for the tea, but that isn't what she wants. "Malcolm, why did you tell Father Coughlin about the abortion?"

He looks up, eyes red. He starts to speak but instead lets his hands fall with a slap against his thighs. "I'm sorry."

Julian sits back in her chair and exhales. "Everywhere I go you follow me. And then you expand and overwhelm until I'm just this secondary woman in the background. You can't simply teach at my university, you have to dazzle all the priests, and then convert to the religion. I used to feel I belonged here, Malcolm, spiritually too—but in my *own* private way. Not anymore. You publish your two books. You find your spiritual center. Then it's time to be fruitful and multiply. But meanwhile I'm still trying to write my occasional pieces. I don't think you ever considered how this—how a baby would affect me."

"I guess I assumed you'd love our child as much as you love me." Malcolm's voice catches. "That was selfish, I know. I assumed. I didn't think about you, what you needed or wanted. I'm so sorry, Julian. I *love* you."

Julian looks at his legs, the faded jeans she recognizes. She has always loved his tight wrestler's thighs and even now can't avoid the squeezing sensation of desire. Every sense of him is imprinted on her memory, the pale skin and abundance of hair above his knees, the inky scent of sweat.

They stare at one another until Julian shakes her head once and says, "I can't even tell you now, Malcolm, how I felt then. Or now. I want to, but it isn't safe. I'm afraid I'll lose ground." She stands. "Try to imagine things from my point of view. Why should *I* have to lose all of this—my marriage, or my belief, in whatever fractured state it exists—just to become an independent person? A good person, a wonderful woman, but just someone who doesn't want to have children. Can you empathize?"

"I don't know. I'll try, Julian."

In the ensuing fifteen or twenty minutes, Malcolm moves from the bedroom to his study, jangling hangers, banging the closet door, swearing because he forgot to bring a duffel and has to use plastic Hefty bags. Julian remains in the living room, waiting, listening to the squeaky drawers of his antique chiffonier, a gift from his parents. She knows how much he loved his study. He loved this apartment, his life here. The truth is, Julian thinks, Malcolm's desires are very ordinary. All of his plans, the methodical way he plotted his life from Berkeley to Loyola, from his first book on the 1890s to his second on Victorian love poetry, have been successful. And the domestic parallels: courtship, marriage, children; productivity and comfort in older age. Who can blame him for wanting what so many others want? He's sorry. He wants to change. But can a man change something so fundamental as his point of view? And why must Malcolm, having pulled on his heavy raincoat, walk to her chair, lean over Julian and kiss her goodbye, his luxuriant beard brushing the side of her face, smelling of salt and pipe tobacco, so that she feels the separation palpably once more?

He calls on New Year's Eve. He wants to take her out to dinner at Trader Vic's. Reservations were hard to get and they're early, six thirty, but first let's meet for a drink at Vesuvio, the old Beat poets' bar. It's something Malcolm has always wanted to do, have a drink at Vesuvio on New Year's Eve. Will she join him?

The sound of his voice causes Julian to panic. Before the phone rang, she'd been pondering the hours until midnight. She would clean up, then make herself a nice dinner—she'd bought all the ingredients for lemon chicken. Later, she'd work some more on her article. Julian is growing used to being alone. "I've been thinking," Malcolm says, "from your perspective. I need to talk to you some more." And then after a pause, "It's up to you."

Zipping up her black dress, fastening earrings, Julian wonders what will come of this night. So much remains to be said and understood; and she's skeptical, still guarding what she hasn't dared reveal. Will they sit across from one another in their elegant clothes, speechless, or will they talk—honestly? In the promise of this new year, can they really begin to forgive one another?

Why had it come to such an impossible choice? Julian stands with her palms flat against the bureau, pressing the cool wood. She thinks of the Flemish painting, and of Angelica Huston on the stairs, listening, stunned to silence. And Julian knows now that what these women are feeling is loss. Simple loss. Of the self, of the beloved, of the child. She feels it too, for the first time, but not according to the language of Malcolm's church, the edicts of mortal sin and confession. Her loss is entirely personal. And feeling at last a claim to this grief, Julian is nonetheless surprised by the fullness and force of her tears.

It is just before five. Julian walks up Sansome Street in her high heels. Opalescent clouds, in the last rays of sun, gleam between the towers of the Embarcadero Center. As she walks, a piece of paper flutters past, caught in the updraft from a hot air vent. It brushes her shoulder on its way to the pavement. In an instant there's another. And another. Julian sees that they are desk calendar pages. Another twirls down, and then fifty, a hundred pages are falling all around her, twirling gently to the ground. "Goodbye 2006!" Julian looks up as men and women toss armfuls of pages from their office windows. "On with the new!" cry a pair of jubilant men, and in reply more windows slide open in the buildings all around her. Hundreds of days cascading like confetti, like ticker tape, like snow, the ink of names and numbers falling. There is much celebration now as all around her, Julian hears the voices of people in the city calling out, crying out, and all the pages flung to earth.

Sarah Pleydell

from *"Lullaby"*

Sarah Pleydell is a writer, performer, and educator, and a British transplant who has lived in the D.C. area for the past twenty-some years. She is coauthor with Victoria Brown and Cynthia Matsakis of the *Dramatic Difference*, an award-winning educational book on arts integration; her fiction is currently represented by Rogers Coleridge and White in the UK. She most recently performed in *The Fate of a Cockroach* with Sanctuary Theater, and *The Body* at the Clarice Smith Center for the Performing Arts at the University of Maryland–College Park where she is a senior lecturer in university honors.

Marian

This is for you then, my dab of sunshine, my spot of happiness, my ounce of opprobrium—from a bathtub on the East Side of the city. It's summer. The fridge is buzzing; the weather's humid. I could drink the bath water. Neat. I'm steeping, neck deep, like an old tea bag, running my fingers down the tile. Looking...for what?—scratches in the varnish, claw marks. Initials. I'm vulnerable in here, and exposed—even with the dead bolt on the door. I shan't relax until I'm certain you're rising to the surface and slitting its skin. You're a swimmer: a water baby, your harelip barely brinking the water line, you smack bracelets into the foam, treading time with your fingerless fins. I'll hear your shuffle; I'll hear you shake out, dry off, then perch on the rim to listen, the only one left to me now, poised in the nick of time.

I remember him jogging up the staircase of our Blackheath flat in a duffle coat with a bunch of daffodils stuffed in one pocket. Picked or bought, you could never tell with Joe. He usually carried a paperback in his hip pocket, lifted from Blackwells or the Bod. Stealing books was his single delinquency. Or so I believed. Belief was easy then. Still, he made me feel comfortable, at home. Like an old pair of slippers.

Especially when he laughed. I still have a photograph of Joe that I took in Oxford. His face is drawn up into laughter; laughter he says he learnt listening to old men in Catalonia. His forearm leans horizontally over the arm of a garden chair; his fist is curled over like it's injured, and a large-faced watch is visible, caught in the act of slipping underneath his wrist. I come across this photo all the time; in a book, or loose in the front of an album. I can't seem to lose it, as if I'm meant to let it fade but never finally vanish.

It's Botswana or one of those smaller, more ambiguous places? I said.

He told me he had been offered a job as an economic consultant to a small southern African government—an ex-British protectorate in the heartland of South Africa, a country to which the British had graciously granted full independence in the '60s, he said, so it could go ahead and become totally dependent on South Africa. Up to that point, with nominal British backing, it was sustaining its autonomy quite well, but it's been downhill since. Economically and politically it's a Bantustan, a homeland, a holding pen for women, children, the aged, and the infirm—in effect anyone who isn't any good to the South African economy.

Sounds grim, I said.

An economic conundrum, my kind of place. Why don't you come along for the ride?

I told him I'd already got a teaching job lined up for September.

The job'll keep for another year. If not, you'll find another one. He could be breezy sometimes. Almost glib.

Not if the Labor government loses the election, I said.

You're worth more than politics, he replied.

Aren't we all Joe? Aren't we all?

And I persuaded myself it was just that, a matter of value. That there is a correlation between extremity and usefulness. That a calamity like apartheid would allow me to make a more significant contribution. And that the humdrum of South London life merely blurred things, edged effectiveness with ennui. Why bother with anger and action when it's easier to kick back and watch Wimbledon on the box? As Mtimkulu once said, you guys like your sanctity spelled out in black and white. Like graffiti.

And I believed then in commodities like usefulness, service, making a difference, paying one's dues. I had been raised that way.

Besides, he said, you can teach once you're there. One can always teach, he said, Period.

He must have known I would say yes, have sensed how I've always been one to leap at a challenge, to reach for cut glass.

He suggested we make a holiday of it, stop over wherever possible. The airlines are very flexible, he said. We'd be idiots not to.

Not to what? I asked.

Take advantage, he replied.

But I would still ask him—Do you remember, Joe, do you remember our first morning on Lake Malawi? How the horizon disappeared without a seam, and left water and sky like a pale sheet of writing paper? How the air felt full of tiny hairs? How the black torsos of children poked through holes in the surface of the lake, twisted into strange alphabets?

Joe was preoccupied. He always doubted the felicity of transportation. He was suspicious of passport control and customs officers; always prepared for that missing case on a plane.

As our 747 dipped its sails toward the runway at Jan Smuts Airport, I looked down through the window into the unblinking eyes of swimming pools. So many of them. So remarkably blue.

Jan Smuts Airport is ceiling with glass. We had two and a half hours to wait between flights. We tried napping on the black vinyl couches in the airport transit lounge, but the seats had no give in them, and even with our eyes closed it was impossible to ignore the policemen patrolling the perimeter. They were like boy scouts in their pressed navy shorts—oversized men in children's clothes—their buttocks stretched the cloth out until it shone.

Our flight to Lesotho was late. Mechanical problems. I never had confidence in that plane, even before we hit the turbulence. The hostess came back around and collected the cups of coffee that were starting to spill.

Because the radio was scratched out by the weather, the pilot missed the runway twice. Too windy, Joe said—I could see that for myself. The plane wobbled and swooned in upgusts of cold air. The airfield itself was sunk like a bucket between the hills of the Free State and the Drakensburg Mountains. And the wind had closed her palms, had refused to lower us—a miscellany of representatives and tourists—into that interior space.

When the plane did eventually land at Bloemfontein Airport, I disappeared and threw up in the Whites Ladies Only room.

They put us all on a brown rusty bus which ricocheted along tarmac roads—a straight shot, they said, to the border. Only we broke down twice. This was a landscape of sunflowers and high standing maize; the farms were set back from the road, white fenced and white washed. Every twenty miles or so we passed the settlements of farm workers and their families. These homes are constructed of corrugated iron, tarpaulin, and cardboard. The wind might have blown them away like our plane, except they were weighted down. With stones and cinder blocks.

The afternoon was overcast but still oppressive, dry, and hot. You could see flies on the children's faces. The media records that detail well.

Fifty kilometers from the border the bus broke down for the last time and it began to rain; the first rain for two months someone said.

It was dusk when we arrived at the border, and raining. The streets leading up to the border post were congested with cattle and chickens; figures cloaked in blankets were sidestepping the puddles the bus splashed through.

Behind us was the Orange Free State built of bare hills—huge, nippleless breasts rising into a broad, blue sky. The Boers experience them as mystical. They're dry and ugly at first. They grow on you. Ahead of us was a barbed wire border fence, gleaming like a hairpin. Beyond that this tiny country that called itself a kingdom.

Let's find a decent hotel and sleep this whole thing off, Joe said as he took the passport out of my hand and stuffed it into his wallet.

We agreed it was a dive. The linoleum was coming up at the corners of the bed, and the curtains, which were a livid orange, gaped and bunched around the window. Green and red disco lights from a bar across the road reflected in through the windows and onto the sheets and the mirror. Joe went out and picked up some beers.

Early in the morning there was a tapping on the door. Then a soft voice. A tiny voice—*Hee-llo Ba-bee, Hee-llo Ba-bee*. Joe was quick. Not tonight, thank you. I started giggling; I couldn't help it. Joe fell back into the center of the bed and covered his face with a pillow. For a while it continued, while we lay drumming our heels against the mattress, that low voice repeating itself, *HEE-LLo BABEE, Hee-llo Bab-ee* and then it left us alone.

The next day Joe and I kept retelling the story as we walked arm in arm through the city streets. Children we passed or crossed caught our laughter from us.

I hardly need tell you how much things changed, how estranged we later became, lying in bed, back to back, like two faucets turned off.

Hadn't we better let someone know we're alive? I said, as we swung into the foyer of the Holiday Inn. Joe muttered something about a contact person from the Ministry of Agriculture. Straight ahead of us, leaning up against the reception counter, was a stocky man in faded khaki shorts, one hand in his back shorts' pocket, the other flipping noisily through backdated issues of *Time* magazine. Bob Mcphee Joe said in a register that could have been surprise.

Bob Mcphee flipped around. *G'day* he snapped enunciating his Australian brogue. He wasn't to be confused with a South African. Not by a pair of Brits.

I hope you haven't been waiting long, I started to say but he cut me off; he was never one to stand on formalities. Of any kind. He proved that point much later, the night he brought me back to this same hotel, procured a key at this very same counter. It was all a crock as far as he was concerned. So what did Bob Mcphee stand for? I'm still not sure. I wonder if he knew either.

Mcphee—that was his preferred mode of address; he didn't care for Christian names—Mcphee whistled for two boys who scuffled up like a pair of shoes to load our stuff into the back of his Volvo.

As we were pulling out of the hotel I noticed all the other vehicles in the car park had South African licenses.

Gambling and prostitution, he said. They're both illegal in the Republic, so everyone lines up at the border on a Friday night for a helping of knickers and knockers, he said, a little knees up. You were lucky to miss the crowd.

Let me explain how the Anglo-Saxon complexion responds to an African sun; how the glare of that black globe sharpens shoulders, shears the flesh off collarbones until they cave in like cardboard and must be concealed under protective garments. Yet we insist on exposing our calves and forearms; we're stubborn. We roll our sleeves up to the elbow; wear shorts that swing at the knee. But it fails us, this skin, grows loose and extra to the bone, and wide blotches of raspberry and plum develop on its surface, the swaths of a summer pudding. A bathing suit exaggerates everything, and when a tan does eventually wear into tissue, it takes on the color of defeat.

I developed this opinion, sitting by Mcphee's swimming pool on a Sunday morning, pretending to read the *Johannesburg Post.* I didn't put it into words then. I let it wipe me out, wash me away until I was purely listening, listening to the metronome of tennis balls on asphalt, the din of young children in water.

Joe and Mcphee were picking up a set at the club. Mcphee said it was worth joining for the facilities, the tennis and the squash. They serve curry for Sunday lunch and show Disney films to the kids in the afternoon, he said.

He talked nonstop, fucking this and fucking that. Whatever came into his head. His place was a 1920s colonial with creepers climbing up one wall and fading rhododendron in front. His wife, he divulged, was a South African Colored from Natal. This didn't seem to get in the way of his pronouncement that until the blacks took their fingers out of their arse holes they'd never make anything of this crock of rock and shit.

She was quiet, insouciant, a large-boned woman who seemed to shrug her husband off like smoke. On the weekends, he said, she liked to sleep in while the maid entertained the children. All the relaxing by the pool exhausts her, he added and winked at me.

About eleven that morning she appeared on the patio, a long-legged, wide-angled woman in a striped sundress and dark glasses. Want some lemonade? she asked easing herself in the lounge chair next to mine.

Don't move, she said, I could hear the amusement in her voice. Eugenia'll fetch it.

There'll be a stream of women banging on your door as soon as you get your own place. They can be quite a nuisance.

I drew a blank. Domestic servants, she interjected. It's a fact of life around here. You'll get over your scruples when you realize that an entire family can live off one maid's salary. I'll help you interview if you like.

I told her thank you but I wouldn't be needing a maid.

We sat a while sipping drinks in the shade, the sky so blue it was almost turquoise: I picked up the book Joe had left spine up on the deck, *The Making of the English Working Class*, he'd "borrowed" it semi-permanently from the British Council Library.

It would be easy, I mused, to grow accustomed to service. Sitting in the morning sun, having someone bring you coffee on a tray.

Bob Mcphee worked for the Ministry of Agriculture, but his real passion was photography. That evening he asked if we wanted to see his collection. He was hoping, he said, he might get them published in Sydney or London. He knew the brass he said at *Life* magazine. No one buys black and white anymore. That's the fuck up!

We sat on the sofa nursing another round of South African beers while he passed around the contact sheets.

This was the real coup…my lucky day, he said. The rows of black and white stills followed a mass that looked like a striped centipede moving closer at first and then retreating into the background. Through a magnifying glass we could distinguish a group of young women smeared with white mud and wrapped in wads of cloth and bark. They were bound to one another with twine.

Female initiation, he said. My first time too! Mcphee enjoyed his own jokes.

Hands cover faces; heads are bowed. They think we'll steal their spirit, he explained. As soon as they saw the Land Rover they tried to skedaddle, he said. Had to use the telephoto. They don't all take themselves so seriously. Some'll even dance for you if you pay them enough.

Upstairs his kids kept running in and out of their bedrooms naked and laughing and bouncing Sotho phrases back and forth to the nanny. The African in their blood was more pronounced than the Caucasian, particularly in the girl whose features were plump and dewy like her mother's. They hadn't learnt Sotho from their mother though, they'd learnt it from the maid.

Mcphee took beautiful photographs, especially of women and children—though women and children are the majority of the population because all the able-bodied men migrate to South Africa for work. There were shots of a party of village children dancing in the mud with their hands joined over their heads pulling their sweaters up over their waists to expose their dusty genitals.

There was another series of a young woman wearing a floral print dress which she'd belted with a plaid blanket; a paler print kerchief covers her hair, knotted to one side. She's leaning up against a tessellated mud wall: at first she's so dark in her thought that the camera reads the detail in her clothing but shies away from her face, leaving it a blur; then gradually, in the second and third shots, her features come into focus and break into a wide smile. Her cheeks lift and blanch, her eyelids elongate and crease, the dark junctions between her teeth disappear. Suddenly like silver foil she's reflecting so much light, growing whiter the more available she's become to his lens.

Could I have a copy? I said.

Sure thing, he said. Come over after work tomorrow and I'll show you how to use the darkroom.

I already know, I said.
Bully for you!

We dipped into the fixer, dabbled with the developer. I was absorbing his technique, when he leaned over my shoulder and traced the edges of my prints with his fleshy sunburnt forefinger. Could have got that image a little sharper, he said, too softly, far too confidentially. I flinched. My vision is a very private possession; the only one I still could call inviolate. He dotted my nose with a lick of bromide, leaned his face into me while I averted mine and laughed. Light as torn ribbon.

His wife was in the garden outside; I could hear her chatting with Joe.

I framed one of his photos and gave it to my mother for Christmas. It's hanging in her living room. Over the mirror. I can't bring myself to do that; I am suspicious now of the urge to paper one's walls with pictures of the poor, suspicious even of the image of poverty. But then I felt differently; I was obsessed with breaking out, breaking through and touching the other side.

And why did I laugh? Why not spit that acid up into his eyes? Was I really such a fool? No. I needed Mcphee. Even then. I was afraid to snap the threads between us where we hung white paper turning black, images forming underwater.

Little did I know a whole story board was already in place, every frame cut and pasted, laid out in sequence, ahead of me. And last but not least your face, on the horizon, an inkling swinging into view. Calling my name.

Victoria Popdan

Time of the Season

VICTORIA POPDAN is a writer from Maryland. She graduated from Johns Hopkins with a master's in writing, and from the University of Maryland, Baltimore County, with a bachelor's in English. Working as an editor has sapped most of her creativity, but made her a fervid proponent of the serial comma.

It begins as a slight twinge. Subtle, undefined. It lingers between my shoulder blades—whispering fingers, drawing up gooseflesh beneath the surface of my skin—as the five o'clock Y-8 opens its vertical maw and beckons me to enter from the corner of University and Georgia.

The air on the bus is close—moist and clingy in clouds of recycled breath. It is crowded, but not yet overcrowded—not many practicing the fine art of urban surfing, still a few seats open. A light drizzle wanders listlessly from the sky, bathing the late afternoon in an inescapably dismal hue. The window is cool against my cheek. The bus stops and goes, stops and goes. Flecks of rain land, collect into rivulets, and run down the glass. People get on; people get off. I listen to the traffic as it travels around me—heavy tires on wet asphalt, the occasional horn, the thin *whoosh* of smaller cars as they pass the heavy frame of the bus. Advertisements line the interior walls—*Enjoy Coca-Cola*; the *Washington Post* Classifieds, where you can find a new car or a new love; pictures of faded children asking *Have You Seen Me Lately?*

With a hiss of air brakes, the Y-8 pulls up alongside the red and blue Metro Bus sign, just before Randolph Road crosses over Georgia Avenue. The tingling sensation grows legs, runs up the back of my neck on a thousand prickly feet. The periphery of my vision dims, blurs, dissolves into darkness. By the sign, a mob of people waits to board the already crowded bus. They file on, pay their fare, make their way down the aisle—a tall man, a stout woman, a teenaged girl in a red jacket pulling a reluctant toddler with a runny nose, a guy with a crusty baseball hat, a man in a dark suit. Up front, the door whisks closed behind them.

As the bus roars to life, taking off from the curb, the guy in the grungy baseball hat settles his weight into the red vinyl seat in front of me. He hums a tune under his breath—familiar, yet indistinct. I can almost, but not quite, identify it. Long, wavy auburn hair kicks out in wiry tufts from beneath a grayish hat, which might once have been blue. A coppery beard covers the sliver of cheek and jaw I can see. The tingling in the back of my neck is eradicated by a sudden and pervasive weight that ensconces my body. It soaks through my pores and down into every cell, consuming all sensation, leaving only numbness. All around me is open air, but a claustrophobic grayness surrounds me, weighs on my limbs as if they were stuffed with mounds of wet sand.

His hair, mottled with flecks of gold and copper, catches the muted light from the windows, contrasts against the lifeless gray sky and dirty hat, brushes the silver metal bar that crowns the back of the bus seat. Intermittent images flutter in and out of sight like a camera's shutter opening and closing. *Flash*: Water. *Flash*: Duct tape. *Flash*: Sunlight. *Flash*: Blonde hair. *Flash*: Closet.

...and the bus around me disappears.

A swimming pool. An enormous, indoor swimming pool. The heavy grayness is gone from the body I am in. Bright summer sun streams through the glass walls. The reek of chlorine stains the air, stings the eyes. Laughter of children bubbles up from the water. Feet splash in puddles; the lifeguard's shrill whistle blows. Warm, damp air clings to the skin. Bile rises, bitter, in the throat. Only a few feet away, three preteen girls splash and play in the shallow end of the pool. The humming tune echoes, familiar yet indistinct.

Two girls have brown hair; the smallest of the three has pale blonde hair and sits on the side of the pool, demurely dangling her feet into the water.

The edges of the vision flicker, suffuse with a deep crimson glow. A quick jabbing in the gut of this body radiates warmth, drips down into the groin where it collects into a pulsing mass. The hands itch.

Hiss. The bus brakes. My body rocks forward slightly as the bus lurches and rolls to a halt before Hewitt Avenue, where two people wait beneath the blue and red sign that stabs brightly into the dreary evening. *Swish, swish.* The doors open and close. The two, androgynous in their heavy winter clothing at this distance, do not pass by me; they take the narrow seat directly behind the driver.

Around me, the peoplescape has not changed—tall man, stout woman, man in suit—all are still here, now barely distinguishable from the bland crowd that was already part of the bus when I boarded. The runny-nosed toddler looks up at me with the wide brown eyes of a fawn. The teenaged girl he sits beside peers at me with the wary eyes of a hunted doe.

With the two pairs of inspecting, conflicting eyes still wet upon me, my attention ebbs, flows, eddies in the seat before me. A glance at the auburn hair, the soiled hat, and his afferent guilt settles over me as the driver reenters the busy flow of Georgia Avenue.

Through dark green leaves and bristly pine needles, metal and sturdy molded plastic converge in a vibrant rainbow of playground equipment. The air is sweet with honeysuckle. The body shifts against a rough tree trunk, crunches decaying foliage under the feet. Warm evening air laps at the skin I am in. A young girl pumps her plump legs in and out, pushing the swing higher and higher into the air.

A deep blush impinges the edges of the vision—a throbbing, blood-red background to white-hot sparks of excitement that glimmer and dance. The sparks are invigorating, infectious—they urge the body into motion.

Swinging, slow arcs traced through the air, punctuated by the flip of a blonde pigtail and a squeal at each end.

Itchy hands measure precise lengths of sticky, silver tape.

The empty swing glides listlessly in the dusk.

The Y-8 opens its doors to no one in front of the Gate of Heaven Cemetery, just before Georgia approaches Connecticut Avenue. Three passengers dislodge themselves from the background and descend the three steps into invisibility, into the night. Out of the night, uncounted impalpable riders board before the double doors snap shut.

The man with auburn hair shifts in his seat. I am suddenly afraid that he might feel me in his head, that he might turn around and look at me. Quickly, I drop my gaze to the floor. I trace formless shapes into the wet dirt with the toe of my shoe. The dull murmur of coalescing conversations makes it difficult to hear if the man in front of me is still moving. So I can look without looking, from the corner of my eye, I tilt my head up halfway and smile at the snotty-nosed kid. His big, brown-eyed fawn stare remains unchanged. The bus rumbles under me, inertia pressing me back as it takes off. I shrug a little and look away from the kid. My eyes return to the shaggy head in front of me, and his palpable guilt welcomes me back like an old friend, draws me in.

Hard, solid, gritty, cool; the body I am in leans with its back against a brick wall. All around, tall buildings reach up to the starless black sky. Vibrations beat through the wall, echo through the rib cage—steady, deep; persistent bass. A narrow black alley stretches out to the east; a green Dumpster stands between the body and a heavy, gray metal door to the west. The door bursts open, as if repelled by the flashing colored lights and busy electronica that comes spilling from behind it into the alley. Muscles clench. The heart falters, drums uncertainly, then speeds off uncontrollably, pumping icy blue fear through the veins.

Voices. The door swings closed, and there are voices. A thick, almost sweet burning wafts through the air.

"No, no. I can't!" says a voice like blown glass as it breaks into giggles, "I'm already so *wasted*!"

On the other side of the Dumpster, only two shadows spill over the wall opposite the door. Cold blue trepidation begins to subside, to thaw, to give way to the sharp, burning desire. Feet slide like whispers along the dry pavement. Itchy hands clutch a heavy brick.

Two teenaged girls are huddled around a fat joint, long blonde hair flipping in the cool wind. The arm swings—two birds with one brick; the messy one goes in the Dumpster, the limp one goes in the trunk.

My head snaps back as my body lurches forward when the bus stops at Georgia and Bel Pre Road. Scattered across the bus, heads pop up from their seats and people move into the aisle. They file out, heading toward the apartment buildings, where they will fill other seats and be living scenery for other people.

On the corner, more than a dozen people wait to board the Y-8. Seven of them follow a haggard-looking black woman like a row of mismatched ducklings—three Latina girls fighting over a Barbie doll that had seen better days, a tall black boy wearing his baseball cap sideways, a pair of sullen boys with angry red hair and a splash of freckles, and a little blonde girl with muddy shoes and a dirty face. They spread out over the empty seats across the aisle from me as the bus pulls away from the curb. One of the red-headed boys melts begrudgingly into the seat beside me. I smile down at him. He glances up at the black woman, who is otherwise occupied, looks back to me, and gives me the finger. Across the aisle, his freckled clone laughs.

Diagonally ahead of me, the blonde girl shares a seat with the tall black boy. Her seatmate took the window, which left her the aisle seat; which also left her sitting directly across the aisle from the humming, auburn-haired man. He's turned enough in his seat so that he nearly faces her, and watches her unabashedly. From his profile, I can see that the curved-in brim of his dirty hat is pulled low on his forehead, obscuring the upper half of his face. He could look at anything he liked, without being noticed.

The heavy grayness, the guilt, I'd felt emanating from him, has nearly disappeared. It's been replaced with something I cannot quite identify—hesitant but persistent, a vague green. Curiosity, perhaps. Deeper, somewhere underlying, I still sense that same feral anticipation building into desire. I can't see it on his face, but I can certainly feel it. His fingers work rapidly, balling his hands into fists and reopening, snatching at the air.

The bus takes a sharp right into Leisure World for its Clubhouse stop. Y-8 veterans grab handles, balance in the aisle, brace themselves for the turn while the unsuspecting passengers are tossed about like popcorn in a popper. The Latina girls topple like dominoes into the tired black woman. The little blonde girl floats like an air current across the aisle, nearly landing in the auburn-haired man's lap.

"Sorry," she says, without so much as looking up at him, and scrambles back to her seat.

He gives a pleasant little chuckle and says, "That's okay, not your fault," in a soft voice that is disturbingly normal. He resumes humming to himself. *It's the time…*

The Y-8 pulls up in front of the Clubhouse, waits. No one boards, no one leaves. The bus swings around the U-shaped driveway and heads back toward Georgia Ave. As the bus makes the right turn, back onto Georgia, I feel a tickling anticipation build up in the man. I watch the man watch the girl. When the tall black boy holds protectively onto her as the bus turns and its contents pitch left, the tickling fingers of anticipation bear down, scratching in anger.

I concentrate on the back of her little blonde head for a few moments, but feel nothing from her.

As the Y-8 approaches the Norbeck Road intersection, the interior lights flicker on, at once obliterating dark and mysterious areas left swaddled in shadows by the encroaching night. But the darkness has not left the man before me. Again, I peer into it.

Dim. Drawn curtains. Dank, musty. Old cigarette smoke. And it's cold. Piles of refuse—papers, articles of clothing, food in varying stages of decomposition—litter the floor, the chest of drawers, the narrow bed. From somewhere close by, the slow gyrating of an old Zombies song takes on a distinctly sinister tone. The mouth forms around the words, perverting the lyrics with a miscreant tongue, sings along with the now familiar tune, "Time of the Season."

The bright chrome of a metal bar bolted into the cinder-block wall above the bed stands out, glinting in the weak light—it is the only area in the room not drubbed into dullness by its surroundings.

Muted whimpers come from behind a thin plywood door next to the bed. Heavy guilt tries to surface in the body, but is quickly squelched by the competition of more powerful sensations.

The hand pulls the door open. A cramped room, a closet; dark, full. Packed in tightly, skin against skin, a dozen intermingling shades of blonde strewn across the occasional glint of metal, red welts, blood.

The hand reaches in, grasps a chain at random, pulls. At the other end is a thin, teenaged girl, naked but for the chains that bind her. She emerges hesitantly, but moves more quickly as he tugs at the leash. The hand reaches out to touch her, but withdraws. Instead, it fastens the chain to the bar above the bed and goes back to the closet.

It selects another chain, pulls out another, younger girl.

The bus stops in front of Olney Manor Park. The man with auburn hair still watches the blonde girl. His vague humming has taken on words. Softly, to himself, as if practicing, he asks the girl about her name and her daddy.

The black woman has gathered up her ward. The kids follow her down the aisle, out the door, into the night.

I concentrate on the man. Any hint of the guilt I sensed is gone. Now, there is only the anticipation, the desire. He rises from his seat, joins the motley line of ducklings, and follows them off of the bus. As he moves down the aisle and into the night, the softly sung word echoes in his wake:

Loving…

Joy Reges

from *"Stollen Kisses"*

JOY REGES has spent many years writing short stories and plays. She has worked as the Director of Visiting Christian Science Nursing Services in New York City, Minneapolis-St. Paul, and now in the metro Washington, D.C., area. When growing up, Reges worked as a stage assistant for her mother, a professional storyteller and puppeteer. Watching thousands of hours of master puppeteers, magicians, clowns, and storytellers perform made her want to become a writer. "Stollen Kisses" is her first novel. She lives with her husband, Wolf, who is a German native, and their two dogs, Cody and Pepper, in Reston, Virginia.

I didn't want to wake up in the morning, but I kept hearing a pounding. I rolled over and put the pillow over my head to try to muffle the sound, but it was insistent. I sat up in bed, trying to comprehend everything that Bjorn had told me. It all made sense to me and it didn't make sense. It made sense to my head, yet my heart didn't want to believe it. I wrapped my arms around my knees and rested my head on them. The pounding was coming from outside and it didn't stop. I looked up and saw the top of Echo's head walking past my bedroom window. My bedroom window was on the second floor. I couldn't believe that the tree house was up that high. I went to the window and looked out. Echo was right below. I opened the window and leaned out.

"What are you doing?" I asked. She looked up and smiled at me.

"I know that you won't be able to understand this. I have to go back to my origins. I need to blend with my spirit tree. I've been tarnished by the friendships that I've been keeping and I need to purge myself of their contaminating effects. I need to experience the tree itself to restore the flame that was burning inside of me."

"What are you talking about, Echo?" I looked around at all the materials she'd brought up to the tree house. "I don't understand what you're saying."

Echo gave me a pitying smile. "That doesn't surprise me. I'll say it more clearly. I moved into the tree house and I'm not coming down. The only way you can reach me is through this window or by a ladder."

I couldn't believe it. "You're going to stay up here in the tree house?"

Echo nodded. "Until I've been cleansed of all the inner poisons that have contaminated me."

"What are you going to do when you have to go to the bathroom?" I blurted out, as that was the only thing I could think of to say. I couldn't believe she was going to live in Margaret's tree. I wasn't sure if it was even legal for her to move in like that.

Echo tossed her hair aside. "Is that the most important thing you can ask?"

"How will you stay warm?" I didn't know what I'd do if she died outside our house on a cold night. I didn't know if I'd be liable.

"I'm building my cocoon up here so that I can stay out in any weather. Bjorn set things up for me before he left."

"Bjorn?" I felt a surge of anger and jealousy sweep over me.

Echo smiled happily and walked away to work on another part of the tree house. "Who else?"

My mother was not pleased.

"You should have called me sooner," she said, when I phoned her after I discovered that Echo was holding herself prisoner in our tree. "I can't leave right now, or else I'd fly out. You'll have to wait a few weeks until I can get there."

"I'm not sure what to do," I said, looking out at the tree. Echo was continuing to work on the tree house, but the only way we could reach her was to use a ladder to get up. "What if she freezes or starves to death out there?"

"Then maybe she'll come down," my mother said and hung up.

When I went into the bathroom to wash up, I looked in the mirror expecting to see the word CHUMP written across my forehead. I felt so stupid.

I couldn't believe that I'd been so blind. I went down to the kitchen and sat at the table. Margaret came in and sat opposite me.

"We have to do something," she said.

I sighed. "I know, Margaret. I'll get ready to have a baking lesson in a moment. Just let me rest here for a second. I need to think."

Margaret frowned. "No, that's not what I was saying. We need to do something with Jessie. She needs to come back here."

I stared at her. "But Margaret, she is here. She's upstairs."

Margaret patted the table. "Here. She needs to come back here. She needs to come watch us bake."

I sighed. I didn't know what to do. It seemed insane of me to be trying to take care of Margaret and Jessie without Bjorn. It looked like I'd made a mess of everything. Echo was living in the tree outside, Bjorn was off to the Caribbean, Margaret wanted Jessie to come downstairs and bake, and where was I? What did I want in all of this since it wasn't going to be Bjorn?

I looked at Margaret. "Margaret, I want a bakery."

Margaret nodded. "So did Papa. But he never got it."

I felt a surge of strength inside of me. Having a bakery might not be much, it might not be fascinating or alluring or even interesting, but it would taste good and I wanted to do it. I decided that I was going to bake Bjorn right out of my life or at least my heart. "I don't know how, Margaret, but someway, I will get my bakery."

"Will it be in Linden Hills?" Margaret asked. "That's where Papa wanted his bakery."

I nodded. "I know, but I don't even know where Linden Hills is. Let's start with a bakery right here. Can you teach me?"

Margaret looked at me seriously. "It depends. Sometimes you're not always a good student."

I paused. I wanted this bakery, wherever it would end up. "I want to learn."

Margaret nodded. "Then I'll teach you."

Since we had walked Jessie down the stairs on New Year's Eve, she wanted to go down every day. It was funny, after Bjorn left, Jessie started to do better. Bjorn had arranged for a physical therapist to come and work with Jessie. We all would lie on the floor and do the exercises with Jessie, except for Margaret. She'd sit in a chair, primly dressed and she'd cheer us on. The therapist showed us how to get Jessie down the stairs. Once she had her first taste of freedom, she didn't seem to want to turn back.

One morning, after we had walked Jessie down the stairs, I had Kateesha, Margaret, and Jessie all sit at the kitchen table which was loaded with a number of baked goods that I'd made. I put out paper plates in front of them.

"Are we going to have lunch first?" Kateesha asked.

I shook my head. "No, I need you guys to be my taste-testers. I need to make up a menu. I need you to be hungry so that you can try these. Here are a few things that I've been making with Margaret's help. I want you to taste them and tell me which one you like the best. Then it will go on the menu."

Jessie mumbled something to Margaret.

"She said that she's not sure she'll like everything," Margaret said.

"I understand. That's what you're supposed to do. Let me know if you like it and why and if you don't like it and why."

I pushed a strawberry flan in front of them. "Here's the first one. It can be made with apricots, peaches, apples, gooseberries, or cherries."

I cut a small piece for each of them. Jessie scooped hers up with a spoon and tried a large mouthful. She shook her head.

Kateesha took a bite and thought for a moment.

"I think I like this," she said.

Margaret carefully tasted the pastry, the fruit, and the custard filling. "Not quite Papa's," she said, "but good."

"Two votes fruit flan," I said and marked it down.

I brought over another cake. "This is a hazelnut ring," I said, carefully cutting small slices for each. "Let me know what you think. Then I'll ask you to try the Linzer torte."

After three hours, I had a full menu of ideas that my jury liked. Most of them I was able to make. I just needed to perfect how I made them.

I got up to wash the dishes as my jury sat sipping coffee. I noticed a crowd of people in the alleyway and in the backyard.

"Uh oh," I said. "Looks like the neighborhood found Echo."

That was the end of any privacy for us. Margaret, Kateesha, Jessie, and I were the prisoners of the house, while Echo was center stage in the backyard. People were coming on a regular basis to ask her about the progress. Sometimes people would knock on the door and ask about Echo, but I would just point towards the direction of the garage. I put a sign up on the door that said "Tree House in the Back." Soon they didn't knock.

I thought of putting up a black sheet over my bedroom window so that I didn't have to see what was going on, but I couldn't make myself do it. My bedroom window had become my Echo-cam. Much as I hated myself for it, I couldn't stop watching her in her habitat. I would creep out of my bed at night and sit under the window, peeping out. Sometimes Echo would work into the night. She was carving parts of the tree house and painting the rest. Other nights I would watch her crawl into her cocoon. Sometimes she would wave at me, but for the most part, she ignored me. I hated myself that I couldn't stop watching her. I would stare at her as she built her tree house and I would wonder why there wasn't more to me than what there was. And why the little there was of me was so dull and uninteresting.

I was working on perfecting a poppy-seed cake and some iced rum biscuits the day the reporter from the *Star-Tribune* knocked on the door.

"We hear you have a woman living in a tree in your backyard."

I nodded and pointed to the backyard. The reporter and her photographer left me standing at the door wondering what was going to happen next.

The story ran on the front page of the *Star-Tribune*. There was a picture of Echo looking off towards the sky with her hair blowing back in the wind. In the background you could see Margaret, Jessie, Kateesha, and me staring out the kitchen window. We looked bewildered.

When the wire services picked up the story, we started getting the TV news reporters. I couldn't keep track of how many came. The neighbors kept visiting and were being interviewed about what they thought of Echo in the tree house. Someone started an Echo Watch where people kept track of the number of days she stayed in the tree. I didn't stop baking. It was my only way to cope with the flood of people coming. It was overwhelming to me. I had to go get my ingredients in the middle of the night at the Cub grocery store, which was open twenty-four hours. During the day we were trapped in the house.

Except for Kateesha. She began selling T-shirts out front. She bought a disposable camera at the drugstore and went out to the tree house one afternoon.

"Hey, crazy girl," she shouted. "Come here a second."

Echo leaned over the edge of the tree house. "Are you needing me?" she asked.

"Smile," Kateesha said and snapped her picture. She blew it up and had it put on the T-shirts. She had the words Crazy Girl's Tree House put on the front and on the back she put, I Saw the Crazy Girl. She sold them for $7.38.

"Why $7.38?" I asked one morning when she came in to ask for some change. I wiped the flour off of my hands. I was attempting to make a Prince Regent cake and I had cake layers all over the kitchen.

"Because those are my lucky numbers," she said. "You got any more of that sticky bread?"

"The stollen?" I asked. I'd gotten up early and had made a marzipan stollen.

Kateesha nodded. "Or how about some of them cookies you made with all those nuts in them? Or you got some of those sponge cake slices that you make?"

"Why?" I asked.

Kateesha pointed to the people outside. "'Cause I want to sell it."

I thought for a moment. "I'll get you the card table and the tablecloth. Give me a minute to make up a sign on my computer. What about coffee? Want to sell that?"

Kateesha nodded. "We'll sell whatever you got. Those people are getting hungry staring up at Crazy Girl."

In a half an hour, Kateesha and I had set up a bake stand outside. Margaret bundled up and started to serve the coffee out of a massive old electric coffeepot that she had. I think she used to use it for church functions when it was her turn to serve refreshments.

We layered Jessie and helped her into her wheelchair. Once outside, she'd stop everyone who was going to see Echo and motion to the baked goods. No one really understood what she was saying, but I think she shamed them all into buying at least a cup of coffee.

Margaret was wearing her ratty old fur coat and a tall hat with a brown feather that arched around her head. She put an apron on over her fur coat and was constantly trying to keep her coffee area clean.

I supervised from the kitchen, redoubling my baking efforts. The only thing I asked my crew to do was to keep track of what people liked and what they didn't. What sold and what was leftover.

At the end of the day, we all sat around the kitchen table and counted out the money.

"Three hundred thirty-seven dollars and eighty-five cents." Kateesha looked pleased. "I think we would have done more if you could have kept up with us."

I was exhausted, but exhilarated. I wanted them to tell me everything.

"What did the people want?" I asked. A card table outside of Margaret's house wasn't necessarily the bakery that I was thinking of, but it was a start.

Later that afternoon, I was looking out the kitchen window at the crowd that was continually watching Echo. I noticed that a couple had set up a table near the garage and people were milling around it. Much as I didn't want to, I went outside to check it out.

I approached the couple, who were dressed for the coldest weather. The man was wearing a plaid hat with the earflaps fastened under his chin. He was small and his eyebrows seemed to bristle on his forehead under the hat. The woman was on the plump side, with a soft face that looked anxious. She was arranging things on the table.

"May I help you?" I asked them. I looked down at the table. It was filled with things from Echo's apartment.

"Want to buy a souvenir?" the man asked.

"Who are you and how did you get Echo's things?" I asked. I may not like it that Echo was in the tree outside my window, but I didn't think she should have property sold without her permission.

"We're her parents," the man answered. "Joe Jackson from Sleepy Eye and this is the better half, Sally. We were reading the newspaper and realized that Susan was holed up here. We figured we'd sell some of her things to pay for her rent and the money she owes us."

"Does she know this?" I asked.

Echo's mom nodded. "We told her when we got here and she gave us the key to her place."

I noticed the garage door was open. "Are you staying here?" I asked. "This house and garage belong to my great-aunt."

"Oh you must be Helen," the mom said. "Susan's told us so much about you. You've been finding yourself out here, haven't you?"

I felt myself getting angry, so I looked down at my feet. "We need to keep the car in the garage during the day." I looked into the garage. It was filled with Echo memorabilia. It was crammed full. I think the Jacksons thought they would be able to make quite a killing off of Echo's stay in our tree.

I went upstairs and looked out the window. Echo was still going strong. A vegan group started feeding Echo. They tried out a number of recipes and would share them with the news crews that were there. I hadn't tried to have a conversation with her since I stuck my tongue out at her. I opened the window and leaned out. I felt it was only fair to tell her what her parents were doing.

"Echo," I called. She stopped hammering for a moment and looked up at me. "I just talked with your parents. They're selling all your things."

Echo smiled. "I can't be sold," she said. "Only traces of my being can be left for others so that they knew I'd been here." She paused for a moment and pushed her hair back. Even though it hadn't been washed in weeks, it still looked full and vibrant.

"They're selling your Echo-time clocks," I told her. She stopped for a moment.

"How much are they selling them for?" she asked.

"Twenty-nine dollars and ninety-five cents and if you want to add a picture of you at your prom, it's only $34.95."

Echo frowned. "That was my statement about the limits of time. The price should have caused others to reconsider their views on existence and the self-imposed boundaries we live under. I was going to price them over a hundred dollars."

"Well, they're almost all gone now," I said. "And I think they're getting ready to sell your lamps and your togging platform.

Echo looked down at the garage. "They never could understand my being," she said, disdainfully. "Where is all the money going?"

"Apparently you owed them some money that they loaned you."

Echo waved her hand. "Currency exchanged doesn't mean that I'm tied to the earth. But if this makes them happy and leaves me to my inner solitude, then I don't mind."

I hated to admit it, but the tree house really was beautiful. I'd never seen anything like it. She'd suspended part of the building with ropes from the upper branches. She braced the main level against the roof of the garage. She had rope ladders going up to the different branches, where she'd hung her hammock and had made a lookout. A carpenter who lived in the neighborhood came over and gave Echo advice on how to create different views. He set up his saw in the garage and she'd lower down the wood that she wanted cut. Together they added an archway that led to the hammock and a window that was shaped like a sunrise. She'd added bird feeders, and a local pet store stocked her with birdseed.

Echo watched me as I stared at the tree house. "Look what I made last night," she said and went to another part of the tree house. She came back lugging two huge objects. She held up two large wings with straps. "Aren't they beautiful?" she asked. "I can become one with the sky in them."

They were beautifully made. She had used real feathers. I wondered where she'd got them.

"Are you going to try to fly with them?"

"I'm not sure where they'll take me, but I know I'm ready to soar."

I looked over at a shelf that she'd made between two trees. "What's that?" I asked, pointing to a mug that she'd placed there.

She smiled happily and brought it over to me. "He gave it to me today. As a symbol of affection and love."

My heart sank when she held up a carved wooden mug with the logo of the Jumpin' Java Jive Boat on it. I'd put mine on my dresser as well.

"Very nice," I lied, wondering when I would ever stop believing that Bjorn thought I was special. "He brought that to you?"

She smiled dreamily. "I know that he's missed my presence. He rushed back here to be with me. I showed him my wings."

I closed the window as she sat looking out at the trees, holding her mug. I picked mine up and walked down to Kateesha's room.

"Want a wooden mug?" I asked her. She was propped up on her bed watching *Divorce Court*. She shook her head.

"I put mine over there," she answered, pointing to a similar mug that she'd put on her dresser. "So I'm going to be helping you with the cooking?"

I sighed. I was beginning to wonder if Bjorn had bought them in bulk and for a discount.

"Yes," I said. "I could really use some help getting these orders done."

"We gonna talk salary yet?" Kateesha asked.

I paused for a moment. I hadn't thought about that. "I don't know what I can pay to start," I said, thinking that I still wasn't getting paid myself. All my money went to buy the ingredients.

"You best talk about benefits as well," Kateesha said. "I want to know what this company's offering me. Braids of Glory gives me free braiding when I want it."

"How about a free poppy-seed cake or a stollen?" I asked.

Kateesha started channel cruising. "Free braiding is better, but I'll think about it. We can start tomorrow when Bjorn brings Madelyn."

"Who's Madelyn?" I asked.

Kateesha shrugged. "Another one of Bjorn's."

I sighed and walked away. I put my cup in the trash can. Normally my heart would thump when I thought of Bjorn. Now it went chump, chump, chump.

Bjorn arrived early the next morning with Madelyn. Bjorn walked into the kitchen and smiled. "I brought something special with me."

I looked at him and tried to smile. I could barely make my lips move. "What did you bring?"

He motioned towards the doorway. "A Madelyn."

A slim young woman walked into the kitchen. She held her hand out to me and smiled. "You must be Helen Agnes," she said. "I'm Madelyn."

Madelyn had a soft, clipped British accent. She had short braids all over her head. They looked beautiful on her. When she smiled, one large dimple appeared in her cheek and she looked as if she were a naughty child. Her skin was the color of dark honey.

Bjorn put his arms around her. "I met Madelyn on the Jumpin' Java cruise. She's a singer. She's from the British West Indies. This is her first trip to Minnesota."

"Oh," I said, trying to recover as quickly as I could. What little warmth was left in my heart for Bjorn quickly melted. "I hope you like it here."

Madelyn smiled. "I think I'll love it."

Bjorn took her hand. "I'm going to take her up to meet Jessie."

Madelyn turned and waved at me as she walked out. "I'm sure I'll be seeing more of you."

I sighed. I knew I would be.

They went up to Jessie's room for a while and came back down again to make themselves breakfast. They helped themselves to coffee. Margaret and I quietly watched them from the kitchen table. I was getting ready to start baking, but I didn't want to begin with them both there. While I could see that Madelyn was a nice person, I wondered if she knew how many Madelyns there had been before her.

Later on in the morning, I picked up the phone to order more boxes from Restaurant Depot. I heard Slim on the line.

"I can't believe you'd do such a thing," he was saying. I was shocked. Who was he talking to? Then I realized it must be Bjorn. I knew I should hang up, but I couldn't.

"Why would you bring Madelyn there? Why would you do that to her? Hasn't she helped you out enough? She doesn't understand and yet you walk right in there, parading Madelyn around to everyone, not caring what she might think. I can't believe you'd do this." I quietly hung the phone up and went back into the kitchen. Margaret looked at me.

"Are you ready to bake?" she asked.

I nodded. "Yes, I guess I am," I said, but what I really wanted to do was to think about what Slim was saying. Did he mean me or Echo? It had to be me. Who else would he be talking about? A warmth started around my heart and I smiled slightly. No one had ever stood up for me before. I started humming as I began creaming the sugar and the butter together.

I don't think Echo saw Bjorn arrive with Madelyn, but they stayed most of the day, visiting with Jessie in her room. I went out on a bakery delivery with Kateesha. Margaret stayed close to Jessie, eyeing Madelyn carefully.

"Does he do that all the time?" I asked Kateesha when we left.

"Do what?" she asked, looking down at the map.

"Constantly have new girlfriends?"

"Like I told you. Since he was twelve. They've always been around Bjorn. They just don't last long. He only has room for one woman in his life."

"Who's that?" I wondered, realizing it would never be me.

Kateesha looked surprised. "Who do you think? Aunt Jessie."

I wondered how he was going to tell Echo.

Echo tried out her wings after Madelyn came to check out the tree house. I was in the kitchen, getting ready to start Kateesha on a baking lesson. Bjorn had gone out to do a delivery for me and Jessie was upstairs snoozing. I was at the kitchen sink when I saw Madelyn stroll by, checking out the backyard. I watched her wander over to Echo's parents and visit with them. Then I saw her staring up at the tree house. I could see that she was admiring it. I started to go towards the back door to tell her to stay away, but then I changed my mind. This was Bjorn's deal. This was for Bjorn to take care of. I went back to the kitchen sink and turned the water on full blast. I didn't want to hear what they would say to each other. I looked up a few moments later and saw that Madelyn had caught Echo's attention. I turned to Kateesha.

"Time to make rum cakes," I said, putting an apron on.

I was sound asleep that night when I first heard a crash. I thought the whole tree house was coming down and I bolted to the window. Echo had climbed out up to one of the farthest branches, wearing her wings. Bjorn was looking up at her from the lowest tree house level. He was shaking his head. He started climbing up towards her.

"You can't violate my spirit," Echo yelled at him. She kept pulling on her left wing, which was caught on one of the branches. "You can't blend with my spirit and then leave without explaining why." She turned and looked at him. Echo straddled the tree limb with her legs. She kept pulling on her wings, but she was having trouble getting them to open up. "What do you see in her that you don't see in me?" Echo struggled to get her wings free. I wasn't sure she was going to stay in the tree.

Bjorn started climbing up after her. "Echo, I never promised you anything. If you read more into it, that's your problem, not mine," he said.

I opened my window. "Echo, be careful," I yelled. I meant it not only because I thought she might fall out of the tree, but also because I couldn't believe he was telling her the same thing that he had told me.

She tried to shake her wings loose, but one was still caught in the branch. She started to fall, but Bjorn was able to grab her as she dangled from the branches, her wings holding her up. She looked like a thin, redheaded parachutist caught in the branches of the tree. She seemed scrawny and helpless as she struggled to get free. She started crying as he pulled her down to the floor of the tree house. I could hear her. Bjorn shook his head. "You needed me to get you the garage and help with the tree house. I did that. You got what you needed, but if you thought there was more, I'm sorry." He looked up at me as I slowly closed the window and went to bed. I tried to sleep, but I couldn't. I couldn't stop crying, only I didn't know if it was for me or for Echo or for Madelyn.

Jessie Seigel

Her Own Kind

JESSIE SEIGEL's fiction and poetry have appeared in *Gargoyle*, *Élan*, *Response—A Contemporary Jewish Review*, and the *Boston Jewish Times*. Her unpublished novel, "Tinker's Dam," was a semifinalist in the 2003 William Faulkner Creative Writing Competition, and an excerpt from the novel appeared in *Ontario Review* in 2005. Seigel has received an Individual Artist's Fellowship from the D.C. Commission on the Arts and Humanities, as well as residencies at the Tyrone Guthrie Center and the Virginia Center for Creative Arts. She has an MA in writing from the Johns Hopkins University, has taught fiction writing in Georgetown University's continuing education program, and is an associate editor at the *Potomac Review*. She also practices law in Washington, D.C. "Her Own Kind" is excerpted from "Mr. America," a novel in progress.

1. So, What Do You Do?

Okay. You've been to the movies. You've been to the movies at Mazza Gallery, that small, somewhat upscale shopping mall in Friendship Heights. The one with the Neiman Marcus, the Krön Chocolatier, but also with the McDonald's tucked away in a corner by the exit to the Metro.

You've just come out of the movies with your friend—call her Ann—and now you're going out for a late dinner.

But you both need more cash.

So. You've been to the movies—it's about ten o'clock at night—and you go to the money machine on the lower level of Mazza Gallery. Your friend Ann gets some money out of the machine. You've just seen some adventure comedy and you're high on the mood and talking about Johnny Depp who was in the movie. You're engrossed in your fun. You get some money out of the cash machine, about two hundred dollars, because they make you pay a two dollar fee and dammed if you're going to pay two dollars every time you get forty out of a machine. You get two hundred dollars in twenties and you count it to be sure it's right, which anyone with sense, including you, knows you're not supposed to do *at* the machine, but you're with a friend, you're in a mall, you're not on the street, and even though it's ten o'clock at night and all of the shops except McDonald's are closed, there are still people around.

And you're counting your cash and all of a sudden there's a woman practically at your elbow. There's this woman at your elbow, saying: "do you know how to open a car door? I locked my keys and my purse in my car."

Okay. So, what do you do?

The woman seems all right. The woman is nicely dressed. She's wearing a small, straw bowler hat, a nice T. She's not young, not old, could be white, could be a very light-skinned black person, has light brown freckles. Looks pleasant, cool, starched. She's wearing capri pants, sandal heels, a ring with a large, jagged stone. Nicely manicured nails. Real ones. But still, she's at your elbow, in your space, right on top of you when you've just got this money from the machine. When you've just stuffed it in the small Eagle Creek purse pouch you always wear over your right shoulder and cross-wise across your body so you don't have to think about someone grabbing it.

You ask where her car is. She says it's in the parking garage. You don't know how to open a locked car door, but even if you did, you're not going into any parking garage with a stranger, even if she is wearing nice suburban capri pants and a ring with a large stone.

Your friend, Ann. The lawyer. She suggests the woman call the police or Triple A for help. The woman says, no, no, she couldn't do that, she couldn't possibly do that; they'll only pop the trunk; she locked the keys and the purse in the trunk; and if they pop the trunk it will ruin the electrical system. It's one of those fancy cars that locks electronically.

Ann, the lawyer, asks, couldn't they move the backseat out to get at the trunk, but the woman doesn't want to hear about anyone jimmying open the door to get at the backseat.

So, what do you do?

It's ten at night, the mall is going to close, and here's this woman—however unreasonable—that's maybe stranded without her keys, without her purse, without any money at all.

The woman with the straw bowler, the capri pants, the big ring with the sparkling jagged stone is going on about how she'd asked some men for help. How they just kept walking, walked right off, calling over their shoulders, "good luck." She says people these days are so suspicious. Unasked, she recites, quickly: she's an antitrust lawyer, she works for Blah, Blah, Blah & Blah on K Street; she just wants to go home; she's got an extra set of keys at home; she wants to go home and come back for the car.

Ann. Ann, the lawyer, says the woman was volunteering information you never asked for, wouldn't consider any help you suggested, was talking fast and furious. Ann says this later. But this is now.

This is now, and you, the great philanthropist, the good Samaritan, ask the woman: "where do you live?"

"Aspen Hill," she says. "Aspen Hill, Maryland."

You've never heard of it. You have absolutely no idea whatsoever where that might be. Though it sounds posh. Has a ring of two-story Colonials. You ask her: what would it cost to get there? She stops, figures, says: two dollars to the end of the Metro line. Then twelve dollars at the other end for a taxi cab.

Fourteen dollars. A hell of a lot. Or not so much. Depending.

Here's this woman in the straw bowler, the capri pants, the starched, white, v-neck T, who says she lives in Aspen Hill, who has suddenly turned up at your elbow when you just got money out of an ATM, who wants fourteen dollars to get home, which you have, and could probably afford to give someone if they were really stuck, but would rather not give to someone who's just conning you.

And why do you think she might be conning you?

Does she talk too fast? Does she talk fast because she's panicked or to keep you from asking questions? Was she studying you for a split second when she computed the amount she needs? And just how is she going to get into her house to get that spare set of keys if all her keys are locked in the car? And why isn't there even one single person, one single friend, she could call to help her? But you only think of that later. You don't think much about that now because now you're too busy weighing: should you tell her, "call the police or forget it"?

But it's ten at night, and if you insist she call the police, you'll feel obliged to stay with her until they come. In case the mall closes. And you and Ann are on your way to dinner and you don't want to stay. But you would stay. You would stay because you're a woman and you know how you'd feel if you were in this situation, at ten o'clock at night in a mall that might close at any moment, miles and miles from home with no money, no purse, no ID. Do you dare take a chance on not giving her the money? Will you be waking up in the middle of the night feeling mean and ornery and worrying yourself over her predicament?

So, what do you do? Quick now. What do you do?

You think to yourself, do I have fourteen dollars in cash because I'm sure as hell not giving this woman one of the twenties I just got from the machine. You turn sideways to her while you ferret through your Eagle Creek pouch purse, while Ann is looking on, and the lady in the straw bowler is going on about how kind you are, and asking how will she get the money back to you. You don't have a pen or paper to write your address, and you probably wouldn't give her your address if you did. And she's asking, do you have a cell phone? She could call you to get your mailing address. You have a cell phone, but you wouldn't give her the number any more than you'd give her your credit card, so you say no, you don't have one. And she says, well, will you be around the mall? She could bring it back to you. Yeah, like you're going to hang around the mall at this time of night until she goes all the way to Aspen Hill and back. What are the odds?

You tell her to forget about it. Just do something for someone else sometime, if they need it. And she's all smiles and grateful words. You give her the fourteen dollars, and she gives you a hug, says something about good deeds coming around again, and for a moment you feel the warmth of giving. She asks your name. You tell her. What harm? She says her name is Bonnie English. Benita. She gives you another hug. She wags a finger at Ann. Says, "I know you're a doubting Thomasina." She sees Ann's taken aback, so she takes back her words, says no, no, it's okay, she'll give Ann a hug too. And she goes off down the Metro escalator.

So you've just paid fourteen dollars for a guilt-free evening and the warm feeling that giving gives. But you can't leave well enough alone.

So, what do you do?

The next morning, you call information. Do they have a number for a Benita or Bonnie English in Aspen Hill, Maryland? No? How about a B. English? There are a number of Englishes in Beltsville, but no "Bs." An unlisted number? No. Any English in the District of Columbia? One. In Northeast. On the seedy side of Union Station. B. English. You dial the number. You let it ring, see who answers. Phone machine. That's the voice. That's our girl.

So, what do you do?

2. Work Ethic

She's come out of the Union Station Metro and is walking along First Street N.E. in the direction of the bus station. It seems like there's someone asking for a handout every twenty feet. She passes them all by.

She's a small woman with freckles and a healthy, almost orange glow to her complexion. She's wearing a light straight-line beige summer suit. A white, V-necked T. Sandal heels. She's looking smart. Cool. Starched. Neat. Very neat.

She passes a first man. He's singing off-key outside the entrance to the Metro—some loud religious gospel song—and shaking coins in a tin can as percussive accompaniment. *God. Someone pay him to shut up.* She rolls her eyes as she passes him.

A second man is sitting just beyond the street venders. Sitting against the stone wall that runs the length of First Street below the tracks where the trains come in. He's sitting cross-legged, staring at nothing, his upturned cap on the cement in front of him. The woman steps past as if he weren't there.

There's another one across the street. This one's wearing a second-hand suit too large for him. His shtick, apparently, is feeding the pigeons. And looking old, and sounding amiable. His tin can sits on the street nearby.

The fourth one comes out of nowhere. A tall, thin, black shadow, slightly stooped in the shoulders, who holds out his hand, tentatively. "C-c-c-could y-y-y-ou sp-sp-spar—"

"Get a job."

She steps around him. What a moron, she thinks. What a *bunch* of pathetic morons. You just want to take 'em and *shake* 'em. Look at them. They haven't got a clue. Dirty. Ragged. Standing in pigeon shit. Do they think they're gonna sit there like dead men with a hand out and someone's gonna drop money on them? In this town? It's penny ante. It's pathetic.

Those who look for pennies in the gutter are always gonna be in the gutter. Where's the ambition? Where's the pride? She is tempted to shout at them: *pull yourself up by your damn bootstraps and get on with it, God damn it!* But she's a woman in a hurry. She strides on. Big, furious strides.

It's the number one principle of business: you have to spend money to make money. You've got to invest something in the process. Anyone who doesn't know that is too dumb to live. Period.

It's like going to an interview: you have to sell yourself; you have to look the part. And you've got to know how to talk to people. People don't operate based on pity. They relate to their own kind—to people who are like them. Those dirty, pigeon-poop, ragtag torn-jeans sad sacks. How the hell do they expect to get anyone to have confidence in them if they don't show confidence in themselves?

And does she give a damn?

She does not. Except for the annoyance. The hindrance. They get in her way. And she's a woman in a hurry. On a schedule. Got to get to work. Lunch hours are short here. People are already heading back to their offices.

"Excuse me," she says, to one woman walking down the street, a woman in a tailored beige summer suit much like her own. "Excuse me, I left my car in the Union Station parking garage and I locked my keys and purse in it. I wonder, do you know how to open a locked car door?"

Debra Sequeira

from "Origin and Ash"

DEBRA SEQUEIRA is an Indian Canadian writer, born and raised in Saudi Arabia, and educated in the United States and Canada. She received her BA in political science and French literature from Duke University in 1990 and an MA in international studies from the University of Toronto. She is currently an MFA student at George Mason University. Sequeira works for the International Finance Corporation in Washington, D.C., on issues of environment, social equity, gender and culture, which are key themes in her novel. She has coauthored numerous publications in the field of International Development. "Origin and Ash" is her first novel.

The last time Serena made this trip was as a young girl, sleeping across her mother's knee. Now, as they traveled together some twenty years later, their roles were reversed. The leather case which held her mother's ashes sat heavy in Serena's lap, never shifting despite the long journey and the empty seat beside her.

Goa emerged as if from behind a curtain: a countryside wet and lavish with green. Fringes of coconut palm leaned inward like nosy neighbors hoping to catch secrets whispered in the breeze. Rain-fed streams gushed through quiet glades while slender-legged egret idled among grazing buffalo.

It was just as she said it would be.

Out the window of the bus, women readied themselves to work the flooded paddy, tying up hair and saris before wading, calf deep, into the silted waters. In the distance, the Western Ghats loomed over a waking skyline. Whitewashed churches and villas reminded Serena that this was once Portuguese India. This tiny Catholic pocket, nestled quietly on the western coastline, was the place her mother had called home.

She had measured time—days, weeks, months—in relation to this day.

Now, as they approached Hanolim, Serena felt a quiet excitement rising through her like a breath. She slid open the window to let the humid air embrace her skin. Tropical flowers flashed crimson, blood orange, saffron. And somewhere in the mingled breeze, Serena could smell the ocean.

When she got to the house, an elderly woman was waiting by the gate. Serena recognized her grandmother instantly despite the years that had passed. Nana was small-boned with silvery hair and a heart-shaped face. "Sylvie's child," Nana said, her eyes shining with tears and disbelief. "Finally you've come."

Serena's gaze left her grandmother for an instant, drawn by the sprawling garden and the sight of the house rising up behind her. It seemed strange yet familiar at once, like recognizing a face in a crowd without being able to place who it is or what it means to you. Serena could not be sure whether this sense of knowing came through the breath and eyes of her mother, her constant narration whispering in her ears, or from early childhood memories of her own. Whatever the source, she felt an instant connection that could not be explained in words.

It was a large three-hundred-year-old house built in Portuguese times with shuttered windows and a verandah that wrapped around the sides. The exterior was whitewashed with a lime concoction made from crushed sea snails and oyster shells, but streaked with grime as if someone had cracked a large gray egg yolk on top and let it ooze down the sides. On top, the gabled roof sat like a tattered hat, its slanting rows of baked tiles victim to the salty air and falling coconuts.

"You remember me, your Auntie Vinoo?" Her mother's younger sister, Veena, dressed in a checkered housecoat came rushing down the walkway and kissed her on both cheeks. "My God, she's a picture of her mother," Vinoo gushed. "Looks just like Sylvie."

"I was going to say the same about you," Serena said, though Auntie Vinoo was a less worn, slightly plumper version, with frosted lipstick and too much perfume.

Serena noticed her grandmother eyeing the leather case. "Let Vinoo take your bag," Nana said. "Must be heavy carrying it all the way from

Canada, no?" Serena felt a stab of anxiety. She didn't know how they would react to the news of the cremation. "That's all right. I prefer to keep it with me," she said.

They made their way past frangipani trees and oleander bushes. In the center, a stone well dripped with a living upholstery of moss and lichens. Everything, it seemed, was alive. If she looked closely, Serena could see fat black beetles peeping out of porous rock, imagine amber roaches scuttling under heart-shaped leaves sweaty with dew. Before coming, she had wondered whether she'd be able to go through with it: leaving her mother in this place, scattering her, like she'd asked, among the grass and the flowers and the leaves and the bugs. But with the sun out, the garden looked so lush and enchanting that Serena could almost see the appeal of an eternity passed in this way.

The steps leading up to the house were wide at the bottom but narrowed as one ascended into the shade of the *balcao* with built-in benches that flanked the front door. At the top stood Serena's grandfather, struggling to control the emotion in his face when he saw her. Serena went to hug him, but he offered his hand instead, pulling her forward with an eagerness that caused her to stumble and step on his foot. His kiss, intended for her cheek, landed on the side of her nose. They laughed. Serena had forgotten that hugging was not the custom in this part of the world. "To look at you it's as though our Sylvie had come back to us," he said. Serena tried to imagine what it must be like to lose a child in a far-off place and then be confronted in such a tangible way by her memory. Papa was just as she remembered him: tall, slender, seemingly unchanged by the years.

Her cousins, Clara and Jacinta, were a different story. Time had transformed them from unremarkable children into astonishingly lovely women, not too far in age from herself. Jacinta, the younger of the two, had a round, girlish face with a pair of exuberant dimples that sprung into being when she smiled. Clara's prettiness was more sophisticated, shining hair more brown then black, and a beauty that derived from the perfect symmetry of her features: light brown eyes, angled cheekbones, delicate lips, all spaced with mathematical precision against a backdrop of flawless skin, the color of milky tea.

"Just see, we all have the same nose!" Jacinta giggled. It was true. With Serena standing among her aunt, cousins, and grandmother, there were in fact three generations of the identical nose on display, each shaped like a small, pointed arrowhead with nostrils that tended to flare in times of emotion. It was a strange yet comforting thing, the novelty of sameness, Serena thought, especially for an only child.

The kissing and greetings continued until Serena had met everyone in the house, including the servants. "This one is Ermelinda whom you won't know," Nana said, presenting a stout, middle-aged woman with thick ankles and a smile full of rotted teeth. "But this one you may remember? Esperanca. Espu we call her." Nana motioned to a tiny woman wearing oversized eyeglasses and clutching a broom. "Espu, you remember Sylvie, no?" she said, then caught herself. "*Serena*, I meant to say. See now, you've only just arrived and already I am mixing up!"

Espu was brown and puckered as a date, but her eyes flashed mischief. "I used to give you gram flour baths and oil massage when you were small baby," she informed Serena through toothless gums.

Nana gasped. "Chi, Espu! Where are your teeth?" She rapped Esperanca on the head with a rolled newspaper. "Go put them on, you hatter! You want to frighten the poor girl or-what?" Espu shrieked with embarrassed laughter, covered her mouth with both hands, and ran out of the room. Nana shook her head and sighed. "At our age we become forgetful. What to do?"

After a wash and a vain attempt to run a comb through her hair, Serena came back out into the sitting room to join the others for tea. She felt overwhelmed, not by fatigue, but by the happy realization that she had an entire family whom she scarcely knew. Growing up without a father or siblings, Serena had spent much of her childhood envying those with big, boisterous families. How odd it was to think that halfway around the world she had a ready-made family just waiting for her to turn up and claim them. She glanced around the room and saw a half-dozen variations of her mother's face smiling back.

Afterwards, Nana led Serena to the room they had prepared for her. It was a large house, much grander but more dilapidated than Serena had remembered as a girl of ten. Now she was thirty and many of the rooms appeared to have aged as well. There did not appear to be many doors in the house, instead floor-length curtains in cheery floral prints hung down from wooden transoms. The curtains fluttered in the breeze, allowing Serena a voyeuristic peek into each of the rooms. Nana brushed aside a daffodil curtain and ushered Serena into her bedroom.

"Your mummy used to sleep here," she said, "we've had it done up." It was a corner room with lots of light and a lovely verandah that faced the road. The window next to the bed overlooked the garden, the very view Serena had heard described so many times before. The walls were freshly painted and there was a dressing table in the center with a long narrow mirror and a wooden armoire which Nana called an *almirah*. The room welcomed Serena as though it were her own, as though it too had confused her with her mother. She felt a lump rise in her throat.

The bed struck her as unusually large. On closer inspection it appeared to be three single beds pushed together. "Wow, that's a big bed," she remarked.

"Well, three of you must fit, no?"

For a moment Serena thought she had misunderstood. "Three?"

"We didn't want you to feel lonely so Clara and Jacinta are going to sleep with you, at least for the first week. That way all the cousins can sleep together again, just like when you were small girls, you remember?"

Serena was not quite sure what to say. While it was true that she had returned to India to seek refuge in family, sharing a bed and the same air while one slept was a level of intimacy she had not had with anyone in years, except Ethan. And now he too was gone. "Oh, that's sweet, really, but it's not necessary," Serena assured her. "I'm used to sleeping on my own. I live by myself in Toronto, you know." Serena expected her grandmother to be impressed, but instead Nana consoled her.

"I know. You poor thing, all alone like that with no husband to look after you. Mummy wrote to us about it. Tch, such a pity." Nana pointed to a pair of thick rubber slippers at the foot of the bed. They were fluorescent pink with scalloped edges and flecks of green and yellow. "I sent Papa into town to buy those specially for you. Just see if they fit properly," she urged.

Serena removed her sandals and tried on the slippers. They were a perfect fit. There was no excuse not to keep them. "Thank you, Nana," she said, remembering her manners. "But you really should not have taken the trouble."

"Trouble? Hut! We all have *chapals* to walk around the house. You shouldn't have or-what?" She pointed to her feet. "Papa bought you the fancy-fancy type. See ours only, so plain." She stuck out her foot. Her slippers were thin and black, much more sober and practical than the show-stoppers on Serena's feet. "We are simple people, we don't need all this extra *jigrafisk*. But I know you people from abroad like to have all the latest fashions."

As soon as Nana left the room, Serena flopped forward onto the bed, nearly shattering her pelvis in the process. There were no springs, no bouncy cushioned mattress, just a thin layer of cotton wool between her and the hard, wooden base. Serena rolled onto her back and grinned up at the ceiling. She'd forgotten about Indian beds.

Once she was alone, Serena opened the leather bag and unpacked the urn from its casing. It was made of pale green onyx with a glossy surface and a smooth contour that she had grown to love. Serena set it on the windowsill overlooking the garden. "Only a few more days in the jar," she told her, "then you can be out there forever."

Serena remembered how bitterly she had cried when her mother first lost her hair. It was not as though she hadn't seen cancer patients before, their baldness startling yet dignified. Somehow she'd thought it would happen that way, that is to say, all at once. Her mother would go to sleep with a full head of hair and wake up one morning with a smooth shining scalp. But instead it had been ugly, messy, like everything to do with the disease, coming out in ghastly uneven clumps until they couldn't bear it anymore. In the end, Serena had been the one to do it, to shave her mother's head late one night in the upstairs bathroom with the curtains drawn so that the neighbors couldn't see her beautiful black waves falling soundlessly into a pile at their feet.

"We all need constants in our world," her mother liked to say, "something unchanging, immutable, that we can cling to, return to. For all time." The Goa house was her constant, the place to which her spirit would fly the instant it escaped her ravaged body. "People's fear of death is really fear of the unknown," she told Serena in one of her last clear moments. In those final days her eyes shone like polished rocks from deep within their darkened sockets, even as death had begun to nibble away at the muscles in her face. "I don't want you to worry about me, Serena. I'm going back home." She had said it casually, as if they were parting ways, mother and daughter, after a day of shopping at the mall. "I'll go on ahead and then you come and bring whatever's left of me."

It had taken Serena almost a year to make good on that promise. The trip to India had to be put on hold while she attended to the practical imperatives of death: funeral arrangements, the house to pack up and sell, legal documents to sort through, taxes and medical bills to pay. It was another type of grief altogether and nothing had prepared Serena for the exhaustion of it. She'd spent the year having to grovel to her bosses at the magazine. She'd needed time off to take her mother to the hospital; to care for her at home; to be at her bedside on especially bad days. "Surely there must be someone *else* who can help?" She could see the question flickering in their eyes, just beyond the pity. There were, of course, neighbors and friends. But for the important things, both big and small, there was no one else, just the two of them, as it had always been.

When Serena awoke the next morning she found Jacinta and Clara gone from the bed and three sets of eyes peering at her through the curtain in the doorway. Auntie Vinoo was straining to see over the head of Nana who was peeking from behind the shoulder of Espu who was tottering to keep her balance with the other two bearing down on top of her. Serena wondered how long they had been watching her.

"There! She got up! Go bring tea," Nana shouted directly into Espu's ear. Serena wondered if Nana had to shout because Espu was hard of hearing or if it was Nana's shouting that had made Espu go deaf in the first place.

"My! How much you slept. It's almost three o'clock," Nana chuckled and came over to the bed. She drew back the curtains and sunlight flooded the room. With the curtains drawn, the urn sat in plain view on the windowsill. Serena's heart skipped a beat. Had she forgotten to put it back in its case before going to bed? She watched as Nana leaned over to unlatch the window, the folds of her dress brushing against the urn. Serena's mother had wanted to wait to tell the family about her cremation. They were devout Roman Catholics and traditional in their thinking, so she felt the news would be easier to take if delivered in person. Now the burden of telling them fell to Serena.

"You slept all right, Serena? Not too hot?" Auntie Vinoo asked.

Espu came in with tea as Serena struggled to sit up in bed.

"After tea, go for your bath. You'll feel fresh," Nana said, "I've told Espu to keep well water ready for you in the *mory*. Then we'll have our lunch on the verandah."

Serena nodded, but with her heart beating so fast she'd barely heard a word Nana had said. Auntie Vinoo left first, followed by Espu. But Nana lingered behind. She fluffed up one of the pillows and threw it back onto the bed, then smoothed the top sheet with her hand and tucked a stray end under the bedding. She wandered over gingerly and straightened the row of shoes under the almirah as if she had all day and nothing better to do. On her way out, she spotted a towel on the floor and hung it back onto a hook behind the door. Serena sipped her tea and tried not to draw attention in her direction. She could feel Nana taking one last look around the room to make sure everything was in order.

"What's that you've brought?" she asked. This was not how Serena had planned to tell her grandmother that her eldest daughter was there, quite literally, in their midst. "I'll tell you about it over lunch," Serena said casually, as though the urn were nothing more than a stray knickknack picked up on holiday. The response seemed to satisfy Nana. She brushed aside the curtain and walked out.

ॐ

The mory was a small dim room with gray tiles and a pink Western-style toilet in one corner. Serena was secretly relieved to discover this, having used the servants' bathroom the night before with a keyhole toilet in the ground over which she'd had to squat and hover while the muscles in her thighs trembled with the effort. The mory also functioned as the laundry room where the servants beat sudsy garments against the floor to get them clean. Serena had to duck under a row of dripping undergarments, dangling from clothespins, to get to the plastic bucket that contained the water for her bath. She dipped her finger into the bucket. The water was cloudy and cold. As if reading her mind, Espu rushed in with an enormous kettle and poured steaming water into the bucket until it overflowed.

"Geyser is broken so I had to boil water," she explained.

"Geyser?"

Espu pointed to a rusted metal contraption mounted on the wall. "Hot water heater."

"Oh, I see."

"For head bath must have little warm water otherwise will catch cold," she said.

"Head bath?"

"You're going to wash hair, no?"

Serena nodded.

Espu pointed to a small wooden shelf that was crawling with black ants. "Shampoo is there." She handed Serena a translucent bar of Pear's glycerin soap.

Serena thanked her and latched the door behind her. Even with hot water, the temperature was still tepid at best. She shivered a little as the first mug of water splashed against her neck and breasts. Her skin erupted in goose bumps. She listened to the sound of chickens in the courtyard and the squeaking of the well as water was drawn. She dumped a second tumbler of water over her head, conscious that this was how her mother must have bathed. And the act, simple as it was, made Serena feel closer to her.

~

There was an airy quality about the house that came from its lofty ceilings. Given the right conditions, Serena imagined, it seemed quite possible to float. Nana said the house was designed this way, to capture the westerly breezes from the Arabian Sea while warding off the rising damp during the rainy season. Serena trailed behind her as she pointed out the elaborate mosaic floors fashioned from bits of glazed tile and broken crockery into the shapes of butterflies, gargoyles, and horses. She informed Serena with pride that many of the original windowpanes were still intact. They were thin, translucent ovals made from shimmering oyster shells which filtered out the harshest rays of the afternoon sun and flooded the house with a soft, colored light.

The sitting room was butter yellow with floral motifs stenciled along the walls. Less attractive were the dark water stains, the cracking paint, the profusion of fungus that had sprung from the dampness in a grayish green web of mildewed veins and capillaries across the ceiling. But these disfigurements were only noticeable if one looked up, and since the ceilings were so high it was quite possible to go about the day keeping one's gaze at eye level and ignoring the specter of decay hovering overhead.

The far wall in the dining room was decorated with porcelain plates. "Priceless antiques," Nana said. It was clear from the discolored patches and holes in the plaster that many of the plates had been removed. "Before we had such lovely heirloom pieces from Macao, Portugal, Belgium, and Italy. My father's father used to collect. But these few are all I have left now."

"What happened to them?" Serena asked. The question was barely off her lips when Nana's face turned pained and so full of regret that Serena wished she could take it back. Nana explained that the plates were broken or stolen over the years. When she said this she sighed heavily in a way that made her tiny frame rise up then sink back down into her shoes.

"Tch. It's a sin what happened to those plates. I never should have left this house," she said. "If they want me to leave again, they will have to tie me up and drag me out by the hair."

She waited for her grandmother to elaborate, but Nana had nothing else to say, and Serena knew enough not to ask.

❧

The weather was perfect, sunny and warm with a light breeze that made it pleasant enough to lunch outside. Nana had already eaten but she kept Serena company as she gobbled down the spicy *pomfret* curry and boiled cauliflower that Ermelinda had prepared.

"When Sylvie was small she would say 'I want my children and their grandchildren to grow old in this house. I'm never going to leave.'" Nana put down her teacup and dabbed the corners of her eyes with a napkin. "But then she met your father and left." She rubbed Serena's leg and gave her a playful slap. "This is what children do. They grow up and leave. What to do?"

"She had plans to move back here," Serena said, "before she got sick."

Nana started shaking her head even before Serena could finish her sentence. "That Sylvie was always promising she would come back. When she got married and left for Canada she told us it was just for few years. Then when your daddy was killed in the accident, poor fellow, we thought definitely she would come home. You were still so small then and we thought how can she manage alone with a child in a foreign country like that? But your mother was a stubborn donkey. A bit like me." Nana chuckled to herself. "She told us, Stanley and I came to Canada so our children could have a good education. If I don't give Serena at least that, what was the point of coming all this way?"

After lunch, Ermelinda brought out a wooden bowl full of fruit—guavas, custard apples, sweet limes, and red bananas. "Try a *chickoo*," Nana said. "They were your mummy's favorite." Serena knew of her mother's fondness for chickoos but had never tasted one herself. It had the shape of a plum but its skin was brown and smooth like a new paper bag or a kiwi without the fuzz. Nana sliced it open to reveal a black glossy center seed. The texture was grainy on the tongue but its bursting honey flavor was unlike any she'd tasted before. If Goa could be captured in a taste, surely this was it.

"In the beginning your mummy told us she'd stay in Canada and work until you finished the sixth standard," Nana continued. "But after elementary school it was secondary school, and after secondary school it was college. Then when you finished college we said to her: enough now, Serena is a grown woman! Why you want to go on staying in that cold-cold place with all those foreigners? Come back home. And you know what she said?" Serena shook her head. "She said, how can I come when Serena is still unmarried? If I leave her on her own, God only knows *whom* she'll land up marrying." Nana was smiling now, clearly amused by the recollection. "So Papa told her, why don't you bring her here and find her a nice Goan Catholic boy? And you know, I think that's what she was planning somewhere in the back of her mind. That was her hope, before the cancer took her of course. But probably she never told you?"

"Never told me?" Serena laughed. It was her mother's favorite topic.

Nana smiled, but it was a sad smile. "You know all that time she never told us how serious it was?"

Serena knew. "She didn't want you to worry."

"If we had known we could have sent Vinoo to be with her," Nana said. "Doctor says I cannot fly, but still I would have come."

Serena pushed aside her half-eaten chickoo. "All she talked about those last few months was the Goa house and how precious it was to her."

Nana's face puckered instantly. "Enh! It's easy to think in such a rosy way when you have been gone for so long. This house is nothing but one headache after another. The roof leaks, the pipes are rotted. And the moment you fix the roof, the termites come and eat the floorboards. Chi! Who needs this botheration? I get fed up." Nana lifted the quilted cover off the teapot and poured them both a cup of tea. It was steaming hot but she sipped hers straight away. "And maintaining it is not like the old days, baba. These days all the repairmen are crooks. You should see what big-big money they ask for doing such small-small things."

Serena felt her palms perspiring. "Nana, I don't know if Mum ever mentioned this, but she wanted to be buried here."

Nana clucked. "What for? You've seen the state of our cemeteries here?" She shook her head. "We had a big funeral mass for her this side. You should have seen. So full the church was."

Serena plucked up her courage. "I know this may come as a surprise but Mum decided, sort of at the last minute, that she wanted to be... *cremated.*" She tossed out the word like a live grenade and waited.

"That urn in the bedroom you were asking me about?" Serena added, "those are her ashes. She asked me to bring them here, to scatter them in the garden."

A dark frown spread across Nana's face, slowly, like an ink stain seeping into cloth. She set down her teacup, hands quivering with the effort. "What are you saying? That you haven't buried her all these months?" There was genuine disbelief in her eyes. "That she's gone and desecrated her body?"

"This way she can be here with you," Serena said, "close to everyone and everything she loved."

"Have you both gone mad?" A thick green vein in Nana's forehead began to bulge. "How does she expect our Lord to raise her up on Judgment Day if she is scattered here and there?" Nana asked the question in all seriousness, waving her hands for effect. "One arm under the chickoo tree, an ear behind the well, her legs Godknowswhere. And what if some parts are missing? Blown away in the wind or washed into the Mandovi by the monsoon? What will she look like for our Lord and the Archangels, tell me? A fright, that's what!"

"Nana, it's done," Serena said. "It's what she wanted. Shouldn't we just accept that now?"

Nana scowled.

"I was thinking we could have a small ceremony here at the house," Serena continued. "Invite a few close friends and family to be present for the scattering of her ashes."

"Don't talk to me about ashes and fashes!" Nana said, her irritation returning. "I don't know why that Sylvie had to go and get cremated.

Catholics don't go in for such things." She pursed her lips. "I'll have to check with Father Agnello, but I'm sure this whole burning business is a sin. What does she think, we're Hindus or-what? In that case why not behave like a Parsee and get the bloody vultures to come eat her flesh?" Nana began muttering to herself in Konkani.

Serena recognized the language despite only knowing a handful of words in either Konkani or Portuguese, the two languages her mother grew up speaking in addition to English. "I'd like to do it on Wednesday," she announced.

Nana bolted upright in her chair as if some invisible hand had reached over and pinched her backside. "Wednesday? You mean *this* Wednesday? That's impossible," she said. "We've already arranged for Father to offer a memorial mass in the church. It's our tradition for the one-year death anniversary. Ashes can wait."

"Until when? I'm here for less than three weeks," Serena reminded her. She had originally hoped to stay six, but with her position at the magazine already precarious, she hadn't wanted to push her luck.

"How can you give us a shock like this and then expect to do things in a mighty hurry?" Nana said.

Serena knew her grandmother had a point, but what choice had there been? Her mother had insisted that telling them earlier would only upset them at an already difficult time. "Mum felt it wasn't the kind of thing we could tell you over the phone," Serena said. "You have no idea what I've gone through to make it here in time for the anniversary. I really want to scatter her ashes that day."

Nana crossed her arms over her chest. "You may *want* many things," she said. "But Father Agnello will not like last-minute changes."

"What if I talk to him?" Serena offered. The conversation was turning out to be rather unpleasant and she suddenly felt unprepared.

"Nothing doing!" Nana snapped. "And anyhow, now is not the time to be doing things in the garden."

Serena started to protest, but then she saw the look on her grandmother's face and it stopped her. For the second time since her arrival, Serena was reminded that the loss was not hers alone. She decided to try a different approach. "I know it might seem rushed, but just think of Mum. For her the wait must be unbearable." She watched Nana's face for any sign of softening. "Now that I'm here, I don't think it's fair to make her stay in that urn a moment longer than she has to. Do you?"

Nana spoke in a gentle tone but her mouth was still drawn tight. "You know, Serena, we have a saying here about a servant girl who through her own haste breaks the pot of water on the doorstep of the house after having carried it all the way from the river."

Serena stared at her grandmother, trying to grasp the intent behind the gray-green eyes. "Is there something you're not telling me?" She preferred directness to metaphors.

"I *am* telling you, but you don't want to listen," Nana said. "People who rush to do things that later cannot be undone, often live to regret."

Sheryl Stein

List Served

SHERYL STEIN is a music-obsessed mom, writer, and web strategy type who lists among her proudest moments the day her kids sang with X. She is currently revamping her first novel and completing her second. Keep up with this product of the New Jersey public education system at her website, www.wrekehavoc.com.

I've been a bit of a shy geek all my life: the wallflower in seventh grade who only went to the dance under pressure, only to spend most of the evening in the bathroom, hiding out; the valedictorian who barely knew anyone in high school (except for members of the chess and physics clubs, who were pretty much all the same people) because I spent my time with books, libraries, and symphonic music. In college, I discovered computers. They spoke to me rationally, cleanly, and in a way nothing else had. They seemed to hold the answers to most of my life's questions: "How will I support myself?" [Answer: Become a programmer, then ultimately help others construct logical, functional websites.] "How will I meet other people?" [Answer: I've met a lot of friends, and even my husband, on the Internet. We all see each other in real life, of course, but it all started on my PC.] I've always been a bit mystified by interpersonal relations; I guess I have this single-minded attachment to logic that is somewhat unshakable. People are not always logical. Computers, on the other hand, are. Always.

If children are little people, then they, too, defy logic from time to time. When I became a parent five years ago, I knew I had to find other parents to help me navigate through the treacherous days of sleep deprivation, the terrible twos, perpetual potty training, and hearing the word "No!" a thousand random times a day. It started out as an email list among friends. I invited a few parents I knew to join me on this adventure where we could post our questions and our triumphs and hold each others' hands, virtually anyway, as we walked through our kids' childhoods.

The list became quite the lifesaver and part of my routine, just as nursing and burping and playing and sleeping had. I vividly recall a post I made, begging the group for help when my eldest wouldn't sleep at a year old. People gave me names of books, videos, sleep therapists, and even night nurses I could hire if I needed to take a break. I was astonished at how we had grown into such a helpful group. Over time, friends invited friends, who invited friends, and so on ad infinitem. Being a democratic sort, I always let everyone in, and we didn't really have much controversy for a long time. The pattern was predictable: a person wrote about a problem, and people wrote back suggestions, which, while not completely value free, were fairly nonjudgmental.

All until HackieSac64 joined our group.

I was never able to trace Hackie's lineage; none of my circle of friends claimed her, and none of their close friends did, either. She signed up, just as everyone else had, with a name and optional city and state (she entered those); but, as the administrator, I felt strongly that I would not reveal her name or location to anyone. I didn't have any legal obligation, of course—this is a private list, and people are free to join and leave at will. But I never put in place any sort of safeguards, any sort of behavioral code.

It all began when a poster asked about sleep methods. See, people who understand lists know to search the archives to make sure that their question hasn't already been asked. Increasingly, though, newbies joined our list and would ask the same questions. Being of good humor, some old-timers took it in stride and would respond, anyway. So a poster asked one of the perennial parenting questions: what do I do when my eight-month-old won't sleep through the night? Some parents told of children who slept and nursed in their family beds until they were two or three; some parents told of reading up on sleep expert books; some told of letting their child cry it out (CIO).

In strode Hackie on a horse of eternal righteousness, wielding a keyboard as a sword:

CIO is cruel, and all parents who practice it are guiltless and unfeeling. Pediatricians know it to be cruel, and more and more leading experts warn against it. Doing that to your child is tantamount to child abuse, and you ought to be reported if you try it. I'll probably get slammed by the working mothers, who don't have time to be patient with their children, but don't try CIO. Try a gentle method. Eventually, your baby will understand and you'll feel better for it.

Our peaceable kingdom was disrupted for the first time. People accused Hackie of being a troll who just popped in to stir up trouble; people reminded her not to be accusatory and to try to be more constructive with her comments. Individuals emailed me as the administrator and asked me to bar her. I refused, reminding people that this was a big world and I had to include a diversity of opinion. Besides, I noted privately to some friends, this will probably be her first and last post, especially after all the chiding, albeit gentle, she had received.

I was wrong.

Hackie showed up again two weeks later after a parent lamented the challenge of returning to work after maternity leave. Most posters empathized with the mother, noting that the transition is challenging but gets easier as time goes by for most. They gave strategies for pumping at work; they gave tips for some great daycare centers in the area; they shared some more books and resources to help the new mother make it through. One poster even gave nutritional advice to help the mother feel stronger! But not Hackie:

Perhaps this guilt is due to the fact that mothers ought to be with their children? It is, after all, the natural order of things. Motherhood is perhaps the most important job you will do in your life, and already you are parceling it off to someone else to accomplish. Of course you feel awful about it. You ought to look inward and see whether there might be a way to make this work better.

This antediluvian attitude just blew everyone on the list away. The response was swift and immediate: "What century do you come from?" "Why don't you provide helpful strategies instead of harmful criticism?" "Are you currently barefoot and pregnant?" List members were furious this time, and even the new working mother wrote to me, asking me to ban

Hackie from the list. Unfortunately, there is no real way to ban anyone from lists, I noted to all. I could bar the email address, but Hackie could resubscribe from another email address. I noted that the best thing people could do would be to ignore Hackie's posts; she clearly wrote with a malevolent, unhealthy streak. This should make us all stronger, ultimately, I wrote.

Some rumblings came from some old-timers about my creating a new list. I really didn't want to create a new list to administer, and anyway, I didn't want one person to think she could single-handedly control this giant virtual support group, now numbering in the hundreds.

But who was Hackie? And why, in the next few weeks, did she write epistles on home-schooling (for it), abstinence (for it for teens), television (against it), and breast-feeding (formula should be outlawed, in her view)? Finally, Hackie went over the line with a vicious attack on a lesbian parent list member. Apparently, Hackie didn't approve of gay parents, or gay people for that matter.

You know, I pride myself on being a logical person, but even I was struggling with Hackie's behavior and her single-minded efforts to tear apart this community of parents. It gnawed at me, day and night. I finally decided I would try to figure out who this person was—assuming she gave me the correct identity! In checking her information, she was listed as J. Merriweather of Arlington. Hmm. I used Google and found two Merriweathers. One was Anita and Robert, the other was simply Merriweather. On closer inspection, it looked like Anita and Robert were living in a community for the elderly, whereas the plain Merriweather lived in North Arlington near Route 50. I suspected folks eligible for social security were probably not the most wired individuals around, so I set my sights on the plain Merriweather.

Okay. I know I sound like a stalker, but I decided I would drive by there a few times over the next few days to see whether I would learn anything. Most days, I just saw children in the yard—lots and lots of children, all blonde, and looking like they were about seven or eight and younger. The idea of anyone watching my children creeped me out, so I didn't stay very long. I only wanted to catch a glimpse of the person whose vitriol was poisoning my little world.

I was driving my three-year-old daughter, Leonora, home from the library a few days later when I took a detour and drove past the house. I saw a brown-haired woman, wearing jeans, a green T-shirt, and an occupied baby sling, packing several children into a battered minivan. She was probably in her early thirties, but she seemed like a worn-out, vintage person. In any event: pay dirt. I drove around the block, hoping I could possibly catch a glimpse into her life. When I came around the block, the minivan was just pulling away, so I kept some distance and pulled away behind it. While the prospect of being a cyberdetective was exciting to me, I wasn't sure what I would do with the information I would find. Something compelled me to follow. The minivan pulled into the parking lot at Lubber Run. "How would you like to play on the playground a little, sweetie?" I asked Leonora. I was praying she wasn't suddenly going to demand a nap. She never liked to sleep, but it would figure that she would want to since this would be the one day in my life I would be happy to forgo the experience. Please, please, please, Leonora. Say yes.

"Let's plaaaaaay!" she chirped enthusiastically. Phew! I parked my car, unpacked her, and walked over to the park. She ran ahead of me. "I'm going to sit down, honey," I yelled to her. "I'll be right over on the bench!"

"Okay, Mama!" she yelled, running toward one of Hackie's children, a little girl who must have been about the same age as Leonora. I moved to the bench, where sling-wearing Hackie sat.

"May I sit here?" I asked politely.

"Sure," she said, a weary grimace creeping onto her face, a baby sleeping quietly in the sling.

Her first word to me. Wow. "What a sweet baby," I said, trying to make conversation.

"Thank you," she replied. "They're so much easier when they're this age."

"Yes, I agree," I said. "My five-year-old is such a handful!"

"Five is a nice age," she noted. "My eight-year-olds can be tough. They want what they can't have."

"Don't we all," I smiled. I stuck out my hand awkwardly. "My name is Lisa."

She took my hand gently. "Marie," she said. "Nice to meet you."

Marie! Not "J." That's weird. Maybe it's a pseudonym? Or maybe I'm barking up a tree from another planet.

"Very nice to meet you. Are these kids all yours?" I asked.

"Yes. I have six kids. I home-school them, and this is their outdoors time."

"Wow," I said. "That's a lot of work."

"Yes," she said, sighing, "it is. But nobody said parenthood would be easy!"

"That's so true," I said, watching Leonora sit in the sandbox with her little blonde friend. "Is she yours as well?"

"Yes," Marie answered. "That's Faith. She's three and a half. Christian and Chastity, my eight-year-olds, are helping my six-year-old, Justin, on the bars. I don't know what Nevaeh is doing—looks like she's about to throw dirt at your daughter and Faith—Nevaeh! Don't throw dirt at people, honey!—She's eighteen months and has a mind of her own, just walking around, trying to do what the big kids do. And this angel," she said, looking at the baby, "is Grace."

"You've got lovely kids," I said. "How do you home-school them—I'm afraid I'm pretty ignorant about that sort of thing—I hope you'll forgive me. Is there a book you follow?"

"We're a very religious family, but I have to teach them also in accordance with the commonwealth's educational goals. I try to add some faith-based information to everything I teach. On Saturday mornings, I go to the library and use the computer there to get curriculum and information for the week. I print out a lot while the kids are enjoying the story hour." She pushed her hair out of her eyes. "Gosh, it would be so much easier if we had a computer at home." Faith and Leonora were giggling wildly in the distance as they built mud castles that Nevaeh knocked down, over and over.

This was a revelation in itself. "You don't have a computer?"

"No," she admitted. No computer. How on earth could she be Hackie? Hackie posts mostly during the week. Marie is only near a computer on weekends, and a public one at that. And if she has six kids in tow, she barely has time to accomplish her tasks at hand, much less sit around composing missives to strangers. Suddenly, I'm lost.

"I have a consulting business where I help people build websites. I bet I could find a computer, a used one of course, but a decent one that could work for you at home. You'd have to get an Internet connection if you wanted to use the web, but at least it's a start." Suddenly, I was walking in this woman's huge shoes. She wasn't Hackie.

"Well, I'd have to ask my husband. I don't know about the Internet access—I know that's expensive. But a computer would probably help in other ways. Thank you. That would be really, really kind of you!" She smiled at me, the first warmth I'd seen from her since we'd met. I imagine we are dissimilar politically, but my gut told me that Marie wasn't a bad person. Just a tired one. She wrote her name and number on a piece of paper and handed it to me. "I don't want a handout, of course. Let me know if there are ways we can somehow pay for this computer," she added proudly.

"Oh, I have so many PCs laying around, I'm sure I can find something. It would be my pleasure," I added. "Hopefully, that'll be okay with your husband."

Marie looked at the sky through her bangs pensively. "Well, who knows. He's not a big fan of our children on the Internet, but I read about lots of controls you can put on machines to keep the kids away from the sites you don't want them to see. He has a laptop that he brings home from work every night. But he's pretty adamant that it's only for church work, nothing else. So the kids haven't been on the Internet yet, and I haven't had any opportunity to even think about it for the kids."

"Really," I said. "What does he do?"

"John works for an evangelical society downtown. He is in charge of public affairs and outreach."

"How nice," I said. John Merriweather. J. Merriweather. Arlington. I looked at my watch. "You know, I have to get home for a client's call, but I have really enjoyed talking with you. And I mean what I say about the computer." I pulled a pen out of my pocket and tore off a scrap of the paper Marie had shared with me. "Here's my name and number.

Please call me and let me know if it's OK for me to work on the computer for you. All free on my end. And maybe we can have a play date for the girls again."

"Yes, I think they hit it off really well," she said, smiling. "Faith! Come and walk your new friend over to her mommy. She has to go home now, but we'll make sure you see her again soon!" Faith dutifully grabbed Leonora's hand and pulled her up. The two girls skipped to us.

"I want to play soon," Leonora said sadly.

"We'll try, sweetheart," I replied. "Marie, it is nice to meet you. Hope we hear from you!"

"You will," Marie replied. "Bless you!" I swooped down, scooped Leonora up in my arms, and tickled her all the way back to the car.

⁂

My husband was working late, so after I put Leonora and Sarah to bed, I went online to check out the list. Everyone was playing nicely that night, discussing cloth versus disposable diapers. I decided to compose an email to Hackie:

> *Dear John,*
>
> *Our list is a list for parents, which I know you are by definition. It is not, however, a promotional vehicle, an evangelical vehicle, or a platform for you to try and push the uneasy into church. I like to be respectful of your views, and I hope you will do the same. If you have genuine issues about parenting to discuss in a nonjudgmental way, we will welcome you in our community, and people will gladly respond to you in kind. However, if you feel you would prefer to stir up trouble and belittle people's choices when they differ from your own, I will be forced to block your email address from the site. I would prefer not to do that, but the choice is up to you.*
>
> *Very best,*
> *Lisa*
> *Administrator*

I pressed *send*, wondering about the reply I'd get.

In the most basic of programming languages, we use words like *if* and *then* in statements. Computers understand that every action results in a reaction, and the logic of that relationship is complete and whole. I believe that life complies with such rules; you just need patience to let each program run to its conclusion. After a few weeks of tranquil conversations on the list, I found my resultant reaction to be permanent silence.

Amy Stolls

from "The Ninth Wife"

AMY STOLLS is the author of the young adult novel *Palms to the Ground* (Farrar, Straus & Giroux), winner of the Parents' Choice Gold Award in 2005. She is at work on an adult novel entitled "The Ninth Wife." Stolls currently serves as the literature program officer for the National Endowment for the Arts.

It's karate that Bess is thinking about as she drives up Wisconsin Avenue toward the Beltway. Her karate school requires students to write a paper before each test for a new belt and the one Bess has due tomorrow is on the concepts of Yin and Yang. She had gerbils once named Yin and Yang, when she was eleven. True to their names, Yin was dark and passive and female, and Yang was a lighter, more aggressive male. They played well together, balanced as they were, and for a time Bess imagined having loads of little Yin and Yang babies, but then Yang escaped the cage one afternoon and was brought back by the neighbor's cat, a prize dropped on the front stoop. Yin wasn't herself after Yang's death. She shed most of her fur and wouldn't eat. Two weeks later, she too took her last breath. Bess felt guilty naming them Yin and Yang as if the labels themselves dictated their fate. Maybe Yin could have survived had she been called Wonder Woman instead, or Cher, or Mother Teresa.

With regard to karate, she would write in her paper, the symbiotic relationship between Yin and Yang manifests itself in several ways, the artistic (choreographed and beautiful) aspects balancing out the martial (physical and more violent) aspects to create a true martial art. Karate depends on a healthy balance between offensiveness and defensiveness, physical strength and mental acuity, competitiveness and camaraderie, patience and determination, an awareness of details (heel down, elbows in, wrist straight, thumb tucked) and a sense of the fluidity of moving through a whole routine. "We are, each of us, teacher and student always," her instructor had said, and Bess liked that idea.

But then in her paper she is also supposed to write about how this particular philosophy applies to her life outside of class, and here she is stumped. "Each serves to define the other and cannot survive in isolation," it said in the reading packet and she thinks, maybe that's the problem. She doesn't feel in harmony with the world or even within herself. *Where is my Yang*? She thinks about her ex-boyfriends. Were they Yang to her Yin? Could Rick be a good Yang? *I Am a Big Yin-Yang Failure* is what her paper should be.

Bess crosses the line into Maryland where the large houses on hills sit atop hoop skirts of perfectly mowed lawns. She is headed to Rockville to visit her grandparents, Millie and Irv. Over the decades, they had moved steadily northward and westward through the district, up from their first years of marriage in the 1940s at Q and 16th near the Jewish Community Center, to Cleveland Park where they adopted and raised Bess's mother in the '50s and '60s, and on into Bethesda over the border into Maryland when Bess's mother moved out and moved in with a Smithsonian museum tour guide in Capitol Hill at the start of the 1970s. In the '80s, when Bess was in her early teens, her grandparents made their final move to their largest home in the Maryland suburbs.

This was a common route for Jews in Washington, D.C., the first of whom migrated from Baltimore in the mid-1800s. Bess had devoted part of her doctoral study to this subject based on the assertion by her mother and later verified through records that Irv's great-great-great-grandfather was among those who fled persecution in Germany and came to the new world, to Baltimore, in 1848—the year a sawmill worker discovered gold and sparked a mass exodus to the West, also the year they broke ground in the District of Columbia to build the Washington Monument. Said Irv: "See? My ancestors come and suddenly they run for the hills or get the idea to build a big shlong." This was the first acknowledgement, in fact, of his true heritage after the made-up stories he spoke into Bess's tape recorder. She had gone back to her grandparents with some evidence of their ancestry and, like a cop in an interrogation room, called their bluff. Because it was for her dissertation, they said, and *education is very, very important Bessie dear almost as important as family don't you forget that* they listened to what information she'd gathered and filled in the gaps.

"My family was in the dress business," Irv had said. "Why? Probably my great-grandfather liked to know what touched his hands would also touch the naked bodies of the dames in town. My father told me that. But that's it. Nothing. End of story."

"What's with you, no story," Millie had chimed in. "Always with the no story, he's got nothing to say your grandfather, you believe that one? Ha. I'll no story you, mister. Don't listen to him." She looked like she was about to tell a secret.

"What's with the face? We Steinblooms are normal law-abiding people. Well, except for Uncle Abe, this is true."

"See, there he goes."

"Uncle Abe, boy. He had him some stories. Used to do vaudeville, play fiddle down at the movie houses. I was too young to go into those places, but I could hear him from the street. He's the one taught me how to read music. Only ones in the family with any musical talent, me and him. He drank too much, that's what they said anyways, but he was a good musician, and you know what? They asked him to be part of this new orchestra they were putting together back then, and you know what I'm talking about, Bessie? It was the National Symphony Orchestra!"

But that wasn't what Millie meant when she hinted he had stories to tell. Bess noticed when it came to telling the truth, each spoke for the other. They liked to expose each other's faults and failures in a competition of superiority. She liked to tell about the time he hired the wrong man to run his shop in Baltimore *He was a nice boy, what are you talking about?*, who took to wearing the flapper dresses he was supposed to be selling *I said there was a dress code, so he took me literally* and because Irv hardly ever visited the store like a good manager should *It was so far away* this man in a dress scared women out of the store telling them things like if only they weren't so fat they'd look as good in the dress as he did *Well, someone should tell it like it is.* It's stories like that, said Millie, that shows you just how soon he'd have been out of business had she not been there to knock some sense into him.

Oh yeah, he'd say. He'd say he'd like to see where she'd be if it weren't for him *With Sam Finkelstein, that doctor from Harvard, that's where I'd be, I should have married Sam when I had the chance.* Yeah, he'd say, the poor Russian Jewish girl who didn't even have a penny in her pocket *I had everything I needed thank you very much,* who walked into his shop and rang his bell in her torn pedal pushers *Torn, my tuchas,* whom he took pity on and hired as a salesgirl *I was your best salesgirl,* who all day long punched clack-clack-clack-ka*ching* at the heavy black cash register *I always paid you back whatever I borrowed* and holy mackerel if someone could just have told him what he was getting into, boy oh boy.

Sometimes it's in fun, their bantering. But often it turns to bickering that turns to vicious verbal attacks. Nine times out of ten the argument begins with a nasty comment from Millie. "Nobody cares, Irv," she'd say, or "Shut your mouth," as if the anger inside her—an anger so deep that it is before Bess's time and beyond her comprehension—has no choice but to bubble to the surface in small explosions of hostility. The tension, like smoke, makes anyone else in the room cough and leave. Bess thinks maybe the anger stems from their inability to have children of their own (she doesn't know which one of them had the problem), but then it could be anything, for what does Bess know about keeping a marriage afloat for sixty-five years? What does she know about marriage, period? She would like to believe that her grandparents loved each other once, deeply and passionately, to know they were happy in their lives as a whole, but then what does that say about marriage, that the descent into misery is directly related to the number of years a couple spends together, the accumulated anger and grief winning out in the end? Where is the Yin and Yang in old age? It's as if Millie and Irv's imbalanced inner state manifests itself on the outside, the way they walk slowly and diagonally, bumping into things and losing their footing.

And still, despite all their fighting, Bess feels lucky to have them. They adore her (and she, them). They shower her with all the love they withhold from each other, it seems. How important it is to have family nearby, thinks Bess, as she turns onto their street. She's glad she can drive up a highway and in twenty-five minutes see them opening the front door the moment they hear her pull up to the curb, smiling and aching to hug her, saying *come, come dear* as she shuts the car door and walks into their embrace.

"How's my birthday girl!" Irv yells out, beaming, squeezing her shoulders. "It's good to see you, sweetheart. We haven't seen you for ages."

"For God's sake," says Millie with almost ludicrous exaggeration. "You just saw her last week. What's wrong with you?" She knocks his chest with the back of her hand and shoos him aside. "Bess dear, you made good time for getting such a late start. Was there traffic?" Millie grabs Bess's face in a tight grip and gives her cheek an exaggerated kiss. Whereas Irv is slow, soft, and gentle, Millie is feisty, strong, and hard angled. Her hugs can be suffocating, her pinches send shots of pain to the brain as if she pressed on a black-and-blue mark.

"No, not really. I'm sorry I'm late." Bess rotates her jaw and rubs her cheek where Millie has pressed on it. She wipes her shoes on a doormat that has ducks around its perimeter. "I brought some berries." Bess feels like a giant standing next to her grandparents. She figures they must be down to under five feet by now, and they can't weigh more than a hundred pounds each. They were never big people, but lately they seem particularly small and getting smaller, like thawing snowmen: their wrists thin as twigs, their clothes too big for their frames, their bulbous faces now sallow and sagging so their crooked noses stick further out. She can look down and see the brown sun spots on Irv's scalp through thin rows of gray hair and the bits of dandruff stuck to the outside folds of his big ears, wrinkled and reddish like dried apricots. Millie's silver hair is thinning, too, but she has it styled and sprayed into place each week, preserving its poof by sleeping on a special satiny moon-shaped pillow. At eighty-six, Irv couldn't give two farts what he looked like, his white dress shirt hanging haphazardly over his belt, his fly undone. But the day Millie, who is four years younger, gives up on her appearance is the day she gives up on life, she likes to say. The women's fashion magazines still pile up at her bedside, her closets are still full of seasonal ensembles that haven't yet gone out of style. She dons her pantsuits for appointments in the city and her jogging suits for her morning walks around the neighborhood or, when it's too cold out, around the top floor of the mall before it opens. Today she has on a black sweater, pearls, and gray slacks with a perfect crease down the front and back of each leg. "I like your sweater," says Bess, making conversation. "Where'd you get it?"

Millie takes the bag of berries and places it in the kitchen sink. "You like it? I don't remember where I got it. What size are you? You want to try it on?"

"Bessie, come see my latest acquisition," interrupts Irv. "Downstairs. Come." He takes a book from the shelf and motions for her to follow him. "Mildred," he yells, flicking on the light at the top of a dank staircase. "We're going downstairs, we'll be right back."

The spiral wooden stairway to the basement creaks with each step. The walls are cement and the air is considerably cooler. Irv pulls a string from a bulb in the middle of the room and the harsh light shines on dozens of pairs of eyes surrounding them, staring blankly in their direction—an eerie, unsmiling audience of stiff anorexic bodies, some pointing their accusatory fingers at Bess, some looking upward as if in contemplation, some about to take a step, a few missing an arm, one in the corner disturbingly headless, all upright and female and frightening in their thinness, their nakedness, their having been crowded into this cell like prisoners of war. "Jesus, Gramp, your mannequins freak me out every time. I don't understand why you still keep them."

"They keep me company, these ladies. And they keep quiet." He smiles and winks at Bess. He must have about thirty or forty of them, Bess figures. He started bringing them home from his dress shop when they got scuffed or broken and had to be replaced. He would have five or six mannequins at a time on display in the shop's front windows, each with its own distinct wig and dress and maybe a shawl or handbag. He liked seeing them each morning, even gave them names. *Hello girls,* he'd say, *keeping an eye on the store, are you?* He grew attached to them and felt in some odd way it was his duty to bring them home after they'd served their purpose. But after a while, he started to buy them quicker than he needed them, looking for unique ones with distinct markings or more movable parts. He had been known to offer exorbitant amounts to other store owners if he saw one he liked in a window display. It's a good thing, Bess told Millie once, that he never took to using the Internet. *And don't you tell him*, Millie had said, *he's sick sick a very sick man your grandfather*. Once he retired, he slowed his purchases down considerably, mostly because he was running out of room and Millie was on his case about it to no end. Bess had the feeling he spent a lot of time down here amongst his harem.

"Look," he says, pulling one out from behind a box in the corner. "Isn't she lovely? I just got her from a store in Northeast." She is dark brown with long thin fingers and—as her grandfather proceeds to point out—moveable at the wrists, elbows, shoulders, neck, waist, and knees. She has full lips and black, painted-on eyebrows, but her most noticeable feature is her afro, as she is one of the few mannequins in the room with hair.

"How old is she?"

"I think she's probably a '70s model. She's a bit scuffed at the joints, but other than that she's in perfect shape. Look, someone drew a peace sign around her belly button."

"But she's supposed to wear clothes. What's she doing with a belly button?"

"That's the beauty of it. They probably needed the belly button to show off low miniskirts or high halter tops. Remember halter tops? I'm going to name her Peace."

Bess stares at her eyes, which are gazing confidently up toward a corner of the ceiling. Her stillness is spooky, as if when the lights go out and the humans leave she might come alive and incite her fellow mannequins to revolt.

Irv leaves the room for a moment and returns with a cassette player. He plugs it in and presses play and the room suddenly sounds like a smoky bar. "T-Bone Walker," says Irv. "He's the best blues player there ever was. Peace, would you like to dance?" He positions her arms—one around his waist, the other around his neck—picks her up, and with closed eyes dances her around to the old scratchy recording of Walker's "Hypin' Woman Blues."

Bess watches him. The reasons for her grandfather's fondness for female mannequins is probably not all that difficult to figure out, she thinks. Students in a Psych 101 class might comment on his loneliness, his need for ownership and control, to savor the past and forget about the aging process, to create a safe haven among friends, not to mention any sexual overtones that Bess doesn't want to contemplate in depth. But what's puzzling is his interest in this particular mannequin, this African American '70s beauty, which makes Bess think she really doesn't know her grandfather well, or at least the man he was in his younger days. Maybe he was a swinger. Maybe he dated women like Peace before he married Millie. Maybe he didn't do a whole lot of what he really wanted to do in the eighty-six years he's been on this earth, which is why he's dancing around his basement with a mannequin in his arms, humming, swaying, smiling, imagining.

Bess taps him on the shoulder, feeling a sudden urge to be part of this imaginary world that makes him smile so broadly. "May I cut in?" She means could she dance with him, but he nods and hands her the mannequin, stepping back to clap to the rhythm. "Oh," says Bess, face to face with the woman's perfect plastic cheeks. "Okay then." She grabs onto the figure's tiny waist and slowly twirls her around like a schoolboy at his first social. "Look, Gramp," she says. "I'm giving Peace a chance." Either he doesn't hear her or he doesn't get it, for his gaze is off to the distance and Bess can tell he is alone somewhere, out there, where she can never reach him.

Mary L. Tabor

Riptide

Mary L. Tabor's story "Riptide" appears in her collection *The Woman Who Never Cooked*, which won Mid-List Press's First Series Award. New work will appear in the *Missouri Review*. Her fiction has recently appeared in *Chautauqua Literary Journal*, *Image*, the *Mid-American Review*, *Chelsea*, *Hayden's Ferry Review*, and *American Literary Review*. She has just completed a novel and teaches at the Smithsonian's Campus-on-the-Mall and George Washington University.

My mother died on a Wednesday. I sat in my room for a month after she died. I didn't go to my office. I didn't do my laundry. I didn't answer the phone. In Washington you can get most everything you need delivered by strangers, wearing caps, speaking with accents. I tried not to order twice from the same place. I didn't want to know anyone. I developed a kind of system. A delivery rotation system to make sure the one who came to the door wouldn't know me, even if I remembered him.

My answering machine piled up with messages. I returned some of them. I told my father I was okay and would go to work soon. I kept in touch with my office. Sara, my aunt and my mother's only sibling, called every day the first week, then once a week.

She told me stories when I was little, when we would sit on the sand in Ocean City. She would talk of Neptune and his armies of the waters, of rivers on the ocean floor, and later of the man who fished for forty days and didn't catch a fish, the man with just a boy to help him with his skiff, the boy who stayed his friend when luck had left. Later I read that story, and her telling lingered in my head, the way she told about the boy.

I didn't call Sara. I remembered the boy in the story. I know it's not meant to be his story. I used to like to think it was, pretending I could choose, the way my mother did when she adopted me.

On the Wednesday one month later, I went outside and commemorated my mother's early death, my loss of her when we were both still young. I stood in front of my apartment in Georgetown on the cobblestone path. I watched dust swirl in sun. I thought about how, when I laid my face against my mother's arm the day she told me I was adopted, I could feel the sun on her skin and smell the sea. Then I went back in the house and called my friend Francisca.

Francisca and I drink together. I've known Francisca for a long time though she and I are very different. Francisca cleans houses. She's a middle-class white woman, thirty-one years old, honey blonde hair, long polished fingernails, always manicured. Hands like my mother's. I once asked her how she could clean and still have hands like that. She said her nails were like iron—that it was inherited. Her mother's nails were like that too. They never broke. "In fact," she said, "I use them like tools when I'm cleaning. Maybe I'm not human," she said. "I have claws like a wild thing," and she laughed.

Francisca doesn't laugh much. She lost a baby when she was in her twenties. The baby was three years old when she died from a congenital heart defect. There was nothing Francisca could do. And then there was no way she could recover. She divorced her husband. She started cleaning houses and has a good business now. She still does most of the work herself. She says, "It's like cleaning out the closets in my head, like fixing things." But I know that Francisca will never be fixed.

We went to Morton's, an upscale steak house, a block from my apartment. The maître d', George, flirts with me. He's about fifty-five and thinks I'll probably sleep with him someday. He said, "Sasha, where have you been, my love? Come sit at the bar with me for a few minutes before we get busy."

I'd gotten there early. I wanted to walk in alone. I wanted to sit by myself, get ready for Francisca, ready for talking again. I told George I'd been away. I didn't tell him about my mother. I would tell him eventually but not that night. He brought me a glass of red zinfandel, my favorite, the Jack London. I once bought a bottle for Sara, and she recalled the story by London, a story she'd read to me, the one about building a fire.

She didn't appreciate the wine. At Morton's I sat at the bar and thought about the man in the snow, the matches and sticks that wouldn't light. I sipped the wine George handed me, enjoyed the berries on my tongue, the way the wine warmed my throat. And then Francisca arrived.

She'd just showered. I could see moist strands of hair at the nape of her neck. When we kissed hello, I could smell the soap on her skin. Her makeup was heavy around the eyes, too heavy, I thought. That's how I'd done mine, how I'd needed to do it.

We sat together at the bar.

"Rough time, huh, Sash?"

"Um, but at least I'm out."

"I've missed you," she said. "I've needed to talk to you."

I needed her to need me this way. I understood that Francisca was what I needed because she was unlucky.

"How's Richard?" I asked. I knew he had to be the problem. Francisca had met Richard at Morton's. He bought her a big steak and a thirty-dollar bottle of red wine to go with it. She thought that showed her something important about him, about his staying power. Francisca is looking for staying power. She thought she'd found it in Richard, but I knew it couldn't last because Francisca has to lose to keep her grief alive.

"I got a detective to follow him," she said.

"Whatever for?"

"Sash, he got soft in bed. Now I realize he's forty, but still that's not supposed to happen. And I told him, of course. I mean I have enough problems without feeling like the guy can't get it up for me. You understand."

This was classic Francisca. She told me this detective followed Richard to his ex-wife's house, saw them open a bottle of wine in the kitchen, that he stayed all night. That was it for Francisca. She booted Richard out, told him he couldn't commit and she could never trust him.

"You're sure about that?"

"Yeah, he's not worth it."

"I like that about you, your certainty." That's what Francisca's child, that perfect gift she'd lost, had given her. "It's your best quality. My mother had that. Your turn."

She laughed. “Your best quality? True blue. You stick.”

“Yeah, well, Sara keeps calling and I don’t call her back. Weird, huh?”

“Yeah, considering.”

Francisca knew I used to go to Sara’s house for dinner once a week, every week, that I started having dinner with Sara and her husband Ben and their teenage daughter Rebecca when I started school at Georgetown U. I ate with them at the long wood table in her kitchen in Chevy Chase. I didn’t tell my mother about the visits. I didn’t go home to Baltimore much. Just occasionally on the weekends or when I had to, when my mother was in the hospital. She was in and out most of my life, most of Sara’s life.

That was the year I started drinking, the year I met Francisca.

“Sash, for God’s sake, find out how she is.”

“I know how she is.”

Once, in the hospital, when my mother was on the gurney on her way to another operating room I saw them, no words—just eyes and fingers that made me think of a photo in the album: Sara, a little girl in baggy shorts, white anklets and canvas Keds, sitting on an old glider on the narrow porch of their row house; my mother perched on the railing, wearing a halter top and pedal pushers, her hand reaching for the glider’s metal arm. In the hospital’s linoleum hallway, I watched their fingers part, saw their hands stilled mid-air when an orderly wheeled my mother down the hall. I remember how I thought that I could hear a glider squeak.

Francisca said, with an edge in her voice, “Yeah, sure, you know. And you’re sure, right?”

I filled Francisca’s glass. “Yeah, I’m sure like you’re sure.”

I thought of my mother on the surface of the sea. Before the crutches, before the wheelchair because they turn sand into quicksand, we went to the beach at Ocean City, Maryland, every summer. She swore she could sense the exact times within a day when the moon pulls the sea forward and back. We’d go down from the boardwalk, down to the edge of ocean and shore to watch the tides bulge up on the sand and slide away. When she died, it was like a rip in the surface of the ocean, like a current pulling out to sea, water caught between two sandbars underneath, a trap that, if you're in the ocean, you can't see.

The next day I couldn't go to work. I sat at my desk by the window and took out a long yellow pad. With my head clear of the last night's wine, I started a list of everything I know about myself when I was little.

Here's what I wrote: I kept my eyes closed for a month when I was born. (My mother said it was because I had an eye infection. Sara said I was waiting to be sure to see my mother. My mother loved when Sara said that.) I have dark green eyes. Like the ocean. (My mother used to say that.) Like leaves in spring. (Sara says that.) Deep, dark brown eyes, amber brown. My mother's eyes. (Sara's are like hers but lighter, yellow-brown in the center.) My white ocean of hair. (What Sara called it. Like a peroxide wish, my mother said. She had dark hair she'd once tried to dye and loved the way my hair changed with light, ran her fingers through it, French braided it while it was wet with sea and salt.) My new Mary Janes, yellow patent leather, that I wore to bed. I didn't talk until I was three, then spoke in full sentences. I'm strong-willed like a bull. (My mother said that. Like her, she said.) A sea goddess who came to earth full blown. (Sara said that. She said I came with my own history.) And then I wrote: insulin syringes on the sink, the smell of alcohol on skin. Oranges and grapefruits. Teaching me to put the needles in their skins. The smell of acid in my nose. Piles of pills beside her bed. The way she yelled. The day she hit me when I drank the last orange juice from the fridge. The way her blood ran hot for fighting. The way her blood ran slow inside her narrowed veins. The pain inside her legs and hands. The pills. My drinking. Dinners at Sara's house.

I was at the bottom of the page. Words trailed down the yellow pad, black ink, off the lines, off center, all over the page. I felt smothered, sucked under, choked.

I longed to talk to Sara, to sit across from her. I could see her in the middle thwart of her safe skiff, her oar lying in the sea, waiting for my hands to wrap around, take hold, be pulled across the side.

I called her.

"Sasha, Sasha." That's what she said when she heard my voice—just my name, again and again, and then she waited.

I asked her to lunch.

We agreed to meet at the Mayflower Hotel in the restaurant off the lobby. I wore one of my black suits. I was perfectly put together, understated gold earrings, flat suede Ferragamo shoes, black stockings, swingy but professional black skirt, elegant ivory and black patterned vest with scroll-wrapped tiny buttons, and an Armani tailored jacket. I was sitting in the lobby waiting for her when I glanced down and noticed the smudge on my cuff. Had I inadvertently wiped my nose on my sleeve or, more likely, dragged my cuff across the foamy top of my morning cappuccino?

I was alarmed by my sleeve.

Sara was wearing a black sweater and slacks, oddly casual for her job. She directs one of the research departments at the Library of Congress. I like to think she works in an attic room, a book open on her lap, a window filled with rustling leaves. Quiet work. "Unlike my noisy childhood," she'd said once. "Noisy how?" I'd asked, and after a long pause, the silence before speech that is the sound of sadness, she'd said, "Illness makes a lot of noise." And I sat silent, thinking of my mother's sickness, how it must have filled her house the way it filled up mine.

"I took the day off," she said. I gave her my cheek. She tried to hug me, but quickly stepped back when I pulled away. I stood and looked at her. Sara is three years younger than my mother, tall and thin, prettier in an odd way—strong bones in her face that give her a look of knowing. It's the way the bones dominate in her face, not the flesh, as if I can see her core, her skeleton. I don't have that kind of bone thinness. My mother didn't either. My mother admired Sara's bones and her skin, smooth and fair like their mother's. My mother had skin that tanned and wrinkled. She sat in the sun all summer managing the pool near her house. She couldn't have a job like Sara's or mine. The illness that took over her life when she was twelve and finally took it away when she was forty-six and I was twenty-five marked her territory—the way her death marked mine.

"Yeah, well, I've taken the month off," I told her.

"Yes." That was all she said. Then she waited. That's her way. Not like my mother at all.

"But I'm okay now. I've been back to work for a week. I just needed to be alone, really alone to think."

"I've been worried," she said.

"I got your messages, but I just couldn't talk. I need to be alone," I said again. I wanted to explain why I couldn't let her help me. But how to put in words what I had yet to understand: this pull, this tow?

"Without me?" she asked.

I didn't answer. Instead I looked at her and wondered if she went outside when she was little to get away from the noise inside her house, if she sat on the curb, if she wished herself away.

We ate. She picked at her salad. A chicken Caesar salad. She'd ordered what I'd ordered as if the food didn't matter to her and then she didn't really eat it. So I guess it didn't. But then I thought, That's why she's so thin. Never eats. My mother used to say that. She'd say, "Sara gets throat lock when she's nervous. Can't get anything down and since she's nervous most of the time, she's thin like a rail." She'd say to Sara, "If only I could get such an ailment." And then my mother and Sara would laugh, a kind of private, morbid joke. My mother, after all, was sick.

I'd made it hard for Sara to eat.

When we left the restaurant, she suggested coffee in the lounge in the lobby. She said, "You could smoke there and we could talk some more."

Sara stopped smoking fifteen years ago when my mother had the first operation on her leg. My mother told Sara she had to stop smoking because she wanted her alongside. And Sara did because my mother had to stop. Sara never started again. I was only ten and couldn't go on the trip. I stayed home with my father who said he had to work, who worked more and more as my mother got more sick, more often. They went to Milwaukee because the veins in my mother's body had all narrowed and even the doctors at Johns Hopkins didn't think they could find new veins to save her leg. But there was this doctor, as my mother said, "in God-awful Milwaukee," who could do it.

We got our cappuccinos and it was as if Sara read my mind as I lit up. "The first thing your mother did after the first operation on her legs was put a cigarette in her mouth. What a pistol she was. She lit it up just the way you're doing now, only she had an IV in her arm and she did it right in front of the doctor. She lit it and when he told her not to smoke, that it would only make things worse, she smiled wide and showed those great teeth of hers and said oh so sweetly, 'Fuck you.'"

I laughed. Sara had never told me that one before.

"Still," she said, "I wish you wouldn't smoke."

"It's one of the advantages of being adopted," I said. "I don't have to worry about heredity."

"How does that make any sense?"

"Because I don't know what it could make worse."

I looked down into the white cup and stirred the foam and cinnamon. I watched the fluid circle round my spoon like a little whirlpool. The cup had a gold rim like the Royal Worcester mug, the one I gave my mother one Mother's Day. She always used it, at least when I was around. She never put it in the dishwasher because of the fourteen-carat gold rim. She used to warm her hands around the cup, her long red nails, how the polish always glowed. She took such care of her hands, getting manicures once a week. Those perfect nails around the peaches and the grapes on the mug, the purple blue veins in her frigid fingers. I began to weep, right there in the Mayflower coffee bar.

Sara put her hand on top of mine. She didn't say anything. Just put her warm, perfect hand on mine. Her fingers are small and narrow. She keeps her nails trimmed, unpolished. I pulled my hand away.

I remembered the other "Milwaukees" that came one after another—when I was grown like Sara, when I was the one who sat by the bed, when I was too old to find a curb to sit on—when my mother pulled me to her—and when the pull was more than I could bear, how I found another way: with a drink in my hand. I remembered how I laid down a fog inside my head and slept.

Alcohol was the only drug my mother didn't use. She had to kill the pain in ways she understood. That meant prescriptions written out by doctors, purchased in drugstores. She disapproved of drinking. She thought it was low and dirty. It was my drug and she knew it. She knew it because, when I came home, I came home drunk. She waited for me alone, while my father worked his second job, the night job. She never slept even with the drugs. She'd drop off now and then, but the pain in her legs and hands would soon take over. I asserted once, "You use drugs and I use booze and there's not a whole lot of difference—still get a good high," but she didn't agree.

One night I came home and stood at the end of her bed. I reeked from beer and bourbon. I could smell it on my skin, rising out of my pores in sweat. My mother lay dozing in bed, her hair, cut in layers, feathered out on the pillow, her profile defined on the cotton pillow slip. I could see the curve of her nose, the angle of her brow, the parting of her lips. I couldn't believe she was really asleep. I thought she was dead. I walked to the edge of her bed and kneeled down in my rocky, boozy haze. I put my face next to her mouth. I could hear the air inside her lungs. I smelled her breath. It was acrid with smoke and chemicals and loss. She opened her eyes and reached out for me. I thought she was going to hold me, embrace me. She took my long hair into her hands and pulled me screaming on top of her on the bed. She pulled my jaws open and pushed her face into my mouth. She wrenched my head and neck. My back arched. My body shook. I quivered with her anger, lying on her stomach, her breasts pressed against mine. She was strong. She could break me in half.

"What are you doing," she screamed into my open mouth. It was a curse, not a question. "What are you doing to this body that I saved and raised. What right have you. Who do you think you are."

And then the questions: "You think you know pain? You think you hurt? You think you need to numb your mind?"

She threw me on the floor. I reached up to her bed stand and with my heavy, drunken arm swept all the amber, white-capped bottles to the floor. Then I got up and went into my room to sleep it off.

And once a week I went for calm, for respite from the noise of illness. I went to dinner at Sara's house.

After we'd finished our coffee, when I'd pulled myself together, after Sara had paid the check, she said. "Let's go for a walk."

"I'm sorry," I said. "I have to go now. It's been good to see you."

"But Sasha, I've got the whole day. We could go outside and just walk the way we used to."

Once we walked along the Tidal Basin in early April when the gnarled cherry trees bloom. It was early morning before we both went to work. I was hung over and needed to talk. She met me. She walked alongside me. The morning was cold and it sobered me, reminded me of my mother like an upwelling current from the bottom of the sea.

"No, we can't do that," I said. "We can't."

"Why can't we? We can. Of course we can."

"No." I put my hand up like a signal that she shouldn't come any closer.

"Will you come to dinner then, maybe next week?"

"I'll call you," I said, and then I went for a walk, a long walk but not where Sara and I used to walk. I walked the long downtown blocks, one after another, down L Street, over to K, all the way to Georgetown as fast as I could. The sun was high and hot. I pulled off my suit jacket and slung it over my shoulder, kept walking until I got to my apartment. My ivory silk blouse stuck to my skin. I pulled it off over my head without unbuttoning it, pulled my bra off the same way. Unzipped my skirt, kicked my shoes into the wall, ripped off my panty hose and threw them in the trash. I got in the shower and let the water run down my body. Then I lay down on the floor in the shower stall, curled up, wedged into the square of tile. I smelled water, soap, and mold. I cried. Tears and water in the drain.

I longed for the force of will that would give my life a seamless, silent glide through space and time. I longed for my mother's will.

My mother lost a baby before she adopted me. Sara was sixteen when my mother lost the baby. She said that one day about a year after the baby had died she went to the movies at the Crest Theater across from the diner on Rogers Avenue with two girlfriends to see *The Young Doctors* starring Ben Gazzara. She told me how the white light flickered off the screen like

Ben Gazzara's white coat, like all the white coats rushing past her when her face was pressed against the nursery glass. How he delivered a baby. How he placed the crying child in the mother's arms. Sara told me she began to cry, that she wept uncontrollably, unable to explain. How her chocolate-covered raisins rolled on the floor. She said she remembered it as a moment of excess that lingered inside her, disturbed her and slowly developed like a strip of film in solution in a darkroom. I didn't understand then what she meant, but the memory has slowly revealed itself, made me see how much my mother lost before she found me.

When she was pregnant she went to the hospital more than two months before her due date to ensure a safe delivery. My mother told me the doctor put her in a section of the hospital for the terminally ill. She said he did that because the patients there were allowed to walk outside or ride in wheelchairs to a garden, and visitors weren't limited by special hours. But my mother wasn't terminally ill, or that's what people thought in those days about her disease. Like me, they didn't understand how sick she was, how she would die, that she would die young. In this special place my mother waited for her baby to grow and form. The doctor said he was taking the baby early because he feared an oversized baby, hard to deliver. He said diabetics have such babies. But he took it too early. As my mother lay recuperating from the cesarean section, the doctor told her that her baby's lungs hadn't fully formed. My mother told me she watched the baby's chest heave up and down behind the nursery glass and that the baby died after twenty-three hours.

Since my mother had a disease, it was hard for her to get a baby from an adoption agency. It was possible but hard, and my mother wasn't good at waiting. She found a doctor, an obstetrician who told her there were other ways to get babies. And with his help, she got me. A woman handed me over in a hospital. I know because my mother told me. A woman gave me like a gift. That's what I think on a good day. Or like returned merchandise, on a bad day.

On the Wednesday night one week later, I took with me to Morton's the little ceramic box edged in silver that Sara had given me one birthday.

It was hand painted with a soft, gray-green design. It was quite elegant. In the note, she'd said, "This little box reminds me of the undersides of new-blown leaves like the color of your eyes."

I gave it to Francisca after we finished a bottle of the Jack London zinfandel. I told Francisca that the box reminded me of the child she lost, though I had never seen her.

"It's small and light in the hand," I said, "like a memory."

Francisca wept, remembering.

I ordered another bottle of wine for the two of us. George, the maître d', brought it over himself. "For you, my love," he said, "I'll pour."

"It's Wednesday," I said. "Let's drink to my mother. Let's drink to motherhood."

I waited two weeks to call Sara. I called and asked if I could come to dinner. She said, "Any night you want." I said I wanted a night when Ben was working late so we could be alone. I knew Rebecca was away at school, Wesleyan in Connecticut.

When I went away—though not far enough away at Georgetown—Sara, living in Washington, made it convenient for me to stop in and I did it more than I thought I would, told myself it had just worked out that way. Now I understand I went to Sara's house instead of going home.

I would come early and help her cook. We were often alone in the kitchen fixing dinner for the others.

Copper pots hung from the ceiling over the stove, tarnished, scratched. She has a rough, tin Foley grinder up there on the rack. She uses it for mashed potatoes. She hangs strainers and ladles and a stock pot from the hooks.

She showed me how to season the old cast-iron frying pan we used for hot peppered fish. She never washes it. Just pours boiling water on it and then wipes it down with oil and hangs it up again. I loved the hot peppered fish. Sometimes I would stop on my way and buy the halibut. When I got to her house, she would be in the kitchen, pounding the pepper for the coating on the fish, heating the frying pan until it smoked. I would take the fish out of the ice and butcher paper and roll it in the crushed pepper on the long waxed paper on the counter. I would lay the fish in the smoking pan while she chopped cilantro for the garnish. I remember the bottle of extra virgin olive oil in her hand, its clear green color in the bottle, the way it glistened when she drizzled it across the blackened fish. I remember the smell of burnt pepper and cast iron.

It was a Tuesday night when I arrived at Sara's door again. I'd brought nothing. No offering, no flowers, no wine. She didn't seem to notice. She was wearing the blue faded apron she always used to wear when she opened the door. She had the long white strings tied around her narrow middle so the knot came out in the front, just below her hip. The front was smudged with flour. Her face was bare, no makeup at all. She was always careful with her makeup. Never wore very much but made sure that the bare truth of her age was covered. That night I could see the lines around her eyes, the shadows underneath.

We went into the kitchen. She poured peanut oil into a big pot. A pile of raw, sliced potatoes floated in a large pot of cold water on the counter near the stove. "French fries," she said. And then she looked at me. Remember, her eyes said.

And I did.

"Suntan lotion and french fries, my favorite smells," my mother used to say. My mother loved the honky-tonk of the lower end of the boardwalk. She loved the crowd, the noise, the dark, greasy air. She was the french fry expert and would buy them only from Thrasher's where they fried them in their skins in vats of peanut oil. The fries filled up in great big paper cones. She poured salt and vinegar on top. Then we went to Dumser's Dairy for a custard ice cream cone. We always had vanilla. She used to lick mine around the edges, catching the melting sweetness while I ate from the top. And then we'd ride the Ferris wheel. With our stomachs full, we'd take the slow slide around the sky. My mother loved the swaying stillness at the top when the wheel stopped turning to let the others off at the bottom. She used to say, "I hope we get stuck up here. It happens sometimes. It happened to me and Sara once. Maybe we'll be lucky like that."

Sara lowered french fries into the oil with a large slotted spoon. I said, "You still went, didn't you?"

"To the beach? Well, sure. We took Rebecca. But it was never the same, Sasha."

While we rocked up there on the Ferris wheel, alone together, my mother always put her arm across my shoulder and held me. I could see kites flying on the beach in reflected light from the boardwalk. I could hear the waves in the sea in the quiet of that waiting, airy moment. I could smell the sun on my mother's skin.

Sara stirred the fries with the spoon. I could smell the peanut oil. And then she said, "You went too with your friends when you got older."

"Oh sure, we drank and caroused. On the loose, you might say."

"Wild, like your mother."

"Like my mother," I said, "right." At the end of the boardwalk in Ocean City, the sand stretches out so far, it's hard to see the ocean. My mother is that place. She's the end of the boardwalk where the old wooden boards stop and the cement walk begins, where the food and the rides are, where the honky-tonk begins, where the Ferris wheel takes its slide around the sky.

Now Sara pressed freshly ground pepper into the tops of hamburgers and sautéed them on a bed of hot salt in a sizzling frying pan. She added lemon juice and Worcestershire sauce to the pan when the burgers were browned. She put a piece of butter on the top of each burger and I watched it melt. I watched her make a salad. I watched her chop garlic and put it in a wooden bowl. I watched her pour in balsamic vinegar and Dijon mustard. I watched her use a whisk to swirl in olive oil for the dressing. I watched her do all the things my mother never did.

At the long wood table in her kitchen, I sat down and she poured me a glass of wine. I drank from her green crystal glass with the clear white, delicate stem and said, "I came here too often, when I should have gone home."

She said, "Your mother was very sick, Sasha, for a long time, for most of the time."

"And I'm my mother's child," I said. It was the only way I could explain. It is the explanation, the only explanation.

After dinner, I didn't help her with the dishes the way I used to. I didn't carry one single plate to the sink. I sat and drank my wine and watched her wash the dishes, scour the pan, pour the used oil into old coffee cans she'd saved under the sink. I didn't help her lift the heavy pot. I watched perspiration form at the edge of her white upper lip. I watched her move and walk in her big, wide kitchen. I looked for my mother in the angle of her back. But they're so different. I could see the tiny bones in the back of her neck. It was like looking through her skin. I thought of my mother in a shroud beneath the ground.

When it was time for me to go, I stood at Sara's open door and looked out into the night. She was at my side and I could smell her skin. It was not the smell of my mother's skin. I could smell her breath, fragrant with wine and garlic. It was not the smell of my mother's breath.

"I'm my mother's child," I said again and thought how I'd always known that I was all she had.

The tide rises to its apogee in answer to the moon and sun and earth when they align. A rip defies this call. My mother used to say, "If you get caught, you need to know the trick of swimming parallel to shore—the best way to get out. Or just let go." She meant just float and you'll get out.

Sara turned me toward her with her arms on my shoulders. She grabbed me and pulled me to her chest. I could feel her fine, thin hands against my back.

"Her only child," I said.

"Yes," she said, "you are."

And now I moved away, light and free inside the tow. However far it goes.

Julia Thomas

Imperfect Crimes

JULIA THOMAS 's fiction has appeared in *StorySouth* and *River Oak Review* and was awarded the 2005 Washington Prize in fiction. She holds an MA from Johns Hopkins University and was a waiter at the Bread Loaf Writers' Conference.

It takes us about forty minutes to get to the state park where seven-year-old Kendra Wishard's body was found. My eyes ache from squinting in the late afternoon sun and I close them as Margaretta lets the car glide to a stop in the small parking lot, the gravel popping and exploding beneath the tires.

"Here we are," Margaretta says and pulls the key from the ignition. I try to rub the tired ache from my eyes, setting off fireworks of pain in my face. I am beginning to regret giving in to Margaretta's desire to come here. For months, our town has been consumed by the disappearance of this one small child, who sledded over a hill in Memorial Park and was never seen again. Reporters from all the big national outfits descended upon our town, taking over restaurants and bars and the only public Internet access at the municipal library as though they had lived here all their lives. The story, the innocence and familiarity of launching a pristine new sled through banks of freshly fallen snow—how could that be dangerous?—captured the rest of the country's imagination. It was the biggest thing that had happened in our town in years, some said the only thing.

Margaretta and I step out of the car and into the parking lot gingerly, tentatively, the way people tour the nearby Civil War battlefields, awed by the sense of walking across ground that has seen events so much larger than themselves. There is only one trail out of the parking lot, its opening marked by a wooden sign that said "Pine Cone Trail" and a matching wooden-slatted trash can overflowing with plastic soda bottles, beer cans, Doritos bags, and torn condom foils. People come up here to party now. One of the last television reports had been about the parties—the boozy, smiling faces lit up by the camera lights; beer cans raised in defiant toast; eager voices crowding the reporter's microphone, jockeying for their one chance to be heard on the other side of the world.

"There's no shame anymore," Margaretta mutters as we hurry past the mess and into the woods.

Margaretta and I have been friends a long time, forty-eight years to be exact, ever since the day I caught her shoplifting lipsticks from the corner drug. We spent the rest of that afternoon rubbing the color into our lips and cheeks, discussing movie stars and boys and teachers. Margaretta's family had just moved to town, a fact that gave her a certain short-lived glamour and celebrity. She'd been short and plain and a little tough-looking, which had appealed to me. By the age of twelve, I'd grown weary of the girlishness my mother had cultivated in me.

It was that girlishness, of course, that had attracted Margaretta to me. I gave her advice on what to wear, how to walk, when to approach a boy. My efforts were pretty successful, if I can say so myself. Margaretta grew up to be the dominant Avon lady in town, although people still shake their heads in wonder when they see her lugging her Pandora's box of potions and powders door to door.

We are sixty now. *That says it all*, as Margaretta is fond of saying. Margaretta's weight has settled in around her hips and thighs. *I'm a pear, honey, a good old Bartlett pear.* Margaretta has lots of these little phrases that she uses over and over.

She looks younger than I do now, which I don't mind. My figure has both spread and receded over the years, as if filling in some invisible rectangular field surrounding my body. I've aged the way my mother did, the way lots of small-town women do. There's a certain hardness and severity that come from trouble and disappointment. Margaretta is forever trying to get me to consent to a makeover. She says she can diminish my fine lines and wrinkles. That some blush would soften my look. She offers me free samples but I take just the tiny vials of cologne. I'm sixty, I tell her. Sure I could look better, but who would care?

Fifty feet in, the Pine Cone Trail narrows and becomes darker and less welcoming. The trees on either side are taller and more closely packed together. Not as much light gets through here, making everything look like old faded fabric. We walk for half an hour before stopping to rest against two moss-covered boulders. Margaretta opens her purse and rummages out a package of foil-wrapped brownies.

"Here," she says and hands me a brownie. "Teresa gave me these when I dropped off her order this morning. You know, the Bumbaugh girl."

I nod and bite into the chocolate. It is dry and bland. I have never been fond of brownies. Either most people can't make them or they are a flawed idea to begin with.

"I wonder what it was like, finding her body. They must have been excited." Margaretta is looking around at the woods. "What did Cal say?"

Cal is my husband. As is the case in these situations, our town had formed multiple search parties to look for Kendra Wishard. Cal had the misfortune to be in the final, successful party.

"We really didn't talk about it," I say. Cal and I have been strangers living under one roof for a long time now, communicating primarily through gestures, sighs, and dishes and mail left out on tables and counter tops. The day his party found Kendra's body, he came home smelling of vomit and sour death. He took a long scalding shower—I could tell by the steam leaking out from around the bathroom door—and went to bed. He slept for fifteen hours.

"How could you not talk about such a thing? Such an important thing?" Margaretta says.

"We don't talk about the unimportant things anymore either."

Margaretta cocks her head and looks at me over the top of her glasses.

"He didn't volunteer any information and I couldn't think of a graceful way to ask," I say. "All I know is what I read in the paper." I am not being entirely truthful with Margaretta. While it is true that Cal has not said anything directly to me about finding the little girl's body, I did overhear a conversation between him and one of the other searchers. They sat on our back porch and drank and cried and talked. I sat by the window in the bathroom, which is on the second floor of our house, directly above the porch, and listened.

"Well shoot, D. That's why I asked you to come along today. I thought you would know where we were going."

"Well, you should've asked before we got here." There was a time when Margaretta and I had been like two sides of the same coin. We knew what the other was thinking, could finish each other's sentences. Those days are long gone now. Sometimes I can still anticipate what Margaretta is about to say, but it's never what I myself would say anymore.

"You're not very curious, Dorothy. I would have gotten Cal drunk, plied his tongue with strong drink."

I watch Margaretta finish chewing her brownie and then proceed to pick bits of walnut out of her teeth. The sight of it irritates me so, I can barely stand still. When John died six months ago, I had hoped our friendship would return to what it had once been. But that may have been overly optimistic, considering all the silt that has accumulated in our lives, like plaque in an artery. We have spent our entire adult lives sharing one man and dividing our hearts between him and each other. I guess it is unrealistic to expect our arteries to simply clear, now that he is gone.

When I graduated from high school in 1963, my mother packed me off to Ohio to care for her sister, who had come down with lung cancer. I had been going with John Nunemaker since junior year. He drove out to visit three or four times in the eight months it took my aunt to die. Those visits had been my only respite from the daily rounds of spoon feeding, sponge bathing, linen changing, and Bible reading.

My mother telephoned once a week to see how my aunt and I were doing. When she told me that she had seen John and Margaretta at the Tastee-Freez, and, days later, in the bowling alley parking lot, I thought nothing of it. John and I had often taken Margaretta along with us on dates, trying to fix her up with John's friends, pushing her to mingle at parties and dances. Of course, John would take care of Margaretta and Margaretta would keep an eye on John while I was away.

When I returned to town after my aunt's funeral, John and Margaretta were already married, Margaretta blooming with child. I tried to be calm. I went to the machine shop where John was working, to return his class ring. But when I saw his familiar blue sedan sitting in the parking lot—the car in which we had kissed and gone for long afternoon drives, discussing our future together—something in me snapped. I unsheathed the ring from its small velvet bag and threw it with as much force as I could muster against the windshield of John's car, willing the glass to shatter into a million pieces. Instead, the heavy ring simply nicked out a tiny chip of glass, bounced off the hood, and fell to the ground. I picked up the ring and threw it again and again, leaving a spray of scars across the glass, until John's boss ran out of the machine shop and I turned and fled.

My mother packed me off again, this time to a healthy sister further north in Pennsylvania, near the Poconos. When I returned a month later, the edges of my anger blunted by long walks in the woods and hours spent contemplating Bushkill Falls, Margaretta had miscarried. I baked a lemon meringue pie and took it over to Margaretta's house one afternoon, while John was at work. Forgiveness was not a word that came up, but we patched up our friendship and went on from there. I tried to be practical. I would most likely find another man to marry. Margaretta might not.

In this way, our friendship has gone on ever since.

"Look at that," Margaretta says, stopping in the middle of the trail. According to my watch, we have been walking for over an hour, huffing and puffing over a path laced with snaking vines and protruding tree roots. Neither of us has had the breath to talk much.

"What is that?" she asks.

Margaretta is looking at a lean-to nestled awkwardly between the trees, cobwebs draped like a white valance from the front edge of the roof. A blackened fire pit sits in front.

"You've never seen a lean-to?" I ask.

She walks around the structure and then back to the open front, an expression of wonder on her face. "Why aren't there four walls?"

"I don't know. So bums don't live in them, I suppose. They're for campers and hikers to use."

"Huh."

"You've really never seen one before?"

"I've never been an outdoor type, D. You should know that by now."

I sit down on the edge of the lean-to. "Let's rest here. I used to be the outdoor type, but I'm too old for this now."

"Why don't we build a campfire? I've never done that."

"You want to build a fire?"

"Yes, why not? If we're going to rest here. Look at all the wood around." Margaretta produces a lighter from her purse.

"All right," I say and go off to gather up twigs and branches to burn. "Scoop up some pine needles to get the fire started. Dry ones, preferably."

When I return, Margaretta is squatting next to a pile of small branches and pine needles, igniting it with her cigarette lighter. She looks up at me and smiles, and I am momentarily hopeful for our friendship. "This is nice. It's quiet up here. You were always getting to go off and do things like this when we were kids. I was never allowed. Camping was for boys."

I dump my armload of twigs onto the ground, then add a few to the fire. Margaretta's mother had always fought her daughter's plainness by drawing strict lines around her life. I am glad I never had a daughter. I sit next to Margaretta on the soft ground and stare into the flames until a random thought pulls me back to reality.

"You know, should we be doing this?" I ask. "They say murderers often come back to the scene of their crime."

"Oh D, you know it was her stepfather. It's always the parents. They hit a kid too hard and then have to make up a story about what happened."

"Not always," I say. "Did you ever hear about Louise-Ellen Martin? She was a girl who disappeared from town, before your family moved here. They never found her body or figured out who killed her."

"I've heard people speak about it. But it was probably someone she knew."

"Well, yes, you're right. I think it was someone she knew. Someone you probably knew, too, a few years later."

Our little fire cracks and pops in the gloaming, releasing sparks that extinguish almost as soon as they are free of the flames. When I woke up this morning, when I met Margaretta for lunch, when we embarked on this silly hike, I certainly never intended to drop this bombshell on her. Immediately, I want my words to disappear like the sparks, but they hang there between us in the concentrated glow of our fire. Margaretta is not a person to let this sort of thing go.

"What do you mean, 'someone I knew'?"

I stall for time, picking up a twig and poking at the fire. The fire blooms for a moment, spraying my arm with bits of hot ash. I had been tempted once to tell John this story but then I didn't. It seems fitting that, in the end, it will be Margaretta to whom it is told. After everything, it is still us, together.

I was just eight years old when Louise-Ellen Martin disappeared. I don't recall being afraid, though I remember clearly that my parents—indeed, all of the adults in town—were. Louise-Ellen lived in a neighboring town, a town my family had no particular need to frequent and so might as well have been a town in China for all I was concerned. Though my parents sat me down and reiterated the importance of not talking to strangers and not taking shortcuts to and from school, I did not change my behavior in the least. I continued to go to school via a long alley that snaked through the town for blocks and blocks.

In a small town, there is so little opportunity for variety or privacy that one has to take those things where one can find them. I found them in the shady darkness of that alley, pretending to be Nancy Drew, carefully setting each foot into loose gray stones, passing old wooden garages and sheds cautiously, taking note of missing planks and shingles, rusted padlocks, broken windows, peeling paint, tire tracks in the hardened mud. If the double doors to one were open, I would stop, my heart beating hard and mouth dry. I'd stand still for a minute, listening to the blood pulsing in my ears, then take a deep breath and sprint past, hugging my school books to my chest and kicking up stones behind me.

It was near the end of the school year, in 1953, that I awoke one morning giddy and breathless in anticipation of summer. I dressed quickly and rushed through a bowl of cereal, as though moving faster would speed up summer's arrival. There was no make-believe sleuthing now. I hurried through the alley, walking as quickly as I could and still be reasonably ladylike.

I remember the cat like it was yesterday. A black and white cat sat staring up at an old garage at the end of a deep yard dark with overgrown bushes and knee-high weeds. Long skinny fingers of ivy stretched up the corner of the garage, as though they were trying to pull the shabby building back into the earth.

As I passed, the cat let out a long meow and I turned to look back at it. Behind the dust and condensation on the garage window was a girl's face, scratches burning ugly red tracks across her cheeks and forehead. A lavender hair ribbon hung off the side of her blonde head, its bow undone. The girl stared at me, her eyes so wide and unblinking that, for an instant, I thought it might be a doll, a reward for some lucky girl's final report card.

The girl blinked and I broke eye contact with her. I looked at the new padlock on the garage door and turned and ran, the cat at my heels. When I reached the school, I was out of breath and sweating. I leaned over a water fountain, drinking, then let the stream of cold water drill my hot cheeks.

I stuck to the streets the rest of the week. Even the anticipation of summer couldn't keep the girl's face out of my mind—the stark whiteness of her skin, the dark dried blood, the lavender ribbon. I gave a wide berth to trees and bushes, looked back over my shoulder at the slightest sound. I slept with the bedroom window closed, despite the heat, and woke with my nightgown soaked and clinging to my skin.

I had been certain the police would find her. That's why I didn't tell anyone. To a child steeped in Nancy Drew, of course the grown-ups would look in an old falling-down garage. Of course someone would search in the alleys, would notice the shiny new lock on a rusty latch. But no one did. And with each passing week, it became more impossible to say anything.

How to explain my delay, which had in all probability cost a child her life? How to explain what I was doing in that alley in the first place?

When I finish the story, Margaretta doesn't say anything. I feed the fire with more twigs and pine needles. It burns quickly. Finally, Margaretta does speak.

"They never found her?"

I shake my head.

"And you never told anyone?"

This is not what I want her to say. I want her to be sympathetic, to say that I was just a child, that I was young and scared, all the things I knew my parents would not have said.

"It was Mr. Henderson's garage she was in," I say and dare to look at Margaretta's profile in the firelight.

"Mr. Henderson down the street from my parents' house? Bill Henderson?"

I bob my head up and down but have to turn away from looking her straight in the face. Somehow this seems like the worst thing I have ever done to Margaretta, keeping this from her and now—when it is too late—telling her.

We let the fire burn out. The woods beyond are now a liquid, inky black.

"You don't have a flashlight, do you?" Margaretta asks.

"No. Afraid not."

Margaretta turns and looks doubtfully at the lean-to. "Have you ever slept in one of these?"

John and I made out in one, once, but of course I keep this to myself. "No, but it's probably like a platform tent."

"Does that mean hard and uncomfortable?"

I climb up into the lean-to and use my foot to scrape dirt and pine needles off the floor, shuffling back and forth until an area roughly six feet by six is clean. I gesture toward the clean spot and Margaretta joins me. We spoon like lovers, like old tired lovers who can't muster the energy for anything more than this. Margaretta smells like pine and smoke and—faintly, sweetly—perfume.

Against my chest, I feel Margaretta take a deep breath and then exhale. She does it again and then says, "Have you heard from Greg?"

Greg is my son, my only child. He is also John's son, his only child.

"No. I thought I might, what with all the publicity." Greg dropped out of high school after his junior year and left town. I have not heard from him since. Every year that passes with no word from him carves a bigger hole in my heart, but I understand what he did. Greg's parentage was always an open secret; he is the spitting image of his father. I think he left simply to avoid the mess John and I had dropped him into.

"He'd have to be someplace pretty remote to have missed all that news coverage."

"Yes, he would," I say flatly.

Margaretta used to buy birthday and Christmas presents for Greg, for "my best friend's son." Greg and I, both, accepted them awkwardly. I think part of Margaretta wanted to claim Greg as her own, as her husband's son, as the child she and John had been unable to have. But I was never able to share him in that way. She had John. Greg was to be mine.

Margaretta drifts off to sleep, snoring lightly. Low-hanging branches scrape the roof of the lean-to. A howling noise rises and falls in the distance. In the morning, I will take her to the spot where Kendra Wishard's bones and clothing were found in a shallow grave, hastily covered with dirt and brush. We passed it less than ten minutes after we left the car. Whoever killed her hadn't had the energy or the fear to carry her body very far. The rest of us have to carry our crimes, the ones that go on and on for years, much farther.

Stretched out on the hard floor, I listen for the snap of a twig underfoot or someone crashing through the brush, until I fall into an intermittent sleep. But my limbs and spine refuse to arrange themselves into any comfortable sleeping position and every time I awake, I look out at the sky, watching for any change in color, any sign that morning is closer.

Sheila Walsh

Peter and the Olives

SHEILA WALSH manages the alternative medicine center of a health website. She enjoys wearing sequins and playing fullback for the Twisted Sisters, a Washington women's over-thirty soccer team, though not at the same time. Her nonfiction has been published in the *Washington Post*, and she was once paid $10 for a cartoon about tongue scrapers published in the Takoma Park, Maryland, Food Coop newsletter.

There was once a photogenic olive industry association intern with whitened teeth who had very little to do at work all day. The intern, Peter, was damned if he would spend the rest of his summer making copies for a patronizing, middle-aged, nearsighted marketing associate. Surely he was destined for better things than this! One day, while lingering by the copy machine, Peter read one of the witch's memos. It was a project proposal, addressed to the association's president: a book about the transformative powers of olive oil. Peter made an extra copy and filed the idea in his mind. He simply could not imagine this proposal being approved—who would want *her* picture on a book jacket?

One morning near the espresso machine, Peter casually mentioned his book idea to a company executive who was a college friend of his father's. They did lunch and shook hands and a call was made to a fine New York literary agency owned by another of Dad's college chums, and nine months later a book was born: a mélange of science, self-help, celebrity testimonials, heartwarming personal stories about supermodels' folksy Greek grandmothers, beautifully typeset bulleted lists, and sidebars for short attention spans. Luscious photos: sun-dappled pictures of beautiful people of leisure stroking each others' tongues with olives. Greek massages, you know, are better than Swedish.

Foul, foul, the bastard STOLE MY IDEA, Jane the marketing associate cried. Sour grapes, hysterical woman, said the execs. You should have brought up the idea first. You're just jealous. You let a twenty-four-year-old outsmart you, and besides his idea is different from yours. Unlike yours, it's marketable.

It helped Peter's case that his face was made for fame, so he was allowed to keep his byline on the condition that he undergo media training and a full-body paraffin wax and weekly nose-hair clipping. No problem, Peter said. Oh yes, said the execs, we like your can-do attitude. Just sign here, and here, and...what? Oh, that's nothing, just some technicalities, pain-in-the-ass legal department...just-sign-here, superstar! No problem, Peter said.

Peter's agent assembled a snazzy press kit and held a killer kickoff party with tons of free food and martinis with, you guessed it, olives. Hired models dripping with indifference and olive oil. How could skin be so luminescent? They drank olive oil before photo shoots. That was their beauty secret, oh NECTAR OF THE GODDESSES! Low-carb, antioxidant olive oil to maintain their girlish skeletons and their sexy protruding hipbones and scapulae.

Thanks to the agent's machinations, Peter had now morphed into a metrosexual named Pieter, age forty-two. On the list of suggested questions for the media: "Pieter, how do you retain your youthful glow, your baby-fresh, kissable most-eligible-bachelor face? You have hardly aged at all! You look like you are in your twenties." "Olive oil," he replies every time. Olive oil, olive oil, I love olive oil. Not just any olive oil, no cheap crap that you find in a grocery store, but olive oil of the Greek Isles, home of the gods and goddesses. Olive oil with a green tint, not a yellow tint. The olive oil that just happens to have my picture on the label. Only that brand of olive oil works. Follow my diet, and you too can glow. A gaze directly in the camera: YOU TOO can look like a sexy Mediterranean mama if you follow this diet of the gods. Isn't it incredible? Yes, it is incredible.

The appearances on TV, the confident drape of the arm along the back of fashionable couches on a TV set. The flash of a Rolex and gold cuff links. The killer smile moving in for the kill: "Oh [insert name of attractive TV show hostess here], your face is so effervescent...I *know* you've been dipping into the olive oil!"

The sound bite: Sylvester Stallone's Rocky drank raw eggs, the Greeks drink olive oil. So if you want to be strong and good-looking, why not drink olive oil with raw eggs? Cross-industry synergy. Olive oil and dairy products. Brilliant. More products: muffins, cereals, sandwiches, hamburgers, french fries, cosmetics, air fresheners, pet food...all made with olive oil. Better living with olive oil.

A frenzy for olive oil erupted all across the United States: everything now had to be dripped in olive oil. Bread, fruit, staplers, toes...there was nothing that could not be improved by a coat of fruity, glistening, smooth olive oil. Ladies on TV commercials licked each others' shiny olive oil–covered faces.

The stock of olive oil companies rose, along with Pieter's net worth. Everyone, it seemed, was happy except the vegetable oil industry (which is déclassé anyway) and the middle-aged marketing assistant who had been scorned. Jane spent her forty-hour workweeks cooking up new ideas for revenge and a book that would topple Pieter off the bestseller list. She had olive industry connections in Greece, so she convinced them to band together and raise the price of their product. Yet the increased price only enhanced the product's prestige, and thereby, consumers' demand.

Jane sent a press release to all the TV program hosts whom Pieter had visited. Now covered in pimples and weighing a scandalous half-pound larger since starting the olive oil regimen, the hosts were eager to pass on Jane's message: Pieter is Peter from Mahwah, N.J., he is twenty-four, not forty-two, and the photogenic "nutritionist" whom Pieter quoted in the book is actually a male escort with carpal tunnel syndrome.

The bad publicity caused Pieter's book sales to drop, but he was so rich by then that it didn't matter to him anyway. The ladies still loved him for his money and bone-white teeth and the authoritative way he signed the check at five-star restaurants. But Pieter knew something was missing. Olive oil, quite frankly, was beginning to bore him. He needed something more in his life. Food cooked in vegetable oil, or possibly peanut oil, would be a start. After a heart-to-heart with his hot yoga teacher, Pieter decided to quit the rat race. It was about time that he devote himself to something more meaningful, or at the very least, something more satisfying, such as basking in flattery and massages from gift-groveling women. Sure, Pieter was no fool; he had followed the career trajectories of enough B-list celebrities to know that, in time, as his money and his good looks inevitably slipped away, the women would grow increasingly homely and middle class. Pieter reckoned that by the time he got that old, he'd be happy with a lap dance every week or so from just about anyone with a heartbeat, recently cleaned teeth, and two semi-firm mammary glands.

Tell them I quit, Pieter commanded his agent. I QUIT! No more media appearances. No one may ghostwrite for me ever again. Faster than a chakra cleansing treatment, the superstar was whisked into a boardroom where he was surrounded by politely gloating lawyers sitting comfortably in really nice high-backed leather chairs. The lawyers were holding the papers that Pieter had signed during his first full-body paraffin wax, back in the good old days. At the time, Pieter's eyes had been covered with organic, free-range cucumbers, so he didn't notice section 42.602f of this pain-in-the-ass, no-big-deal technicality. The attorneys were right, if you scraped off that little bit of wax and trained a magnifying glass on the small print, it really did say that Pieter had to chug eight ounces of olive oil mixed with raw egg every day, twice a day, in front of a webcam for the rest of his life. Perpetuity…what an odd word, Pieter thought.

It didn't matter to the attorneys that the mere sight of olive oil made Pieter barf, and that he more often than not barfed on camera, once even on the camera itself, and that he now had scurvy and shingles, and that his skin was as slippery as a fish in an oil spill. There was no way out, unless Pieter would kindly return all of his royalties, including compounded interest and legal fees. That's what the small print dictated. Maybe this life isn't so bad, Pieter told himself. Webcam performances only twice a day, and the rest of the day is mine. Pieter's volcanic acne, the doctor said, could be controlled, or at least reduced, with a pharmaceutical cocktail of tetracycline, Viagra, estrogen, and ginseng swallowed every six hours.

So every day, twice a day, in front of the webcam, Pieter drank olive oil and barfed and ranted against the entire legal profession, wishing premature wrinkling in non-Botoxable places on all of his enemies. Pieter's website, its page views multiplying each day thanks to word of mouth, eclipsed his sales of the olive oil book, which could now be easily found at garage sales for a dollar, or twenty-five cents to skillful hagglers.

An essayist for the *New Yorker* deconstructed the growing cult appeal of Pieter's website: "It's a digital-age zoo for pasty young men who don't leave home…Microsoft's version of Kafka's ape." Indeed, an audience survey revealed that the majority of visitors to Pieter's website were single young men, ages twenty-five to thirty-four, who work in the information technology industry, drink between six and ten sodas a day, and have a difficult time meeting women who share their interests and, yes, would be delighted to receive a FREE trial subscription to an exclusive computer dating service connecting American hunks with the subservient babes of the Mongolian steppes.

Not to be forgotten, however, was the most devoted webcam fan of all: Jane, now a marketing executive at a different publishing company, thanks to the success of her coffee-table book on the magical powers of ginseng. Every day, twice a day, Jane watched Pieter's show on company time, her cackles so menacing that no intern dared mess with her again, or, heaven forbid, linger by the copy machine.

Riggin Waugh

The Woman Who Didn't Get Out Much

RIGGIN WAUGH lives on medication in Takoma Park, Maryland. Her tote bag-winning writing has appeared lots of places. She is the editor of *Dykes With Baggage: The Lighter Side of Lesbians in Therapy* (Alyson Books, 2000) and *Ex-Lover Weird Shit: A Collection of Short Fiction, Poetry, and Cartoons by Lesbians and Gay Men* (Two Out Of Three Sisters Press, 1994). Visit her website at www.RigginWaugh.com.

A bright orange pantsuit opened the door to the small clapboard house. The slender woman looked about twenty-five.

"Hi, Lenny," she said to my boyfriend. "Ernie's in the living room." She flashed me a big smile. "Come on in. I'm Ernie's wife."

I resisted all temptation to say, *Hello, Ernie's wife.*

"Alice," she added, as an afterthought.

"Hi. I'm Donna—Lenny's girlfriend."

Alice untied her apron, made from the same pattern as one I'd sewn in seventh-grade home ec. A large hem at the top that the sash wove through, and all pockets at the bottom, made of a different, yet complementary material. My *mother* didn't even wear aprons anymore. And this woman with the frosted flip hairdo was wearing brown loafers—with pennies in them, heads up.

"Ernie, Lenny's here," Alice called over her right shoulder. She winked at me. Not a flirtatious wink, but as if we shared some amusing secret. Perhaps a wink picked up from a late night movie, then practiced numerous times in the bathroom mirror. "We can talk girl talk while the boys play."

Lenny glanced at the pained look in my eyes and headed into the living room. He set his guitar case across the arms of an olive green plaid recliner. No sympathy from him. I was on my own.

Alice and Ernie weren't anything like our regular friends. Usually I could at least catch a buzz and have a few laughs at Lenny's jam sessions. But Ernie was clean-shaven and straight. His hair was cut above the collar and barely covered his ears. And Alice wore aprons and penny loafers. Didn't Ernie and Alice know that this was 1975, *not* 1955? Of course, Lenny hadn't warned me. All he had said was that Ernie was a dynamite bass player and Fay's brother. Fay's nickname was "Rip-Off." She and her husband, "Bandit," were cool. They were bikers and rode with the Phantoms. Ernie must have been adopted. Or else Fay was. No, I wouldn't be smoking any reefer tonight.

Lenny and Ernie plugged their guitars into the amplifiers.

"Donna, can I get you a cup of coffee or a soda—or beer?" Alice wrinkled her nose a little when she said "beer" as if it were the booby prize on *Let's Make a Deal.*

"Soda, thanks." I managed a smile and hoped it wouldn't be Grape Nehi.

I pointed to a photograph on top of the television of two happy, but goofy-looking, children sitting underneath a Christmas tree. "Cute kids," I said. "They yours?"

Alice beamed. "Oh, yes. Jennifer's four, and little Ernie just turned two."

"Are they asleep?" I asked. They wouldn't be for long, I thought.

"No, they're staying at my mother's tonight. She took them to a movie. Thank goodness for mothers."

"Right." How would I survive the next few hours? This woman was just like the ones in that movie we saw last week—*The Stepford Wives*—where all the happy housewives were actually robots. Why hadn't I just stayed home? Why? Because, at seventeen, spending an evening in the same house as my parents constituted cruel and unusual punishment. And I was so afraid of missing anything. Since I was obviously not going to miss anything here, maybe I could beg Lenny to take me over to Roberta's or Judy's. Anywhere except here—stuck with June Cleaver without the cookies. But, no, I wouldn't complain to Lenny. Otherwise, my nineteen-year-old boyfriend might not bring me to jam sessions anymore. And God forbid he should go somewhere without me.

Alice started off toward the kitchen, then turned around in the doorway and smiled. "You coming, Donna?" I followed her and took a seat at one of the four mustard-colored chairs with the floral pattern. I noticed that the can opener, toaster, and blender base were also mustard colored, as were the walls. But the tea kettle was avocado. How had that happened?

Alice placed a glass of ginger ale on a mustard-colored coaster in front of me, talking the whole time. "Fay and Leroy are getting a new dining room set, and they're giving us their old table as soon as we can borrow a truck to pick it up." Leroy must be Fay's husband's real name—no wonder he goes by Bandit.

"Is it mustard colored?" I asked.

"What?" Alice looked around the kitchen. "Oh, you mean Harvest Gold. No, it's brown Formica. It'll go well in here."

I noticed a thin catalogue on the kitchen table.

"I sell Beeline Fashions," Alice said cheerily.

"Hmmm," I said and smiled. I pulled at a thread on the hole in the knee of my dungarees. Before I could change the subject, Alice opened the Beeline Fashions catalogue in front of me. Polyester pantsuits in every hue of the rainbow, to be bought and sold like Tupperware in living rooms across the nation. Alice was wearing the pantsuit on page 32. I politely looked away and pretended not to notice, but she sensed the recognition.

"My bonus gift. It comes in rose, turquoise, violet, and navy." She looked down at her own outfit. "And, of course, tangerine. If you'd like to order anything—"

"No," I cut her off quickly and closed the catalogue. Self-consciously, I added, "I don't work." Translation: I can't afford to buy brightly flowered pants with elastic waistbands that would make me the laughingstock of Hillcrest Heights. I wondered if Alice realized that I was still in high school.

Alice smiled sympathetically. "You could host a party." She opened the catalogue again, right to the "Bee-a-Beeline-Hostess" page. "If enough people came, you could get a free dress."

"I really don't think so." I could just see myself wearing some gross houndstooth jumpsuit to my graduation party next month. Actually, I couldn't picture it at all.

This time, Alice closed the catalogue. I started to relax, but then saw her reach for an Avon catalogue. Inadvertently, I shook my head.

Alice smiled a little sheepishly. "I'm sorry. Ernie says I get carried away sometimes. I don't get out much."

I burst out laughing. I couldn't help it. Don't get out much? *Don't get out much?!!* I couldn't have put it better myself.

Alice looked a little puzzled, but genuinely pleased that she had amused me. Ernie and Lenny came in from the living room on the tail end of my laugh.

Lenny raised his eyebrows, then kissed the top of my head. "Having fun?"

"I'm *all right.*" I gently tugged his ponytail and hoped that Alice and Ernie didn't hear the surprise that I recognized in my own voice.

Alice added, "Oh, we gals are doing just fine." I tried not to roll my eyes. My friends and I considered ourselves "women" (as in "Lenny's woman") or even "chicks" or "girls," but never "gals."

"Taking a break already, boys?" Alice asked.

"Just getting a beer, honey." Ernie and Lenny continued discussing amplifiers on their way back to the living room. I acted interested because they were guys so this must be important. The truth is that I found amps about as interesting as Beeline Fashions.

"I also sell plants that don't need dirt," Alice said. Plants without dirt—imagine that. Although the idea intrigued me, I didn't encourage her. Alice tried again. "Would you like to see some pictures?"

"Sure." I always have liked looking through people's family photos—how they've changed, what they choose to photograph. I figured that Alice and Ernie's wedding pictures would be a hoot. And at least she wouldn't try to sell me anything out of a photo album.

Alice led me into the bedroom and lifted two large baby blue albums off the top of the white dresser. Each album was about three inches thick, and I somehow knew that not a single adhesive page was empty. What had I gotten myself into? We sat down on the lime-green bedspread. For each picture, Alice provided first and last names, dates, ages, cities, states, previous relationships, and a numbing stream of anecdotes that had no conceivable connection with any given photo.

Forty minutes later and halfway through the first book, I tried to stifle a yawn.

"I'm sorry, Donna. I'm boring you, aren't I?" Alice flipped to the last page: three Polaroids of a man lying dead in a casket in a funeral parlor. I was repulsed, but no longer bored. "We don't look at *these* very often. Ernie's father."

I couldn't imagine anyone taking pictures of their dead father, let alone putting them in a photo album with all the weddings and birthday parties.

"Oh my God," I whispered.

Alice continued. "He was gunned down in Texas six months ago."

"Wow, you're kidding." I immediately regretted saying it, but people always say that when they hear shocking news.

"But he looks good, don't you think?" Alice asked matter-of-factly. "I mean, you can't even tell he was shot in the head." Then Alice's face changed, and she looked like she was about to cry.

"I'm sorry," I offered. "You must have been very close."

Alice looked down at her hands. "No, not really. I mean, I liked him, but I didn't know him all that well, them living so far away." I waited for her to go on. "I met Ernie's parents at our wedding, and we saw them about once a year after that. We couldn't afford to fly down there much." Alice returned the photo albums to their place on the clean dresser top and sat down again. Her hands were shaking.

"What is it, Alice?" I asked.

Alice shook her head. "You know what really got me about the whole thing?" She stopped. "No, you'll think I'm crazy."

"No, I won't," I promised. But I had my doubts.

"The funeral was the same weekend as the Pillsbury Bake-Off."

My mouth started to drop open, but I caught myself and bit my lip. This woman really was crazy.

"I was a finalist. Pillsbury picked a hundred recipes, from all over the country, and one was mine—my Crescent Roll Surprise. I send in twenty-five recipes every year, and it was the first time I made it to the Bake-Off. It was in Orlando, less than a mile from Disney World. They had already sent me my free airline tickets, and they were going to pay for the hotel, all my meals—and even give me a hundred dollars spending money. The grand prize was a brand-new kitchen worth thirty thousand dollars."

"I've always wanted to go to Disney World," I said. "I bet it's a real trip."

"I was really looking forward to it. The *Prince George's County Journal* was even going to interview me. But I had to go to the funeral in Laredo instead. I told Ernie that I didn't mind—he was so upset about his dad and all, but—." A tear rolled down her cheek. "Does this make any sense at all?"

"Yeah, Alice, it does. It makes a whole lotta sense." And in some strange way, it did.

Alice started to reach for my hand, but stopped herself. I reached over and put my hand on top of hers, still folded in her lap. We sat there for a few minutes without saying anything. Then I reached over to the bedside table and handed her a pale blue Kleenex to dry her eyes.

"Hey, Alice," I said softly, "how *do* you grow plants without dirt?"

NC Weil

Laundry Fugue

NC WEIL knew she would be a writer at the age of seven. Since then she has devoted her energies to studying language(+s)—not only English but Spanish, Latin, Russian & un peu de Français—and acquiring life experience. She's put over ten thousand solo miles on her thumb, and presently lives surrounded by Takoma Park in Silver Spring, Maryland, with her April Fool husband. She's written several novels but hasn't broken into print until now (agent, please call), is a member of the Women's National Book Association (her sons were surprised to discover she's in the WNBA), and plays a mean game of Scrabble. She believes that breaking rules involves knowing first what they are.

After Budge was jailed for knifing a cop, Ginger was on her own in the trailer, and became nearly a shut-in. At school she kept her head down and did her work, thinking there must be more challenging reading than *Up the Down Staircase* and *Lord of the Flies.* Parkersburg was close to Ohio, so some of its opener air leaked across the river to tell her the existence of Vonnegut and Heinlein, *Cat's Cradle* and *Stranger in a Strange Land*, of Arthur C. Clarke's *Childhood's End.* The school librarian took her to Cincinnati to a huge used bookstore, where she stocked up on the wild prose and blinding covers of Tom Wolfe's *Electric Kool-Aid Acid Test* (blue), *The Pump House Gang* (hot pink) and *Radical Chic & Mau-Mauing the Flak Catchers* (orange). She brought home *One Flew Over the Cuckoo's Nest*, *Sometimes a Great Notion*, *On the Road*, and *Been Down So Long It Looks Like Up to Me.*

Reading about Kesey and the Merry Pranksters off in the woods of La Honda, California, filled her with envy and misery—the only day-glo in West Virginia was blaze orange during hunting season, which no one would mistake for a psychedelic frame of mind. She could get ugly drugs in Parkersburg—PCP, quaaludes, or speed—but nothing mind-expanding like LSD or psilocybin. Smoking pot made her feel alternately stupid and paranoid, especially because Dickie, the Parkersburg High dealer, thought making a sale entitled him to hit on any female customer. Dickie had bad skin and hollow eyes, smoked a lot of cigarettes, and had a repertoire of nervous tics that drove her nuts. Her friend Dor had taken her recently to sample before buying a nickel bag; once they were sitting in Dickie's pickup stoned, his restless hands traveled from the steering wheel to the Bud beer-pull mounted on his gearshift knob, to the radio that crackled with Steppenwolf and Rolling Stones, to the back of the seat, messing with Ginger's long red hair.

She told him to cut it out but his fingers crept back like ants after crumbs, and pretty soon she wanted to squash them like an invading trail. Dor being the buyer felt entitled to pull rank, making Ginger the designated grope-ee—when Dickie told them to pile in, Dor aimed Ginger ahead of her into the tobacco-smoky cab, to the middle of the seat where the gearshift bumped her knees, giving Dickie more excuse than he needed to let his hand slide thighward. Ginger pressed against Dor til her friend pushed back for fear she'd bump the latch and end up out on the pavement as they rode up 50. Taking a county road, they lurched through potholes and wound downhill, into the woods out of sight of the highway. There Dickie rolled down his window and fired up a j. Stubbing out the roach on the windshield he turned up the radio…

The worst thing about pot, she concluded later, was it made a repulsive guy less so—made his saliva-slick kisses tolerable, the tobacco grains in his mouth miraculously inoffensive. He didn't even taste bad, which shouldn't be possible given his habits. Next time Dor was gonna have to find another sucker—she'd be damned if she was making a habit of that. The high only worked as long as she didn't think, but it was an effective block to thought—she just floated out on the radio—somewhere people who wanted to be together were listening to this same song, getting off on it, and years down the road they'd be nostalgic for it the way Mom was for that Don Gibson song "Sea of Heartbreak" that she said reminded her of being newly wed. For Ginger, the memory of "Angie" would be forever tied to this attempt to escape Budge's trial—Dickie's stench and lust, Dor singing along off-key from her safe spot, the gearshift in the way every time she moved, Dickie's hand up under her T-shirt, his rough fingers scratching the sensitive skin around her bra.

"Jerk him off so we can go," Dor grated in her ear—Ginger'd come along for the high and because Dor was her friend, but if they were both going to use her, screw it. In a flash of rage she shoved an elbow into Dickie's gullet where his neck met his body, and as he fell back choking, she reached the other way, opened the passenger side, and scrambled over Dor, out. She spun off-balance on gravel and the new growth of spring, and staggering to right herself, she took off up the road, running not so much from the pickup as from everything, her feet light under her finally, and though they'd come a good ways down off the highway she felt easy in her stride, feet picking spots out of the mud but also avoiding the clusters of wild violets and those little blue flowers that looked like giant blackberries or tiny bunches of grapes. She heard the truck engine, the whine of low gear as it climbed the grade in pursuit, and while a curve still hid her she jumped off into the woods on a path she barely realized was there—like it just appeared when she needed it—and she bounded like a deer, far enough back to be out of sight. She stopped to catch her breath while in blinks of turquoise the truck went on by—the windows were open and Dickie was hollering hoarsely he was gonna git her for that—not that she'd wanted to hurt him but what the hell! Dor had some apologizing to do.

She felt contaminated after being in his truck—clothes, skin, and hair all stunk of cigarette smoke with an after-tang of Dickie's own sour sweat—so once she'd showered and her hair was about half dry—it took forever to dry, thick as it was—she wadded her laundry into Budge's Army duffel and shouldered it for the hike down to the Little Kanawha, across the bridge into the main part of town, and down the side street to the Slosh'N'Wash. Before Dad died they had a house with its own washer, though they had to dry stuff on wires suspended from the basement pipes, but after the insurance money thinned out and Mom still couldn't do better than clerking at the drugstore, they moved to the trailer. It was just her and

Ginger at first, Budge being off in Vietnam, and the once-a-week trek to the laundromat became one of Ginger's chores.

Coming in with her load of dirty clothes and sense of stain, she saw Zippy. She didn't know what to think—a man with stubble and a pointy head, wearing clodhoppers and a dress—nobody in Parkersburg looked like that. His eyes were weird—shining without intelligence. She couldn't decide if he was an imbecile or knew something the rest of them hadn't figured out yet, but once she had her machines loaded, he sat in the adjacent chair and fixed his gaze on the swirl of soap and plaid shirts and jeans and T-shirts in one of the round glass doors facing them. Of the three loads, one was white stuff which included the net bag of bras swimming by, and socks and sheets; another was the heavy stuff: jeans and flannel shirts and other dark things; the third washer had her school clothes in it—the lone skirt she wore about once a week, the pantsuits the principal allowed as long as they were some other color besides blue, her blouses, and her vest.

"Laundry is the fifth dimension," Zippy said in a low thick voice, as though his throat was full of applesauce. She couldn't look at him because she'd just end up staring, so she watched her clothes turn over in the suds, shaking in syncopated time left, right, left, dropping then tossed. Without being truly hypnotic it was fascinating. She could feel his intense regard for the colors and patterns of the clothes going by in the window, and as though she'd gone through a phase-shift, the bank of washers suddenly resembled a ship, the row of portholes offering a view into the heart of an ocean usually hidden.

"Red and gray plaid flannel shirt," she said, the words spilling out unconsciously, and the pinhead grinned so immensely she could feel the glow of it without even looking at him.

"Red and gray plaid flannel shirt," he chanted, "red and gray plaid flannel shirt, red and gray plaid flannel shirt."

Then she did turn to stare—she couldn't help it—and noticed he had six or seven hairs near the tip of his pointy head, tied up with a narrow blue ribbon like some delicate bouquet. The ribbon failed to match his dress, which was orange with large pink polka-dots, which failed to make ensemble with his white gym socks and yellow—now what were those things? Not boots—more like clogs, only they didn't look like slip-ons. No laces—in fact, no evident way to remove them. Clodhoppers truly, smooth and clean, curved instead of flat on the undersides. The material was flexible, it seemed—they actually looked comfortable—maybe they were rubber, some stretchy stuff. The dress looked comfy too, and he was utterly unselfconscious wearing it, even though he was a guy and it was hideous. The most pathetic hick at PHS didn't look so hopelessly out-of-it.

"Where's your laundry?" she asked, grasping at the likelihood that he was wearing the "uniform of the day" because everything else was in the wash.

"It's all clean today," he said in that voice like a thick milkshake. "I just come in here to travel."

"Travel where?"

"Into the laundry dimension. It's the best place to be if there's no Krispy Kremes."

"They got those at the Circle K," she said.

"But I have to have taco sauce with them, and they don't have the right kind."

"You *don't* put taco sauce on doughnuts," she said firmly.

"*With* them. And Ho Hos are good too, but they didn't have the pink ones."

"No, the pink ones are nasty. Anyway, you shouldn't eat crap like that—no wonder you look so weird." Wow, she didn't mean to say that—she'd seen that happen before—peculiarity was contagious somehow. But he didn't appear insulted—he didn't seem to be aware he had *any* appearance, as though he'd never looked in a mirror or didn't realize that was himself, or didn't have the capacity to judge how different he looked from everybody around him. An imbecile, a retard.

"Why are you wearing a dress?" she demanded.

"This is a muu-muu," pronouncing each letter so it came out "moo-oo-moo-oo."

"Which is what?"

"This," as though she was the stupid one. "Polka-dot muu-muu, polka-dot muu-muu, polka-dot muu-muu."

"One of us is crazy," she said. He sounded like an engine that wouldn't quite turn over.

"Oh look, it's the Rinse cycle," he said with all the excitement that voice could produce, so she turned back to the washers which were nearly flooded, the drums not turning for the moment as the water level rose. She thought of people drowning—Budge was like a shirt in the wash, about to be submerged, and all she could do from the other side of the glass was watch. The trial was winding down, they'd probably sentence him tomorrow or Friday. Warrick was a cop with a clean record, popular on the force—and he'd been a star halfback on the PHS football team in '66 and '67, just a year ahead of Budge in school—they were gonna teach her brother a lesson, make an example of him, and with Mom off in Portland with her new husband, Dad in the ground, and Ted's kinship a secret, she was having to watch the show all by herself. The only people interested in talking to her were nosy assholes from the paper—she had nothing printable to say to them.

This life was too nuts for her—made about as much sense as Krispy Kremes with taco sauce, or a pinhead in a polka-dot muu-muu. The washers began to turn, first the heavy clothes then the white wash, finally her school clothes. She thought about what order she started the machines—not this sequence, she was pretty sure. Weren't machines supposed to be consistent? the same? You couldn't tell a laundromat Speed Queen how long to spend on the Wash cycle—after you set the water temperature, lined up your quarters in the slots and pushed the tongue into the cash box, the machine did all the rest, including chew holes in your shirts and shrink things.

The clothes cascaded behind the window, trailing comet tails of suds. A Levi's pocket with that distinctive orange stitching slewed into view, then rubbed the glass like someone leaning on it from inside, and that struck her as funny—she could be in that washer herself, in the fifth dimension, having a conversation with her shirts, relaxing. Maybe it wasn't actually wet in there, maybe it just looked that way from out here. She was the one drowning while the clothes were fine. Actually they looked like they were dancing at a party, sleeves shaking, pant legs kicking unexpectedly in the churn. Listening she could hear, above the growl of the motors, the click of buttons on glass, a faint version of the sound Judge Gilpin's gavel made. The judge wasn't shy about hammering for order, these buttons were just suppressing hostility better.

"Where d' ya live?" she asked suddenly. "An' what's your name?"

"I live where I am, and I am Zippy the Pinhead."

"Y'are huh?" She slitted her eyes at him. "Yeah, y' sure are."

"I like diners, and salad bar sneeze guards."

Yeah, he did look like he could spend his whole lunchtime watching a slab of acrylic deflect germs from their destiny among the cucumber slices.

"Y' got a job?" she asked.

"Chores—no job."

"What kinda chores?"

"Laundry, and bowling."

"That's a chore?"

"My creator thinks it is."

His *creator*? Whatever God the Baptists and all prayed to Sunday mornings, that Almighty had nothing to do with bowling—ever. Or giving this guy marching orders.

When she got home, she opened her new dog-eared copy of *On the Road*, and a postcard fell out—of Zippy the Pinhead, standing in a laundromat, wearing that polka-dot muu-muu and yellow clodhoppers, a slender ribbon tied into a bow around his thin little sprout of hairs. Mrs. Heflin had contributed this book to the stack Ginger bought two weeks ago, but she hadn't got around to reading it yet—she was too absorbed in Tom Wolfe's manic prose to look any further. The librarian had been giving her meaningful looks while Budge rotted in jail awaiting trial—her warm brown eyes, magnified behind heavy glasses, gazed at Ginger the same way Lassie looked at Timmy when she had something important to tell him, but like the dog she wouldn't come right out and say it. Even on the trip to Cincinnati she just attended to her driving. Of course she knew about the Raleys—wasn't a soul in Parkersburg uninformed on the topic—she held her tongue out of respect for Ginger's feelings, or else out of worry that Ginger would react to questions by withdrawing even further.

On the back of the postcard someone had written:

Dear Rodney—

Today we rested up between marches. If you were here I know you'd

was all it said—along with the mystery of Zippy was the puzzle of the unfinished message—did Rodney show up, so sending this became moot, or had the writer already trespassed, claiming to know what he'd do, and changed her mind? Or did she get some bad news about Rodney, then stuck the postcard in a book and forgot about it?

The sentencing came on Friday just before noon—she guessed the jury wanted to take the afternoon off—mid-May, all the mountain laurel and such were in bloom, the woods as pretty as they ever got. This time of year you'd see twin fawns with their neat rows of white spots, their mother somewhere nearby, and all the birds were nesting—cardinals, blue jays, kingfishers, and herons down on the Ohio and Little Kanawha. The skeeters weren't bad yet, the only nuisance was wood ticks—if you were out with your honey that made a good excuse to touch each other. All the higher animals traded grooming—why did humans need an excuse?

The twelve jurors and two alternates filed in, everyone in the gallery on their feet for the judge. He sat and rapped for order, the foreman stood. The head juror was Phil Fraser, owner of Fraser Auto Body—Ginger knew his son Turnly, a year behind her in school til he dropped out at fifteen to help his dad in the business. Mr. Fraser was a stiff sober type, but Turnly was a jerk—showed up at school always late, sometimes drunk, mouthed off to teachers, and scratched his crotch and armpits like a monkey. If he bothered to say anything in class it was some obscenity, and you could always spot his test paper in a pile—crumpled and tattered, his printing big and sloppy as a second grader's. She wondered did Mr. Fraser dread seeing his own son where Budge now sat, or was he invoking this trial to scare the kid straight? Trouble was a plenty busy train in this town, new passengers all the time.

Gilpin ordered Budge to rise, then said to the jury, "Have you reached a verdict?"

"We have, Your Honor. We find Richard Raley guilty of all charges—assault with a deadly weapon, possession of a concealed weapon, and resisting arrest."

Budge was staring at the judge like he was figuring out a way to kill him with hate—Gilpin glanced at him, then toward the jury.

"Your Honor," Fraser continued, "we recommend the maximum penalty in this case—we find no mitigating circumstances."

The judge hitched himself around in his seat, eyes back on Budge. "Mr. Raley, I sentence you to ten years in prison for these offenses. Have you anything to say for yourself?"

Budge looked at the jurors, fixing them with his stare one by one, then said, "You don' know shit." He spat on the table in front of him, his lawyer yanking his papers from harm's way too late. The gallery flooded with noise, and Ginger thought of the Rinse cycle at the Slosh'N'Wash. The image of Zippy filled her mind so completely she was unaware of the sheriff taking Budge out the back door—his leg-irons clashing and dragging the hollow-sounding wood floor were like buttons and zippers tossing in the washer—she came back to herself to discover a reporter closing in—she went the other way down the row, pushing her way blindly through the crowd exiting Courtroom 2, down the broad wood stairs and out into a brilliant day. She walked fast to shake off curiosity-hounds, and instead of going home discovered herself coming through the doorway of the laundromat. There was Zippy, staring at empty washers with their doors gaping open. All she had to wash was her bandana that she'd cried and blown her nose into all week, but she placed it in the machine directly in front of the pinhead, bought a little box of soap and put in a sprinkle, set the water to Hot, and loaded a pair of quarters.

She settled in the chair beside Zippy's, and together they watched the washer fill then tumble, the red cloth with black and white paisley markings billowing into view then away, soapsuds developing, the water dancing freely with almost nothing to wash.

"There any good laundromats out West?" she asked after while.

"Good laundromats are everywhere," he said solemnly.

"Thanks for helpin' me make up m' mind."

"Make up anything you want, but use low-sudsing soap."

"Low-sudsing soap, low-sudsing soap, low-sudsing soap," she said, meeting his witless smile. In his eyes she saw her reflection, tiny but clear—a woman far away with ocean behind her, penumbra of red hair lit by midday sun. There was no Zippy looking back at her, no consciousness in this room but her own. He was some scrap of raw absurdity invented by her mind—going West was better than going nuts. They watched the Wash cycle proceed, and when the drum had spun empty she popped the door and peeled the bandana free, studded with indentations from the drain-holes, folded and plastered together so it held its shape stiff as leather, almost dry already.

Mary-Sherman Willis

Dogs Will Be Dogs

Mary-Sherman Willis was born in Washington, D.C., in 1951. Her poems and reviews have appeared in the *New Republic*, the *Iowa Review*, the *Hudson Review*, *Poet Lore*, the *Plum Review*, *Shenandoah*, and *Archipelago.org*. Her poems have also appeared in two anthologies, *Not What I Expected: The Unpredictable Road from Womanhood to Motherhood* (Paycock Press, 2007), and *Cabin Fever: Poets at Joaquin Miller's Cabin 1984–2001* (The Word Works, 2003). She was a longtime writer and editor at Time-Life Books and at Michell Beasley Publishers in London. She teaches creative writing at George Washington University and lives in Woodville, Virginia.

Toward the end of the afternoon Mickey would let me know it was "cocktail hour at the dog park." As he patrolled the garden, he barked through the iron fence rails at the passing dogs headed up Bancroft Place for the park. I could hear him from my study become louder and more frantic. Time to get the leash. I was well trained.

From all around Dupont Circle they come. That woman with the cleavage and her sheepdog Quincy parade in from somewhere on 19th Street. Jupiter and Zeus, a pair of bulldogs, came with one or another of those nice boys who lived in a big, flounced-and-furbelowed townhouse on R and 22nd Streets. Once they had me over to tea, fussily, and were surprised I knew what *gen mai cha* was. I told them how cheap it was in Nagasaki after the war! Nice boys, though. Kelly and her border collies (particular favorites of Mickey's and mine) came to the park from Florida Avenue. She had them trained to come at a whistle and to lie down like dropped stones or sit or fetch, all at a hand signal. They would even do it for me. Kelly is friends with that irritating Oliver with his Jack Russell terrier, Bingo, a matched pair if there ever was one. And there was Robert, our old State Department friend. These days I watch them from my perch here in the yard, a real cocktail clinking in my glass at the end of the day.

Why did I go there day after day? It's a scruffy place, grassless in the summer, a windswept tundra in winter, and always faintly reeking, even if everyone is responsible and picks up after their dogs. It sits high on a hill at the edge of what's known as the Piedmont Plateau, or so I learned at school, the geological raison d'être for the City of Washington, D.C. The plateau arcs through the city to the north and west, bisecting the Potomac River at the Falls, where it becomes unnavigable. The city had to be here, said The Father of Our Country. You couldn't go any further upstream.

We are an accident of geography, I guess. And of necessity. During the Civil War there was a hospital here, safe from the pestilential miasmas of Foggy Bottom—what people called "Potomac fever." It was from that old elm stump that we stood and watched the smoke rise from the burning Pentagon that September morning, into a pure blue sky.

At any rate, it's a dog park now, so decreed by former landowners in memory of their departed pet—a toy poodle, as it happens, as was Mickey.

On a hot summer afternoon like this one, after work (for some of us) and as the heat begins to loosen its hold, we'd assemble. The light is turning pink and orange at that time of day, and the shadows stretch across the parched ground. Young dogs, cooped up all day, would run in circles in the dust around the older ones, who would stare morosely at them, panting. If someone threw a ball, a furious barking stampede would ensue, sometimes ending badly. The humans, the owners, would be standing on the park's perimeter under the shade of the old piss-bleached trees, like chaperones at a dance, watching to see what would happen. And just like fifth grade, we had our little clusters, our cliques.

There are skills you develop of necessity. After years of Embassy practice with Herbert, I can put on my hostess face, walk into a room of strangers, and strike up a conversation with whomever. At first, I wore my hostess face at the park, spoke to everyone, introduced myself, "Hello, my name is Celia. How are you?" But honestly, what's the point? Herbert's gone. I can do what I want. And frankly, not everyone is attractive or interesting enough in such a random sample as the dog park to warrant the effort. We were united there by our dogs, our furred and fanged proxies, mongrels and purebreds alike. Much like this city, transient political backwater that it is.

So I had my coterie, my little dependable cohort to walk over to and talk to. They were: Kelly; the nice R Street boys; Angela, an attractive young black paralegal. I included Robert, when he, and not his new wife, brought their standard poodle puppy, Rocket. And by default or association, Oliver, because of Kelly. I suffered Oliver, you might say, and his dreadful little terrier for as long as I could. Oliver himself was appealing, in a diminutive way. He was trim and tidy, like his dog, with glossy black hair and ironed blue jeans, even in the park where anyone's dog is liable to jump up on you. He was a good raconteur, rather open about his amorous adventures when his surly boyfriend Eric wasn't in tow. He tended to squabble with his employers, but was never out of work for long. "Gotta keep those benefits," he's say.

And there it stood for several years, for most of the Clinton administration, in fact. What quarrels we had over *that* little scandal, my goodness! American provincial prurience at its worst. Kelly agreed with me, but she's lived in Europe and seen a bit of the world. You can tell when you see her, a tall elegant blonde, easy in herself. Fluent in French, married to an economist. As progressive as this neighborhood is, with nonprofits and advocacy organizations on every corner, I'm often surprised by how reactionary my neighbors can be. How they jumped all over Clinton! Aren't they sorry now, with this pious administration in the thrall of an out-of-control Pentagon. The new Crusades, for heavens sake!

But I'm digressing. It's my own small battle that I'm concerned with here. Or rather, Mickey's battle with Bingo, which happened quite suddenly, on an afternoon much like this one, in a ball-chasing melee just like any other. Mickey could be aggressive, as I said, but usually from behind the safety of his fence. The two dogs were certainly matched for size, but a toy poodle is not a terrier. Both went after...a Frisbee, I think it was. Mickey got there first, and I watched, horrified, as Bingo lunged for him, right for his throat, Mickey on his back under him, kicking, screaming.

That is what I saw and heard. But after we'd pulled them apart and assessed the damage—a gash on Mickey's shoulder and numerous puncture wounds, resulting in a triple-digit vet's bill—Oliver refused to admit his dog was in the wrong, refused to pay, and finished by accusing me, by *yelling* at *me* that *I* was overreacting, that Mickey attacked Bingo, that dogs will be dogs.

Dogs will be dogs.

Mickey of course was traumatized. His wound became infected. I nursed him, but he was not a young dog. He limped along for another year and then got pneumonia, and I had to put him down. Herbert had given me the dog for our last Christmas together, ten years earlier. There was no point getting another, no more reason to go to the park. So that was it.

If anything good came of this at all, it's the little visits that Kelly pays me now and then at home. She seems to have an open heart for a cranky old woman like me, or rather, the woman I've become. This solitude has crept up on me. My house has darkened and grown quiet—though at times I'm sure I hear the clicking paw steps, or see a shadow of dark furry movement around a corner. Strangely, I miss the dog more than I miss my husband. Herbert was time served, a kind of contract to acquit myself of satisfactorily over the length of our life together. Then it ended, just as I'd expected. A dog is also a companion for a span of time, a companion you chose, that you plight yourself to, a shared life for ten or fifteen years. I know my life will never have another such span. I'm on my own now, counting down the years.

About a week ago, the dog park cocktail hour was well under way, the usual cast of characters assembled. Robert was there with Rocket—who knows where the wife was. He really needs supervision, poor thing, with that wild poodle ready to knock him off his pins at any moment. Kelly and Oliver and Angela were sitting around a picnic table, waving away the gnats and talking. Bingo was lying in the shade under the table. I remember how you had to keep an eye on that dog when he was anywhere near your feet; he was liable to pee on your ankle without warning. Angela was there in her work clothes—a suit (the jacket off), pointy black sling-backs and a Coach purse big enough for the assortment of dog toys she brings to the park. Her springer spaniel, Juno, is a vigorous ball chaser, and Angela had turned to lob a yellow tennis ball high in the air for her. Suddenly Rocket was racing Juno for the ball, running from one end of the park to the other. He twisted into the air to catch the ball, sprang to the ground, and, as he landed, came close to slamming into someone's legs. Dogs scattered away from him, but he pranced around with the ball clamped in his teeth, shaking his pompom tail to entice another dog to play. From the wide red collar around his neck, a matching red leash flapped and dragged in the dirt.

Angela rose from the table and walked to where Robert stood staring somewhat vacantly at the ground in front of him. I watched him listen to her, pull himself erect, and say in a loud voice something about "full control," "neighborhood for thirty years," and "Anacostia."

Before Angela could say anything, Oliver was striding toward Robert. Him, I heard more clearly.

"Listen," Oliver said to Robert. "You don't have to be rude. Your dog is clearly out of control and we're only looking out to see that it doesn't get hurt. Or hurt anyone else. So watch what you say." At this point, Oliver was standing close enough to Robert that he had to lean back a bit to look his taller adversary in the eye.

Robert took a moment to register this small man chastising him from below. He leaned forward, opened his mouth. "Bark bark bark bark," he cried out. "Bark bark bark, you faggot!"

As if the air was suddenly sucked out of the park—or sucked into Oliver—everything went still. Even the dogs stood still. No yapping, no panting. Not a breeze stirred the leaves. Overhead, the sky was hazy white, a luminous tent over a surreal tableau. Oliver's face was white, his eyes narrow. I couldn't look at this face. It was as if everyone was waiting for him to breathe.

Robert broke the spell by suddenly staggering back, his eyes losing focus, as Oliver lunged for him.

"Why you fucking bigot...you fucking Nazi...you sick old fuck..." he snarled. "Racist," I heard in the garbled invective. "Homophobic..." Bingo would have been gnawing my old friend's calves, leaping for his throat. Horrified, I jumped from where I sat to save him, prepared to vault my own fence—at my age! What else can you do when fangs are at the throat? But at that moment, Kelly was at Robert's side, threading her hand under his arm to lead him away.

"Come on," she said firmly. "Come on, time to go home." Robert reluctantly allowed himself to be led. Angela, actually, intercepted Oliver. She grabbed his arm and said something to him as she walked him back to the table.

"Don't come back, you asshole!" Oliver turned to yell, waving his free arm. Rocket was retrieved and brought to Robert, and the pair was aimed down the hill on Bancroft Place and toward home. As he tottered past my house, I met him at the bottom of my steps to walk him home the rest of the way. I don't think he ever recognized me.

Kelly came to tea several days later, and I heard the rest of the story.

Before the scene with Robert, the three had been discussing Bingo's health. The terrier, who must have been at least thirteen by that point, had developed a tremor in his hind legs.

"What's the matter with your dog," Angela had asked. "Is he okay?"

"Oh nothing," said Oliver. "Just old age. The vet says the nerves in his hips are wearing out." He leaned over to rub the dog's head.

"He's getting gray around the snout, isn't he?" Kelly observed.

"Yeah. Too much bungeeing and bouncing around, you little bastard," Oliver said to the dog. "Gives you the shakes. Gotta learn to chill, right? Gotta take your glucosamine, your chondroitin." Bingo sprawled out, his legs splayed behind, belly on the cool dirt.

"Well, it happens to us all. Sucks to get old," said Kelly.

He looked at her. "I wouldn't know," he said.

"Oh that's right. You'll always be thirty-two, right?" Kelly joked. He didn't answer.

"Here, let me throw that ball," Angela had said, and we know what transpired next.

What had Angela then said to Robert, I wondered. "She said that when Rocket runs around with that leash on, he might hook it on something." said Kelly. "'He might snap off his head,' I think were her words."

"Hm. Not particularly provoking," I said. "But Robert never did like being told what to do, as I recall."

"Robert is a sick old man, Celia," Kelly said. "He must have dementia, to start barking at Oliver like that."

"I'm afraid you're right. 'Barking mad,' as the Brits say." I joked feebly. "Still, Oliver didn't need to take off on Robert either. Think how humiliating it was for him. He looked like a cornered rabbit. What does it gain? Who wins in such a situation?"

"Oliver felt very badly, I should tell you." Kelly said. "He sat back down at the table with us and said nothing for a long while. He was very upset. I remember it took a while for his breathing to quiet down. He was rolling the tennis ball on the tabletop, around and around. I asked him if he was okay.

"But he said, 'God damn it.'

"And then he said, 'Oh, shame on me. I shouldn't have done that.'

"Angela said, 'What! After what he said to me, after what he called you? Of course you should say something back, even if he *is* nuts. Maybe not beat the guy up, but he *dissed* you! He dissed me!'

"'Yeah, but you were right to hold me back,' Oliver said. 'Thank you for that.'

"'No problem,' she said.

"Then Oliver said, 'I've got a temper. I know. I always have, and it gets me into trouble. But after I got HIV, I began to think, why should I care *what* I say? What can anyone do? Kill me? I'll be dead soon anyway. I can say what I want. Fuck 'em! And *that* was cool!'

"They were able to laugh at that.

"'But now that I'm surviving, I have to learn to behave,' he said.

"Then he cocked the ball to throw it for Bingo, who streaked out ahead and was there before the ball could bounce.

"'I'll probably outlive my dog,' Oliver said. "That's the part I can't stand. '"

Robyn Kirby Wright

After Grandy, That Bastard, in an Airport

ROBYN KIRBY WRIGHT's fiction has appeared in *Five Points* and *Best of the Fiction Workshops 1999* edited by sherman alexie. she has just finished a novel and is currently working on a memoir called "sweeping beauty." she lives in reston, virginia.

He's the kind of ugly I sometimes find attractive, rangy and spry, someone in the early stages of heroin addiction—before the safety-pin thin arms. I can't justify the attraction. But why should this time be different? It's like Grandy said, "There's no explaining fucked up." That bastard. I'm almost over him. But this guy, he's different. A religious nut or something. One of those types who defy generalities: a religious nut/heroin addict with a stunningly precise bobbed hairdo. He's wearing leather thongs with a little ring fitted around the big toe. (I can hear Grandy right now.) And he's looking at me. This is my new beginning. I've been dry for eleven hours. Away from Grandy for eight. I have a bruise the size of a Georgia peach on my ass. I don't need anymore trouble. Don't fuck it up. Don't smile at him. There's no need to reapply lip gloss. I'm wearing a straw hat, something that implies an enthusiasm for holidays. Believe me, I dread everything. I'm one of the few people left in the world who wears a hat for sun protection. I have freckles on my scalp. I've spent hours studying my part. It's shameful what I do in the privacy of my own bathroom. The nut's playing the harmonica. The lady beside me is wearing mouse ears. She's been to Disney. I'm drying out. Clean and sober next to Disney. Just looking at him makes me long for the drink. Dry, I say to myself. It sounds like starved. I smell my armpits. They are damp. They are thirsty. Goofy glitters on the lady's big breast. Are we in the same country?

Grandy and I liked to see what depths human beings could fall to and still keep a job; the only rule was that the job part didn't apply to him. I had the job because someone had to pay for the drinks. Grandy and I, we'd sit on stools at a hotel bar and get drunk, fishing all the cashews out of the nut mixture, feeling elevated because the barman had done a Jell-O shooter off my belly the night before. There's nothing more depressing than a hotel bar, except maybe, a regular at an airport bar, someone with the pretense of going somewhere. At least we knew where our asses were parked. We had no illusions. There's a satisfaction in apathy, so long as you call it by its name. Here's the thing about me, though. I have the kind of face that makes other people feel good about themselves. It holds up over time, after seven Jaegermeisters and two shots of Grey Goose Vodka. It doesn't impose, it's plain as a bar of soap. Sometimes it's downright transparent.

Nut has a black box. Not large enough for a body, but it's not an accordion either. He's wearing a white, muslin shirt. A shower curtain. Breezy. All the trappings of a music man. Upon closer inspection, I notice he has little braids woven in his bobbed hair, scattered willy-nilly. I hate the cliché of it all. (The braids, my straw hat, the DTs.) Three more minutes until boarding time. He has the kind of calf muscles you are either born with or develop after miles of walking on soft sand. Maybe a crabber. Better that than a musician. He's looking at me again. I take the hat off. My hair is in pigtails. I left the mouse ears at home. My last defiant act after the breakup. *"And you can keep the mouse ears,"* I yelled, letting the car door slam on my foot.

"Are you all right?" he asks. I notice he walks on the balls of his feet, also good for the calves.

"I wish it were that simple," I say. "But I have a plane to catch." I fiddle with my tickets. My water bottle falls and leaks on his thongs.

"Sorry about your sandals," I say.

"They're thongs," he says. "And my feet were hot. I have sensitive feet."

"Better toughen them up. The island sand's hot."

"You want to know what's in the box?" he asks. "I saw you looking."

He has a slow deliberate way of speaking which makes me feel like he's showing me how to stroke him. It pisses me off. He opens the case and pulls out a wooden Buddha the size of a small dog.

"Can I rub his belly?" I ask. I say this but don't want to. Grandy said my biggest downfall was my mouth. He also said it was my greatest asset.

"I must have been wrong about you," he says. "Usually I can tell."

"Tell what?"

"Who's an asshole."

"Guess you're not that good a judge of character," I say. "Because I'm definitely an asshole."

"Hey," he says. "Are you from the Midwest? You have a Midwestern face. Wide as cornfield."

"And I'm dumpy too," I say. "Look. I've had a shitty day. I need a drink. And don't need to be reminded I'm an asshole."

I used to tell Grandy that *love wasn't supposed to hurt*. And he'd say, *it can if you want it to*. That was the last time I tried a slogan on him. It's crazy. He broke my jaw in two places. It actually lines up better now. I'm like one of those ventriloquist dummies whose mouth gapes open at inopportune times.

The Nut's seated on the aisle seat across from me; thongs tossed carelessly in the aisle where anyone could trip over them.

"You know I can levitate people," he says. "It's really a matter of mind over matter."

The drink cart is three rows back. I can feel the water beading on the green bottle of beer. I need this. Just one. I'll hit my other ass cheek and call it even.

"Bend this spoon," I say. "Let me see you do that."

"I only know how to levitate."

"Then bending a spoon should be easy."

"You have a bad energy," he says.

"Give me the spoon back then," I say.

The flight attendant hands me a sack of Eagle nuts. "Honey roasted." I have my eye on a beer. My heart feels as if it's going to jump out of my chest. I'm weighing my options—throw myself out of the airplane or pop the top off an icy one.

"What are you going to do with the spoon?" Nut asks.

"I'm going to snap the damn thing in two," I say. "Like this." Nothing happens to the spoon but the propeller catches a bird and sputters.

"Soda or wine?" The flight attendant scoops a cupful of ice out of the bucket.

"I'm clean," I whisper. "Better make it a beer. And another utensil."

The beer sits on my tray. I hold the spoon in front of me.

"Maybe you should try levitation," the nut says. And laughs. He has a beautiful mouth, like Grandy's. Trouble. Beyond trouble. Familiar.

"What time is it?" I ask.

"Twelve thirty, " Nut says.

I hold off twisting the top off the beer. Grandy, that bastard, must be rolling out of bed right now. I can see him clearly. Combing his seven strands straight back, plucking tobacco from his teeth. I'm inclined to be disgusted, but I know just beyond my mind's eye view, I'm there. Spread out on his eagle blanket with the burrs embedded on the fleece. Smelling a lot like wet dog and last-chance sex. And here's the scary part: I like it.

"Do you want to see me naked?" Nut asks. He's tapping his bare foot against my armrest.

"Only in a headlock," I say.

"You're not looking so much like Kansas anymore," he says.

I open the beer. Sober twelve and a half hours. Grandy eight hundred miles away. My car up on blocks in a south Miami parking garage. Louise Becker typing my briefs and phoning in orders to Big Chow's Asian Buffet for lunch. The barman saying, "What the fuck? Is it Christmas? Where is she?" My pink tropical fruit dress bunched up my ass, threatening to rot from the hypocrisy. My hands shaking. A spoon wedged between my foot and sandals. Still not bending. The beer shines like a promise. I can have one sip. Just one. It's all I need. I make a bargain with God. One sip and he can take Grandy out. I laugh out loud.

The nut says, "I can't get my head around you."

"I'm an alcoholic," I say. "And I'm going to take this drink."

"You deserve it," he says. "I mean, really." He shrugs.

"Do me a favor," I say. "Don't ever man a suicide hotline."

"Deprivation creates nothing but depravity," he says.

I'm in no mood for philosophizing. The beer sits there. I've got maybe ninety to one hundred pounds on it. It's kicking my ass. The nut has a new interest in me. He hooks his finger around his baby toe. I want to do something desperate, fling him against the window and put my mouth against his. I want to taste his tongue and whatever substance has been there. He has a long neck bottle of Heineken tucked between his thighs. I want to go there. I want to feel his precise, dirty hair against me.

It's obscenely bright inside this plane. The nut plays his harmonica. Boz Scaggs. I don't find this the least bit odd. The beer is waiting. Have you ever noticed beer smells the same as nuts until you drink it? I have an ache. To be filled. To be sloppy. To live the illusion one more time. I reach for the beer. I think of Grandy rolling his own weed, smoking it out of anything—cabbage leaves, tortillas. He seems so far away. Barbados is a tiny speck outside my window. So much God-forsaken reggae. I dare to dream up. About meeting a guy with a boat. Who spears fish and filets them for dinner. A good-natured man who wears canvas shoes. No laces. About holding a stick over a bonfire and roasting a marshmallow. I picture myself sunned and wind-whipped in search of grouper. It boils down to grouper. A sandy man carrying my tackle. I spill the beer all over my dress.

The nut has his hands full.

"Will you carry the Buddha?" he asks.

I'm hesitant, but the sun is shining on my shoulders. It feels like good karma.

"Yes," I tell him. I am light in the world.

We wander inside the dismal little airport. I carry the Buddha facing forward, my backpack slung over my shoulder. Thirteen hours and no drink, but I smell like a brewery. If I get desperate enough, I'll wring out the dress. One step at a time. The Nut is halfway through customs, rummaging through his bags. A pack of ramen noodles falls on the floor. It is strange what courage a Buddha will give you. Grandy wouldn't understand about enlightenment. They wave me through and stop me. I can see the taxi man in his open-toed shoes and cotton shirt loading bags. The agent pulls me aside.

"It's nothing," he says. "A formality."

Three pairs of underwear are bunched on the conveyor belt. He squeezes out a tube of my toothpaste. A man with a dog is waved over. The dog looks hungry. He looks like a government official.

"Is he on the payroll?" I joke.

"Don't move," the man says.

I look for the nut job, but he's nowhere to be seen. A woman is selling bananas in the corner. The policeman takes a hammer to the Buddha's tummy. It splits open like a coconut. Cocaine spills all over my feet.

I start to laugh.

"Crazy girl," he says. "You look so young. Like a baby."

"Yeah," I said. "That's not the half of it."

I lean over to dust off my feet. This is it. I suck on my fingers, tasting the drug, feeling the grit between my teeth. Believe me, I know this. This is not even how far I'll go.

Hananah Zaheer

Interlude

HANANAH ZAHEER is a Pakistani writer who has completed a collection of short stories and is currently working on her first novel. She teaches creative writing at Montgomery College, Maryland, and is associate fiction editor for the *Potomac Review*. She lives in Rockville with her husband and three-year-old son.

There is no explanation for what I did. Period. But Ari says he wants to know how it happened, and why it happened, and all those other questions that one asks in the sort of rage he was in. And he is still my husband. So I tell him.

It was the way he said my name that made me stop and turn around. A short sound that conveyed urgency, and desperation; a sound strangled at the end, drowning in silence.

"Can we talk?"

"No, I don't think so." But I didn't move away. A draft from the entrance burrowed through my clothes.

"Why not?" He was wrapping his arms around himself.

"I just...I don't know."

"Maya, I have something to say. Please?"

He watched me, his hands frozen in mid-motion as if my next words would either break the spell, or break him. And I perceived such earnestness in his eyes, heard such longing in his words, that I stayed.

I forgot that Ari was waiting for me at home, ignored the impatient sighs of the frozen pedestrians who were trying to enter, past me, and seek refuge in the relative warmth of the coffeehouse. The disbelief in his face was apparent, the green in his eyes becoming brighter momentarily before he too, like me, dropped a guarded look over his face.

"Would you like to sit down?'

I said nothing.

"Something to eat with that?" He persisted, motioning to the two cups of coffee in my hands; one mine, the other Ari's.

"No."

He sighed and lowered his head. I tried to make out his face, wondering if he really did have the little scar just below his lip that I remembered. A shaving accident, he had called it, when really, Ari had once flung a razor at him, drawing blood and tears in a twisted game of tag.

The intimacy of my memories surprised me, but perhaps it shouldn't have. Perhaps I should have known that seeing him would never be easy, or simple. I thought about leaving. And then he looked at me, caught my eye with his. My feet were paralyzed where they stood, my tongue in my mouth. I thought I heard tires screeching outside, perhaps a muffled thudding of someone beating their hands against the hood of a car. But then again, it could have been the rush of sound in my head, burning my ears.

He pulled a chair towards him and sat down, pushing one back with his feet for me. I followed, placing Ari's cup between us on the table.

"How is…" He hesitated, rubbing the underside of his chin with his thumb.

I raised my eyebrows. "My husband?"

He nodded, his eyes flitting over me but refusing to rest on mine.

"Ari is fine." I rolled my coffee cup in my hands. "We're fine. Happy." I lied.

"Happy?" he repeated.

"Happy," I insisted.

I can't say why it was that I felt the need to make that assertion. Something about his presence, the reality of him, sitting before me, the dark frown still sitting over his eyes, the jaw that still jumped with every shift in emotion, made me uncomfortable. Perhaps I just wanted to remind myself that Ari still existed.

Why did you acknowledge him? Ari asks. He is whacking my favorite sculpture, a three-inch exquisite rendering of a naked Indian woman, against the side of his head. He is resentful, I can see that. But he asked for the story, the reason, as he called it, of betrayal.

Do you want to hear this or not, I ask him, distracted by the thumping of the hollow wood against bone.

He puts the sculpture in his lap, her face down on his crotch, and leans back on the sofa.

Anyway, I continue. I didn't. I tried to ignore him. I was minding my business.

We sat across the table, hesitating, wondering, I think, about the serendipity of our meeting. His legs, long, lean, strong, touched mine from time to time, and I pulled back, retreating into my chair until my back was flat against it. But I couldn't stop looking at him. I took in his dark unruly hair, so different from Ari's neat brown crop, the darkened edge of his index finger, stark against the whiteness of his palms. He clasped his hands on the table and then withdrew them to his lap.

"You still bite your nails?"

He nodded, his eyes still intent on mine. I stared at his lips, severe in their tightness, belying the faint upturned corners that were meant to suggest a smile; the same lips that had crushed mine, trapping my breath in my own mouth…when was it?

Years ago…

I wonder why you started talking to him. Ari is talking at the ceiling. His hands are locked behind his head, cradling and rocking it from side to side.

I don't know, I tell him. I really don't. I was curious, I guess, whether he would apologize, you know, for…

Curiosity killed the cat. Ari straightens his head until his eyes are level with mine.

Don't worry about me, I say. I've got eight lives left.

Seven, he counters, blue eyes glinting.

If my children had survived my body, living inside me, I would have used that moment to pull out snapshots of my life: beautiful brown-eyed children with golden brown hair, a little like Ari, a little like me, rolling in the grass, hanging on our arms. The last one almost made it too. And then Ari lost him, a boy few months from being born, for both of us. He had been angry, in that inexplicable way that I have come to accept from him, and drove faster down the curved street that led to our house. At the end, in the midst of screaming and skidding, he had plowed into a parked car on the side of the road. I lay in the hospital bed for weeks, dangling between moments of confusion and stark clarity, never really able to figure out which one of us was to blame. Either way, it was something Ari and I both accepted, because who is to say that the picture in my head would have been reality anyway.

He shifted in his chair.

"I've moved back here." It sounded more like a question than a statement.

I considered his words, the intention of them unclear. Perhaps he was confirming that he indeed was here, with me; maybe it had nothing to do with me at all, just a query to himself, questioning the correctness of his decision.

I could feel the cold slipping in between my shoulder blades. The sky was darkening fast outside. I knew Ari would soon be worried.

"It's close to…where you used to live."

I shivered. The memories ran through my veins in short bursts. I remembered the building where we had lived as neighbors and friends, before Ari and I had discovered each other, a few days before I had realized that perhaps it wasn't Ari but his Indian roommate I was meant to be with. Ari saw the possibility that hovered in the air between his friend and me, I think. I could never be sure if they were jealous of each other, Ari certainly was the type, but I stayed with him anyway, lured by the otherness of him, closing my eyes to the fairness of his skin, the darkness of my own. And his friend waited, and I can't say I didn't want him to, and lingered around the edges of our relationship, until…

I remember the purple paisley print of the curtain above my bed, still that night he had sneaked into my room while Ari, then my boyfriend, slept unawares next door. The blinking reflection of the bedside clock on the doorknob had been red and persistent, the numbers flashing three eights, over and over. I think perhaps the bed squeaked, it had shuddered for sure. I had lain in my bed, huddled and bruised as he sneaked out of my room, the hallway light creating a dim yellow halo around his bare brown back, knowing that I was doomed to replay this moment for the rest of my life, wondering what it would have been like if he had been the one I met before Ari.

When he disappeared a week later, and Ari stopped mentioning him, I wondered. I felt betrayed by the silence, on all our parts, angry with Ari that he wouldn't comfort me, angry with myself because I felt deceived, by Ari, by him, by myself.

We fought; I wanted him to care. So much so that when Ari decided he didn't want to move in with me, I proposed to him, pretending that was what we had been headed towards all along.

He watched me, frowning in thought, and pulled at his scarf, loosening its hold around his neck. I had an image of twisting the green wool tight around his neck, tighter than he had held my throat that night, tighter than I had twisted my own hair thinking of him, years after he left. He took the scarf off, baring his neck to me, the birthmark in the hollow of its base as vivid as ever. My stomach crumpled into itself. There it was, the spot shaped vaguely like India, the reddish brown edges ragged against the skin on his neck. He raised a hand to touch his neck, and I looked away, ashamed of having been caught looking. And I think, maybe, he recognized what he saw, the look, the desperation of someone caught in time. He smiled.

The relief in his eyes hit me like a jolt of lightning in my stomach and I retracted my hand suddenly, spilling coffee on my legs. He swam in and out of my vision as I patted at my legs with a napkin, wondering vaguely how my body could feel so weightless and so heavy at the same time. He leaned forward, concern apparent in his face, and I dropped my head, my face burning; I was desperate to distance myself from the revulsion I felt for myself. How could I, still, after what he did, after all these years, still feel…?

"Let's go to my place. To talk." He spoke softly, coaxing with his eyes.

I thought about Ari, and that perhaps I should leave. But he was up and walking away before I could say anything. I stood by the chair, caught between my two lives: one that lived each day inside my head, replaying and readjusting the past over and over, and in stark contrast, Ari's sagging energy, growing resentments, and the occasional and never satisfying acts of love. He turned and glanced at me, and I thought I saw possibility in his eyes. So I left the cups sitting on the table and followed him instead.

He was angry at you, spilled coffee on you, and you still stayed? Ari narrows his eyes at me, his hands tracing the curves of the statue in his lap. If I did that, you would never…

I can see the suspicion on his face, the dark cloud of resentment taking hold of his features.

You wouldn't do that, Ari. You're not like that. I am tired of his whining, his constant competition.

What am I like? His narrowed eyes are challenging.

It was anger, Ari, passion. He was angry because I said I didn't care to talk to him.

He lifts the small figurine from his lap and raises it to eye level.

Passion, huh?

He closes one eye then the other, and I know I'm a blur in the background.

Go on, he says.

And I do.

We stopped in front of an old apartment building, the dull stone front appearing more so behind the curtain of falling snow. He fumbled for a minute with the keys in his pocket while I waited behind him.

He glanced back at me. "Coming?"

I heard traffic behind us, tires grating against snow, wheels churning, turning, crunching the ice already forming along the edges of the road.

A mother rushed her baby, bundled in a red snow jacket, across the intersection. I rubbed my hands together; he kicked at a bit of the snow with his foot. I nodded. Turning, he climbed the stairs, one hand brushing against the wall; I followed him up a flight of stairs, my fingertips wanting to linger, running along the whitewashed walls in his wake.

The hallway was lit only with the faint winter light from the two skylights at either end, reminding me of winter snows from three years ago, when Ari and I got married. Snow days had been dark, and deliciously dreary through the windows of the apartment we shared. Perhaps if we had stayed there, looking out at the world, wrapped in our nakedness and each other's company, perhaps if Ari hadn't been driven to overcome the ugliness of our differences, the brownness of my skin, although he never said it in those words, by moving somewhere more appealing, perhaps...

"Maya?"

He was calling my name again. I realized that I was standing in his living room, surrounded by his things. I could feel him watching me, studying my face. I thought that perhaps I should return his gaze, but instead I watched them...his things. The couch, red, torn at the seams. A pillow at one end of it, dented slightly in the middle as if someone had been resting against it just a minute ago and then disappeared, poof, as we walked through the door. The dusty stereo by the tall window; next to it abandoned CD cases. Coltrane, Davis. A heaping ashtray sat on the coffee table in the middle of the room, surrounded, as if in defeat, by an army of papers.

"Have a seat."

I chose to sit near the pillow. It was comforting, the possibility that I was near where someone might have been. I have always been like that. Excited by the almost could-have-beens, depressed at what didn't happen but someday might. You could say it was what kept me sane...my imagination, the understanding that there might be something other. Other than what, I never knew. Just other.

You should have turned back, Ari is petulant.

I know, I hear myself soothing him. But I had to know what he had to say.

No. He slides between emotions so easily. You wanted something else. He has a sly smile on his face.

He turns the statue to face me. The light of the side lamp glints on her stomach.

Ari touches the tips of her breasts lightly with his fingertips. I shudder.

He grins. Keeps going, one finger lowers itself to her stomach, drawing a straight line down from her navel. You wanted something else.

I am angry. But I owe him this, so I say nothing.

He reached into his pocket and pulled out a packet of cigarettes. I watched his mouth as it curved around the smoke. He inhaled again.

I felt impatient, desperate to break the silence. "What now?"

It was the question that had lingered between us all afternoon.

He sat down at the other end of the couch, framed by the tall windows behind him. The sky was dark, resting heavily on the tired-looking buildings under it. He tapped some ash onto the already burnt pile of cigarettes.

"Now. You are now here. Hell, even earlier I thought I wanted you to be here. Because in my head I saw you fit perfectly. Right there on that spot where you are. I imagined you would sit just as you are, on the edge on the sofa, grabbing your bag, but crossing your legs so I think you are comfortable. No don't move. I don't know what I'm saying."

He dropped his head into his hands. I rested mine on one hand. I counted the ticks of the clock on the wall behind, convinced that the growing silence was intimate and not awkward. After a while, he spoke again.

"I'm not a philosopher."

"Okay."

"I can't make grand statements of love. Or desire."

I felt the prickle of heat rise along my neck. Outside, the snowflakes eased their assault against the windowpanes.

"You love me?"

"I'm just saying. I'm not that kind of guy."

"You desire me then?"

He shrugged.

"We can't pretend we don't have this connection." He refused to look at me.

I wondered whether Ari and I had a connection; were lost children and mistimed gestures of affection a connection?

"A connection?" I repeated.

He blew smoke into the air. "It could have been something then."

"But now?" I was standing on the edge of a precipice that seemed too hard to retreat from.

He shrugged again.

I leaned back against the sofa. "Well then…"

Smoke filled the air between us, and somewhere in that haze, I saw clearly what he was asking for. It's possible that in that moment I felt regret. For being where I was, for not meeting him before, for feeling what I felt. He, who had occupied my thoughts and Ari's too, I think, for all these years, wasn't the kind of guy either of us wanted him to be. And in a strange way, I regretted that too.

Ari sits up straight, drops the statue to the floor.

And, he prompts me.

I have to go to the bathroom. I rise from the couch, stretching my legs to ease the numbness. I can see him in the mirrored wall, his eyes on the back of my head, a childlike eagerness all over his face. He waits, patiently.

I return and lift the prostrate statue from the floor.

He doesn't object.

And then, he asks again.

Then I say, placing the statue on the table between us, then it happened.

He flinched as I reached over and took the cigarette from his hand. The smoke still curled its way out after I buried it deep in the pile of dead cigarettes in the ashtray. His mouth tasted ashy, his lips drier than I had imagined. But his hands were eager.

The snow resumed its descent onto the pavement outside. I moved closer, shifting until I was sitting on his lap, slowly and deliberately taking off my clothes, watching his face melt into the same desire I had seen on it all those years ago. He tried to reach for me, but I held his arms down, enjoying the feeling of him squirming beneath me.

"Stop," he protested when I bit his neck and tasted salt on my tongue.

"No," I said.

He wanted to take his clothes off.

"No," I said again.

The clock ticked loudly as I rocked back and forth on top of him. I couldn't tell if the grimace on his face was of pain or pleasure. But I watched him, and I told him he couldn't touch me. When I was done, I moved off of him, gathered my clothes, and kissed him on the cheek.

He lay on the couch, looking dazed and desperate. "Maya?" His voice was faint.

I turned, impatient to leave.

"I'll see you later?"

I turned around. He had raised himself on his elbows. Evening light fell on his shoulders from behind. He seemed weak, and childlike.

I smiled, and walked away, leaving the door open behind me.

Ari is silent.

I watch him.

He studies my face, perhaps he is trying to decide how truthful I've been. I stare back at him.

So he tried to kiss you? He asks

I nod.

And nothing else happened. I mean he didn't want…he leaves the words unspoken.

I shrug. I don't know. I didn't want anything.

He hasn't changed, has he? Ari wants some reassurance.

I am unsure how to answer, so I remain quiet.

He rubs his forehead. I feel an urge to reach across the space between us and smooth away the frown.

And you, you feel that you …

I resolved something, I say. I'm not lying. Something inside me has shifted.

And he—

He, I interrupt Ari, is just an interlude.

Anna Ziegler

Passages

ANNA ZIEGLER's plays have been produced in New York, and her work published in *Ten-Minute Plays for 2 Actors: The Best of 2004* (Smith and Kraus) and *New American Short Plays 2005* (Backstage Books). *BFF* and *Life Science* will be published by Dramatists Play Service, and *BFF* will be included in the anthology *New Playwrights: The Best Plays of 2007* (Smith and Kraus). A graduate of Yale, Ziegler holds an MFA from Tisch. Her poetry has appeared in *The Best American Poetry 2003*, the *Threepenny Review*, the *Michigan Quarterly Review*, *Reactions*, the *Mississippi Review*, *Arts and Letters*, *Mid-American Review*, *Smartish Pace*, the *Saint Ann's Review*, and many other journals. For more information, please see www.annabziegler.com.

The woman in question never hesitates to pick up the phone when something is bothering her. She's an only child and not particularly close to her parents; in the same way she has many good friends but no best friend. She talks most to Hayley, even though it's long distance. Hayley's married and the mother of daughters. When Hayley speaks to her she's careful not to assume too much and careful, also, not to seem condescending. The woman in question isn't married and hasn't had many lovers. She's thirty-four and inexperienced.

The man in question works nights. He enjoys fly-fishing and quiet afternoons, the lake he grew up on in summertime. He is, quite simply, a man of the world. His favorite memory of childhood is standing with his brothers at the top of Mount Washington in January in what he likes to say was "a mighty cold wind." The man in question is not a man of many words.

The woman in question has never cross-country-skied. She has never snow-boarded or ice-skated or wind-surfed or sky-dived. She hasn't done many things that involve hyphens, or falling.

The man in question was married once. He was even a father, though, according to him, "I ain't one now."

The woman in question isn't very tall. She isn't very quiet either and can frequently fall prone to fits of giggling. She follows three television shows at one time and can be heard uttering the term "devastated" to describe her emotional state if she misses one. The woman in question doesn't understand how to use a VCR and refuses to learn about the Internet. "Oh that thing," she calls it.

The man in question has no hobbies, only "life pursuits." One of them is to play many instruments well. Another is to fall in love.

The woman in question is still embarrassed about wetting the bed one night at sleep-away camp during a dream in which she was being chased by bulls. The next morning, five girls crowded around her cot, holding their noses. One said, "You stink." It is this incident that she cites when explaining why she doesn't think the world is fair, or just.

The man in question took a poetry course once at a school for continuing adult education. He never went to college, or more specifically, he never finished. In the poetry course, his professor was a man his age with much more hair and too many questions. "How should we interpret this line?" he asked over and over again. One day, in the middle of the discussion of a poem by Frost, the man in question stood up and said, "The hell if I know," and walked out.

The woman in question is not stupid.

Neither is the man in question.

The woman in question doesn't think much about what she wears. In the morning, she puts on one of ten or so possible outfits. They all consist of a skirt that falls below the knee, a collared blouse, and a cardigan. No one at work has ever complained about her attire and this is pleasing, especially since a girl named Louise was fired for dressing inappropriately.

The man in question has two brothers, Jake and Dave. They don't live close by. Dave walks with a limp for which the man in question feels responsible. Jake is married to a woman he knocked up; the wedding took place before the baby was born and then the baby died at birth. Above all other things, the man in question misses his brothers.

The woman in question sometimes goes to bars on her own, even though she's seen movies in which women at bars alone are subject to events beyond their control. Still she likes the friendliness of bartenders and the way, at closing time, the lights just go out. In summer, she'll take a book and a pack of cigarettes and finish both while sitting outside at a picnic table in front of McKay's.

The man in question doesn't smoke. He once did, but his ex-wife found it irritating before she began to find him irritating. He quit for her and now begrudgingly wonders if she saved his life.

The last time the woman in question called Hayley, Hayley was in the middle of changing a diaper. "Let me call you back," she said, but the woman in question wouldn't have it. "It's fine," she said, "I'll catch you another time."

Surprisingly, the man in question has never flown in an airplane. He's terrified of them, the way they streak across the sky like birds or gods or apparitions. The way magic must come into play. Maybe once he read a story about a crash and it stayed with him. He doesn't know.

The woman in question daydreams about being pregnant. She sometimes catches herself with her eyes closed imagining the deep closeness of a womb, the darkness, the roaring sound of a heartbeat miles away. She is not as solitary as she seems. At least twice a week, she sees friends; they go drinking or to the movies. Sometimes, they smoke pot.

The man in question works as the night custodian at a local elementary school. Sometimes he wanders the halls staring at pictures by children he will never meet. Hannah, fifth grade; Joel, fifth grade. A girl named Sophie (fourth grade) always draws kites and dragons. But mostly there are common themes: family, pets, war.

The woman in question would like to lose a few pounds. Not too many but enough so that she could wear her skirts from college. There's one in particular that she misses, a white one with brown flowers and light blue trim; she remembers, mistakenly, that it made her feel free.

When it rains, the man in question sleeps late. He knows it's arbitrary, but to him it's as good a reason as any to make oneself happy. He's not a religious man, but he does respect the natural world. He believes in signs.

The woman in question went to the small college where she now works. That's where she met Hayley even though Hayley up and moved to Minnesota. "Why are you leaving me?" she asked when she heard the news. She was drunk and beside herself. "I'm not leaving you," Hayley said, "I just want to go somewhere else."

The man in question was not granted custody of his son because he had a tendency towards unruly behavior, according to the judge. This behavior consisted of verbal abuse (it's documented that he once told his own child to "shut up") and throwing a pot across an empty room.

The woman in question has an extensive library. Her books cover three walls of a sizable room. One wall is devoted to poetry—her favorites include Elizabeth Bishop, Robert Frost, and T.S. Eliot. When she read *The Wasteland* in college, it struck her as sad whereas now it just seems true.

The man in question lives in Brooklin but finds himself in Bar Harbor on a quiet summer evening. He doesn't have to work tonight because the school is undergoing renovations. He buys himself a Guinness and sits out by the water, remembering things.

The woman in question is tired. Last night she stayed up late reading the letters of E.B. White. One in particular stayed with her—a letter to his stepson, an editor at the *New Yorker* after White stopped working there. She can't recall the exact wording, but the line she liked had to do with sticking to your guns and not letting the world dismay you. She liked it for its concision and the implicit acknowledgment that the world is indeed a dismaying place. The woman in question is about to go home when a coworker, Marcia, invites her out for a drink.

At the bar, the man in question orders a second Guinness. Why not feel it a little tonight, he thinks. Why not?

Marcia and a few others, including the woman in question, choose a table outside. Carla, their supervisor, offers to buy the first round of drinks. When she leaves, the remaining women put their heads together and discuss the run in Carla's stocking, her bad breath, her lisp. The woman in question wonders aloud if Carla is happy.

The man in question stands, stretching his legs. It's been a while since he's spent a night like this, alone and by the water. He remembers how, when he was married, his wife insisted they go out once a week, just the two of them. They'd go to restaurants, to bars, to bowling alleys, to community theaters. They may have even been here once or twice. He remembers how he dreaded those nights and at some point realized he was not and had never been in love.

Lust is a strange thing. It takes people by surprise. It is not unlike an empty sky across which suddenly darts a swiftly moving airplane. It comes and then goes and then is gone.

The woman in question notices the man in question first. He is standing by the water. He has strong calves, muscled. His back is to her. The hem of his shorts is frayed and he wears socks under sandals, the way her father did, an act which always triggered her mother to chide, "Harry, must you?"

The man in question returns to the bar for a third beer. The breath of the woman next to him smells like garlic consumed out of loneliness, so he takes a step to the side. She orders a round of Miller Lites "for the ladies." The man in question wonders what kind of ladies these are. He orders his drink and wobbles a little as he walks.

The woman in question remembers being nine and drawing a picture on the front porch. The wind is blowing. The stone holding her paper down isn't enough and the paper blows away, her little masterpiece adrift now on the front lawn. She runs to retrieve it as it floats but she trips on the steps, gashing her chin on the slate and pebbles of the walkway. She screams and screams but no one comes. Finally, she walks inside, wounded, and sees her parents in the kitchen. At first she thinks they're fighting but it turns out they're making love.

The man in question studies the table of women.

The woman in question thinks he looks like a younger Harrison Ford, or maybe Clint Eastwood. Either way, he's kind of craggy, rugged.

The man in question recognizes that he's being watched. The woman in question is attractive with round cheeks and the kind of eyes that usually get hidden behind glasses. He likes the red of her cardigan, the way it looks against the light, which is fading quickly. The man in question knows that if there's one thing he's learned, it's that every day ends.

About a year ago, the woman in question complained to Hayley that she'd screwed up a date with a perfectly eligible man. "What'd you do?" Hayley asked. "I stared at him," she admitted, "I couldn't stop looking at him."

The man in question hasn't dated since the breakup of his marriage. In fact he's been known to curse women over the phone to his brothers. They try to settle him down. "Don't worry—you'll feel differently eventually. Don't worry—you won't always work nights. You'll go to college; your life will change." When he hangs up, he feels the pressure of a thousand mistakes.

The woman in question thinks, "Fuck it."

The man in question isn't surprised so much as flattered. He's feeling his drink now and wonders if that third beer was yet another in a long series of bad decisions.

The woman in question says "Hello." She wants to be simple, direct. She doesn't want to play games. The last time she enjoyed a game she was thirteen and beat her father at chess.

"Hello," the man in question returns.

It's one of those nights when the moon is visible before darkness falls. For a few moments they stand in it, neither knowing what to say.

"Are you waiting for someone?" she asks.

He's torn. Should he risk crudeness ("You") or risk being pitied?

"No," he says.

"Oh," she says. She seems for a moment pleased. A whisper of a smile. A quiet illumination like lightning in the next town over.

"You're with friends?"

At first she doesn't know to whom he refers. She looks around and focuses again on the table of women. Right now they are staring at her and speaking softly; surely they are being unkind.

"Yes, well—coworkers."

And of course, if he could, the man in question would take this woman's arm.

Of course, if she could, the woman in question would ask for this man's number.

Instead, for the moment, they stand together while the outdoor tables at McKay's fill up and a blinking light up above—a plane, perhaps, or a dying star—reminds each of them, separately, of the harshness of time.

Christy J. Zink

Taking Cover

CHRISTY J. ZINK is on the faculty of the University Writing Program at George Washington University and has twice been awarded a grant for fiction writing from the D.C. Commission on the Arts and Humanities and the National Endowment for the Arts. Her work has appeared in such journals and anthologies as *American Literary Review*, *Spoon River Poetry Review*, the *Gettysburg Review*, and *The Bedside Guide to No Tell Motel.* She teaches writing workshops in Washington, D.C., public high schools and is a senior editor with the *Next American City* magazine.

The second time a hurricane came through Pensacola I thought I'd won everything, but instead I lost my luck. Even though the house stayed, I guess it took everything good that could've happened to me to keep that damn thing standing. I'm convinced of it. Because by the time the third hurricane hit—Hurricane Emilia—I didn't care that it ripped my house off its foundation. By then, I'd given up on the world and everything in it.

I met Travis during Hurricane Jarvis two years ago at the Red Cross shelter set up in the basement of First National Bank and Trust. We were both there as volunteers, but he'd been there both longer and too long, so he bossed me around in a mean voice. "You," he said, pointing at me and then to a dwindling stack of gray blankets, "go get more."

I did it without blinking. I'd like to say I was just preoccupied with helping people however I could, that I was some kind of generous person with this big selfless heart. But I'm at the point in my life right now I don't care to lie. The truth is that I stood there along those long rows of army cots and children wrapped up in blankets and felt guilty that my own house came through without a scratch and guiltier still that I took pleasure in the fact that the storm had veered mere miles off the course towards my house at the last minute and hit someone else instead. It seemed not providence, but the work of something darker that I was going to have to pay for later. Turns out I was more right than I could have known.

Travis raised up a sheet to fold it. His blond hair was going in a hundred different directions. He looked, then, like a kid who'd just pulled off his ghost costume at Halloween and had too much sugar in his system already. I found out later that he was almost always disheveled, even when he was calm—how he'd turn out that other look he had, like he'd just climbed out of bed from good sex. But that night he was crazy-eyed, barking orders at me and the other people who'd come to work. He was intense and strong and sure of himself, and I found him irresistible and infuriating at the same time. He kept on folding sheets, unfolding them just as fast when a new cot got set up. He yelled at young women, old women, men of all ages, people of all colors. "You," he shouted, along with whatever command was going to occupy you for the rest of the night.

When morning light crept in through the windows of the old bank we were stationed in, I felt more awake for the light, and just as suddenly stumbled back in the full weight of exhaustion.

"Time for a break," he said, looking my way. "How about some coffee?"

I nodded, surprised. That was more than he'd said to me at one time all night.

He waved at one of the college kids who had a whistle around his neck—in some attempt to look official, I guess. The kid probably had a summer job as a lifeguard and thought the whistle might come in handy, but it just looked silly dangling there. "Taking a break," he said, but he didn't invite the kid along.

We walked over to the Dunkin' Donuts across the street, and when we stepped through the door, my nose filled up with all that yeast and powdered sugar and sticky jelly until I felt full just smelling the inside of that place. But I was too tired to even think about eating, and I knew that kind of food would only make me crash that much quicker. I ordered a large coffee with extra cream. He ordered himself a large coffee, no cream and half a dozen chocolate glazed donuts.

I watched him while he ate them, slowly, one by one, not saying a word to me, but letting himself smile a little more after each one. "Ah," he said when he was done. "Breakfast." He brushed his large hands off one another. "Nothing like chocolate glazed to start your day off when you've got absolutely nothing left."

I blinked hard at him. I don't know why I'd just assumed he was with the Red Cross doing relief work, like me, out of guilt. Instead, I realized, he was there out of fear and loss, because he didn't know what else to do with himself.

"It's all gone?" I asked. I was careful not to push it. He was talking now, talking to me, and this couldn't be easy for him to put into any kind of words.

He bowed his head down. "Timber," he said towards the Formica table. "My house is timber." And then he dropped his head all the way down onto the table, on top of his folded arms, collapsing beyond exhaustion and whatever else he was feeling that I couldn't imagine. His shoulders rose and quivered down. Here he was, crying with this little moan, a man who'd irritated me for hours on end, but once I understood why, I felt like I'd learned the single thing I needed to know. I moved across from where I was sitting to the booth where he was and put my arms around him but looked straight ahead. I knew he was the kind of man who wouldn't want to be seen this way. I didn't move my hands at all; I just held him there. He let his whole weight fall against me, and I pushed back against him to hold him up. There's that point of breakage and leaning you get to as a couple when both of you buckle and you forgive each other for whatever had already happened and whatever might in the future, and I took it in at that moment for what it was. But it had happened so early between us—way too early—that I would have been smarter not to trust it.

There are dangers that come of living on the Gulf Coast. You know this the second you decide to stay here and put the kind of money down that's going to tie you to this place for any amount of time. You take one good look at those mortgage papers and the official insurance papers all together and see that they mention Act of God like 18,000 times, each and every time making sure you know how it's going to be your fault, not theirs, for any disasters that befall you. Life here is about assuming responsibility and risk and knowing that the two, more often than not, are exactly the same thing.

Down here, it's up to you to protect yourself. For one thing, you don't go and offer a man you just met the right to your bed, but I did. I called it *giving him shelter* because, let's face it, he had none. And after making up so many of those cots with scratchy, army-issue blankets I wasn't going to make him sleep in that temporary Red Cross shelter, not with all those strangers. I suppose that place offered people some small solace, but to me it seemed depressing and pitiful and I was full of shame and happiness and I was embracing this life of risk. How, then, could you blame me?

"I wanted to come home with you," he said. "You seem like someone who needs being taken care of."

"Me?" I said. "You're the one without a house."

Still, I thought it was sweet. I wasn't that kind of woman who was just waiting around for a man to take care of her. I'd done fine so far, living with men as long as they were worth it. Moving on when they weren't. I was in my early forties, so I'd bought a house, determined to be happy being on my own. But still.

At first it was amazing between us. He was good to me in bed—attentive in ways I didn't know I needed until he showed me. I was no innocent when I met him, so it wasn't tricks that he did or ways that we did it. But that I felt like his skin had a fever right underneath it and that when I'd wrap my legs around him I'd feel like I was keeping a volcano going at a fast rumble, but keeping the whole earth from changing because I'd allow him release in some other way that he and I both needed. We'd seen trouble and we'd worked against it. For that reason alone, I thought that together, we could keep disaster at bay.

He was a man who talked in bed, afterwards; I didn't know that kind of man existed. He told me stories about how he was a mariner, how he'd traveled with the Merchant Marine out of San Diego, California (he said it just like that, as if I'd never have heard of San Diego and he was just making that place up). Actually, I didn't know the Merchant Marine existed anymore; as far as I knew it was just a job that the characters on soap operas had in their pasts. But when he told me about the time they'd docked in Panama, under strict orders just to deposit their cargo and go, I believed him and the life he was telling me he lived.

"So you see," he said to me that night in bed, "I didn't need to go ashore to know that place. Just being on that dock, it was enough to off-load those crates and then look out at that little town from the tanker and watch it wake up. All those people who came up out of sleep and cooked some kind of breakfast that's not even anything I'd want to eat first thing in the morning and they're speaking some language I can't understand a word of and never will, and getting ready for their days in this world that's so far away from anything I know that there's nothing I can touch there, nothing I can do that's wrong, so long as I do my job unloading crates and staying quiet. I mean, that's a pretty powerful thing," he said. 'When you can see that things can be safe from harm, at least a few minutes at the start of the day someplace else in the world."

And then it'd be morning before I knew it, and I'd wake up to him turned back quiet as the day I met him. I'd heard him myself call out orders with authority in his voice about cots and blankets and even bandages and hydrogen peroxide for when someone came in hurt, so it made sense that he'd been some kind of military man, and I felt like I learned something else that explained him and felt closer to him again, and again, like there was always going to be more to learn late in the night, that it was always going to bind us tighter and explain him better, so that by the time we'd lived out our lives together, he would be a completely solved mystery. By then he'd have seen every clue in me, too, and we'd know everything and be simple for each other in our old age.

I didn't care that over the next year we didn't walk down the aisle or that he wouldn't even use the words *wedding* or *marriage*. I was a woman of the twenty-first century. Independent and aware. I wouldn't use the word *feminist* for god's sake, but I knew that I was a woman who knew what she wanted and, sometimes, even how to get it.

It all started with the storms, when hurricane season picked back up in September. He turned even quieter than usual, and the more I tried to soothe him, the antsier he got. In the middle of the month, he came home slobbering drunk with some story about the docks foreman being a sonofabitch, and after six cups of coffee, he finally told me he'd been fired.

"But why?" I asked. "What happened?"

"Don't ask me that," he said, and his bloodshot eyes seemed to get redder and his face go madder. "Don't you worry. I'm still gonna pay my share."

I wasn't worried, but the truth was he hadn't paid much of anything around here other than to buy an occasional case of beer or carton of cigarettes. He'd put his insurance money in the bank, and I knew he went over to his old house and worked on it now and then like a weekend hobby. I was still giving him time, and space. It's a lot to lose your whole house out from under you, and he was at home here now, with me. The last thing I wanted to do was chase him away, so I'd made allowances, because everyone had always told me that's what love was.

There's something about hurricane season on the Coast where everything slows down and people get all cautious and worried. People aren't hiring, that's for sure. I suppose part of the problem was that Travis had too much time on his hands, too much time to build up that intensity of his into a kind of fury.

I'd come home, exhausted, from my job at Anderson Brothers, where I typed in numbers into tiny boxes all day and kept the spreadsheets clean and correct. And I'd be worn out when I came into the house carrying sacks of groceries with no will to make the dinner I knew I'd have to slap together. Travis and I—we weren't enjoying each other anymore in those days. We hardly slept together. Meals were a matter of merely feeding ourselves. He glared at me across the table and spoke fewer words by the day.

"You're late," he said to me while I separated three frozen meat patties from each other.

"I had to go to the grocery store," I said. "I told you that this morning."

"It doesn't take an hour and a half to buy three bags of groceries," he said, and took my wrist in his hand and yanked it.

"Fuck," I said, and yanked back. "How would *you* know? When's the last time you did anything around here?" I knew I didn't mean it the minute I said it. I was tired, and I wanted it to be like things were with us before, when he was slowly unfolding himself to me, when I could gather everything he was into me in the deepest part of the night.

And just like that, he hit me. Not a slap or a shove, but a cold cock in the nose, and the blood came immediately, before I even knew what happened.

"Damn it," he said, like it was my fault I was bleeding. He hurried off to the bathroom and came back with a towel that he held out to me. "Hold this tight against the bridge of your nose. Press down." I saw him turn off the stove out of the corner of my eye and grab his keys.

"Come on, now," he said. "We've got to get you to the hospital." It was like I was a child who'd done something stupid like fall out of a tree. That's how he talked to me. I was too full of the taste of my own blood and the shock of that punch to be as afraid as I should have been, and I followed on out of the house right after him, just like he told me to.

What he did over the next six months didn't take trips to the hospital. After my eye swelled up and the blood vessels under my eye broke the skin, after all that bleeding, even though he didn't break my nose, I looked bad enough it must have spooked him. He apologized and watched over me like a nurse for days. After that incident, he was just more careful with his violence: bruises on my skin that for the most part the world couldn't see. Bruises, though, that he must have thought would keep me from sleeping with any other man. But I kept telling myself that he never meant to do it, that it all came unexpectedly out of this red-hot anger about loss and his broken house that he didn't know what to do with, that what he did wasn't all that bad. I probably provoked him most of the time. He wasn't taking a knife to my throat or slitting my skin anywhere. He didn't keep me afraid. I never, ever, ever thought he was going to kill me. That's important, now. I want you to understand. He was just a man of certain passions that were too big for his skin, and I happened to be the body in front of him when that time came. I was going to take it, because he needed me for that. I loved him; he loved me. He needed to call out to someone in that secret language of his and for someone to listen and answer him with the simplest of actions, to show that he'd been heard. And even if this was a little extreme, is that really so different than what we all want out of love?

By March, with the weather turning warm and balmy, he turned sweeter again. He found work with McAdams Shipping Company. He grew tender in bed. He asked me what I wanted and I told him and he gave it to me. He bought me an elegant red dress. He left the price tags on—$134 for that thing. So I slipped it on, and the minute I saw it fit, snipped off the tags before he could change his mind. He took me out to dinner at the fanciest Italian restaurant in town.

"I'm thinking about selling my house," he said after our entrees had come.

"Really?" I asked. I had no idea what that meant for us.

"Well, the developers want it. And I thought maybe I could work on fixing up our place. Get some stronger storm windows. The nice kind. And think about what we might want to do with that extra room that's filled up with junk."

I still didn't know what he was getting at, and I was pretty tentative with this new Travis, all sweet on me instead of sullen.

"You know," he said, "we could have a talk about having a family. Making that room into a nursery."

I just about dropped the lasagna in my mouth out onto the table. Here we were, treading water all those months, and now he was talking babies and family and a real, new life together. I looked him straight in the eyes to see whether he was drunk, but he had on this little-boy blue face like he meant every word straight from his heart.

What can I say? I caved. I'd been building up strength for months to leave him; I'd even decided I was going to ask him to pick up and move out of my house and my life next week. But it all disappeared, just like that. He even, God forbid, paid the check.

It was a Saturday night in May, and he'd taken me back to the place we'd come to think of as our restaurant. He was still paying for me, and I let him do it. There were summer storms here and there, but they didn't seem to get under his skin the way that the fall weather did.

"I'm thinking about changing careers," he said.

"Really?" I asked. "To what?"

"I was thinking I could be a schoolteacher."

I couldn't help it. Before I could stop myself I laughed.

"What?" he asked, hurt.

"It's just, you know. Kids. I'm not sure you've got the patience for it, honey." I thought about one loudmouth kid bugging him the wrong way in the wrong month, and knew exactly what lay ahead of that path. He wouldn't be able to get away with what he'd do the way he'd gotten away with it with me.

I had no illusions. I'd calmed him down, some. But everything was still there, under the surface. You don't put out a rumble like that and still have the man he was before you.

He didn't speak another word to me throughout dinner. He slapped the bill closed after he paid it.

"C'mon," he said. "We're getting a drink."

He drove us to the Kentucky Downs Bar. I do not know what Kentucky and horse racing have to do with coastal Florida, except that lots of people who don't belong here lay claim to this place, and no one is going to call them on it.

Straight off, he ordered a whiskey with a beer chaser and pointed to me to order for myself. I asked for a rum and Coke, and I handed the bartender my credit card to start us up a tab for what I already sensed was going to be a long night.

We drank like that for a while, one glass and then another, not saying anything to each other. When I went to the bathroom to freshen up, I got a good look at myself in the mirror while I put on my lipstick and saw some woman looking back at me from the glass who looked like she had no idea how she got to this place and needed some solid directions to get herself home.

When I came out, I knew it wasn't good. Travis was leaning forward with his shoulders pulled back; a burly man in a cutoff T-shirt leaned right back at him. I've seen that pose on Travis before and knew exactly what was coming. I saw him cock back his fist and get his muscle warm in his arm, like he was ready to go. But then the burly guy yelled at him, and there was this back and forth of words—you can guess what kind. I sat down on my bar stool and scooted my purse over closer to me for when I needed to grab it and chase after Travis, when he got thrown out of this place, or for when he really hurt this guy who was testing him.

But they just kept on yelling. And all of the sudden, the guy turned on his boot heel and waved Travis off. Stormed off to the jukebox that had red neon piping on it in an upside-down U. I watched the man and the metal CD that spun in the top of the machine setting off colored light like a diamond. He cracked his knuckles and put his hot hands on the jukebox, staring down into it, then hit the button to watch the options spin past him.

And like that, it was over. I let out a big sigh of relief. I put my hand on Travis's back and rubbed it. "Sweetie," I said, "you know I love you."

He nodded down at the bar and relaxed into my touch. I thought things might just turn out okay.

"I need cigarettes," he said, and I was quick with my wallet to give him the dollar bills he'd need. Anything to keep him happy.

After he got up, I turned to the woman at the seat next to me. "Hi," I said. "Sorry about that nonsense earlier."

She smiled and tossed her hair. "Missy," she said, putting out her hand to introduce herself. "Men. What *can* you do with them?"

"He's really quite sweet," I said. "Really."

"Oh I know. They just have their moods. That's our job, right? Handling them?"

I nodded back at her. She was probably in her mid-twenties. She had these little delicate wrists and ankles, with a gold bracelet on her right wrist and a gold anklet on her left ankle. She'd bleached her hair just shy of white—it was that blonde—and it made her look wispy and a little like those angels on the Hallmark cards at the drugstore.

I was so taken with her that I lost track of Travis. I hadn't met anyone new in a long time. Travis and I mostly kept to ourselves. So I asked her where she was from, and she started telling me this story about how she'd come here from north Georgia, from the mountains. I told her I didn't even know that there *were* mountains in Georgia.

"Not only that," she said, turning her head so that she looked like a pretty little puppet, "but there's this little town close to where I live called Helen. And it's all done up like an alpine village. All the houses are supposed to look like German houses. The hotels and motels, too. Even the Wendy's Hamburgers is supposed to look like it's some kind of European chalet."

I laughed with her, mostly because I was surprised she knew the word chalet or what Europe was even supposed to look like. Don't get me wrong. She was cute and nice, and I was drawn to her. She just didn't seem to know much about the world, and she certainly didn't know what she'd gotten herself into coming to this town, a place that had been hit by four tornados over the past five years.

Travis came back over, and I introduced them. He started talking to her in this soft voice I remembered from when we first met and he was first letting me get to know him. And in that sound I heard some kind of roar in my own head, that this girl was going to need saving, but that it was none of my business.

While Travis and Missy kept talking—and don't think I didn't see the two of them flirting, too—this man I had never seen before walked over close to us and then winked at Travis and pats his own pocket. Then he walked back away. I didn't know what it meant, but I knew something was up.

A few minutes later, I was on the way back to the bathroom (too many rum and Cokes for my tiny bladder to handle) when that strange man followed me. He was a heavyset guy with a biker's body—longish brown hair pulled back with a raw rubber band, and face in need of a shave. He was kind of handsome, in a redneck, reckless kind of way. I could smell cheap cigarettes on him and cheaper whisky.

I hurried into the bathroom and closed the door and was so thankful that it was just a one-toilet job so that I could lock the door right behind me. I didn't know what that guy was up to, but I didn't want him following me in here, that's for sure. I did what I came in here to do and spritzed up my hair and put on some powder and some more lipstick. Under the florescent light, I saw that I did not look delicate and pretty, like Missy. I looked like what I am: an aging, semi-married woman with dark hair and dark circles under her eyes who was getting more tired with her life by the minute.

I was not surprised that when I came out the door the biker man was waiting for me. I held my breath and pushed past him.

"Wait," he said, so sad-sounding that I did just what he asked.

"Can't I just meet you?" he said. No harm in that, I thought. I told him my name was Amanda, but when he asked for my last name, I just shook my head. "Amanda for now," I said.

"All right, Amanda for Now. I'm Dudley Anderson."

I looked up at him and almost laughed. "Really?" I said.

"Are you laughing at my name?" he asked.

"No," I said. "It's just that I would never have taken you for a Dudley."

"Why not?" He looked at me with this little furrow in the middle of his hard forehead. "What's wrong with it?"

"Nothing's wrong. I'm sorry. Forgive me." But still I laughed a little. He was being nice to me, and I lost my doubt of him for some reason. I recognized there was no push in the air like he was going to hurt me or that he'd come back here for anything bad. He was just a man who wanted to talk to me. To *me*. That hadn't happened in a long time. I guess that laugh just happened out of flattery and my own strength coming back into circulation through my veins. I missed that part of myself, and I was happy she wasn't all the way gone.

I noticed the tattoo of a tiger on his right forearm. "What's that for?" I asked and touched him there.

"Princeton," he said.

"Princeton? The university?" When he nodded back, I said, "Well, now. A scholar."

That I didn't believe, but I wanted to keep him talking, hear this voice I was starting to like the sound of. He had a sweet face, I noticed. Bright blue eyes.

We stood there in the back hallway where the air was still and dark, and he told me how he wanted to go to graduate school, but got sidetracked, so now he was reading through the books to give himself that kind of education. How he's reading this writer named Franz Kafka, who's really not that hard to read, because his sentences are short and to the point, but it's only when you're lying down later on and you think about his stories that he can blow your mind.

"He wrote in German," the man said, "even though he spoke Czech."

His talk was interesting, but it gave me a headache after all that liquor I'd drunk. I'm not a book person, and I didn't have that much to add. I only read the *Good Housekeeping* magazines that kept showing up in my mailbox even though I didn't have a subscription. And I hate those. All that *here's how to make a perfect cookie, and all you need are some pinking shears and homemade jam* sorts of stuff. But it's the only mail I got other than notices about how I owed people things, and deep down I didn't mind it, because it was some sort of connection with the world that helped me pretend I was a woman in charge of her own household.

"German, huh?" I said. "Maybe you should talk to Missy over there at the bar. She's from an alpine village."

He looked over at her. "The blonde? Nah." He shook his head.

I smirked. "An alpine village. In Georgia. That's what she told me. Anyway, I should be getting back."

"Looks like you're boyfriend's kinda occupied," he said, and pointed a finger up off his beer. When I looked back towards Travis, he had his arm around Missy and leaned forward to kiss her cheek.

I thought a whole lot of things, but the one thing that didn't rise up in me was that I wanted to fight for him. Fine, I thought. He's her problem now.

It was the strangest thing. I knew I loved that man with all I was, but he'd used me up. It's true that he hadn't hit me in over two months. Even so, fall wasn't that far away again; every last part of my body that he'd hurt over the past two years knew he wasn't at all good at keeping himself out of trouble.

When Dudley brushed my hair away from my face and cupped his hand under my chin, then leaned in to kiss me, I kissed him right back, best I knew how. It was like a bargain that said maybe I could learn to read Kafka and talk books, and my life would open up instead of keep shutting down.

I spent three grand nights at Dudley's place, after he'd invited me back to his ramshackle house from the bar and after I'd seen Travis and Missy sway off together an hour before. In bed together that first night I told him how I'd always wanted to go to nursing school, and he listened and said he'd help me sign up for classes the next day, and he did just that, driving me up to the registrar's office to fill out the paperwork to apply for starting up classes in September. I realized what it meant to be with a good man you weren't the least bit frightened of, and on the fourth day, I dialed him up on the phone and called him sugar and told him I thought I loved him. He took a second without saying anything, let out one big heavy breath, and told me he was busy and couldn't see me for a while.

I waited at home in my house for some man to call or come through the door—I didn't care whether it was Dudley or Travis, maybe because I knew it would be neither of them. I waited all through June and July and into August. I tore up the envelopes that came from the local college about enrollment and tuition for nursing courses at the college. I went out and bought a pretty nightgown—it said Diaphanous Blue on the price tag above the cost I knew wasn't worth it unless I could make it work. But Dudley would not return my phone calls, and though I could tell Travis had been in the house to pick up clothes the few times I wasn't there, I had no idea where to reach him. Most of all, I wanted him to do the coming back to me.

I sat there on a beautiful, late August night in that thin nightgown and poured myself a tall glass of whiskey from the kitchen cabinet. I watched out at the window as the sky went from clear to cloudy, the air pushing down, and the sunlight getting compressed down into sunset, like a quiet, long fire. I kept my eyes out the window when the sky let loose and rain set in with a vengeance. I'd heard the sirens all afternoon, but I didn't move when that fierce wind whistled up then rumbled through, even though a sound like that belonged to nothing less than a hurricane. The whole sky shot up with lightning. My old, bad windows rattled, and the house seemed to bend to the side easy as a tree.

It felt like the last minute on earth that I yanked my nightgown over my head and threw on jeans and a sweater and got in my car and hit the gas to get to the church the car radio was telling me was providing shelter. I leaned on the accelerator and gripped the wheel hard to keep control. I had to squint and strain my eyes to see through the windshield, the rain was coming down so hard, and I knew I was a fool for waiting there all that time like I did for Dudley to call me or for Travis to come home. I was a fool for thinking that I get to be the woman who is allowed happiness instead of fear, and I was a fool for almost dying and if I did die, then I was a foolish fool for believing in anything good and for everything I'd done since the last hurricane claimed its due in this town.

I walked into that church, soaking wet and chattering my teeth. I knew somewhere Travis was holding that woman Missy quiet and convincing her that he was going to keep her safe, and here I was empty handed without even a suitcase packed up or a change of clothes to my name.

I put my hand up against a window because I want to feel the storm rattle through me the way that I felt Travis when he was taking care of me, both for good and for bad. Some stranger came up and pulled me back, "You've got to get away from the window, miss," he said. "It's not safe." And I turned to him, half-expecting to see Travis, but just seeing some scrawny college kid trying to do good, and so I pulled back to myself.

I think even then I knew there wouldn't be anything to go back to. I looked up to see women all around, scurrying to help people like me, the lost and scared and lonely ones, and knew I was no good at taking care of anyone and never would be. I couldn't even take care of myself. But there were alpine villages in Georgia. There were kind men who used their hands in gentle ways, and if you went slower with your gratitude just might stay. There were all sorts of impossible places that weren't supposed to exist that did. All I had to do was find one, and with no roof over my head and nothing solid under my feet, I had every excuse now to do just that.

Richard Peabody, a prolific poet, fiction writer, and editor, is an experienced teacher and important activist in the Washington, D.C., community of letters. He is the founder and co-editor of *Gargoyle* magazine and editor (or co-editor) of fourteen anthologies including *Mondo Barbie, Conversations with Gore Vidal, A Different Beat: Writings by Women of the Beat Generation, Kiss The Sky: Fiction & Poetry Starring Jimi Hendrix*, and *Grace and Gravity: Fiction by Washington Area Women*, and *Enhanced Gravity: More Fiction by Washington Area Women*. He is the author of the novella *Sugar Mountain*, two short story collections, and six poetry collections including *Last of the Red Hot Magnetos* and *I'm in Love with the Morton Salt Girl*. He teaches at the Writer's Center and at Johns Hopkins, where he has been presented the Faculty Award for Distinguished Professional Achievement. Peabody lives and works in the Washington, D.C., area. You can find out more at www.wikipedia.org and www.gargoylemagazine.com.

Cover artist Jody Mussoff has been exhibiting her drawings for over twenty-five years and is represented by Gallery Neptune in Bethesda, Maryland, and various museums and collections in the United States and abroad. More recently, she has been working in ceramics as well. She lives outside Washington, D.C.; her website is www.artworkphotographer.com/jodym/home.htm.